The
Harvest
King

 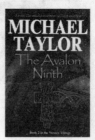

The Harvest King

MICHAEL J. H. TAYLOR

FICTION

The Harvest King
AN F4M BOOK

Published in 2009 by F4M Publishing
(Farringdon, Fore and Marshwood)
Farringdon House, Nr Langport, TA10 9HT, England

A CIP catalogue record for this book is
available from the British Library

ISBN 978-1-874337-10-2

Cover design Kevin Oatley
Typeset by M Rules
Printed and bound in Great Britain by
CPI Bookmarque, Croydon

F4M is a fiction imprint of
Bestseller Books Ltd
publishers

Dedication

To all unselfish and stout-hearted people who stand firm against insufferable 'meddlers' interfering in the quiet lives of others in scenic rural villages.

Acknowledgements

Many thanks go to the proprietors of the Holman Clavel in Culmhead for their kind permission to describe their premises in this novel and for offering invaluable detail on its historic importance within the area of its location. The author also wishes to acknowledge the contribution made to chapter 22 by Mr Eddie Upton, Director of Folk South West. The Somerset Apple Play featured in this chapter represents fragmented extracts from a play written by Mr Upton as part of the traditional and on-going Wassailing Festival performed on the 6th or 17th of January (Twelfth Night old style) each year to encourage a good apple crop. The extracts are reproduced in this novel with Mr Upton's kind permission. Thanks also to Mr A Bricha for technical back-up, Mr Archie Thomas, and television celebrity and broadcaster Johnny Kingdom.

THE WESSEX TRILOGY

Book 1: The Angel of Wessex
ISBN 978-1-874337-08-9, first published in 2003
as ISBN 1-874337-08-X and first reprinted in 2005.
Third print 2008

Book 2: The Avalon Ninth
ISBN 978-1-874337-09-6, first published in 2007

Book 3: The Harvest King
ISBN 978-1-874337-10-2, first published in 2009

Wessex Trilogy Boxed Set
ISBN 978-1-874337-11-9, first published in 2009
and containing all three novels detailed above

Available direct from the Publisher, at better bookshops, and at
promotions and book signings nationwide.
Orders can also be placed via the web-site www.michael-taylor.co.uk
or by email to mjhtaylor@hotmail.com

All correspondence regarding foreign, television, motion picture and
any other rights must be in writing to the Publisher in hard copy.

"They roamed our land with jealous thoughts and deliberately, monstrously, prepared to scheme against us. But they could not understand our customs, or our ways which relied upon the power of imagination"

CHAPTER 1

The secret — 1872

A perfect Sunday afternoon in July was nearing the moment of change, as delicate wisps of pure white cloud began to fragment the blue sky above, heralding the first cooling breeze to soften the heat of the day. Around the ancient village of Cadbury acres of farmland bathed in the light, green in a variety of shades and colours, made pale only by the few nearby hills which appeared almost illuminated at their peaks.

At the centre of the village, in this secluded region of Wessex that had once been the rallying point of Arthur's army defying the Saxon invaders, were the unmistakable slopes of an ancient hill fort. An old rowan tree stood half-way up the steep defensive embankment, rooted solidly to its precarious position. To all appearances it was dead. No slender leaves were left hanging to be swayed by the breeze wafting against the earthwork slope and which, finding no way through, exhaled over the top and through the rowan's uppermost limbs. Not a red berry had graced the rowan for as long as anyone could remember, its serried branches thick and twisted, lifeless and, yet, they still reached out as arthritic fingers, warning foragers not to take its wood for making spinning wheels.

At the plateau of the fort, where in ancient times a settlement of buildings had stood surrounded by wooden posts set into crushed stone, two of the rowan's highest branches overhung the edge of the vacant space. For, as all could see, everything man-made had been levelled centuries before, leaving an area of uneven grass and absolutely no sign of former occupation. A handful of cows grazed lazily over the top pasture, having trudged up a narrow path recently gouged into the embankment by a farmer, who had breached the old defences to increase his working acreage.

On the rim of the fort scampered two boys of very different circumstances. The younger and smaller was from farming stock, while the other was the local magistrate's son. They had played around the rowan for years, hanging ropes from its branches to swing out and over the drop. It was only when the frayed rope finally broke under their combined weight and the boys plunged to earth did they notice for the first time how the soil had eroded from between the heavy tentacle roots of the rowan, leaving small cave-like voids. Shaken, but unhurt, they pulled themselves back up the slope to peer inside. Here was a ready-made hideout, a secret place from where to plan new adventures.

Returning to the hideout later that afternoon with pockets stuffed full of cheese and cake, plus a bottle of ginger ale and two candles, the smaller boy saw something metallic half-buried in the mud wall. Digging it out with his fingertips, the disturbed soil slipped away to reveal a further opening beyond, penetrating the embankment itself. The larger, more intrepid boy, having pushed his friend aside, clawed around the hole until he could wriggle his head and shoulders through.

"What can you see?" asked the smaller excitedly.

"Nothing. It's too dark. I'm coming out."

Squeezed together among the roots, the boys stared at the object, taking turns to rub it against their clothes until it shone.

"Is it money?"

"I suppose it must be. Roman, perhaps. I could show it to my father. He will know. He knows everything."

"Do you think there's more to be discovered, if we look for it?"

"How would I know? There jolly well could be."

"Perhaps we should keep this place secret after all. You know what grown-ups are like. They would say it's too dangerous and stop us coming. Anyway, it's Sunday and we shouldn't be playing anywhere. We would be in terrible trouble if they knew what we'd been up to."

"I'm for exploring now, just in case. It might lead to more treasure. Have you got the matches?"

The smaller boy felt in his pocket.

"Good. Now, we need to be brave like real explorers. And, for goodness sake, keep your candle away from my trousers. My father will stick you in jail if you set me on fire."

"I'm not sure we should be doing this. I'm a bit scared of the dark and I hate tight places. It might cave in on top of us and nobody would ever find our bodies."

"Do what you like, ninny, but I'm going in. The candle glow will be enough light for me."

The small boy gave way and duly tied one end of the broken rope around a root.

"What are you up to now?" asked the larger boy in annoyance.

"Don't you remember the stories from school, when adventurers were saved by making a rope trail? If the candles go out, we can feel for the rope to lead us back to the entrance. It's not very long, but, then, we won't go far in, will we?"

"Come on," his friend replied enthusiastically, choosing to ignore the question. "I'm the biggest, so I'll go first. If I can squeeze through, you certainly can."

The hole looked black and uninviting. A candle was plunged into the dark space ahead, its flickering light showing nothing but walls of mud, embedded with small stones and fibrous roots. The boys crawled in on their stomachs, immediately experiencing a sharp drop in temperature.

"What can you see?" asked the smaller boy nervously from the rear.

"Give me a chance. My eyes need to become accustomed to the dim light."

"I don't like it. I don't think it's safe."

"Nobody's making you stay, ninny. Go back if you're afraid."

"Are you going on?"

"Why not? This is terrific fun."

The smaller boy turned his head the best he could, reassured by the sunlight illuminating the roots behind. "Alright, just a little bit further."

As the hole twisted to the right, causing the last of the outside light to fade from view, and with stones scraping their knees as the floor became uneven, the boys decided to give up. The air, too, had become thin and unpleasantly damp.

"Can you turn around?" asked the larger boy, now in considerable discomfort.

"No!"

"Nor can I. We'll have to crawl out backwards."

The smaller began to whimper.

"Stop that! We're not stuck. Just keep calm and go back the way we came in. Can you feel the rope?"

"No. It ran out a few feet back."

"Why didn't you say so before?"

"Because you wouldn't take any notice if I had, and you would call me a ninny again."

"Even so, there's absolutely no need to panic. We're perfectly safe. We haven't come far. It just seems like it. Reverse slowly on your hands and knees and I'll follow you out. Talk to me if you're scared, but keep your voice down in case the walls are fragile."

"Aren't you frightened, just a little bit?"

"Certainly not," swallowed the larger boy, his heart thumping hard beneath his shirt.

Lying outstretched on the grass at the top of the fort, the boys rested on their elbows as their pulses slowed to a normal rhythm and their spirits soared. They finished the food, washed down with ginger ale, feeling exhilarated at the thought of having had a real-life adventure. The larger boy again reached deep into his pocket, this time pulling out a half-smoked cigar.

"Where did you get that from?"

"Where do you think, ninny. Let's have a puff."

"I don't know," replied the smaller boy. "Won't your father notice it's gone?"

"From his bin? Don't be daft. We have other people to do the cleaning. Anyway, if he does, he'll think it was one of the servants who took it. They're always nicking his stuff, or so he says. Come on, get a match going. I'll have the first smoke."

The lighted match was brought into contact with the tobacco. As the boy sucked, the flame was irresistibly drawn to the cigar and the end began to glow. After a few puffs he handed it to his friend, who drew hard. Coughing, it was handed back without enthusiasm. The gesture needed no explanation and the cigar was finished by one.

All around the countryside lay open below them, hills to the left but perfectly flat for miles in all other directions, their views restricted only by distant uplands silhouetted as grey against the azure sky. It was a scene of generous fertility, where streams rarely dried and grass remained a rich green even when elsewhere a sustained period of heady sun might bake the land brown. To such a landscape as this, where even a fine artist could do no justice, the smell from the cigar only added further serenity, a sweet stillness to the timeless views enjoyed by both boys in silent contemplation. No sounds could be heard that were uncommon to nature, apart from rhythmical chiming of a church clock.

"Glory, did you hear that? It's five o'clock already. Come on, we'd better get home or we'll be in for it."

"How do we explain our absence and the mud on our trousers?"

"Say we were collecting leaves for a school project. We'll get away with that. We can pick up a few on the way home. Do I smell of smoke?"

"You do, a bit. Here, swill the last of the drink and spit it out. With any luck, the ginger should take it away."

Bad weather forced the boys to abandon the rowan for several days. They used the intervening time to draw-up detailed plans for another expedition into the hole, spurred on by the metal object which had cleaned up well and now glistened with an incandescent quality, although the metal remained cold to touch. Although, when first discovered, it had looked to be a large and well-preserved coin, it was now quite obviously a different type of object of unrecognisable purpose. On one side was moulded in relief a strange, almost human-like creature with four beating wings, while on the reverse a similar creature was shown floating on the surface of a pond below the stunted branch of a tree. A single hole pierced the centre, passing through both bodies. Perhaps it was an ancient charm of sorts, or part of a necklace from the time when the fort had been occupied. Whatever it was, the boys decided to keep the treasure secret, hidden by the small boy in his parents' barn.

After school on the following Friday the weather was dry, but the boys had a long-standing date with a large fish which occupied a deep hollow where a river ran steady and an embankment of trees cast lithe shadows over the water. Many times they had leaned over the bank, running their fingers over and between the stones where the fish hid. Once, the smaller boy had felt the cold flesh of the fish with his fingertips, but had been too shocked to hook a finger into its gill. Instead, his sudden movement had sent the fish temporarily darting downstream and the prize had been lost. This same bad-luck continued that Friday, but at least they were heartened by thoughts of visiting their hideout the next day.

But, Saturday turned out to be a typically wet start to the weekend, when any hope for sustained sunshine had given way to the reality of deep puddles and the threat of more rain to come. Even so, the boys had grown impatient to return to the tree. As they began the ascent of the embankment carrying bundles of wood to shore-up the hole, intended to give them the confidence to probe deeper, the rain again turned heavy. Soon, it was streaming down the slope and cascading over the toes of their boots, guaranteeing any greater adventure underground in such weather conditions would be an extremely dirty experience. This would bring angry reactions from their mothers and many awkward questions. And so, instead, they decided to store the wood amongst the roots for drier times.

On their return along muddy lanes, and as the first glimpses of brighter sunlight began to creep out from behind dispersing clouds, a strange-looking cart came unsteadily towards them, taking up most of the width.

The boys skipped to one side, but, finding the grassy edge slippery, they vaulted a low bramble hedge where they stopped, straining to make out the driver as he approached. At a distance, they thought it was a boy at the reins wearing a scarf, but as he came closer they could see it was a very small man, his beard parted by the earlier rain into two long points. He was partially hidden under a soaked, wide-brimmed hat which flopped as a cupola over his eyes. Behind rode several other kindred folk on white horses, their heads nodding to the jingling of silver bells hanging in rows from the harnesses. The boys giggled. The procession pulled to a sudden stop.

"Tengmalm Lane. Come to know the name, young man," said the driver of the cart in monotone, staring at the smaller boy but pointing ahead.

The boys looked at each other doubtfully.

"Was he asking me a question, or telling me something?" whispered the smaller boy through the side of his mouth.

"Shush!"

"I don't like the look of him. He's a monk, isn't he?"

"No, he's not. More like a nutcase. Ignore him and he'll go away," said his friend, almost inaudibly.

"What? All of them nutcases?"

"How would I know? Stop imagining things. You're such a cry-baby. Just stop chattering."

The driver dismounted, pushed back his hat and pulled a measure of loose hay from a truss suspended under the cart, tossing it ahead of the animal. His eyes, now seen as unusually misty in their perfect paleness of yellow, yet sharp in movement, were almost owl like.

"We ride the old Fairy Rade, having come from Pitminster market," he said with no friendship in his voice.

"Sorry, Sir, fairy what?" replied the larger boy in a pitch that assumed a scoffing tone somewhere between derision and embarrassment, heartened at now seeing the old man's small physical stature. "This is plain-old Cadbury, where I live."

"Then, you know the whereabouts of the deepest den?"

"Begging your pardon?"

"*As seconds pass in hurried hour, I go to find the solemn bower.*"

The boys stood confused, unsure what to do or say. The man stared, as if reading their innermost thoughts. It was not his intention to frighten, or waste any time in idle conversation, but probe for answers using the power of the boys' own imagination.

"*Nor laugh at me or act as silly, a curse on them that takes the gild and spoils the lily.*"

"Sorry?" the larger boy replied once more.

"I'm afraid of him," whimpered his friend feebly, hoping the man would not hear. "Don't speak to him anymore. Just let him go on his way. They might be a band of cut-throats."

"*The mildest man if taken wild, will fright with fear as any child; but a boy who stole and then has fled, will shake and scream with trembling dread.*"

At last the man came very close. To the boys, his strange appearance and unpredictable ways overcame his small size. They stood frozen to the spot. Despite his ageing hair and beard, his skin was fresh and plump.

"I have a window into your soul, Cornelius. Return the thing you covet."

"Sir?" replied Cornelius nervously, trying to pass the treasure behind his back to the smaller boy, who was unaware his friend had taken it from its hiding place in the barn.

The man sniffed loudly, turned, remounted the cart and flicked the reins. The procession began to move forward.

"What are you to meddle in my world?" asked the man as he passed the small boy at very slow pace.

"Scared," came the honest reply.

"*No good comes from things that gleam, lives lost in the opposite of a dream.* Remember, Oswald, losers will be weepers. The future is an already trodden path, known only to the forgotten people who once lived in a place of wonderful things before it was taken away."

"Sir?"

The cart trundled off, grinding its buckled wheels on the uneven road. The riders followed behind. The boys stood, staring, until the last horse was out of sight.

"He knew our names, for goodness sake!" cried Oswald.

"Do you know him?"

"Of course not. Don't you?"

"Never seen the old buzzard before."

"How come he knows who we are, then?"

"Creepy, wasn't he."

"It's witchcraft!"

"Don't talk daft. There's bound to be a simple explanation."

"I don't like it. I really don't."

"Come on. We can be home before he thinks of returning. My father will know if any lunatics have escaped the asylum."

"What's the opposite of a dream?" panted Oswald breathlessly, as they sped along the track leading to the big house.

"Take no notice of the silly old duffer," replied Cornelius, slowing the pace to put a reassuring arm around his friend's shoulders. "We'll tell my father all about him. He'll know what to do. You worry too much."

"But, what *is* the opposite of a dream?"

"I don't know. A nightmare, I suppose. No, that can't be right. It's not the opposite. Maybe he meant a living nightmare, a real-life tragedy. Like being run over by a runaway horse, drowning, or something similar."

"I want to go home, to my own home. . . Now!" said the smaller boy in distress.

With the evening spent in the comfort of his grand, warm home, Cornelius quickly dismissed the strangeness of the old man and his words. He would not tell his father, after all. Oswald, on the other hand, remained troubled as he huddled by a glowing stove in the kitchen of his cottage, eating a meaty broth. He had tried to tell his father of the incident, but had received a clip around the ear for making up stories.

The next day the boys returned to the rowan, but for very different purposes. Cornelius was still determined to explore even deeper than before and believed Oswald was similarly committed. But, Oswald was disturbed and secretly carried the treasure in his jacket pocket, intending to bury it where it was found, without Cornelius ever knowing. Afterwards, he would never return to the tree.

But, the scene which greeted them was one of devastation. The latest rain, which had begun with the full fury of a storm but had now eased to nothing more sinister than a light shower, had caused a mud slide and the spaces within the roots were filled. Most of the shoring timber, too, had been buried, the few pieces to have survived now strewn in a heap at the foot of the embankment.

Dispirited, Oswald took the treasure back to the barn, placing it in a small box and stuffing it deep amongst piled rubbish in a disused corner, away from the adults. It was the conclusion of the adventure.

The rowan was left to stand in peace.

CHAPTER 2

Twelve years later —1884

The sultriness of mid-Summer demanded all interior shutters should be flung back and every ground level window of Partington Hall should be fully opened, filling the indoors with the richest fragrances of the garden. Gentle breezes stirring amongst the climbing stems of honeysuckle carried a heady perfume into the drawing room that was redolent of childhood, while elsewhere in the house roses and other more delicate scents vied for favour and space.

Reclining on a chaise longue in the centre of the opulent surroundings was a woman in her late forties, a small occasional table conveniently close at hand laden with chocolates, a glass of lemon water and a silver tray. A bowl of fruit rested comfortably on her stomach. In a darker corner sat her husband, his chair moved from the brightness of the sunlight. He was content to be ignored.

"My dear Mr Fairfax, have you ever felt so good about a day?" asked his wife, steadying the fruit bowl with one hand as she stretched to return an opened letter to the tray. "Why, if only every day could be as this." She awaited a reply. "Are you listening to me, my dear, or am I alone in the room?"

Mr Fairfax looked over the top of his newspaper through tiny wire spectacles, before folding the paper in half and lowering it to his lap. "Yes, yes and no," he replied languidly, feeling his neck steaming around his stiff white collar.

"Your meaning?" she returned impatiently.

"*Yes*, I have felt better on cooler days, *yes* I am listening and *no* you are not alone. The latter is most certain, as you give me no peace to enjoy my reading."

"But I have such news of my own."

"And you want to tell me?"

"Naturally. Don't you want to know what excites me so much?"

"I have no such curiosity, but I have a dreadful foreboding I am bound to listen anyway."

This was agreement enough to continue in feverish tone.

"Why, I have news from Cornelius. Our boy is planning to come home for a month or two. He has a new business idea he wants to put to us. Splendid! Now, what do you make of that?"

"I suppose it was too much to hope he would stick at farming or any of the other false starts I have recently funded. Why can't he take up something serious, become a sawbones, for instance? There is a need for doctors about these parts and he might find himself useful to someone for a change. No, we have to face it, we have ruined the boy."

"We?"

"Alright, you!"

"Excuse me? That wasn't what I meant at all."

He smiled into his lap, taking back the newspaper.

"Put the paper down, Rufus, and tell me what you meant by that remark."

He gave way. "How old is he? Twenty-four at the last count and still he asks me to pay for all the little schemes that last only as long as my money allows. Business is to make money, not waste mine!"

"You always had a mean streak. My aunt warned me I would have a hard life at your hands."

He looked across at her repose, with every luxury at her fingertips. He conjectured an amusing reply, but kept it inside his head.

"This time it wasn't his fault," she continued.

"How so?" came the indifferent voice from the corner.

"He says he was let down by others. Apparently, he had an understanding with a neighbour, in which he would grow fruit and swap small quantities for a little of his neighbour's time helping around the farm and loaves of bread. He says the arrangement took account of the seasonal nature of his crop."

"And? There has to be an *and*."

"And, last week Cornelius found an entire colony of rats in an outbuilding, so many that he wouldn't enter alone."

"And?"

"The neighbour agreed to help and said he would fetch a bag of poison. But, right in front of Cornelius's eyes, the neighbour stepped backwards and slipped into the undershot gully feeding a waterwheel, falling most awkwardly and sustaining a fractured skull."

"Good heavens! What did Cornelius do?"

"Oh, don't worry, he put a match to the outbuilding and razed it to the ground."

"I meant, what did Cornelius do to help the neighbour?"

"He doesn't say in his letter. Typical of you to worry about others before your own flesh and blood. You are so unlike my dear, late uncle. He would do anything for me and Cornelius, having an inclination to see everything in an upbeat way through rose-coloured spectacles."

"Then, it must have come as a severe blow to him when he popped his clogs!"

"I believe it did. Death has a way of spoiling one's plans. Anyway, we must make ready. I'll sit a little longer and think of the things you need to do. It's all too strenuous," she sighed, ringing a bell to have her glass refreshed. A man-servant entered. "More lemon, Jenkin, and plenty of ice this time to cool the jug."

"I'll send Mary to the ice-house, Madam." He bowed and left.

"I suppose he's leaving farming?" asked the husband with little genuine interest.

"I would have it no other way. People dropping injured around him. Whatever next?"

"My thoughts exactly!"

A full fifteen minutes passed before the maid knocked and entered. She had hurried from the garden where the brick-built, domed ice-house was buried in a woodland corner, and re-entered the main building through a series of low 'snob' corridors keeping the servants away from the main reception areas. It was as if the servants didn't exist amongst the general household, but merely scurried about like so many tamed mice in tunnels.

Breathless, the maid curtsied and lifted a cooled jug of lemon water from its carrying bowl, made heavier by silver-handled, glass chillers packed with crushed ice. Once the drinking glass had been filled to everyone's satisfaction, the entire apparatus was left on the occasional table. Only then did the wife raise a hand, in an act of careless dismissal. The room fell silent again, except for the rustling of turned pages.

"Do be quiet, Rufus. Can you not see I'm thinking?"

He shook his head in resignation, folding the paper once again and placing it on the arm of the chair. The noise of the final folds caused his wife obvious annoyance.

"My dear Constance, it is a mystery to me how you think I would be privy to know whether or not you are engaged in thinking, as all activity is within your own head. I have often observed in others that thinking leads to some outward expression, such as a furrowing of the forehead, a slight wrinkling of the brows, or movement of the eyes. Yet, in you, no such indications are present."

"Meaning? Are you saying I'm empty headed?"

He shuffled awkwardly in his chair, deciding retreat was the least confrontational course of action. "Meaning only, for a woman to maintain a level of beauty, with porcelain skin and cheeks of rose petals, free from lines caused by too much exaggeration of the muscles, it is necessary not to think unless it cannot be avoided. Intellect and beauty are at war on a woman's face. I was only reasoning how wise you are to think little and keep a natural beauty, so rare among your contemporaries."

"You mean of my age!"

"Indeed, Constance. Nobody can stop the march of time. We can ignore it and hope changes we see in others are not similarly vested in our own features, but in truth ageing is unavoidable."

"And where do you fit into this great scheme of things?"

"Oh, I am beyond redemption, my dear. My face bears the scars of knowledge. My nose is large and red from having my glasses perched on the bridge for long periods of time, and the crow's feet framing my eyes are so large that no bird of the type could ever hope to become airborne if they were on the extremity of its legs. No, I am scarred by intellect, as are men in general."

"All men?"

He pondered the question, amazed his wife had engaged in meaningful debate. "Perhaps, not all men. No, I can accept there may be occupations requiring little intellect, so preserving gentle features. A Member of Parliament may be a prime example. An enquiring mind could be deemed a positive hindrance to advancement in politics. Similar must be true of the Church. A vicar learns the doctrine of the Church at a tender age, and it becomes his duty thereafter merely to repeat it time and time again. It is, therefore, not the vicar but the congregation who suffer the consequences as a clergyman ages, for, with the passing of years, the flames of fire and brimstone become ever fiercer in a vicar's sermon until an old clergyman sees redemption as being virtually beyond the reach of any of his flock and delights in saying so in fearful language. In so doing, a vicar may inflict the ageing process on his congregation, but he remains of kindly appearance, even if he is not being entirely compassionate. How simply a vicar warns of hell-fire and then, as his flock trembles, he asks the children to stand and sing *All things bright and beautiful.*"

She looked at him suspiciously. "I cannot tell whether you flatter or mock me."

"Believe me, Constance, you are better off not enquiring as to my mind. Sufficient to say, I am as one with most other men. Males see the female pursuit of eternal beauty to be a race without a winning post. Ageing cannot be stopped, or hidden beneath paint and powder. They are only temporary masks, and pretty poor ones at that. Physical destruction is guaranteed by the passing years, whereas intellect and the accumulation of knowledge are like building a great house, each brick added to the last until a great height is reached. Men, in my opinion, have the best of it. We do not run the race against fading beauty, and in not looking for victory we cannot suffer defeat. A woman past her prime suffers losing the race on a daily basis, as she stares into the looking glass. No, I am content with my nose and my lines and enjoy the peace accompanying them. You, on the other hand, have kept your looks better than most and should, therefore, remain nebulous."

"And, what of Cornelius in all this?"

"Oh, as long as I have money to spare, he will have the skin texture of a child's doll. For that, we must blame ourselves. It must be my endeavour after he arrives to place a frown between his eyes."

So it was that one week later Cornelius arrived. Things about him were different, though, strange and unexpected. He had driven into the courtyard on a farm wagon, a fine grey trotting behind on a tethering rope. His possessions occupied the rear of the wagon, covered by a tarpaulin bearing signs of an earlier light drizzle.

Constance hurried out to greet him, stopping under the huge overhanging portico. She was shocked by his shabby appearance as he jumped off the wagon to hug her tenderly, all his usual swagger gone and his dark hair in need of urgent grooming. His father followed, with hand outstretched. The shake was strong and sincere.

"There is much of importance to tell you, Father, after I have settled the horses."

"Leave them, my boy. Others can do it."

"My clothes and things are in the back."

"Jenkin will bring them inside. Come, let us talk."

"Give me a moment, Father. I have a little thing to retrieve which I can't entrust to anyone else. It's of the greatest importance to me." He returned to the wagon. "It's my little baby." He lifted a corner of the tarpaulin and pulled out a small wicker basket, which he balanced between both hands.

"What did you just say?" his father blustered, as the basket was lowered to waist height.

"It's the reason I'm not farming anymore and the most precious thing in the world to me." Carefully, he gathered both handles in one hand, leaving the other free to grab the corner of a small blanket covering the inside.

"Is that what I think it is?" enquired Constance fearfully, hardly daring to look more closely. "It looks very much like a Moses basket."

Her husband, whose face was now ghostly pale, put an arm around her shaking shoulders. "Whatever it is, or rather whoever it is, it is Cornelius's and therefore ours," he whispered. He turned to look full-square at the basket. "Show us. Have no fear of our reaction."

Cornelius pulled the blanket away.

"My word! What is it?"

"Clearly not what you expected, judging by your expressions. I'm sorry for pulling a bit of a stunt. I couldn't think how best to break the news to you regarding what I've been doing with your money, so I took a bit of a liberty with your emotions instead. Knowing how you are bound to react to what I have to say, I decided to lessen the impact by first making you believe something worse. I find such a ruse often makes the truth an easier pill to swallow. Clearly, I succeeded beyond my wildest dreams."

"But, what is it?"

"Let's go inside. I'll explain there."

In the comfort of the drawing room, Cornelius lifted a wooden box with no lid from the inside of the basket. From this he removed several frail objects and a small jar.

"There," he said with pride, "what do you make of it?"

"It's a broken toy and a jar of Dundee marmalade!" exclaimed his mother.

"Tell her, Father."

"Looks like Dundee marmalade to me, too, my boy."

"Well, that's not surprising, because the jar is, indeed, the remains of many pleasurable breakfasts."

"And the point of this foolery is, Cornelius?" returned his father, showing some annoyance.

"The point, as you so readily scorn, is that there is something more inside. I keep it well hidden from prying eyes. First, though, we must look at the rest of my stuff." He carefully rearranged each individual piece taken from the wooden box until they formed a single, discernable shape on the floor.

"What is it, Rufus?" asked Constance.

"Looks like nothing I've ever seen."

"Goodness, don't you ever read the newspapers? Why, when properly assembled it becomes a flying machine, or at least a tiny model of one. It's my baby, created by my own fair hands."

"And the point of it is?" returned his father, dazzled by the fragility of the object.

"Its purpose is in its name. It's a machine that flies, built to prove the possibility of a full-sized version carrying a man up into the sky."

"Well, I'll be dashed. Does it work?"

"It flies a little, on the power of a rubber band that I twist until it is so tight that it is ready to break. I find oiling the rubber helps, but I get through quite a few bands. Then, by throwing the model skyward, I release the wings and they flap furiously. Note, the wings are not stiff. They are merely linen fabric of the lightest quality held in place by wire supports around three sides. I don't yet know why, but having the back edge unsupported seems to help, as the motion of flapping billows the fabric. Everything has to be kept as light as possible or it would drop like a stone."

"It has four wings. Why four?"

"I started with two, mimicking the birds, but it wouldn't rise. It just flapped to the ground, dragging itself along. So I tried four wings because of an inspiration gleaned from something I keep in the marmalade jar. Anyway, the back two seem to be necessary to stabilise the machine. But, it's still a long way from being satisfactory."

"Have you tried something larger? I can't see this has any practical use."

"Not yet, Father, but I have high hopes of doing so, eventually. The design needs improving first and, I fear, financing."

"Ah, money! The evil word returneth! This is more like my son. Welcome back, old man."

"Please, Father, take me seriously."

"Like all the other times you mean, farming and the other projects preceding it?"

"I can explain."

"I wish you would."

"Did it never occur to you to wonder why I chose to farm in Chard, rather than take up one of the estate's smallholdings?"

"I rather hoped it might be because of a woman," said his mother, with a countenance that showed disappointment at the shake of his head.

"I've no time to waste on such things."

"Make time! There are a good many well-bred fillies hereabouts, sensible girls who eat heartily, enjoy long walks and avoid excessive thinking."

"Good grief," spurned her husband, still able to be astounded by the asininity of her mind after thirty years of marriage.

"I'm entirely serious. If marriage is to be happy, a man must select a woman of considerably higher or appreciably lower intellect than he, for this guarantees no likelihood of protracted conversations involving lofty issues. Ideal, one might say."

"Take no notice of her," said Rufus in frustration. "I would love the company of someone of equal intellect."

"Equal, or higher than myself?" replied Constance through a scowl.

"As always, I am lost by your reasoning, dear. You outsmart me again." He cast a sly wink towards his son. "But, returning to you, Cornelius, should I have deduced any significance from Chard? As I see it, it's as good a place as any in Wessex to squander your future inheritance."

"You should realise, Cornelius," interrupted Constance again, not to be so easily distracted, "a single man is of the greatest attraction to unattached ladies. Indeed, now I think on it," she chuckled, "a married man might sometimes be of equal interest to a woman if past her best years and likely to be left a spinster." She smiled, knowing she had been uncharacteristically witty.

"I would prefer to be left in peace. Such dalliances are for the distant future."

"Ah, if you deliberately want to be unattractive and ignored by the opposite gender, my advice is definitely to get married. I can assure you, since our marriage your father has become the most unattractive man I know."

Cornelius looked across to his father, who shrugged in resignation. Cornelius continued.

"Chard is by far the best of places, Father, but not for reasons of soil and climate."

Constance stood, ruffled at being ignored. "It strikes me, men do not admire women who offer an opinion rather than listen submissively. That said, and since we talk at cross-purposes, I think I'll leave you two to debate the merits of flying sticks."

"No, Mother, I want you to hear all I have to say. It's very important. No, more than that, it's vital."

"I'm intrigued," said Rufus. "Pray go on. We are all ears."

"Well, forty-odd years ago a man named William Henson took out a patent on a steam-powered flying machine, which he called the *Aerial Steam Carriage*. It was designed to carry paying passengers and merchandise all over the world. Imagine if you can, Father, a truly huge machine to be built as a vast wooden framework, with wings no less than 150 feet wide, strong but light, covered in silk. Hanging below was to be an enclosed boat-like hull for carrying the precious cargo and housing the engine, the steam power intended to drive two rear-facing propeller-screws looking like giant windmill sails. It was to be a modern wonder of science, the like of which had never been seen before, one to rival Noah's ark in magnitude and magnificence. Why, the newspapers were full of it at the time, even though it had not been built. Artist's sketches were produced and published by the bucket load, showing it flying over the Egyptian pyramids and a great many other places. I've seen back editions of these papers, so I know what I'm talking about. In fact, I have a copy of a sketch with me." He unrolled a drawing from a tube. "As you can imagine, it caused huge interest and much anticipation. Even Parliament debated the matter and passed an Act covering the proposed establishment of the Aerial Transit Company, intended to handle the construction and operation of replicated full-size machines."

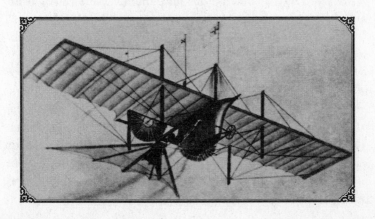

"Gracious! Whatever happened?"

"As a first step in its development, Henson and his colleague, a chap by the name of Stringfellow, produced a scale model to test the design."

"Much as you have," interrupted Rufus from the edge of his chair.

"Now you are getting the point! Henson's model was fitted with a miniature steam engine. But, when tested time and time again at Chard, it hardly flew at all. They even tried launching it from a ramp to help it into the air, but, alas, it was a flop. I've actually seen the model *Steam Carriage*. It's been exhibited.

"So, that was that. A huge white elephant costing a good man his reputation and the Government some considerable embarrassment."

"I suppose it did. According to reports I have read, there were plenty who poured scorn on the whole project, but, then, even Brunel had his failures and thereby attracted his fair share of enemies. You see, for those with little imagination, Henson was no more than a fatuous dreamer. But, for those who salute the brave men who progress science by trying new ideas, however outrageous in concept, and begin new industries by their perseverance, he was merely ahead of his time. It became inevitable someone would succeed where Henson failed."

"Are you saying someone *has* since triumphed? I've not heard of it."

"No, I can't say that. I wish I could. But I have no doubt someone will, and in the not too distant future. For my part, I want to be in the race. There's a fortune to be made and a place in history equal to Brunel and the French Montgolfier brothers. You see, Father, the problem of mechanical flying lies in the production of enough energy to turn a propeller or flap the wings. The correct engine choice is vital. Steam engines are great for locomotives, factories or for pumping water, but I think they're just too heavy to use on flying machines. It's all a question of power-to-weight."

"Hold up, can't you speak in terms I can understand?"

"How much power an engine can produce compared to its standing weight, if that's more digestible. It's a simple mathematical equation. Think of it like a catapult. The rubber when stretched back will fling a light object a long way, whereas the same rubber will only fling a heavy object a short distance. That's a crude example, but it makes the general point."

"You mean a heavy engine can't produce enough power to lift its own weight?"

"Or the weight of the flying machine itself. Bravo, you have it. More to the point, without creating surplus power, such an engine could never lift the added weight of a man."

"Perhaps it's for the best. What silly person would want to fly?"

"I would, for one."

"No, Cornelius, you are altogether too adventurous, nay, foolhardy," pleaded Constance. "Expend your energies finding a wife. She will give you trouble enough to keep you well occupied."

Rufus ignored her, more concerned to convince his son of the error of his ways. "People already fly using balloons. Surely, the race has been won?"

"Not so, from any practical viewpoint. Look, let me try to explain. A balloon is not mechanical. It merely rises by the hydrogen gas it carries in the spherical envelope, the gas itself being lighter than the surrounding air. Older style hot-air balloons work in a similar way, using fire instead of gas. Think of it like this. You must have seen a shirt billowing when dried in front of a fire, or ash being carried up a chimney on waves of hot air from the flames. Well, that's how a hot-air balloon works. Stop feeding the flames and down it comes. But that's all a balloon does, of either type. A balloon travels only where the wind blows it, making it a fine play thing, but, as a serious means of transportation, it's a complete dead loss."

"I'm impressed. I had no idea your education was worthwhile."

"I've learned most of this since leaving school, Father."

"Are you telling me there is no way whatsoever of making a balloon more adaptable, to force it to fly in the direction you want it to go? Because, if there is, a heavy flying machine would be entirely surplus to requirements and nothing better than an expensive indulgence. It seems to me your time would be much better occupied finding ways of making a balloon steerable. Such a new direction for your energies would also prove considerably cheaper for me, I'm sure."

"Father, listen to me. It's pure luck where a balloon finishes up. That will never change, I promise you. However, in fairness, I should tell you there are various Germans and Frenchmen who would agree with your thinking and believe they can solve the problem of directional flight by building the gas-carrying envelopes in long cigar shapes, instead of the traditional ball. They call them ships of the air, or airships. Then, by fitting a propeller turned by hand or by an engine, they hope to exert control over direction, even when flying into the wind. They could even fit several engines to such craft."

"There we are! Listen to yourself. You have made my point."

"No, Father, I haven't, but to prove my eyes aren't closed to all sciences of the air, I will tell you something amazing. Only last year a Frenchman put an electric motor on such a cigar craft, but it wasn't very successful. However, two officers from the French Corps of Engineers have copied the idea and have adopted electric power to drive a new airship, which they call *La France*. Incredibly, just a couple of weeks ago it lumbered over a circular course of five miles, like some great monster crawling through the sky. Although I am not encouraged by it, the flight was something quite marvellous. From what I am told, it had been set free of its moorings at a military balloon ground in the late afternoon. Despite the vastness of its gas-bag made from varnished cloth, it ascended only slowly, perhaps even threatening to fall back heavily and crush the men left behind who had worked furiously to get it airborne in the first place. But, in the event, no such accident happened and it rose perfectly well to the height of the surrounding plateaux. Then, the engine was set into motion, sending a shudder through the hanging bamboo gondola in which the aeronauts occupied an open space. The craft was steered away from trees, eventually floating along at a thousand feet and casting a menace on those watching below, eclipsing the heavens from the good meadows over which it held dominion. After rising and descending for more than twenty minutes, a 250 foot length of rope was finally released and the big propeller was raised to stop the blades breaking as the airship came back to earth. Awaiting soldiers grabbed the rope and hauled the monster in until all was secure. Those on board walked free with their lives spared."

"Goodness, Cornelius, you have described the future."

"You are right in one thing, Father. The year 1884 *will* go down in history, believe me, but only as the pinnacle of a dead-end idea. After all, what good are a few miles covered at a circular crawl? No, I strongly believe anything requiring gas to make it rise has no long-term applications. Gas airships will always be unpredictable, extremely slow, highly dangerous because of the risk of an explosion, and limited in use because of their massive bulk."

"So, the French are barking up the wrong tree. Excellent!"

"Don't run away with your national pride. In this area of science, as in all others to do with aeronautics, the French are beating us hands down. We must concentrate on practicality. The future of flying lies squarely in what we call heavier-than-air machines. Forget the rest as bunkum."

"The German Empire? What about the Germans?"

"Lots of experiments, but no real success. A certain Count von Zeppelin is interested in airships, but he hasn't built a thing yet. I think he will, though, eventually. Apparently, his interest was sparked by the use of balloons during the American Civil War."

"I'm still to be convinced, Cornelius. Anyway, tell me, what happened to Henson? You didn't complete the story."

"Because he was so dejected by failure, I suppose, he emigrated to America in 1848, after trials with the model ended. However, by then Stringfellow had already designed his own model. It was about half the size and far less elaborate. Because it was as light as a feather, even with a miniature steam engine fitted, it actually flew at Chard after being released in the air from a suspended cable. It is said the method of launch was chosen to reduce the risk of fire, but I'm not so sure. I think it was chosen because Stringfellow still encountered the same problem, namely the engine could not produce enough power to raise the machine off the ground. Remarkably, when taken to London, the machine steamed its way over a distance of more than a hundred feet. But, Stringfellow, too, was unconvinced anything larger could be built and gave up experimenting for a long time."

"So this is a Chard connection, way back in the 1840s. But why now?"

"Stringfellow only died last year, having designed better craft. He even won prize money at the Aeronautical Society's first exhibition at the Crystal Palace. I found the old man to be free with his knowledge for the short time we corresponded. It's the unwritten law of aerial experimenters. So, you see, I spent your money to fund my own trials, which I knew you wouldn't approve of if I told you first. And that's why I've lived in Chard. I needed the ambience of a place where others had almost achieved their goals, just in case there was something in the air that helped. Of course, I now know a 'flying miasma' was a ridiculous thought, even for me. Anyhow, I took up the challenge, veiled in secrecy. I grew a bit of fruit, but only to hide my work. I never sold any, just swapped it for labour."

"And bread."

"Yes, the stuff of life."

"Have you any of my money left? Anything at all from the hundreds of pounds I loaned you?"

"Nothing. That's why I'm home. I knew I couldn't ask for more without some form of explanation. And so, with my heart in my mouth, I decided to come clean."

"You understand me well. The strings are pulled tight around my purse. I suggest you leave flying to angels and the balloonists."

"There's more, Father, which might make you realise the importance of my work."

"I doubt it, but you are free to try."

"Picture a world in which the French, Russians and Germans have dominance of the skies, to spy on us or even drop explosives on our cities, or troops in the field."

"It doesn't bear thinking about. Could it ever happen?"

"It is possible, and sooner than you might think. A full-size, steam-powered machine flew in France a decade ago, at Brest. It only managed a very brief hop off the ground because of the engine, but it carried a sailor on board. Others are trying, too. From small acorns. . ."

"Do mighty armies grow."

"And there's worse. A German named Otto has invented something called a four-stroke internal combustion engine. It uses a highly volatile flammable liquid made from petroleum. I'm quite convinced this type of engine will prove to be the key to the future and will replace any further consideration of steam. Otto's engines don't offer much power yet and so they don't meet the efficiency demanded for aerial navigation, but they are very much lighter and ripe for development. If he gets the elusive power-to-weight ratio right, and there's every indication he will, it could be our undoing as a nation unless we are prepared."

"No more rule Britannia?"

"It's a possibility."

"We can't allow that."

"And still there's more. While all this has been going on, a captain of the Imperial Russian Navy has just built a flying machine with two steam engines, which everyone thinks will just manage to rise a few inches off the ground with a man on board. We know about the machine because the engines were constructed in England. It has been assembled at a military field near St Petersburg. We should hear any day now whether, or not, it has flown, if it hasn't already. Mind you, I'm far less impressed by the engines than the design of the airframe. Just imagine if the captain replaces steam with a couple of Otto's engines. What then? A brief hop could turn into a genuine flight!"

"It now seems to me you should be concentrating your mind on producing a suitable engine, before any thoughts of a winged machine."

"Way out of my league, Father. I will have to rely on others to develop good engines. I have no knowledge in that field."

"And Britain? Is anyone else batting for our side?"

"There is an Englishman named Moy. He's managed to coax a steam-powered model off the ground, but it's only that, a model like mine. We are losing the initiative on every front, partly because the British Government is too stuck in its ways to see the need to back our home-grown pioneers!"

"Then search for men with deep pockets, Cornelius. Britain must rule the skies as well as the waves if peace is to be preserved for the next generation. I will help you, now I understand the gravity of the situation, but my resources are strictly limited. I will curb your mother's excesses if it helps preserve our national freedoms."

"Rufus!" screamed Constance in horror, reflecting on the humiliation of having to walk past the latest French fashions brought to Ilminster's premier drapers.

"Oh, do be quiet!" barked Rufus in unusually abrupt tone.

"I've been thinking along the same lines, Father, looking for a sponsor I mean, not stopping mother from shopping. There's an expatriate American who moved to London three years ago. He goes by the name of Maxim. He's an engineer. At the moment he's wrapped up in demonstrating his latest invention, a machine-gun that fires bullets at a rapid rate without the operator cranking any handles. I'm hoping he might show willing to back me. He's exceedingly wealthy and a staunch supporter of our nation. I'm told he already thinks that if a domestic goose can fly, surely a man will also fly one day using artificial wings. But, make no mistake, until such wealthy patrons are involved, it will be left to the minnows like me to carry on regardless."

"Maxim, you say? Don't know the fellow by name or reputation, but I'll find out where he resides and write to him on your behalf. He may take a letter from me more seriously. Once an introduction has been effected, it'll be down to you to convince him of your case." He rose to find pen and paper. "By the way, I suppose you don't mind having your ideas blabbed about to strangers?"

"Maxim's okay, I'm completely sure. However, I've wondered about my personal safety in all this. There's a lot at stake, and I don't mean just money. It could be a question of foreign power interference."

"Spies?"

"Perhaps. Spies, industrial thieves or assassins, don't you know!"

"I expect this Maxim person has taken up residence on a vacant English estate," said Constance quickly, engaged in a little free thinking, which included the prospect of a future invitation from a rich American. "That might narrow down the likely places to find him. And, he would be untitled. I don't think they have aristocracy in America."

"I believe you could be right, dear. How very observant. All Americans claim to be of a single class, although some dress in rags while others are so rich they leave rats to nest among bundles of dollar bills stored in cellars. It's a vast country, where the opportunity to become rich very quickly is ever present."

"Sounds dreadfully parochial. Is it cold?" added Constance, back to her normal voice.

"Is what cold?"

"America."

"Sorry?"

"I just thought it might be, with all the open space."

Father and son shuddered, but let the remark go.

Three weeks later a letter was returned, marked Baldwyn's Park. Cornelius grabbed it from the silver tray and ran to his father's study.

"It's come, the letter from Maxim." He handed it over with excited anticipation, being addressed to his father. "Well, what does he say? Is he going to help?"

"Wait, Cornelius. He writes much."

Three pages of close writing were read carefully. At the end, Rufus dropped into his chair, his hand still clutching the reply.

"Well?"

"He says much. He's clearly a very fine gentleman indeed and a great supporter of Britain. He starts by talking about his present work on rapid-firing guns. His frustration with British bureaucracy is obvious from his tone, given that he has invented a weapon to master any battlefield. He remarks, if the British Government is slow to realise its potential, then other European powers will invent similar guns and destroy us."

"But, what of flying?"

"He congratulates you on your early efforts."

"Any offer of money?"

"Wait for me to finish. He says he, too, has been thinking about a long-term project to test a man-carrying flying machine, for which he is willing to invest up to £20,000 of his own fortune."

"So much! Good Lord."

"However. . ."

"I just knew there would be an 'however'. Give me the bad news."

"He remarks that his experiments in that field of science will be some years in the future, following his present, more pressing commitments. Then he gives a very brief outline of his own thoughts. You had better look at these for yourself. I cannot make any sense of them. He says mechanical flying will always be a question of balance, whatever that means."

Cornelius took the pages and scanned them quickly, becoming steadily more agitated. "No, he's wrong. I can't believe it."

"What?"

"He says, steam engines are the only possible power source at present with the potential to offer sufficient output. He's so wrong."

"I don't think you're in any position to question such an eminent engineer, Son."

"Believe me, Father, he *is* wrong. Steam is a dead-end, a complete donkey. He understands the problems associated with heavier-than-air flight, but has suggested the wrong solution. Instead of looking for alternative types of engine, which would allow the airframe to be kept small and light, he thinks any flying-machine must have at least two absolutely huge steam engines to produce sufficient power to turn massive propellers the size of two fully-grown men, requiring several people to operate them. Can you imagine anyone seriously planning to carry more than one man on board a flying-machine? That means his flying-machine would need truly vast wings and weigh tons. It's impossible. And, even if it did lift off the ground, how could such a machine ever be controlled? He would never achieve 'balance', as he puts it."

"I wouldn't be so ready to dismiss Maxim. He's famous for getting things right."

"But, he is mistaken this time. I'm sure of it. Steam is no good at all. I was wrong to ask for his help. I will write and make my sincere apologies for deciding to go my own way."

"Don't you still need his money?"

"Not if it comes with steam attached."

"Have you learned anything from him?"

"Yes. He intends to adopt fixed wings on his machine. He places no faith in ornithopters with flapping wings. I must walk before I try to run. I will first conduct experiments on the correct shape for wings before worrying about an engine. I must learn to glide and soar!"

That evening the family gathered in the drawing room, ready to be called for a late supper. They hoped the temperature would cool, as they had dressed formally.

"I've not been entirely open with you, Father, or you, Mother."

"Oh, yes?" replied Rufus gravely, rubbing his collar in the accustomed fashion when hot.

"No. Well, you see, there's a deal more to this flying lark than meets the eye. Do you remember as a child I had a friend named Oswald Lane?"

"I do. If am not very much mistaken, your mother let you play with him despite his low social standing. Truth be told, I very much liked the boy."

"We were like brothers and called each other that after we mixed blood from pricked fingers."

"Boys do that," added Rufus, looking at his wife and remembering his own care-free days of youth.

"Boys might show close fellowship, but only after they've called each other a lot of hurtful things first," interceded Constance through a smirk.

"Not boys, my dear. Boys aren't vixenish. They might hit each other and shout a lot, but only *after* real friendship has been established. Then, when the blows have stopped, they immediately return to being the best of pals."

"You always have something to say which denigrates my gender," exclaimed Constance bombastically, patting the curls on her head.

"Not so, my dear. I have only the greatest admiration for those who can make such a virtue of expressing contrition for their physical weakness while storing such enormous capacity for verbal venom towards others of their own gender, often for no better reason than the lack of a formal introduction. It seems to me. . ."

"Enough!" shouted Cornelius, immediately apologising for the outburst. "Can we not return to more important and interesting issues – namely me?"

"Sorry, Son."

"Sorry, Cornelius."

"We were talking about my friend Oswald."

"Weren't his parents our tenant farmers for a while? Is he the boy you mean?"

"Just so, Mother. They packed up and left after he died."

"Oh, yes, poor little Oswald. If I recall correctly, he was on board the train which plunged into the river when the Tay Bridge collapsed."

"He was. One among seventy-eight who fell to their deaths into the icy water below, after a gale had blown away the centre spans of the bridge. It was the poor construction of the bridge that was ultimately to blame."

"Sad."

"Sad indeed, Mother. I have little to remember him by, but what I do have in my possession is of such significance to me that I keep it in the Dundee marmalade jar as a reminder of where he perished, God bless him."

"Significant? What do you mean?"

"First, Father, let me tell you something rather odd, almost unbelievable I suppose. Once, many years ago, Oswald and I were returning home after playing around the hill fort when we were stopped by a peculiar little man driving a cart, who spoke in rhyme and knew our names."

"An escaped lunatic?"

"Only if all the inmates of the asylum broke out at once. He was at the head of a caravan. Certainly the words he spoke were not from a feeble mind."

"Did you recognise him?"

"That's the thing. Neither of us did. He was a total stranger. He rather frightened us, seemingly knowing what we had been up to during our childish frolics."

"You've lost me."

"Have you ever heard of Tengmalm Lane?"

"I don't think so. Have you Constance?"

She shook her head.

"Nor had I when the man seemed to ask Oswald the same question. I thought he meant to go there and wanted directions. My mind later conjured up all sorts of fanciful ideas because of the strange sounding name of the place and his personal appearance."

"Sorcery, you mean?"

"I suppose so, Father. You know how a child's imagination works, after reading scary bedtime stories. I had absolutely no reason to think such wild thoughts, but that's the nature of being a boy with a vivid imagination. Plus, we had just learned about heresy at school, so I suppose it was in the back of my mind."

"It's hard to imagine anything like that hereabouts, but anything was possible in the Middle Ages, I suppose."

"Then, there's this." Cornelius removed the stopper from the jar and tipped out the treasure. It fell onto the chaise longue.

"What is it?" asked his mother, reaching across to take it, but in so doing catching a lamp with her elbow and tipping the table onto its side. The thin glass shade shattered as it hit the floor.

"Damn and blast. Stay still, Constance. I'll ring for Jenkin."

The mess was quickly swept and the spilled oil mopped with muslin.

"Here," said Constance. "Have the silly thing back. It has a curse on it."

"How right you are, Mother. This silly thing, as you describe it, is something Oswald and I found under the roots of a rowan tree. Oswald kept it for years, only giving it to me when he said he was leaving to work on the Edinburgh to Aberdeen railway. He said I should keep it."

"Yes?"

"And when he gave it to me, he said one day I would let my curiosity lead me into unhappiness. Laughing, I took it from him and his mood immediately changed, as if he knew we would never see each other again after he went away. The happy moment suddenly became menacing, not just because it was the end of a long friendship, but something much darker. As I took it, I too felt fear. Still, I dropped it into my pocket and the feeling disappeared. We shook hands. On the day he finally left, I surreptitiously placed it back into his pocket, along with a photograph of the two of us at Sunday school. I could think of nothing better for him to have as a memento of our childhood frolics. It was the trophy of our greatest adventure. Poor Oswald."

"A kind gesture, indeed. But, how come you've got it again?" enquired Rufus.

"He obviously found it in his pocket and decided he still didn't want to be the keeper. You see, I now realise how frightened he was to have it, as odd as that might seem to us. He had written a letter to me saying almost those exact words, which he hadn't got around to posting by the time of the accident. The letter was discovered in his bag, which had been placed in a separate carriage that survived the accident. The letter was unsealed, ready to have the treasure popped in at Oswald's convenience. His intention to dispatch the letter to me was carried out posthumously, but not by post. There's more."

"Go on."

"Naturally, his parents were notified of the accident. I went to see them as soon as I could, to offer my condolences. They asked if I would be willing to accompany them north for the identification of the body and to support them in their grief. Actually, I think they were terrified of the train journey after what had happened."

"What a terrible thing to ask of you."

"I didn't mind in the least. Anyway, I too had received a letter from the authorities, mine saying they had something for me to collect. The 'something' turned out to be the letter and treasure in question. Now, here is the rub. He must have written the letter only a short time before his death, as he was found dead grasping the metal talisman, as he then called the treasure we had discovered as boys. Talisman was a much better name for it, as I became all too aware. So, it never reached the envelope, which he must have intended to post at the end of his journey. Perhaps he wanted one last look at it before sealing it away. Heaven knows whether the railway engine exploded at some point, or what happened that involved heat, but the talisman had burned imprints onto his palm and fingers. Yet, strangely, the back of his hand was not charred in the slightest. I can only think he must have put it down and then grabbed it again when it was very hot. I can't imagine any other explanation."

"My goodness!"

"Of course, I didn't know anything about that when we set off north on our grim task. Then, when I was given the talisman, I was absolutely amazed to see that the image on one side was exactly how I remembered it, but on the reverse it was entirely different. For a while I couldn't believe my own eyes. Where a creature had been depicted swimming under the branch of a tree, the talisman now showed a creature at the foot of a grassy hill. I was completely taken aback, hardly trusting my own recollections. Then, Oswald's mother took his lifeless hand and kissed it for the very last time. She was shocked by its coldness and pale colour. All the lifeblood had drained away, the final assurance that Oswald's soul had departed his mortal remains. It was at that moment of embrace that I noticed the burn on his palm, a mirror image of the talisman as I had known it and not as it now appeared. I had remembered correctly."

"How can it be?"

"I can't explain it, Father. For once, I am completely lost for an explanation."

"Shock, you suffered shock and that played on your senses. That's the rational explanation."

"I suppose you're right, Mother, as always. I should forget the whole thing as so much nonsense."

"It would be best," she replied dismissively.

"Poor little Oswald. He was always such a baby, scared of his own shadow. What it must have been like in the last seconds of his life as the bridge gave way, I cannot imagine. I hope to God the end came quickly."

"Amen to that."

"Enough gloom, you two," cut in Rufus. "All this sad history depresses us. Let's give thanks for our family being reunited, even if I already feel the strain on my purse from Cornelius's ambitions. We must count our blessings."

"And your money, Father, don't forget that."

"But not too much," added Constance with an air of concern. "We already live like paupers and I cannot do without the odd luxury to keep my spirits high."

"Modesty in all things, you mean, my dear?"

"Not all things. You must give consideration to having a wife of position, even if you are willing to wear darned socks. Modesty has its place, but not in my wardrobe."

"Ladies of irresistible modesty are those who make virtue unamiable. Sir Richard Steele said that."

"Meaning, Rufus?"

"I'd rather not try to explain, my dearest darling."

"Do I know him, this Steele fellow?"

"I fear there can be very little doubt that you do not."

"Then we should be acquainted at once, if he's a man of words. Writers are so much ahead of all other professions. They have unequalled intelligence and much elegance at the dinner table, no doubt brought about by their observation of everybody else. Invite him to supper."

"It is exceedingly generous of you to take keen interest in my literary acquaintances, but I fear on this occasion it will be to no avail."

"Why so, pray? Does he not eat?"

"I expect he did, once upon a time. He died in 1729."

"Then, why bring him up in conversation?"

"My foolishness, nothing more or less."

"Hmmm!"

"I agree," said Cornelius, dropping the talisman back into the jar. "We must count our blessings and look to higher things."

"To heaven?"

"No, Father, to flying!"

"And beat the Germans?"

"I tried learning the German language once," proffered Constance through a grimace, "but it is such a vulgar sound, requiring such contortions of the throat and face as to make its use unsuitable for mixed company."

Rufus ignored her. "Where do you go from here, Cornelius?"

"Are you leaving already," said Constance absentmindedly, still replaying the humour in her thoughts. It was her second witticism that day.

"No, Mother, I believe Father referred to my experiments in flying."

"Oh, those."

"I thought I might eventually journey to Paris. See what the Frenchies are up to, first hand. But, I have a lot of arrangements to take care of first, so expect my company for quite a time to come."

"I knew someone who died while abroad," she added independently. "It showed a wanton neglect of duty."

"Then, Mother, I shall take the greatest care not to fall ill."

"And don't stay too long. I am very much against staying in foreign lands too long. It gives people the opportunity to find out too much about foreigners which might rub off on their Britishness. It's a bit like marriage. A long engagement offers too much scope for detecting faults in each other, which is never advisable until the ceremony is over."

"I beg you not to distress the boy with further talk of marriage and women. He will find a good woman when he is good and ready, without any assistance from you."

"A good woman, Cornelius, is all very well, but seeking too much perfection can bring about the opposite of the intention. You see, to be too good is to see the worst in all others. It's merely a question of degree."

"You speak ahead of our time, Mother."

"I may do, but I cannot pretend to be the puritanical type. Being too resigned to finding someone with the incorruptibility of perfect virtue is to seek the unobtainable. Conversely, to be too soft on virtue is to surrender more than just one's peace of mind."

"I think that's quite enough, thank you dear."

"No, Rufus, I am not finished. You see, Cornelius, fair maids are like the month of May, although, off-hand, I cannot exactly remember why."

"I think you refer to Shakespeare, Mother, As You Like It."

"I don't know if I do, like it, that is, without remembering the rest."

"What our boy means, dear, is that maids are referred to as the month of May in the play called *As You Like It*. Although, I believe Shakespeare went on to say, the sky changes when they are wives."

"You do it again!"

"I beg your pardon?"

"Have a go at women."

A loud gong called the party to dinner.

"Saved by the bell," whispered Rufus. "We will talk later, when your mother gets one of her headaches."

"I still haven't told you about the talisman itself, or Tengmalm."

"Later, Son, we can talk then, without interruption."

CHAPTER 3

The fairest lady

The evening remained warm. The windows and shutters were closed only when the family made plans to retire for the night.

"Good night, my boy," proffered Constance, taking his shoulders and kissing him within an inch of his cheek. "It's lovely to be a family again."

"Same goes for me, Cornelius. I'm also for my bed."

"But, Father, you promised we would talk."

"And so we shall, tomorrow."

"No, Father, I have something on my mind that is likely to prevent me from sleeping until I share it. Please, I beg you, spare me a few moments."

Rufus turned to his wife and gestured that he would follow shortly, but would occupy his own separate room. Without curiosity, she left.

"Well, what's this problem you hint of?"

"First, Father, let me pour you a glass of port wine. We have a little left in the decanter."

"I believe I've had sufficient. Please, do the decent thing and finish it yourself before the servants do."

"Would they, without your permission?"

"Probably not, they prefer my champagne. They've been

known to remove many more bottles from the cellar than are accounted for at my table."

"That's awful!"

"Not so, Cornelius. I drink mostly red wine myself and make sure it is always of excellent vintage. Your mother likes champagne, but gulps it down without so much as letting it tickle her throat. So, I buy the cheap stuff for her. If I keep my wine from the clutches of the servants by letting them take champagne, it is theft I gladly ignore for the sake of my taste buds. Only, judging by the number of champagne bottles still in the cellar, I am starting to worry that they too suspect the champagne to be more gas than grape." Laughing, he sat. "Now, what troubles you?"

Cornelius slid forward a large sitting chair which occupied a place close to the empty hearth, throwing its scatter cushion to the floor before sinking into its deep velvet.

"Not a problem, as such. More a continuation of what we were talking about earlier."

"Must we? Your mother was probably right when she put that nonsense down to shock. And who could blame you, given the dreadful experience of seeing Oswald after the accident. You know, news of the collapse reached all the daily papers?"

"Yes. But, when Mother said it was shock disturbing my recollections, I merely let the suggestion go, even though you must have reasoned for yourself the flaw in her argument?"

"Flaw?"

"Of course. If it was a fault of my memory, how come the talisman has an image now that is entirely different from the impression burned onto Oswald's palm?"

Rufus ruminated for a few seconds before looking up. "That's a difficult one to explain."

"Exactly! No, I'm quite convinced the mystery involves Tengmalm Lane."

"I don't understand!"

"Look, Father, can you remember far enough back to your school days?"

"Don't be cheeky, Cornelius. Of course I can."

"And when your teacher talked of Oliver Cromwell or King James, did you ever think of them as real people who lived real lives with real families and suffered everyday problems like colds and coughs, rather than mere tales from history?"

"An interesting thought. No, I suppose their lives were so remote from the present day that it's hard to believe they actually existed in the normal way of things."

"Yet we know they did. It's because posterity chooses to remember only a few historic events from their lives, and none of the everyday things, that makes it so hard to think of them as ever having lived full and active lives. Now, instead of applying that idea only to historical characters, think how it could be applied to matters we regard as folklore, fantasy or myth."

"I don't understand!"

"Do you believe in the supernatural?"

"I don't understand."

"Ghosts, gremlins, witches, wizards and the rest?"

"I don't understand."

"For heaven's sake, stop saying that."

"But, I really don't understand."

"Alright, Father, let me start again. The story I want to tell you began a very long time ago, when Oswald and I found the talisman. We were just boys."

"With you so far."

"The thing is, and I don't wish to repeat myself, the talisman seems to have a hold on anyone who keeps it."

"I don't understand." He looked at Cornelius. "Sorry! This talisman of yours, it troubles you in some way?"

"Well, sort of, I suppose. The best way of describing the feeling that comes from possessing it is that it gives the owner the courage to do things that otherwise he wouldn't contemplate."

"Not marriage, I hope. Nothing so daring."

"Take me seriously, Father. As I said, it seems to give the holder power."

"Power?"

"No, not exactly, I've used the wrong word. Say instead, anticipation."

"As in apprehension or hope?"

"More like preconception, mixed with foresight."

"Goodness. And was it the same for Oswald, when he had it?"

"That's the point. It had even greater effect on him, probably because he was younger and therefore more susceptible. Oswald told me things, strange things."

"Explain?"

"But, you wouldn't believe them."

"Try me."

"I don't think I will. It would only bring ridicule on my head."

"Maybe, but I brought you up under the notion that the answer is always *yes* unless there is a good reason to say *no*. It equally applies here. Who could be harmed by it? Certainly not Oswald, sadly, and you have broad shoulders. I have asked to hear and your reply should be *yes*."

"Alright, but you won't understand."

"Go on."

"But first I warn you. What I say will sound ridiculous and very, very childish."

"I stand warned. Now, get on with it. Once upon a time. . ."

"Stop! I will not begin after such an overture of ridicule."

"My apology. Please continue, but in reasonable haste."

"Very well. I will tell you exactly what Oswald told me, word for word as I remember it, with no embellishments whatsoever. It happened a while ago, a little time before he took the Scottish job, in fact. One day, Oswald was walking alone on top of Cadbury fort, eating as he went, when the grazing cattle suddenly took fright for no apparent reason. As they parted, he saw what looked like a human-sized fairy sitting on a boulder in the middle of a small, shimmering pond. Everything about her appearance was unnatural."

"Good heavens, Cornelius. I think you can stop there. I have no inclination to hear such rubbish concerning bug-a-boos when I am eager for my bed."

"I told you the story would be unbelievable."

"And so it is. Such old wives' tales abound in the West-Country, but nobody takes them seriously."

"Do I continue?"

"Only if you feel you must, to ease a burden. But, remember, I am much tired. If this is a joke, it is in poor taste for the hour."

"I will be brief. As everyone who lives around here knows, the fort has no pond, although maybe it once had its own water supply to serve the settlement. So, we are led to believe what Oswald saw was an illusion. Indeed, this was Oswald's own immediate reaction, caused perhaps by eating bad food or taking too much sun. Anyway, the fairy, for want of a better description, the most beautiful of all women draped in what he described as a spiders' web gossamer gown, raised an arm and called to him without a voice."

"A fairy called him without making any sound? Balderdash!"

"Think what you like, but hear me out. I speak only as he told it to me, in all sincerity. The story needs no elaboration. Now, shall I go on, or are you beyond listening?"

"No, please don't stop now. I'm all ears, big pointy ones."

"Anyway," continued Cornelius with eyes flashing, "he thought the fairy wanted some of his cake, so he threw her a lump."

"A fairy cake?"

"Stop it! As it sank below the water, the fairy dived. She emerged biting a corner, but threw it back as being too stale, for in a second of Oswald's life the cake had turned completely hard. At that, she disappeared and the cattle came out of hiding. The lush grass returned and the water vanished."

"And, so, the story ends. Don't believe a word of it. Goodnight, my boy. Don't dream of gremlins."

"No, I'm far from the conclusion, Father."

Wearily, Rufus returned to his seat. Now expecting a long

session he reached for the decanter as solace, pouring the remaining port into a glass, which he sipped with no real appreciation.

"I know I'll regret asking, but what happened next in this fairy story?"

"Startled, but curious, the following day Oswald returned, this time carrying bread. But the fairy did not reappear. Disappointed by her absence, he tried to think what was different from the previous day, only then realising that before he had carried the talisman in his pocket for safe keeping, as his father had begun clearing out the barn. He had hidden it again that evening after the tidying had been completed. So, on the third day he returned to the fort, now carrying the talisman in his left hand and bread in his right. The cattle duly parted and the fairy sat waiting. He spoke gently to her, but she remained completely silent, the guardian of her own privacy, as is the way of fairies. He tossed her the bread, which sank. Again she dived and this time came up smiling, eating it until it was gone. Oswald was mesmerised, as you can imagine."

"Crazed, I would say."

"Take me seriously, please. Anyway, for several more days he repeated the trick, each time attempting unsuccessfully to engage the fairy in the conversation of mortals. Then, finally, he thought up a plan. So, on the next occasion, after she had eaten half his bread, he offered her something more, the talisman itself. Resting it on his upturned palm, she tip-toed over the water's surface and grabbed it from him, dropping the bread. Then, quite suddenly, she dived, re-emerging seconds later in the company of an old man with a wild beard. They stood together on a rock, as if lifted clear of the water. That man was the very same stranger who had frightened us as boys."

"Well, I'll be. . ."

"There's more. According to Oswald, he was convinced he lived a year in a day, if his memory can be trusted."

"Which, evidently, it can't."

"Oswald believed time for fairies passes incredibly quickly, allowing a minute of our time to fill a day in theirs, an hour for them to pass between the blinks of a human's eye. Like the lifetime of a mayfly."

"And this difference in time manifested itself how?"

"It started when the old man asked if Oswald wanted to marry the fairy."

"That's it! I can't take any more. You go too far."

"Naturally," continued Cornelius without stopping, "he did and said so, if it was possible. 'Anything is possible', the old man replied, 'but there are conditions'."

"And Oswald said?"

"What do you think he said, given her beauty? Oswald agreed to any terms. At that point the old man allowed the fairy to step towards him, adding in a serious voice, 'Lily will be yours, as a human, until such time as you bruise her thrice. But, know this, she lives a fairy's time'."

"What a strange thing to say."

"Strange goings-on, Father. Of course, Oswald pleaded that he could never hurt her."

"Was that it, the end of the conversation?"

"Not quite. The old man started rhyming again, as he had when we first met. He said: '*They mistake who say that fairies die, but thrice a hurt and passions fly*'. After, Oswald took her back to his cottage."

"Oh, come now," said Rufus with indignation. "This has to be a joke at my expense!"

"I can assure you Oswald believed all of it. His sincerity convinced me. And I have the proof."

"Which is?"

"I will tell you that last, when the story is complete."

"I can't wait."

"Weeks later Oswald saw a spider crawling along the fairy's arm. He brushed it aside in a sweep of his hand but she turned, crying, saying the spider had been mending her gown and that

Oswald had struck her once. A bruise instantly appeared on her fair skin, although his touch had been gentle. He pleaded with her, saying he hadn't deliberately hurt her, but to no avail. Then, later, he thought she was about to slip off a low branch as she climbed for apples. He grabbed her tightly to prevent a fall. Bruised, she shook herself free, saying he had hurt her twice."

"Twice?"

"Indeed. He was mortified. Now afraid of his own quick reactions, he thereafter tried to hold himself back from any sudden close contact. Thus, a period of strange disunity entered their relationship which lasted throughout the Summer and Autumn. Then, one Winter morning, he saw her walking towards a disused well that had been left uncovered. He lunged forward to save her, but at the last minute remembered what had happened before and pulled back. With dismay, he watched her fall. A voice from the deep said he had hurt her deepest of all, for he had cared more for her company than for her protection and that of their unborn child. With such harsh words from her lips, she vanished."

"Was that it?"

"For Oswald it was. He returned to the fort in the hope of being given a second chance. And there, most remarkably, he found on the ground the half eaten bread exactly where she had abandoned it all those months before. As I said, they had lived a year in a day, because the bread was entirely fresh, as if just from the oven. Beside it rested the talisman."

"I don't believe a word of it. Foolish boy if you do. You would never have gone a year without seeing your best friend."

"Remember what he had been told, Father – she would live a fairy's time. Anyway, I said I have proof."

"Oh, yes?"

"After Oswald died, I took the talisman to the fort. Believe me or not, there, right in front of me, sat two fairies. I swear the scene was real. One fairy was crying."

"Real tears?"

"Just so. I couldn't understand why. But, I think I now know."

"So, tell me."

"The old man had once said '*losers will be weepers*'. Maybe the fairy lamented having to give up the talisman. For, while she had it, she lived among mortals. The strange man had also said '*a curse on them that takes the gild and spoils the lily*'. I wonder if the gild he referred to was the talisman. For, the fairy was the lily, of that I hold no doubt."

"What of the other fairy?"

"She was of equal beauty and looked directly at me with alluring charm. The old man sitting between them held a baby. To all appearances the child looked human, without any of the diaphanous appearance of the fairies. I wondered if it was possibly Oswald's baby, for it is said fairies must steal or sometimes create human children by interbreeding to add sturdiness to their lineage.

"And then?"

"The one not crying raised an arm, but I turned my back on her and the mirage vanished, but not before I stole a backward glance and saw her brightness fading with rejection. I left it several days before trying again, having planned a better response. But, my being there with the talisman was not enough to bring her back."

"Saints preserve us! You know I don't accept any of this as real, Cornelius. It's impossible, ridiculous and extremely childish. Still, you might as well finish the tale, now we've got this far. Tell me the whereabouts of the place you mentioned, Tengmalm Lane."

"I came to realise it wasn't a place at all! I think Tengmalm was the baby's given name. Remember, Oswald's surname was Lane. The baby was none other than Oswald Lane's child. It all fits."

"You think so? You conveniently forget the fact that you two were nothing more than innocent schoolboys when the old man asked about Tengmalm Lane. By your own submission, the child was years from being born."

"You misunderstand, Father. The old man said '*the future is an already trodden path*'. Should that be taken literally? He had demonstrated that he knew more than could be possible under the normal way of things. No, I think I have it right. I have brushed against the supernatural and survived the experience, unlike Oswald."

"No, I won't believe it. It goes against everything I hold sacred. Show me any solid proof, something verifiable."

"Strangely, I can. I have discovered another account of something very similar. It's part of Welsh folklore. Apparently, a young farmer in the middle-ages famously came across human-size fairies at a Welsh mountain lake. Like Oswald, he married one. She, too, eventually disappeared after being hurt, taking with her the cattle, sheep and horses which had been part of her dowry. She is still remembered to this day as the Fairy of Llyny Fan Fach. The area around Myddfai is regarded as magical. How odd is that?"

"This is all wrong, Cornelius. You shouldn't believe any of it. It goes against rational thinking and rational faith."

Cornelius walked to a bookshelf, where he removed a dictionary. "Let's get the proper meaning of faith. Oh, yes, here it is: *Trust in a belief that does not rely on logical proof or firm evidence*." He shut the book.

"Clever words prove nothing, my boy."

"But why shouldn't it? Does our modern world know everything? Does science and industry make allegory unworthy of an open mind? There is so much from the past that we have lost the ability to understand."

"But here, in our home village of Cadbury, right on our doorstep?"

"Why not? Why anywhere else? After all, Cadbury is said to have been a place connected to King Arthur, and you know the myths and legends surrounding that period of English history. What of Merlin?"

"Show me the talisman again, Cornelius."

"No, Father, it's best ignored. If it ever held magic, I feel sure it's gone. Now, for me, it holds just the memory of an old friend and a childhood never to return."

"Shall we tell your mother about this?"

"I think not. She wouldn't understand."

"And you think I do?"

"Probably not."

"Definitely not. You're always away with the fairies. Sun stroke, I shouldn't wonder. Or a gas released from below the ground both here and in Wales, given off naturally by the rocks, enough to give a person the vapours. A miasma."

"Yes, sun stroke or shock."

"Or the vapours."

"Vapours, yes. I'm sure you're right, Father. Goodnight."

As his father climbed the stairs, Cornelius took the talisman from the jar. It was now lifeless and cold.

"Sun stroke or vapours, be damned. God bless you, Oswald. The strange man had said '*a boy who stole and then has fled, will shake and scream with trembling dread*'. Did he know you would die in such awful circumstances, my oldest friend?"

A loud voice called from the top of the stairs, making Cornelius jump.

"I forgot to ask, my boy. What do you intend to do with the talisman thing?"

"I shall fling it away, I expect."

"That's the ticket. Best get rid of it and all dark thoughts."

Once more Cornelius looked at the image on the front, a human-like creature with four beating wings which had inspired him in his early work. He turned it over. Where once a similar type of creature had been depicted on the surface of a pond, was now, for all to see, something entirely different. Of course, he thought, a shudder of fear flooding through his body. The creature in the original image had not been swimming at all, but had fallen from a great height and lay face down in the water. Perhaps the stunted branch represented a damaged bridge.

Panicked, he looked again at the new image, his pulse gradually calming on seeing nothing disturbing. It merely showed a winged creature resting at the foot of a grassy hill. Nevertheless, Cornelius sweated as he popped the talisman back into the jar and rammed the lid shut.

"My God, Oswald never stood a chance! His fate was sealed the moment he pocketed the talisman," said Cornelius to an empty room.

CHAPTER 4

Old Mr Mortimore

While Cornelius made last minute alterations to his plans for a trip to France, having already spent many weeks that turned into months settling his affairs and seeing a new tenant move into the farm at Chard, a dissolute dairymaid trudged her way towards the rear entrance of the Holman Clavel, an inn built in the 14th century. Quite by chance, she was only eight miles from Chard and two miles from Pitminster, in a most westerly area of Wessex known as the Black Down Hills, a region less than a day from London and, yet, it had remained a place of seclusion.

For the dairymaid, the day had been one of hard walking, culminating in a relentless climb up a steep path where, near its highest point, she had noticed the place partially hidden to her right and entirely isolated from other dwellings in the village. It was a welcoming sight for a weary traveller.

Despite her journey being long since leaving her employer at Westkings for the third time in as many years, the Black Down Hills had afforded inspiring views, even in the month of October, and she had enjoyed all but the last few tiring miles. For, although anyone journeying along such a route might have expected a rugged landscape and harsh conditions, in reality the Black Downs offered a dramatically rolling landscape, with gentle rise after gentle rise, put to the plough or left as lush pasture, each neat field trimmed with hedgerows or forested outcrops too thickly wooded and mature to be considered coppice.

Emmeline Sturry was old in worldly experience for her tender age. Not that she looked old, far from it, but her many bitter ordeals now outweighed any happy memories of the time when she, Christabel, Mary and Louise had been merry together in the fields of the Elvington estate. She had lost in love, not once but twice. Christabel, her only really close friend, had died and a gold ring memento from that friendship had been forcibly taken from her by Charlotte Elvington, Christabel's natural but estranged mother and the wife of Emmie's former employer at Westkings. To Emmie, it seemed she had no friends left who were capable of offering any comfort. Yet, in the back of her mind, she knew she had caring parents who would always welcome her home no matter what she had done to deserve censure.

"Can I help you, maidy?" offered the landlord from a richly smiling face.

"Have you any work, Sir? I need work."

Her question seemed to astonish him. He looked her up and down with grave expression. Her hands and complexion were far from delicate, a sure sign of outside labouring, yet she was hardly capable of standing.

"Why, you are but a bit of a child."

"No, Sir, I am an adult. I'm small, that is all."

"You are that," he replied. Her plea for work, when he could see she had other more pressing needs, touched him deeply. "You say you need work, yet I can see you need sustenance first. When did you last eat a proper meal?"

Her head dropped. "I think it was yesterday. I had some bread."

"Goodness, my sweet child, such goings on will never do. Little wonder you're the size of a dormouse. No, it won't do at all."

Being a kindly sort of man, who counted his blessings daily and was generous to share them with others, it was inevitable from the moment Emmie stood before him that she was saved.

"Have you, Sir?"

"Sit you by the ingle and get warm while I see what I can put on a plate," he added. "No bolting off, mind, when me back is turned. You shall enjoy a meal with Chimney Charlie."

"I am too tired to run anywhere," she replied in soft tone. "I thank you, Sir, for your kindness to a stranger. May I wash a bit first?"

"Wash? Why, I suppose so, if you must. There's a pump out back and you may grab a cloth from the kitchen, though why you would want to bother is beyond me."

"More than my hands are dirty, Sir. The path was quite perilous."

"And the air outside is cold. I can see some point in washing your face. You need clear eyes to see, an unblocked nose to sniff and a moist tongue to spit. But anything else is perfectly unnatural before morning. That's why God gave us waterproof skin, to keep the dirt from our insides and the cold of the day from our bones."

"He also provided water, for what purpose if not for washing?"

"Why, for drinking, of course, and the making of fine ale. It was created to cleanse the inside, not the outside. Still, if you insist on washing legs that won't be seen by another mortal soul, then you will only have yourself to blame if you catch a fever."

Having taken the chance and returned inside thoroughly chilled, Emmie took a seat by the inglenook where the warmth from crackling logs enveloped her entire body. The opening to the fire was huge, not centred in the retaining wall in unusual fashion, but occupying a space to the far left.

"It's a mighty strange name, the Holman Clavel," said Emmie as a bowl of steaming hot soup was placed on the table, together with a wedge of bread and a small selection of cheeses and cut meats. "My goodness, Sir, this is a feast. I have very little money in my purse. I fear I cannot afford such luxuries."

"Did I ask for payment?" returned the landlord.

A tankard was placed beside.

"For me, too, Sir?

"'Tis the milk of human kindness."

Emmie took a long gulp. "It is milk!" she exclaimed, recovering from the unexpectedly thick liquid that spilled from her mouth. "My pardon, Sir, it is delicious, of course. It's just that it wasn't the taste my mouth expected. It caught me by surprise."

"Nothing finer than Wessex milk straight from the cow, and no better place to live in the whole country I am thinking."

"But not what I had expected in an ale house."

"Do you greater good than beer, I can assure you. Now, you get it down and we will talk about a job after I shut for the night or, better still, in the peace of the morning, when you are fully refreshed. The regulars will be gone in a few hours, unless they get stuck into a game of skittles. We must bed you."

Emmie's eye's flared. "Do you live alone?" she asked with more than a little concern in her voice, careful not to imply any doubt to his character.

"Do I heck, maidy. No, I have the company of four. It won't do to be afraid of me. I'm as gentle as a lamb, and never been left to my own company since I took over this place."

With that said he left for the bar, leaving Emmie to tuck into the meal with relish.

That night she took refuge in an unoccupied guest room situated behind the skittle alley. She had been shown the alley before retiring to prevent any alarm at the 'thwack' sounds that would penetrate the wall if the game was played.

The alley was a purpose built room of great length, but narrow. Its rough and windowless walls supported an inclined wooden gully to the left, used for returning the bowls or 'cheeses' to the players after they had rumbled down the length of the floor and fallen into a lower gully immediately behind the skittles. The skittles themselves stood on nine markers within a diamond pattern.

As predicted, Emmie's sleep was interrupted by the sound of skittles being knocked over. It went on until dawn. Thankfully, the landlord left her to oversleep. She was eventually woken by the sound of heavy barrels being dropped into the cellar. It was nine o'clock. Another quick wash in cold water had to suffice.

"So, you are up at last!" the landlord remarked in a kindly way, wiping ale from his mouth with the back of his sleeve and grinning towards the drayman.

"Yes, Sir, I am ready to do your bidding."

"Lord, have mercy on us!" he cried in cheery tone. "You might be the size of a sparrow, but you surely have spirit. Work for you is not on the agenda until after you have breakfasted properly. Take yourself off to the kitchen and pan fry a few eggs and whatever else takes your fancy. There's a goodly range of wholesome stuff to choose from. No sparrow's portion, mind!"

"Do I make enough for two, Sir?"

"Bless you, no. I was up with Chimney Charlie and he won't want any."

"Is he one of the four who live here?"

"He is, so to speak. Now, get you off."

And so, in this framework of young girl in need of help and jolly landlord, a platonic friendship was born that transcended employee and employer.

Mr Mortimore was a man in his early fifties, stout in figure and usually red in face. His nose appeared to have become a sponge for excess ale, swollen in size and with very visible pores. Not a hair graced the top of his head, but his mutton-chop sideburns were thick and gave a slimming effect to his features. He was, in overall consequence, a nice man rather than a handsome figure.

Over the coming days, in this atmosphere of cheery companionship, Emmie fulfilled her kitchen tasks with a light heart, making little actual money beyond the few tips she earned from customers, but enough to get by. Her board and lodging were free. Indeed, the more the locals welcomed her, the more she learned to smile. In this, her character was transformed every bit as noticeably as the change she brought to the general aura of the inn itself, which enjoyed renewed repartee. Custom flourished, for even the rugged farmers enjoyed being served by a pretty face willing to give a chirpy reply to every cheeky remark.

A regular visitor to the Holman Clavel was Matilda Spry, a most respectable spinster of the parish with well-formed features, who availed herself as a spiritualist to communicate with the long dead. She avoided the recently dead, as the possible pitfalls in her advice to living relatives or friends were too many.

"Ask my wife where she left the rent book, or ask Uncle Tom if I am to be remembered in his will," were beyond her capacity to answer and chillingly open to guess work. Once tuppence had parted hands for a communication with the dead, the advice she gave had to be acceptably accurate or, otherwise, unverifiable.

So it was that on the sixth day of Emmie's work, Miss Spry was again seen sitting in her favourite corner. She had ordered her usual plate of stew and beamed gleefully as Emmie carried it towards her, steam rising from the dish.

When it comes to pranks, field hands are among past masters of the sport. It has often been debated as to why this is so, for their daily drudgery would seem capable of knocking out any spirit or spare energy. Perhaps it was their hard-bitten character from working outdoors in all weathers that made their venting of a little steam not just possible, but inevitable. And so it was that, as Emmie worked her way around the tables, a young man of no more than nineteen stuck out his foot in her path. The dish flew from her hand and crashed to the floor, skimming along the flagstones like a pebble on water, followed by Emmie herself in what seemed slow motion. With arms outstretched to save herself, a shard of pottery pierced her palm as she fell flat and hard.

"That was a damned silly thing to do, young Ted," shouted the landlord, rushing from behind the bar with a damp cloth in his hand.

"None harm done, Mr Mortimore, 'tis only a bit o' mess."

"That mess, Master Groat, was my supper," scalded Miss Spry.

"Ah, but you should ha' seen it coming, what with your powers."

"I deal with the dead, Ted Groat, not fortune telling."

"Are you alright, me dear?" asked Mr Mortimore, as his helped Emmie from the floor. She held up a hand. "Oh, I can see you're not."

"It's nothing, Sir. A bit of a scratch, that's all."

"There," laughed Ted Groat, "no harm done to anyone."

The landlord cuffed his ear, the open hand causing a real sting and much redness.

"Mr Mortimore! Enough of that!" demanded Miss Spry. "Violence begets violence. Wouldn't you agree?"

Emmie looked at her palm after Mr Mortimore had plucked the shard from beneath her skin. The wound was small, but sensitive, as painful as the cut from a fine knife.

"I think the young man is a fool," Emmie replied, a remark made more grievous by their similar ages.

A round of laughter greeted her words, causing acute embarrassment to the young man, who threw back his chair, downed his ale in a single gulp, and blustered his way out of the door, causing maximum disturbance as he went.

"Silly arse," said Mr Mortimore at his departure, bending to pick up the broken plate and clear the floor of food.

"Don't 'ee be doing that, Gerald," suggested an elderly shepherd sitting on a wooden settle. "Let me dog lick it clean. He has a tongue like a mop."

The sheepdog, which had been obediently supine by his master's side, looked up eagerly as its master removed the rope leash. In a thrice the floor was clean, the dog sniffing around the legs of the chairs and tables for any scraps of food still to be discovered.

"Better than any brush is my Jessie. I think it deserves a free quart of ale, Mr Mortimore, for saving you the trouble."

"I do believe you are right, Jack Taylor, and so I shall get it."

The shepherd licked his lips. The landlord returned, placing a dish of ale in front of the dog's nose.

"Hey! That was meant for me!"

"'Twas not you who licked the floor clean. Anytime you want to be a brush, stay behind after closing and you will earn your own quart of my cheapest brew."

That night, when the doors had been shut tight and the tables cleared, Emmie sat in a back room with Mr Mortimore, enjoying a tankard of cider.

"I hope you don't mind me asking, Mr Mortimore," she said in an inquisitive tone, "but what's that I heard about the spinster lady being a fortune teller."

"Miss Spry? No, me dear, she's no fortune teller and would come down hard on anyone giving her such a false title. She describes herself as a spiritualist. She talks to the dead."

"My word."

"Of course, each and every one of us has our own opinion about that. I, for one, believe she does have a rare gift. Others, well, they say she's a fraud. I suppose it depends on our individual circumstances."

"How so?" asked Emmie with interest.

"Well, now, let me see how I can explain. Say, for example, a particular person is sceptical about such matters, but, then, a loved one or friend dies sudden like. Not of a long illness or old age, you understand, but in an accident. Unexpected like. It might happen, then, that Miss Spry or others like her could eventually offer comfort to sooth the grieving process and the receiver of such kindness might want to believe it, even if he or she rejected the idea beforehand. 'Tis human nature to fight against something out of the ordinary which isn't understood until it comes home to roost. Oh, mark my words, I'm not saying her powers would suit everyone, or that everyone would need such comforting in the first place. I'm just thinking that I've seen rock-hard opponents of her meddling turn about-face when suffering the misery of loneliness and call on her to offer a measure of solace from beyond the grave, months or sometimes years after the bereavement."

"Which is it, 'meddling with the beyond' or a 'gift'? You said both."

"Which only goes to show how contrary the subject can be."

"But you don't say where you stand."

"If pressed, in the quietness of my own home, I would say I am a believer."

"Heavens!"

"Don't look at me like that. I'm not an easy man to convince."

"You also said 'others of her type'. What is her type?"

"Why, white witches, of course."

"Goodness!"

"There you go again, getting all alarmed. White witches are generally good."

"They are?"

"Indeed, yes!"

"I don't know," she added, troubled by the thought. "Can you convince me? I have the interest to listen, but the heart to spurn."

"And the *conviction* not to believe whatever I say, I think. No, me dear, I wouldn't try. All I know is there are many things we ordinary folk don't understand, even if the evidence is placed before our very eyes. You see, it is human nature to be blind to those things we don't want to believe. Our Christian faith leaves no room for deviation from the one path."

"Miss Spry is mortal too, just like you and me. So how come she understands it all?"

"'Tis a clever brain you have in that sparrow's head of yours. I cannot compete with it. All I suggest is that she has special powers. I hear said through the bottom of a half empty glass of ale that her kind of wisdom comes from spell books and the like, while others equally tipsy say it is knowledge handed down through generations. Well, what I say is, I knew her parents and they were as normal as you and me. Still, it has to come from somewhere. I suppose, in a way, it's like religion. There are matters common folk cannot explain, but something inside tells us they are true anyway. With her, that belief comes from a strange direction."

"The Church tells us what to believe and we listen. It's the job of vicars to strengthen our resolve. No room is left for doubt."

"Well, yes, I think you're right. But I, for my part, don't take a lot of notice of vicars. They hide behind stock phrases when the going gets tough."

"I don't understand."

"Simple, maidy, and here's a good example of what I mean. I once asked a vicar to explain the meaning of eternity. Because, if you ponder upon it, how can anything have no end. Nothing can just go on and on and on. Thinking about eternity when I was but a slip of a lad used to keep me awake at night. It troubled me greatly and, if truth be told, it still does. Now, if the vicar had said eternal sleep for the dead lasts for as long as the sun still shines in the sky, I could accept such an answer. For, once the sun goes cold, *all* life on our planet will expire and, maybe, so might afterlife, wherever it resides. But, then, what would follow, because the end of one thing normally leads quite naturally to the start of something else? There can't be 'nothing' for ever. You get me meaning?"

"I think I understand. What happened then?"

"He just stared blankly. So I carried on. I asked what lay outside our stars. 'The heavens, boundless distance without end', was his reply. 'The heavens', said I? Well, that's all well and good, but, then, how can that be? If the world was to stop spinning and we were all thrown into the sky to float away into space for all time without limit, how could we never come to an end? Yet, if we did, what form could that end take? And, if there was an end to God's creation, what would be on the other side of it? But, if there was no other side, well, how could that be right, either? It makes no sense."

"And he replied?"

"There are more things in heaven and earth. . . You know the rest."

"He had no more compelling answers?"

"None at all, and he wasn't willing to discuss the subject further. He dismissed me out of hand as if he was a self-respecting man who would be lowered in esteem to debate lofty clerical matters with the likes of me, rough and ready as I am. He left me with the feeling of being nothing more to him than an ignoramus who couldn't add two and two. But I showed him, when I shouted *five* as I left!"

Emmie grinned at his irony. "Do you carry religion, Mr Mortimore?"

"Only in me heart. I don't do with Church. How about you?"

She thought for a moment, unhurried in her response. "I pray, sometimes, but I'm not sure it counts. I seem to forget until I need help and I suppose it would be too late by then. I gave up regular church when I left Westkings for the first time. I could see no goodness in the world to celebrate."

"Yet, goodness there is."

"I know, my dear Sir. You have shown me that truth."

That night Emmie tried to sleep, but was disturbed by falling skittles which lasted until daybreak. She slumped into a chair at the breakfast table.

"Are you well today, maidy?" enquired the landlord. "You look done for. I expect it's too much washing."

"Yes, Sir. That is, I am not unwell. I'm tired, nothing more."

"Not sleeping again? You should try eating just before bed.

Gulping late helps me when my mind is disturbed. Cheese, that's what I use. Lays on me guts like lead and fair settles me down."

"I think I'll pass on that idea, and of having anything now," she returned through a yawn, her head cupped on her hands.

"As you like, or is it you still let thoughts of that Edmond Elvington lad being married to another woman upset you?"

"I told you that in confidence."

"And I will keep it secret between us. I see no others here listening in. Take the advice of someone much . . . a few years older than you. It does no good to constantly muse over what might have been, but can't be changed. Mark my words. He's made his choice, and you have to live with it and move on. Leaving Westkings was the best tonic for your heart, of that there's no uncertainty. You should've left earlier, rather than wait in the hope of changing the course of things. Now, when you think upon it, aren't I right?"

"No, not at all. Edmond once loved me and he might've again. Old passions do sometimes revive, you know, if a period apart ends in meeting up again. Anyway, I was kept awake by quite different things. Tell me, who played skittles so late?"

"Skittles? Why, nobody played after we locked up."

"No, Sir, that isn't right. I distinctly heard them falling."

Mr Mortimore fumbled to collect the unused knives and forks from the table. "Then it was Charlie," he said foxily.

"Can't you stop them?"

"Them?"

"There was more than one playing."

Her remark seemed to confound him. He turned pale, offering her a cup of steaming tea with a trembling hand. "This will help wake you. Are you sure you won't eat anything?"

"I'd rather not, if you don't mind. Later, perhaps. What about the skittles?"

Mr Mortimore knew the conversation could not be sidestepped. "The truth is," he uttered aloofly, "I'm unable to prevent their games. It doesn't disturb me any longer, but it did when I first came to the Clavel."

"Is that why I never see them, because they play all night and sleep all day? What hold do they have over you to prevent you from forbidding their unsociable hours?"

"Who exactly do you mean?"

"The four other people you said live here with us. It must be them playing, because everyone else had left when I locked up."

"Oh!"

"And, if I may say, for someone supposedly at ease with the way of things, you look uncommonly worried."

"I admit it's most unusual for all four to play at once, but I don't think it's an omen of anything bad."

She lifted her head from its cupped position, her eyes widened. "What, exactly, is going on?"

Mr Mortimore was respectful of her forceful enquiry and much moved by her genuine need to understand if she was to live among them, and yet he was afraid to reveal more. It might drive her away. For, even more than the additional custom she brought to his establishment, he feared the loss of her company.

He stared her way, considering how best to give the answers she so reasonably demanded. There was no easy way to explain and, so, by coming to this simple conclusion, he felt easier to speak in whatever way the words parted from his lips. No awkward details would be avoided.

"This 'ere inn is five hundred years old, give or take a bit. Its strange name comes from old times. Holman was the name given to any man cutting holly trees for a living, 'helme' being the ancient word for holly. Clavel meant recess, or fireplace, or beam of wood. Take your own choice as to which. So, when a big holly tree was felled to be used as the mantel over the inglenook, the inn took the name of its most recognisable feature. It must have suited the Holmans too, who undoubtedly drank here. However, others think the mantel is made from Holm Oak. I suppose, after all this time, it hardly matters one way or t'other."

"I would've called it the skittle inn!"

"A good name, right enough, but not accurate for the period. Because, you see, the skittle alley was built much, much later. But, lor, you have unintentionally hit the nail on the head."

"I have?"

"Indeed so, maidy. On the exact same spot where the alley now stands, had been a school for the children of unmarried mothers. The inn itself had become a refuge. As fate would have it, one day the school burned down."

"Was everyone saved?"

"There hangs the riddle of the place. The flames consumed three boys aged four to six."

"Three poor little fatherless lads. How sad," said Emmie in genuine pain, her eyes glistening at the image.

"Indeed so. But there is more to the story. The school was never rebuilt. Instead, a skittle alley was erected when the Holman Clavel returned to its original purpose as a provider of ale."

"I see, but, then, I don't see. You still tell me nothing of the four who live here with us."

"Please, let me continue and you will learn all in good time. It can't be rushed."

Emmie nodded acceptance.

"In ancient times the inn was well sited as a resting place for monks making the long pilgrimage from Exeter to Glastonbury Abbey. All was well with this arrangement until, one day, a rogue monk committed unspeakable acts on a girl from the nearby village of Churchingford. So grave was his crime, he was defrocked. According to the story as I heard it, the monk continued to frequent the inn and eventually worked here. But, when he died, it is said he did not pass to the hereafter in the normal way of things. Instead, his troubled spirit took up residence in the chimney of the fireplace, while sometimes being seen sitting on the holly mantel itself."

"Not Chimney. . ."

"Charlie! 'Tis he alright and no mistake."

"You mean to say, he's one of the four people who are supposed to live here?"

He nodded. "In fairness, I never said 'people'. The others are the little lost boys from the fire."

"Ghosts! Then," she shivered, "it's just me and you living here, alone, for I absolutely refuse to believe in spirits of any kind, other than those sold in bottles."

He saw her shudder dramatically and wondered if her conviction was genuine or whether she played to the occasion. The answer came quickly.

"I have been fooled and placed in danger!"

"No, child, believe me as an honest man, they really are resident and completely harmless."

"You don't fear for your immortal soul to believe such nonsense? I would in your place. I would've been out of here by now if I was in your shoes."

"Not in the least. Anyway, 'tis my home and my living, and Charlie is good for business. Charlie and the boys are mischievous, but nothing more. They like to move things about, or hide things for a while, but always in good humour. Oh, and they love playing skittles at night."

"The skittles I heard?"

"'Tis so." He bowed his head in shame, adding reflectively: "I believe I'm to be left by you. Please say I am wrong."

Embarrassed to give the reply she knew would follow, and with the frightening revelation ringing in her ears, Emmie asked if she could return to her room for a while. All had changed and she needed to think. She rose to leave, suppressing any immediate discontent in the matter of her employment. She could see Mr Mortimore was left a broken man, but she could not pity him for the deception. Even if she could believe in friendly ghosts, or disbelieve for that matter, it did not change the undeniable fact that it would do her reputation no good to openly live under the same roof as an unmarried man. She knew Mr Mortimore was well respected, but that alone would not be enough to stop eager tongues from wagging. As a man, he was immune from censure. As a woman, she would be condemned.

That evening the regulars gathered for their usual ale and cider, happy to pass the hours among friends. Miss Spry sat in the corner eating her usual stew. Mr Mortimore, having heard nothing from Emmie since their early morning chat, reluctantly decided to knock on her door at seven o'clock to seek her help in the bar. Standing outside in hesitation, he bent down to pick up the plate of food he had left at mid-day, but remained untouched. It was to join other unwashed dishes piling up in the sink.

Responding to his gentle knock, she opened the door to the width of a hand, peering crookedly through the gap. He could just see past to clothes folded in a pile on the bed.

"You are on your way, then?" he entreated with genuine regret.

"I am," was her only reply, a slight curling of her mouth intended to soften the blow.

"Is there nothing I can say to keep you here?"

"Nothing at all."

"Lord, I wish it was different. You have given me such joy."

"And you me, Sir."

"Where will you go?"

"Wherever my feet take me."

"Swede hacking in open fields in all weathers, labouring into the evenings by the light of burning fires, I shouldn't wonder. Is that really better than being here with me? Am I such a dreadful person for tricking you?"

She stepped back, allowing the door to be opened fully. There stood Mr Mortimore, as glum as can be imagined. She raised her hand and ran the back of her fingers along his ruddy cheek.

"Mr Mortimore, you are a good man and I don't condemn you in the least for the trifling matter of the trick. Indeed, if you knew my own past, I doubt you would judge me at all well in return."

He remained immobile and sad. "I wouldn't care," he whispered.

"I think you would," she replied. "Dear, kind Sir, I can see from your face you think me ill-used and frail. But nothing could be further from the truth. I have been wilful for as long as I care to remember and have showered shame on a good many people over the years, including my parents and employers. Yet, even that condemnation doesn't do justice to my actions towards the dearest of all friends, a gentle rosebud by the name of Christabel Mere. To her I was worst of all." Emmie recollected her face, sometimes smiling with great happiness and other times contrite and deeply scared by her cruel life. "To me, she was like the Summer sun on a ripening field, the glow of warmth on a Spring lamb's back. I cannot forget her and nor will time heal the emptiness I feel. Her memory burns as deeply now as then. Take comfort from knowing that it is as penance to her that I go, and not because of you. I am resigned to be a better person and as such cannot endure scandal."

"I will miss you with all my heart. 'Tis a very bad day."

"And me you, kind Mr Mortimore."

"Will we ever meet again as friends, my little sparrow?"

"One day, Sir, after we are dead and in the ground. I fear not until then."

His voice was one of deep melancholy, his tone having no rise or fall. "Please, I beg you, stay at least until morning. Grant me that much for my peace of mind. By morning, you might judge me less hard."

"Thank you, Sir, I will stay 'til then, but I will not be here by the next nightfall." She gently closed the door.

In the morning Emmie had gone, but not before she had washed all the dishes, pans and tankards from the previous evening while Mr Mortimore slept heavy on undigested cheese, taking a few parcels of food wrapped in muslin in lieu of wages owed. A wild flower placed in a jar and left on the breakfast table was her note of farewell.

As she climbed the hill towards places new, a voice called out to her. She stopped and turned. Miss Spry stood impassively, beckoning her back.

"I saw you pass my window. I knew instinctively you were leaving our village."

"I was carrying my bag! A bit of a giveaway," was her pithy reply.

She tutted softly. "Don't think for one second I mind in the least if you consider me a charlatan, because I don't. What I can do for Mr Mortimore is all I care about."

"I don't understand."

"Of course not. Come, take a pot of herb tea with me."

Emmie looked at her cottage, made strange by knick-knacks dangling from the roof and porch. Dead rooks with wings fully spread hung in rows on the fence, each neatly skewered through the neck and tips. Miss Spry followed her eyes.

"There's no reason to worry about those little things. They're not part of any magic or spells. Just wind-chimes and such like. Toys to be tickled by the breeze. The birds are pests, hung out to scare others from my vegetables."

Emmie remained impassive.

"Very well. We will talk here, if we must."

"Briefly. I must go before Mr Mortimore notices I'm gone."

"Have you taken something you shouldn't?"

"No! I just want to avoid embarrassment."

"I guess you know I have a reputation for being a white witch?"

Emmie nodded. "And a spiritualist," she added.

"Which scares you?"

"I dare not say what I think."

"In case I put a curse on you? Oh, come now."

"How would I know what you are capable of? Some people believe in your powers."

"Including Mr Mortimore?"

"Yes."

"An honest answer to which I reply that, to a white witch, all creation is sacred."

"Except for rooks," replied Emmie unwisely.

"Except for all pests. It's a fine line to tread and one that sits uncomfortably on my shoulders. My belief in the natural world is why I harness the wind for the making of music. And, yes, it is true I practise Wicca, the religion of witchcraft. It gives my life balance and purpose. Wicca is in harmony with nature, the cycle of creation brought about by the changing seasons. Tell me, are you any easier in your mind now you know this?"

"Not really."

"Because, when you think of witches, you can't stop thinking of spells and flying broomsticks?"

"I suppose so."

"And spells mean danger?"

"Of course."

"And no good can come from them?"

"None."

"I see. Perhaps you may live long enough to know that spells can also hasten change."

"I can't see how."

"Then let me tell you this. We have our own rules, our Wiccan Rede. These forbid us from using spells to manipulate or dominate others. We live by the threefold law, meaning that anything done to another person will come back on us threefold, whether for good or ill. White witches act only after considerable thought as to the consequences. We've been around a very long time. Wicca is the old Anglo-Saxon word for witch."

"Saying all that explains nothing."

"Threefold, I said. Perhaps this will convince you, then. A very long time ago, in 1657 to be exact, an old woman put a spell on an apple, which a young boy ate. On biting it, he rose into the air and flew three hundred yards. The old woman was hanged before Wicca took its own revenge. The place has since been known as a place of flying."

"Where is it?"

"She was hanged in a town called Chard. Not far from here."

Emmie shuddered. Miss Spry clearly believed the story, proof found in her look of complete conviction.

"Why did you call me back?" asked Emmie, releasing herself from the woman's suppression. "Not just to tell me a cock and bull story about flying, I hope."

"Because, Mr Mortimore told me last night how you intended to leave and why. He was extremely melancholy. Naturally, as a friend, I had to intervene, although he didn't ask it of me."

"Not by casting a spell, I hope?"

"Of course not, silly child. He felt you considered him to be a liar, someone who had fooled you into living and working at the inn. That hurt him deeply."

"He *did* trick me."

"No, he didn't. Chimney Charlie and the boys are real enough. I know for a fact. Just like you, he too had been disturbed by the skittles when he first took over the place, and by his possessions going missing and returning later in other places. Sometimes Charlie's antics scared off the overnight customers, but generally most people are fascinated by the story. I expect he told you."

"A little of it, but rather too late."

"Well, what he probably didn't say out of courtesy to me was that once, a long time ago, I held a 'communication' at the inn, for want of a better term, acting as a spiritualist. I took my 'true or false' pendulum, but you don't need to know about that or how it works. It was held in the skittle alley. I asked if there was more than one person present and the answer confirmed there was. I did the same for two and three. I asked if the number exceeded four, and the reply was 'false'. I asked if they were close and a sudden chill in the air made me believe they stood between us. More was asked, but that is private between me and Mr Mortimore."

"I don't want to hear any more. It scares me too much. It flies in the face of normal things. Goodbye."

With the words gone from her lips, Emmie hurried away, closing her ears and mind to anything else.

"You see," Miss Spry shouted, "he told you the truth. He didn't lie. Can you not forgive him the rest?"

Emmie refused to make any gesture that might encourage further conversation.

Shrugging, Miss Spry turned for her door. "The boys are happy, that's all I wanted to tell you."

The chimes rang out as she entered her home, although no wind blew.

CHAPTER 5

November march

$\mathcal{E}$ mmie, with all her experience of farm work, had known from the outset how difficult it would be to find new employment so late in the agricultural year. With the pending Winter would go hand-in-hand the shedding of surplus labour, not hiring, making opportunities few. It was the timeless way of the countryside, a burden the poor and destitute had to face in an annual cycle. But, then, perhaps other types of employment would present themselves. Another hostelry would be nice, she thought, offering easy work and comfortable surroundings.

And so the weeks passed as she wandered the leafless countryside that stretched between farms, villages and towns, diverting to any shed or hovel for cover as the raw twilight of each day made further walking pointless, dangerous and bitter. Taking the risk to leave the Holman Clavel when her belly was full and she had food in her bag now seemed incredibly imprudent, but the distance travelled made any return impossible. In desperation, she accepted odd jobs to satisfy her hunger and rest in any available shelter, often among animals brought in from the fields and with nothing more than their body warmth and straw to keep out the cold. For it was now the beginning of November, when the hills and vales appeared to be in headlong retreat towards hibernation as the severe weather took a grip on the fields all about. Soon, gale winds and bitter rain would snap and pinch at the features of the human needy, the frost already nipping at her fingers and toes.

One particular morning, at a place known as Henry's Eyes, where a deep cleft in a prominent rock gave the impression of a face frozen in time, Emmie stopped to take breath. She slackened her boot laces, just enough to enable her toes to be clenched and ankles to be exercised, while throwing around her shoulders an extra shawl that had once belonged to Christabel.

All about was grassland and gorse, where God alone presided over the majesty of the hills and the fertility of the vales below. It was a comfort to her, as familiar as a child's blanket at bedtime and a million miles from the strange goings-on at the Holman Clavel.

Finding none of the bread left in her bag, earned by a day's labour, she flopped against the stone, staring into the wind that flapped her bonnet and dress. At this time, when hunger bit hardest, she might have been forgiven the feeling of despair. Yet, strangely, she did not. The hardship merely focused her mind into finally realising how much she had gained from her time with Mr Mortimore compared to anything lost since leaving, believing for the first time in ages that she could be liked and wanted. True, such thoughts would not sustain her weakening body, but they enriched her happiness.

Before reaching the Holman Clavel, Emmie had been a lost soul, without direction or purpose. Mr Mortimore had changed all that, more so since she had taken his advice to send a letter to the only person she felt she could call upon, other than her parents, that person being John Madden. And, even though she had not received a reply before leaving, she held belief in her breast that somehow he would reach her. But this was not all she felt. She also took pride in keeping her own promise to be a better person, remembering the comfort of the Clavel while all around the temperature dropped and her skin broke out into tiny bumps.

John Madden lived in the village of Nether Bow, just outside Cerne Abbas. Wheat Sheaf Farm, his family's home for generations, lay in the beautiful Cerne Valley. It was more of a small estate than a farm, specialising in rearing cattle and sheep. Surprisingly, only a single field grew cereals for animal feed.

The village as a whole prospered from being one of care and upkeep, some of the cottages owned outright by their occupants, while those tenanted were carefully supervised by resident landowners. Of course, this did not make the Valley impervious to the poor, those families where the number of children born far exceeded any ability to provide for all their needs from farming wages, or where the old relied on the generosity of the parish. But, in general, it prospered. How different it was from many other villages in far flung parts of Wessex, especially those where deficient soil provided meagre returns for their absentee squires. These places, often referred to as starve-acre villages and where wages were suppressed by low returns from harvested fields, were chastened by poverty. But, happily, Nether Bow and those villages adjacent enjoyed better prospects.

John Madden himself had been through a turbulent period in his life and was now emotionally scarred but, also, more resolute. This turmoil had begun with the arrival on the farm of Christabel Mere, whom he had loved with deep passion. Nevertheless, despite his best efforts, he had lost her affection to Edmond Elvington. He had never quite understood what the youth from Westkings had offered that he had not, although he often remembered with embarrassment and pain the stupidity of his actions towards Christabel while attempting to woo her. Then, he had acted as an impetuous suitor, while Edmond, a mere youngster in comparison, had been far more considered towards her, after first breaking off his secret engagement to Emmie. But, in the tangled events which followed, Edmond and Christabel had parted company without ever fully declaring their true feelings, leaving Edmond to marry Lily Stevenson two years later and Christabel to fall into the worst times of her young life.

Yet, there was more John did not understand. At the trial of Christabel's assailants, one of the shackled defendants had pleaded how Christabel had talked straight through him on the fateful day of her death, as if he was glass. It was as if a ghostly figure had stood behind which Christabel, alone, saw. And, earlier, Christabel had told Emmie of a peculiar notion that she had a guardian angel who guided the hands of others to help her at times of severe suffering. Emmie had told this story to John, but, being a practical man, he had dismissed the very idea as ludicrous. Christabel had even put a name to him, Joseph Stone, who she believed she had first met during a long walk to Cerne, when she left her childhood home at Shalhurn.

Whether Joseph Stone had existed or not, the final cruel act of fate had come when John and Christabel finally reunited only as she lay stricken, when their love was declared as life ebbed from her broken body. His heart had been torn from his chest. During the most lonely period of John's life that followed, it had been little Emmie who had comforted him, on one occasion as they sat together on the head of the Cerne Giant, remembering old times with Christabel. They both suffered, Emmie from regret at her treatment of Christabel and John for being unable to save her life.

With such shared experiences, Emmie believed with all her heart that John remained a true but distant friend. Mr Mortimore had penned the letter to John, accurately writing Emmie's sentiments. But her plan had not allowed for her unexpected departure from the Holman Clavel, and it was to this place that a letter was duly delivered a few days later. If it had reached Mr Mortimore, he might have taken bold steps to find her, knowing its importance. But Chimney Charlie had played one of his frequent tricks and had hidden it above a wardrobe in a little used guest bedroom. It was a month before Charlie returned it to the bar, by which time Mr Mortimore had taken on new staff and the letter was burned, unopened.

As Emmie leaned against Henry's Eyes, she noticed a man and woman approaching from the opposite direction, holding hands. The lower portion of the woman's dress and the bottom of his trousers below string ties were discoloured and damp. The path itself had been churned soft by horses, destroying the glistening frost that had given the bridleway an early morning sparkle. They wandered casually off the path and onto the long grass whenever it meandered from their straight course.

In general, the woman was well covered from head to foot. He was less so. His shirt sleeves were rolled up to the elbows, his chest warmed only by a tan corduroy waistcoat half buttoned from the top. A small cloth cap perched on the back of his head, allowing his hair to sweep sideways across his forehead. A leather bag swaggered across his shoulders, from which protruded the long barrel of a gun. Inside the bag bled two rabbits and a pheasant. Emmie observed how the man and woman expressed none of the determined walk of country folk going about pressing business.

The peculiarly slow progress of the couple intrigued Emmie. They appeared from a distance to be unfriendly, except for the union of their hands. Neither looked at the other, as is usual when talking, nor appeared to desire any companionship. Yet, upon closer inspection, this engendered no visible awkwardness between them. Every so often he appeared to rub his free hand against his nose, causing no reaction from his partner, who occasionally strained her eyes to peer into the furthest distance still to be traversed. Clearly, she enjoyed no society from him, but merely bore the loneliness of her walk with fortitude. Only as the distance shortened could Emmie see that he was reading from a small book, using his nose to turn the pages.

Fascinated by the couple, Emmie turned away only when disturbed by the distant sound of a rider encouraging his horse up the hill from the direction she had just walked. From his agitated kicking and grunting, his temper was unmistakably fierce.

As he came into full view, she could see he was a man in good clothing mounting a robust horse of no great size, a type commonly termed a 'heath-cropper' and closely related to the wild Exmoor. Only two hours before, he had passed beneath the arch of a hanging chapel, emerging from its dark shadow to enter the narrow high street of Larkpit. He had trotted through the street purposefully, without as much as a glance at the little terrace shops nestling to either side. Soon enough, though, he was over the bridge marking the far end of the town and heading into the countryside beyond. Once in open ground and the likely whereabouts of his quarry, his pace had quickened.

Now alarmed at her vulnerability, Emmie hid behind the rock, trying to attract the couple's attention by waving, warning how they strolled unknowingly into harm's way. At last the young man raised his stare, but was blinded from any danger by the crest of the hill. He merely returned a wave before commencing his reading.

As the top was reached in a fast trot, the rider lifted his head, clearly disliking what he saw. Gathering furious pace, he swept past Emmie, who remained hidden, and hurtled down the hill, shouting and thrashing his crop in sweeping circles.

The oncoming thunderbolt was now unmistakable, even to the walkers. In quick succession, the young man dropped the book, tossed the woman to one side and drew the gun from his bag with a sleek movement of his right hand over the shoulder. He was clearly a man used to arming rapidly. In a thrice, the gun was cocked and aimed at the rider's head, ready to fire a shot.

Still the rider approached at frenzied pace, now pointing the crop in a final charge.

"Who is it?" screamed the woman anxiously, crawling away to give more distance. "'Tis a game-keeper after your silly hide."

"It might be," he returned. "But, I have the measure of him if he comes any closer."

"Stop!" shouted Emmie with all her strength, finally recognising the mounted figure. "I'm up here."

The horseman, now in the final part of his charge, turned his ageing head at the shrill cry. It was too late. The young man, who had stood his ground in the forlorn hope of frightening the rider, now dropped his aim and turned the gun around, grabbing the long barrel tightly and holding it high as a club. In the last seconds of their closure he took a huge and decisive swing, dismounting the rider in a single blow by crashing the wooden stock against the horse's legs. In a mighty wreck, the rider catapulted over the animal's head as it buckled awkwardly and fell.

Emmie ran down to where the drama had played out, falling on her knees beside the victim, who looked up with pitiful expression.

"I couldn't refuse your call for help," he whimpered. "I came as quickly as I could."

"Father," cried Emmie in panic, taking his shoulders and kissing his forehead. "Is anything broken?"

"Only my dignity," he returned, rubbing his head. "As usual, you've caused me a deal of trouble."

"You know this man?" demanded the assailant, standing over Joseph Sturry in a hostile and threatening manner, the gun again pointing barrel first.

"Of course she does," replied Joseph, aware of a searing pain across his ribs.

"Well, I know neither of you. You just have time to explain before I shoot."

"Please," implored Emmie, "I can vouch for his good character. He has come to help me."

His stare moved back to the fallen rider, who nodded weakly.

"Then, why did he charge at us? What have we done to upset him? What are we to either of you?" he asked brusquely, while slowly withdrawing the barrel from Joseph's temple.

"I can talk for myself," gasped Joseph. "God knows you have caused me injury enough to realise I can no longer be a threat."

"The old man be right," offered the woman. "'Tis enough that no lasting damage be done on either side." She turned to Emmie. "My name be Jane Fuller and he be Peter Lister. You don't know either of us, do you? There's been a simple misunderstanding."

"Yes," was all Emmie said in reply.

"But not so for the brood mare. It looks done for," said Peter, placing the gun on the grass and feeling along its splayed leg.

Joseph quickly turned towards the horse. It was on its side, tossing its head in an attempt to stand. Two legs were broken. Although pained to move, Joseph shuffled to where it lay and stroked its head until the thrashing stopped. The horse's large eyes looked up at Joseph in trustful manner.

"Will it be alright?" whispered Emmie emotionally.

"Can I borrow your gun, stranger?"

"That, you may," was his reply.

A tear ran down the old man's cheek as the trigger was pulled and the animal slumped, motionless.

"It was a good horse. I must pray for forgiveness."

"You would pray over a beast?"

"I would, young woman, for we are all God's creatures, great and small. This tragedy was of my own making. Will you not close your eyes and join me in a moment's reflection?"

Jane sneered contemptuously. "'Tis not the help of the Good Lord you need, but a good knacker."

"God is compassionate love."

"God be heavenly love and animals don't go to heaven."

"Shut up, Jane," commanded Peter. "As to the carcass, if you like you can leave disposal to me. It can't be left here rotting, to be found by walkers," he offered quietly. "That is, if I can have a shilling for my efforts to clear it away."

"A fair exchange," replied Joseph in a whisper. "Mind you have the horse treated with respect. I am placing my trust in you. Now, we should all close our eyes in a moment's reflection. *Animals are such agreeable friends; they ask no questions, they pass no criticisms*," said Joseph solemnly. "*Amen*".

"The Bible?" asked Peter.

"George Eliot, actually."

"Never heard of him," scorned Jane.

"A woman."

"What?"

"George Eliot was a woman," rebuked Peter dryly.

"No! Really? Not one of them funny women who take a fancy to others of their own kind?"

"Jane, you're so ignorant." Peter turned to Joseph, who now stood awkwardly with Emmie's support. "You may count on me to see the animal right. I give you my bond." He smiled reassuringly, taking the gun from Joseph, who had used it as a prop. "And now, if you're feeling well enough, we'll take our leave. It's a hard stretch to Larkpit if we are to get there in time to call out the knacker's cart today."

"Anything else wanted for the horse? A Christian burial in a churchyard, perhaps?"

"Stop your cackling, Jane, before I take my hand to you. We must about our business." He turned to face the others. "My apologies for her rough tongue. That's what comes from marrying too young. A loose-tongued woman can be the ruin of any ambitious man."

The couple walked away with purpose, arguing.

"You might've done for him, Peter," ranted Jane while striding to keep up. "Striking out like that. An inch from the gallows at Dorchester were you."

"It was a calculated manoeuvre, Jane. I've disabled many foe while in the army by bringing down the horse instead of the rider. We were taught how to use a gun as a club once the shot had left the barrel. Anyhow, I'm to be rewarded."

"How? A shilling will barely cover the cost of calling out the knacker."

"Glue!"

"Glue? You would sell the horse for that? But, you said you would respect it."

"I know. It goes to prove what I always say."

"What?"

"That you can't put any trust in strangers!"

"Are we to eat in Larkpit with the profit? I've a mighty hunger going and you've said nothing about food?"

"I didn't mention it before, in case concern for the old man had taken away your appetite. How foolish of me!"

The couple had only been gone a few moments when Joseph turned to his wayward daughter.

"You see, Emmeline, that's what comes of an imprudent marriage. That man's expectations will come to nought with her in tow. There were times in the past when I was bitter at the thought of your elopement with that dreadful Lieutenant Charles. I even disowned you, for a whole second or two. But, as time passed, I came to realise with bitter irony that you were much better off as an abandoned woman."

"Father!"

He flinched. "No, child, I meant you were abandoned by him to your fate, not you were a. . ."

"Stop! This isn't a conversation I wish to have with my own father. Anyhow, how did you know I was here of all places?"

"Ah, that's simple. It was your good friend, John Madden, who told me the measure of what had been going on. The man is a saint."

Emmie could never forget how John had once before tried to save her from destitution and, thus remembered, gladly agreed that he was, indeed, a saint.

"After John wrote to you of his plans to help, but got no letter in return confirming any of his suggested arrangements, he came to me for advice. The distance being long, he stayed overnight. He had my address from the last time you took off. Of course, I thanked him heartily, but said it was my duty as your kin to assist. I can tell you, he took some persuading to let me take over. He urged me most sincerely to let him make the long journey from Stirminster Oak, as it would prove too much for somebody of my age, particularly in my agitated state. He is so thoughtful, a saint as I rest and breathe. Anyhow, I told him I would break the journey and that all would be well. He could see I was not to be trifled with and let the argument rest. Tell me, Emmeline, what on earth possessed you to leave the Holman Clavel, when by staying put we would've known where to find you?"

"I didn't think, as usual. I had to go. Anyhow, I have questions of my own. I repeat, how did you know I was here, and why did you ride so hard at that innocent man?"

"The second question is easy to answer. I saw what looked like a gun and thought you had taken up again with the scallywag, Lieutenant Charles. My eyes aren't as good as they once were over long distances. My blood was up at the very thought of you letting him back into your life. I'm aware the damned rascal made recent contact with you at Westkings. I suppose I lost my head in the fury of the moment."

"How on earth did you know that?"

"Pardon?"

"That Longborne Charles had written to me while I was working in Westkings."

"It was Mrs Redmarsh. She was so worried by the letter you received from the Lieutenant, and your reaction to it, that she wrote to us, as your parents."

"How rude!"

"Now sensible, you mean, and caring for that matter. Not many people would be troubled for the welfare of such a scatterbrained child as you. You would do well to know who your real friends are."

"But she's old. She cooks for the farm hands on the Elvington estate. She's not my friend at all. Not like Mary and Louise."

"I think she's proved that she is, and a good friend too. Did the difference in your ages stop her from worrying? Indeed, not. In fact, now I think on it, it was probably her many years' experience with young dairymaids which gave her the common sense to tell your mother and me what had been going on. To save you from yourself was clearly her only unselfish intention. You have a great deal to thank her for."

"I suppose."

"Anyway, daughter, if you didn't want others to know your private business, you should've paid more attention to your schooling. You're no fool, but you read and write exceedingly badly, and your spelling makes me despair. That's why you have to rely on others to help. I've often asked myself why, when your mother and I can produce fine letters, and Robert for that matter, you can't hold yourself equal to an average seven year old."

"I paid no heed to the teacher."

"Attention, Emmeline, the word is attention, not heed. It's considered to be old English in our modern times. It's the talk of the countryside."

"Where I mostly live."

Joseph gave up the argument. "As for tracking you here, that wasn't as hard as you might imagine. I talked to a certain Miss Spry after visiting the Holman Clavel. She dangled a pendulum over sand and . . . well, I don't say I believe any of it, but she seemed to bewitch the pendulum, which told her the direction you went. As I had no better plan, I blindly followed the advice."

"And now you find me, will I take a punishment?"

"Bless you, no, daughter. It is joy to me to find you in reasonable health."

"Even though I continue to cause you problems?"

"Trouble and you are old bedfellows. Mother and I expect no less. Oh, truth be told, there are times when I curse your stubborn ways. But, then, long periods of parting make me sad, as only a father knows for his child. I remember so well what you were like as a small girl, the prettiest little thing who carried my heart wherever you went; your big eyes and even bigger smile when I held your tiny hand as we walked along. You had a real spring in your step, as if your feet were rabbit's paws. I can see it now. You see, not all the seed one scatters falls on stony ground. Oh, to go back and make amends."

"Amends?" she replied in honest amazement for the sadness in his voice. "Whatever for?"

"For the trust in your little face when I kissed a hurt away and wiped a tear from your cheek with my thumb, only to let you grow up to be feckless with your affections. I blame myself a great deal for your deficiencies, especially as your mother constantly warned me of the consequences of being too lenient. But, how could I be otherwise, when the unconditional love you gave me made no account of my failings. How can my heart hold anything else but love, even if my mind now suffers torment at your reckless deeds."

"Father, I love you so much." She threw her arms around him in a tender embrace.

"You are my little girl and no better ever walked God's earth."

"Was I really that adorable?"

"Probably not. But, then, a father remembers only the good things."

"And now, Father? What is to become of me?" she asked, releasing him.

"Isn't that rather up to you to decide?"

"You offer no help?"

"I offer every help I can, but only if you want to take it freely."

"Can I come home?"

He took her hands in a warm, reassuring hold, his reply withheld for tantalizing seconds. "You shall not," he eventually whispered, unexpectedly.

She pulled free. "Not?" she gasped.

"No. You shall not."

"But Father?"

"Be calm, my daughter, for I have a better proposition should you entertain it. I think it could be your making. But, I feel such an opportunity will only come to you once. Reject it, as I worry you might, and you may spend the rest of your life as a spinster living with your parents, for there is no life to be made for a young, headstrong woman in our village."

"What is this opportunity you dangle so irresistibly before me?"

"It comes from John Madden himself."

"John?" she replied with glee. "I knew he wouldn't let me down."

"He has expressed interest in taking you on at the farm."

"As a servant or field-hand?"

"I don't know. The generosity of his offer left no room for my questioning his motives. We know him to be of good character and, as such, we must trust his judgement."

"John," she repeated enthusiastically.

"Now, what is it to be, home to stay with your parents or John's patronage?"

"Is he married?"

"I think not, but I don't know for sure. Either way, it's of no importance to you."

"No?" she sniggered eagerly.

"He moves with the freedom of a bachelor, seemingly answerable to nobody. But our relationship has been short and, whilst we share good fellowship, I cannot yet call him a friend, although I have the greatest warmth for him and owe him much. Indeed, we both do."

"If I choose Cerne, am I to go straight there?"

"Of course not. You will reunite with your mother for a few days and prepare for your new position."

"Then I accept with all my heart."

"I am much pleased you do. So, my first job when we get back home will be to tell him of your decision. Come, we must walk to Larkpit, where I will hire a gig. Poor Betsy."

"Who?"

"My horse."

"Oh, is that all!" exclaimed Emmie, already striding ahead with her belongings. "Come on, slow coach. John awaits me impatiently."

"I doubt that's true."

"Trust me. He wouldn't offer a job if he didn't carry a torch for me."

Joseph stopped, nonplussed by her logic and more than a little disappointed.

"You really are a little tyke. I said no such thing and he most certainly didn't indicate any emotion beyond a generous nature."

"Ah, Father, I am a woman. I know these things. Believe me, he desires me and wants me close."

"If that was the case, I would receive his attention towards you with the greatest pleasure, despite your age difference. But, I don't believe such a notion has ever entered his head. It's all fantasy."

"We'll see," she smirked, almost skipping along.

Joseph sighed. "Heaven save us all!"

CHAPTER 6

Wheat Sheaf Farm

*J*ohn Madden, having received a letter from Joseph Sturry by last post confirming arrangements, was now expecting Emmie the day after next. He was of mixed emotions at the prospect. His instinct was to help, but he was unsure why he felt so strongly that he should. She was not his responsibility by any measure. He knew of many others living locally in the Cerne Valley who deserved a helping hand far more than Emmie ever could, those who would not betray his help once offered.

Circumstances were entirely dissimilar to that time a few years before, when he had ridden hard to Dorchester in the hope of saving Emmie from destitution at the hands of the interloper, Lieutenant Longborne Charles. He had then discovered to his mortification that the only person he could not save her from was herself. What had been worse, the money he had given to Longborne to help Emmie's prospects had been stolen by that wretched man when he fled her company, and it had been Christabel who had eventually saved Emmie from a life of grind and poverty in a tortoiseshell factory.

So, why was he helping again, he pondered? The thought of Emmie being close made his heart leap, but he equally knew he felt nothing for her as a woman.

He sat by the fire, scribbling a letter in untidy hand on a Killarney writing slope which had belonged to his late mother. Between thoughts he watched the flames dance, gaining inspiration from each pause. A new log was tossed into the grate at the end of a page, the newer wood hissing as the sap bubbled.

Not a day passed when John did not spend time reflecting on his brief, but precious, time with Christabel. It was she who had introduced Emmie into his life. Yes, that was it! At last it became obvious. It was not that he wanted Emmie's company, but that being close to Emmie would make him feel closer to Christabel.

"Oh, God!" he said out loud, throwing back his head and staring at the ceiling. "Why have I been such an idiot? Of course, that has to be it!"

Faintness filled his head, knowing he had stumbled upon the truth. Life without Christabel was hard enough to bear, without having her memory raised time and time again by Emmie's careless chatter. But, what could be done to stop her at this eleventh hour?

John quickly finished his letter, folding the pages around several large bank notes. He wrote *Elizabeth Grant* and the destination on the front and sealed it with red wax. It was not addressed to the manor house belonging to the Grant family, where he had often visited Elizabeth and her parents, but to a hospital near Glastonbury, built a few years previously to honour Queen Victoria's sixtieth birthday.

The hospital was a tiny affair on the outskirts of the town, constructed of local stone. It had a mere two wards within the two-storey section of the building, each lit by one narrow window. The nurse occupied a single-storey extension to the side. An extremely tall chimney took smoke from the nurse's fire to clear air above the roof level of the wards.

"You have a letter, Elizabeth," said the nurse, having knocked gently on the door of the upper ward.

It was received with equal civility.

"You realise, Lizzy, this situation must be resolved. If the Town Clerk got wind of your unnecessarily long stay here, the pompous ass would surely as not shut us down."

"I don't understand, Maria. What is the purpose of this place if not to help the likes of me?"

Nurse Trimby sat on the edge of the bed, watching Elizabeth stare from the window at the hustle and bustle outside. She longed to be free to resume a normal life, but could not see how it could happen.

"We manage only by the good grace of the Town Council and private subscribers, any of whom might withdraw their support if the place is misused. Philanthropy among the great and the good is not guaranteed to be everlasting. Donating money month after month can become a tiresome burden, and some would be quick to find an excuse to end such commitment if one presented itself. Your father's contributions and those of John Madden over the past few months help a great deal, but I have to consider other, larger benefactors too."

"I see."

"No, dear, I don't think you do. This is not a general hospital. The sick go to the Wells Union. We are more an emergency accident place, although on occasions we have taken overspill patients from Butleigh. I have allowed you to stay longer than necessary only because of the money you raise. But, if we needed both wards for genuine cases, I would be forced to let you go."

Elizabeth turned from the window.

"Where could I go?"

"Now, now, Lizzy, don't distress yourself. We haven't got there yet. But, I do think you should start making alternative arrangements."

Crisp bank notes were removed from John's letter and handed to Nurse Trimby, who received them with gratitude.

"He's a good man, this John of yours. Surely he'll stand by you."

Elizabeth reached for a handkerchief, too late to capture the tears falling from her bowed head.

"What does anyone know about anything."

"I don't understand," replied Trimby, tucking the bank notes into her apron pocket. "Was that a question? Because, if it was, I can promise you I've said absolutely nothing at all to compromise your position."

Elizabeth dried her eyes.

"It wasn't. I mean, John doesn't know anything of my particular plight."

"Really? How can it be so?"

"Very easily, as it happens. Because of the shame I have heaped upon my parents, they forbade me from making direct contact with him, ever. I love him so much. That hurts more than anything else."

"Again, I don't understand. You're not a child. Your parents can't exert influence over you. Anyway, surely they would want him to marry you? That's the normal way of things in such unusual circumstances."

"You would think so, but it's not the case this time. They act as if Unity was never to be born. I think they want me to disappear too. As not even John knows anything, I'm sure they think the secret can be hidden from everyone, for ever."

"That's ridiculous. You're not the first unmarried woman to have a child and you certainly won't be the last. Society is changing."

"But, not for the better."

"No, probably not. There's a certain security in everyone knowing and respecting moral subjection. Still, foolishness and accidents happen, even to the best and brightest."

"Tell my parents that."

"This John of yours. . ."

"He's not mine."

"Alright, this John fellow, if he doesn't know, and you don't see him, how come he sends you money every fortnight?"

"I told him I was working as a voluntary helper. He is a generous man and was quick to offer financial support for a worthy charity, knowing my parents to be frugal with money and that I have little of my own beyond my allowance for clothes and those sorts of things. We are old friends, going back to childhood."

"Then, aren't you being rather unfair to Mr Madden? Shouldn't you give him the chance to be a proper father? Your new baby needs a father, you know. All children do. It seems to me, he would do the correct thing by you."

"Not so."

"Oh, I see. He's that sort of man after all, is he? He wouldn't want to know the child. Is that what you're saying? He's a humbug! So, he's got away with it, while you shoulder the burden. Typical of life, that is. Oh, I've seen it time and time again among the rich and the poor alike, and it's condemnation of our society that defames only the woman."

"No!" Elizabeth shouted, distressed at the thought of John's good name being besmirched. "It isn't like that at all. You've got it all wrong!"

"Have I?"

"It's quite the opposite from what you imagine. You see, John never courted me. He was far too wrapped up in a dairymaid by the name of Christabel Mere. He made no secret of his feelings, and I was left in no doubt that she was the woman he wanted as a lifelong companion. When she eventually left Cerne, I felt sure I could fill the void in his life. In those days, John's mother loved me almost as much as I loved myself and she encouraged me to pursue him with vigour. I soon discovered, however, that a misty memory of Christabel was more precious to him than any real happiness I could provide as a living and breathing woman. Yet, my mind would not accept the undeniable truth of the situation. I found myself making excuses for his behaviour, thinking I could change him, and in so doing I followed her advice."

"Most unbecoming to a grand, young woman."

"It was, but I had no shame where he was concerned. I had men falling over themselves to catch my attention, but I had set my cap on the only man who wouldn't see past ordinary friendship."

"What happened?"

"Months passed, but the only change in John was to his personality. His mother had died, you see, leaving him the estate to run. But her written will was not as he anticipated it would be. She had understood his faults all too well and so had placed quite severe restrictions on his inheritance. His immediate reaction to her death and the loss of his expected wealth was to drink, gamble and seek the company of new friends who delighted in his newly found resources, albeit more modest than expected. When the available money became lean, they left."

"So, he became destitute?"

"Far from it. Isobel, his late mother, had been wise in her dealings and by restricting his income she had ensured the survival of the farm. John knuckled down and made a success of things. For the first time in his life, each new morning started before the clock chimed midday."

"And? There has to be more."

"Of course. As I said, with the dairymaid out of the way I thought I stood a chance. But, alas, he grieved for her as fully as any heart could without stopping. Then, just as I managed to regain his slight attention beyond old friendship, something made him up-sticks and search for her all over again. I was cast out into the wilderness once more, as wretched and lonely as a shipwrecked mariner."

"Did he find her?"

"He did. She died in his arms."

"Upon my soul!"

"I know. I am utterly ashamed to say, at first, I felt pleasure at the news. But I learned very quickly that it made no difference to his feelings towards me. I just couldn't break through the barrier he put around his grief."

"So, and please forgive me for asking, how is it possible you became with child when he was so aloof?"

"It was February last. Everyone had just received the news of General Gordon reaching Khartoum to evacuate British troops.

Well, you will remember the celebrations. It was a wonderful time, full of relief and patriotic fervour. Even John broke out of his chains and joined in. For the first time in a very long period he drank far too much, while I stood to one side and watched with purpose. I helped him into my carriage and took him back to Wheat Sheaf Farm, where his enthusiasm for the evening spilled over into more drinking and merry making. Call it what you like – dandling, fondling, caressing, cuddling – but he became passionate towards me in his stupor and I had no will to resist. It was wonderful to be with him, even if he wasn't really in any fit state to know who I was." She bowed her head at the memory, playing with her fingers until they entwined as an embrace. "It was just wonderful."

"He was a good lover?"

"Please!"

"I'm sorry. I misunderstood. I meant no offence."

"It was wonderful to be so close to the man I idolised, that's all. Anyway, what makes a good lover? I wouldn't know. This was my single indiscretion and, I would judge, he had never experienced a woman before."

"Not even the dairymaid? We all know what country girls are like."

"I think not, although I hear tell she had produced a dead child."

"Well then, you have the proof."

"It proves nothing of the kind. The dairymaid had her own life, before and after John. Besides, a man was imprisoned for causing her bodily harm. Blame him, not my John."

"And now?"

"I will give it thought. You have John's money, so please leave me to consider my future."

CHAPTER 7

A voyage of discovery

*M*eantime, since Cornelius Fairfax had left Partington Hall for France and new discoveries, his world had been turned upside down. On the recommendation of fellow flying enthusiasts, his first port of call had been Armainvilliers, where a middle-aged French engineer experimented with gliders that were said to be 'influenced by nature'. In this instance, 'nature' was represented by little monoplanes with bat-like wings of wood and fabric.

Cornelius agreed the workmanship and ingenuity were exemplary, while privately believing the entire concept to be over ambitious and misguided. The Frenchman saw a great future for his designs, including powered applications using steam, capable of carrying a man or even two. He was sure he would eventually obtain the sponsorship of the French military, if he could demonstrate their ability to carry two persons and a few light explosives. Cornelius acknowledged his foresight and left unaffected, believing him to be misguided.

While walking back to his lodgings, taking the long and scenic route that skirted the Forêt De La Léchelle, past patches of lavender made dull by the season, Cornelius was suddenly and roughly grabbed by two men and bundled towards a carriage parked discreetly a short distance north. His attackers offered no explanation, but merely carried out their intention to hold him securely with all required force.

"What the devil's going on?" remonstrated Cornelius, believing from the lack of response that neither man understood English and he was the object of mistaken identity. He considered resisting more vigorously, but was concerned not to give an impression of guilt. "I'm a British subject," he pleaded. "I've done nothing wrong in your country!"

Still they manhandled him towards the carriage, pulling him ever closer to captivity. Perhaps he was being kidnapped or arrested for espionage, he thought through the turmoil of the situation, or maybe it was revenge by the family of a criminal his father had put behind bars.

Moments were now precious. Within a few seconds he would be held inside the vehicle and, then, heaven knows what awaited him in some French jail or other. Any attempt to escape had to be immediate. There was no time remaining for dialogue. Faking capitulation, he stopped struggling and raised himself up from a hunched position of resistance, allowing his arms to straighten. Their grip loosened. Five more paces and then, in an explosion of movement, he violently dug himself into a halt, ripping his arms free and turning to make a dash towards the woods.

His heart raced as he ran for cover, one man in hot pursuit and another somewhere unseen. His pace was fast, allowing only an occasional rearward glance to assure himself of liberty. Fallen boughs were vaulted without slowing, every twist and turn between trees making deliverance more likely.

Where a line of tall trees marked the boundary of the wood, he pulled up sharply, fighting for balance at the edge of a steep drop. With no time for rational consideration, and having peered over the edge to gauge the gradient, he jumped, fighting for grip as he tumbled and slid roughly to the bottom. The landing was hard. His pursuer stood at the top, furious at being outsmarted.

Winded, Cornelius took a moment's anxious breath, doubled over and heaving. It was at that instant of breathlessness, while running fingers along ribs where an acute pain pierced his body, a hand fell hard on his shoulder, the unmistakable point of a revolver sticking uncomfortably into his back. He twisted, sick with disbelief.

"Stay looking forward."

"English? You're an Englishman," he challenged, open-mouthed and relieved, although his face showed strain.

"Now you've worn us out unnecessarily, be a good gentleman and stop resisting."

Cornelius had always believed anything English meant safety, but in this turnabout situation, such a stranger offered no reassurance.

"Come, Mr Fairfax, we have no further time to waste."

"You know who I am?" he asked in amazement.

"Naturally! We don't go around the French countryside picking up just anyone."

"Who are you?"

"You will know soon enough."

"What's this about?"

"Just be patient!"

They began the walk back, Cornelius restrained by the gun. At last he looked properly upon the man. He was the older of the two, with small dark eyes and a clean-shaven but weather-beaten face. His hair was short and neat, quite wavy on top, of the public school type. Unlike his pursuer who had the look of a lackey despite wearing a suit, of someone who took orders rather than issued them, this man was unmistakably in charge.

"How did you get behind me?" enquired Cornelius softly, to begin a dialogue of trust.

"You ran in a huge semi-circle. Lucky for me you did. I merely followed the path around the bottom. Come along and no more funny business."

"I'm going nowhere peacefully until I know what I'm walking into."

The captor jabbed Cornelius's back, as a reminder of having no real choice in the matter.

The second man caught up, appearing from the same direction as Cornelius had entered the wood. "You have him, the blighter?" he panted. "Time's running out."

"Time for what?" asked Cornelius fretfully.

"Just step along quietly, if you please."

"But, I don't please!"

"You could make it worse for yourself," said the younger, "but I don't advise it. We have our orders and Ben, here, loves playing with guns. I, being fitter, prefer fisticuffs."

With no means of further escape, Cornelius acquiesced, relieved when the grip on his arms was finally released. He was pushed forcibly into the carriage. Only after sitting did Cornelius see the 'revolver' was nothing more sinister than the end of a silver-tipped walking cane.

As the horses gathered pace and then slowed again to allow the carriage to bump its way over railway lines, the rougher man stared impassively at his captive for any signs of resistance. His eyes followed Cornelius's stare towards a large lake looming to the right. Empty boats bobbed at its edges, loosely moored to pegs. Unsure whether Cornelius felt fully subjugated, he lunged for the space beside him, making any new escape attempt inadvisable.

"You will notice, young man," said the older, after his colleague settled back, "the door handle is on the outside. The window has to be lowered to reach it. Now, be a quiet gentleman for all our sakes. It won't take long to get there."

"Where is *there*?"

"Just a mile or so now."

The carriage pulled into a courtyard, where the three men alighted in some disarray. A fourth man, who stepped out of the shadows to assist in the movement of the vehicle to the rear of the building, wore full British naval uniform. He had awaited their arrival and made no attempt to hide a holstered handgun. Cornelius watched with alarm as the carriage disappeared from view, realising how easy it would be for his captors to make him disappear completely. There were no friends or family who knew of his exact whereabouts, and he had set no time limit for his foreign adventures.

"What's going on?" he pleaded once more, all aggression gone from his voice.

"You'll know soon enough."

Cornelius was marched into a rather fine ante-room, where one of the two men promptly left, closing the doors behind him. Cornelius sat in silence. The remaining captor stood opposite.

Nervous minutes hung long in the quietness of the room, the only sound coming from the rhythmical ticking of a Meissen mantel clock. Then, after a shuffling noise became audible from the outside, the other man returned. He had exchanged his overcoat for a formal jacket and now strutted with all the bearing of importance.

"Listen to me well, Mr Fairfax. We know all about you and what you are doing here, which should answer at least one of your questions. I intend to answer no others, but all will become clear shortly. We only have seconds to understand each other, so listen to me well. You are about to be honoured in a way far beyond your wildest imagination. Consequently, you must never disclose what is about to happen to anyone, ever. Do I make myself plain? Just nod if I do?"

Cornelius nodded.

"Good, because the consequences for you if you break that commitment will be dire, I assure you. Now, tidy yourself up, speak only when you are spoken to and, for goodness sake, never turn your back. Do you understand?"

"Not really."

"The boy's a simpleton," barked the guard.

The double doors burst open and a small, dark figure entered, followed by two more naval guards.

"Your Majesty," said the first man, bowing at the waist.

Instinctively, more than obediently, Cornelius followed suit, stunned into disbelief. He stared at his Queen. She was tiny, smaller than he had imagined, probably several inches under five feet tall, sturdy in figure and with a fully round face, popping eyes hooded by old eyelids and hair pulled tightly back under a bonnet. Her skirts shuffled along the floor, over which she moved determinedly. Yet, despite any peculiarity of bearing, she commanded complete respect.

"You may sit, Mr Fairfax."

Cornelius stood, transfixed. The guards judged him harshly, but were restrained in their quick movement towards him by the Queen's uplifted hand. She noticed shyness, confusion in his eyes.

"Stand if you so wish, Mr Fairfax, but your Queen prefers she does not have to look up at one of her subjects."

At last Cornelius sat, prompted by the gentle pressure of a guard's hand on his shoulder.

"I detect fear in your eyes, young man. You fear Traitor's Gate and the Bloody Tower if you displease me?" Her mouth curled at the corners. "Please, do not worry, I merely tease you. We are long done with the place. Trust me and all will come clear."

"I fear the unknown, Ma'am," replied Cornelius sickly, almost crying. "Am I accused of something? Have I done wrong? I am here only. . ."

"Please, Mr Fairfax, do not question Her Majesty," said the jacketed man, taking the initiative. "It is not protocol. We already know why you are in France."

"You do?"

"Come, come," the Queen proffered. "Mr Fairfax is a stranger to our customs. Under the present circumstances, it must all appear quite extraordinary. We must show due forbearance and drop unnecessary pomp."

"As you say, Ma'am. If I may be allowed to explain?" he persisted. "We said nothing on our way here and he requires a full explanation. He is in shock, I believe."

"Are you in shock?" probed the Queen, the steel of her character and the sublimity of her face offering no immediate relief to Cornelius.

"Yes, Ma'am, I am," he replied with honesty.

"Then, don't be. That is a command. No, that is not what I meant at all. There, Sir Benjamin," she said, looking his way, "I have again broken the promise I made to myself to be less abrupt when meeting my subjects, just as dear John Brown advised." She turned back to Cornelius with kindness. "I apologise, Mr Fairfax. In my older age I find myself somewhat short tempered, full of spleen. I am learning to be more tolerant, but my advisors continue to frustrate my every wish and, in short, I have become suspicious of everyone. Know, young man, you are not in any trouble. Indeed, we have a favour to ask of you."

"I believe, Ma'am, he might be less dumb struck if I conduct the interrogation."

"So be it, but why say 'interrogation' when 'inquiry' is so much nicer?"

He turned to Cornelius with a dignified air. "As you have just heard Her Majesty say so graciously, I am Sir Benjamin Crow, senior civil servant to the War Office."

"You understate your use to me, Sir Benjamin," interposed the Queen with the slightest hint of rebuke, bringing a sudden halt to his speech and another smile to her face.

He responded with a dignified nod. "As you please, Ma'am." He turned back. "Mr Fairfax, we know of you from a mutual correspondent. I think you will know to whom I refer when I say he is an English-speaking foreign gentleman who holds the British Empire in the greatest regard."

"Do you mean. . ."

"No names, if you please," returned the man. "We are abroad unofficially to the host nation and as such we are not here at all, if you understand my meaning. This is not part of one of Her Majesty's frequent trips to Nice in the south."

Cornelius raised an eyebrow but said nothing, understanding nothing.

"We are used to placing ourselves in some danger for the sake of the Empire," responded the Queen, "having only recently travelled half the world in a quest for trade. I have since discovered that, on that particular voyage undertaken at the express instruction of my Government advisors, the entire entourage came very close to falling fatefully to a natural disaster. What do you say to that, Mr Fairfax?"

"I am astounded, Ma'am."

"A good answer, Mr Fairfax. We, too, are astounded."

Cornelius continued, uninvited. "Astounded that your Majesty's Government would permit any such risk to your person."

"There," responded the Queen, turning to Sir Benjamin. "The truth of the matter has been said. I am similarly alarmed, not least as half the Cabinet was on board the warship with me, and little Winston for that matter. Out of the mouths of babes! Your comment, Sir Benjamin?"

He looked at her with denial on his thin lips, but stopped. "I believe, Ma'am, Mr Fairfax is unaware of the facts. Your Government would never knowingly place your Majesty in jeopardy."

"Ha!" was her single gesture of reply, said doubtfully. A wave of her hand signalled him to proceed.

"Now, with your Majesty's indulgence, we move on to more pressing matters which brought us together," he said, pleased to change the subject. "We will dive straight in at the deep end. Mr Fairfax, taking the international prospective, Her Majesty condemns all forms of war as a most terrible act against humanity. Beyond that generalisation, and knowing such a principled position will not actually prevent war from breaking out periodically in one place or another, Her Majesty further considers it cowardly for any nation to undertake warfare in an underhand manner. That is at the heart of everything I have to say from this point forward."

"Warfare?" said Cornelius with surprise. "I know nothing about war."

"Nobody said you did," replied Sir Benjamin seriously. "Please, Mr Fairfax, just sit and listen. You will understand soon enough where the conversation heads. In keeping with this high ideal, Her Majesty is of the opinion that development of any entirely new means for conducting warfare will only perpetuate aggression. You see, Mr Fairfax, as soon as one nation fields something revolutionary, other nations consider it their grave duty to match that capability, while also trying to defend their own borders against it."

"A spiral of despair and outrageous cost," added the Queen. "I am very much opposed. Carry on, Sir Benjamin."

"If an example of this is needed, I would suggest we look no further than the German Empire, the former Prussians, who have recently developed a mobile field gun which fires skyward, intended to knock out observation and free-flying military balloons. You see from this example, Mr Fairfax, how one new weapon drags in its wake a new counter-weapon. The next step will be to arm the balloon against the gun, and so it goes on."

"The example Sir Benjamin gives is one of adaptation, in this case a simple field gun for other use. But, my greater concern is to stop at the outset the development of major, covert weapons capable of striking while unseen to the defenders. If allowed to progress, such unique weapons could, one day, be turned against us and we may have the most to lose. My mind is mainly focused on sub-mariner ships and flying machines, both of which have recently come to my notice."

"We are an Empire built upon trade and entirely dependent upon the sea," continued Sir Benjamin, "and such weapons would threaten the safety of our merchant ships required for trade and warships needed for our security."

"Yes, but where do I fit into this?" enquired Cornelius.

"It is Her Majesty's personal conviction, to which we dutifully concur, that existing weapons such as field artillery and battleships will be continuously improved to maintain high efficiency, but there is no good to be had from anyone adding anything more sinister to the world's arsenals."

"The sub-mariner ships and flying machines?"

"Absolutely correct. Well done, Mr Fairfax. You see, Her Majesty believes that sea-going vessels capable of attacking a surface ship while fully submerged and out of sight, and flying machines capable of menacing innocent civilians from the sky, or ships at sea, or troop concentrations on the ground, are not only cowardly but dangerous to our survival as a nation, and are not to be encouraged. We happily sacrifice such weapons ourselves in the hope of preventing similar machines from reaching enemy hands."

"We are aware of such goings-on already," added the Queen with serious expression, "and it must be stamped out before it is too late. The Americans in their Civil War attempted to use various submerged vessels to sink great warships. These were mostly unsuccessful craft, more deadly to their crews than the enemy, but the fact that they were built at all is a very bad omen for the future if nothing is done to stop it. Over to you, Sir Benjamin."

"With this in mind, news of your air experiments and of your fact-finding tour has alarmed those who carry out Her Majesty's instructions."

"But, I've constructed nothing beyond a few rubber-band models that don't work properly."

"We are told you have rather clever ideas which show exceptional promise."

"By the same English-speaking foreign gentleman you mentioned before?"

"Yes."

"Does he know your views?"

"I cannot answer that."

"Is that why his letter to me was discouraging?"

"Again, I cannot say. That apart, Mr Fairfax, it is our belief that flying machines, devised innocently for pleasure and commerce by people like yourself, could easily be developed into weapons intended for aggression. At present, air warfare is fairly well contained to observation balloons and unremarkable bombardment rockets. Her Majesty wishes to keep it that way."

"The Frenchman I've just visited believes he can produce a machine capable of carrying explosives, and that the French army will sponsor it."

"Is that so? We didn't know. That is very serious news indeed," said Sir Benjamin. "Then, we must send a diplomat to the French government at once, to put a stop to it. Thank you, Mr Fairfax. The advanced warning is appreciated and goes some way in proving your worth to us."

"I don't see how?" replied Cornelius.

"I will come to that, although you have thrown me into disarray by news of the French. Anyway, we must progress despite it. You see, Mr Fairfax, there are three strands to our little discussion. The first is about you and flying machines in general, a subject on which I will have more to say later. The second involves the politics of the situation, and the third regards the British monarchy. We will now deal with the second. Are you with me?"

"I think so."

"Good. I will press ahead. Her Majesty, in her considerations, wishes not only to keep the sea lanes safe from invisible attack, but keep Britain free from accusations of warmongering. This is the political aspect. We are not normally affected by anything foreigners say about us in their bile, but at the present time in our history we are less ready to sustain it among our own people."

"You look confused, Mr Fairfax," suggested the Queen. "I will say a few words of my own." She gathered her thoughts. "It is like this. Foreign peevish anger does not concern us one little jot, but the trouble it could engender among our own British subjects does. We live in a time of political extremism, railed against our highest institutions of government and state. Political activists are everywhere and they look for causes, any causes, capable of inciting the people into a violent mob."

"We are a great and proud nation, Mr Fairfax," continued Sir Benjamin, "and thereby the target of much foreign envy. Greater envy would undoubtedly accompany the development of anything as revolutionary as flying machines and sub-mariner boats, and every means to hinder us would be levied by jealous enemies. That is politics of an underhand variety."

"You must understand, Mr Fairfax," affixed the Queen, "if great strides were made in flying, news would quickly get out and foreign nations would spy on us in the hope of gaining the knowledge you and others innocently gather. The world would plunge into an inevitable race for arms. Concurrently, while trying to emulate our science, our enemies would initiate a covert programme of disaffection among the British public in order to slow our own progress, using both their own agents and those British subjects known to have foreign-inspired sympathies. We are much afraid of revolution, Mr Fairfax, and of the French variety in particular. One way of achieving this orchestrated mayhem would be to spread false rumours of costly and unnecessary warmongering, which would incite the public against the Government at a time when so many of our subjects battle daily to survive poverty. As a consequence, the monarchy would also be thrown into risk."

"How could trouble be stirred up against the Crown?"

"You see, Mr Fairfax, the poor of London. . ."

"Please, Sir Benjamin, I can speak for myself. Do not interrupt."

There was a stunned pause before he nodded and stepped embarrassingly to the window, looking outside where armed guards stood in shadows behind stone pillars. The Queen continued.

"The poor in London, Manchester and elsewhere need much. A pamphlet entitled *The Bitter Cry of Outcast London* was published last year, written by nonconformist missionaries of the greatest goodwill. My ministers and I were greatly moved by the sentiments expressed. It contrasted the great wealth and glory of our nation against the squalor endured by the poorest of society. A chilling comparison. So, you see, I am aware of the deprivation, but progress to help them is unbearably slow. Much depends upon the goodwill of industry barons and the action of town councils, many of whom seem remarkably unwilling to accept responsibility for social wellbeing. Plainly, they turn their backs on the needy poor. A good dose of cholera often concentrates their minds, however, caused by a general lack of sanitation and clean water, and the poor air, as the disease has no social constraints. Then, in fear for themselves, the great and the good at long last put their hands in their pockets under the banner of philanthropy. I have to admit to pulling down the blinds in my railway carriage as I pass through certain cities, because the terrible conditions and grime affect me greatly. I become very much distressed." She turned to Sir Benjamin. "Now, please take over. I am overcome."

He turned, straightened his jacket, and stood with his hands cupped behind his back. "The poor are simple prey to troublemakers, Mr Fairfax, in their genuine need for re-housing, hospitals and so on. In consequence, they are easy to whip up into an anti-authority frenzy, leading to social disorder, which in turn means the use of force to quell the crowds and. . . You can imagine the rest. The head of state is the Monarch and could be seen by some as the ultimate root of the problem."

"I have questions, if I may," said Cornelius, holding up a hand as any schoolchild.

"Speak," said Sir Benjamin.

"Firstly, I can't understand where you are going with this scheme of yours. Don't you know flying machines already exist in Russia, France and elsewhere? Therefore, isn't all this rather too late? Closing the gate after the horse has bolted. How can the science be stopped now, or forgotten? Secondly, on the matter of derision, why would a foreign nation bother to stir up social strife in England? It makes no sense. Surely, whatever chaos ensued, it would not alter the policy of a determined British government and they would know it? What would be gained?"

"In the first place, of course we know about St Petersburg. We tried unsuccessfully to stop the steam engines from being exported. We are also aware of the part Parliament played in Henson's ambitions all those decades ago. Nether concern us, as we are advised the machines in question never had a chance of success and, thereby, tended to make the whole business of flying look rather foolish. But your work is indicative of a new breed of experimenters, who study the science before plunging straight into building some contraption or other. That worries us. What we don't want to do is alert foreign governments of the genuine technical possibilities of flying."

"As to your second point, Mr Fairfax," cut in the Queen, "our enemies would say dreadful things about Britain in the hope of paralysing our nation into indecision and lawless decay, while they pursue every avenue of warfare themselves. We in leadership would take no notice of foreign muck-raking, just as you say, but the feelings of the British public would be a different matter. Such domestic criticism could fester, if not attended, into matters outside the politics of warfare. Damned if we do and damned if we don't, you might say."

"In doing what, Ma'am?"

"Tell him, Sir Benjamin, just as you told me."

He shook his head. "Why, isn't it obvious, Mr Fairfax? If word of genuinely capable sub-mariner ships and flying machines got out, the British Government would be compelled against its wishes to openly declare its position to the world. If, as a result, we were to say we are not interested in such sciences, although achievable, we would appear weak. Conversely, if we were to openly declare that such sciences are impossible, but other nations then went on to achieve success, we would appear technically backward. In so doing, we would offer incentive to those who plot against us and give succour to their military ambitions against the Empire. Yet, if we went against our better instincts and decided to build such weapons after all, it would mean increasing the Army's military estimates and divert scarce resources from social welfare programmes intended to improve the health of the British people, and begin the arms race we mentioned earlier. That would not sit well with the poor and their reforming champions. No, it has to be faced, alerting foreign nations of our position and science would be a grave error of judgement."

"But, even that is not the end of the complications," interrupted the Queen. "Carry on, Sir Benjamin."

"Thank you, Ma'am. If, sometime in the future, Britain was found wanting in the face of a foreign power which had itself developed such weapons, against which we had no knowledge or defence, this too would lead to open criticism from our own endangered populous. So, you see, whichever stance the British Parliament takes to discourage proliferation, in the worst analysis it could lead to a foreign power exploiting the situation against us for both political and strategic reasons. No, the sciences must be kept secret in the hope of suppressing such new weapons, maintaining the security of our borders and state, and provide the finances to improve the living conditions of the poor."

"You implied there are persons living amongst us who would like to injure the nation," offered Cornelius. "That can't be so."

"Unfortunately it can. Worst are those from abroad who have chosen to live amongst us for entirely the wrong reasons."

"How so?"

"I will answer that," said the Queen. "As a modern nation we face two enemies, those 'without' and those 'within'. Those 'without' are our foreign enemies. Those 'within' are often more difficult to identify. They can be British subjects or foreign individuals residing in our country who are political activists, motivated by 'ideology'. Tell him, Sir Benjamin."

"Sorry?" replied Cornelius.

"Her Majesty refers to individuals living in our cities, towns and villages, Mr Fairfax, who are determined to turn the British people into republicans, or communists or similar. They will take advantage of, and exploit, any difficult situation that can potentially bring our existing order crashing down around our ears. And, in this pursuit of social and political change at any cost, they care little how much their activities assist the aims of foreign enemies. For some individuals, a tiny minority, thank God, their personal aim is to mould our nation into some kind of proletariat society of equal wage earners ruled by unelected representatives."

"Low wages are already common among the poor," commented Cornelius.

"Just so, unfortunately, but we are a nation of business and our enterprising middle and upper classes have to be protected to allow the creation of wealth upon which all of Britain depends. If capital is not raised privately to open a new mine or build a new woollen mill, for example, no jobs are created for those who are without means of enterprise or capital for themselves."

"I can see that, but where does fairness end and exploitation begin? Cannot all share in the creation of wealth?"

"You begin to worry me, Mr Fairfax."

Cornelius's eyes flashed between Sir Benjamin and the Queen. "No, you have me wrong," he added quickly. "All I meant to say was that surely it is not unreasonable to encourage a little more of the wealth created to be used to raise the living standard of the poor."

"And you think another system of government and industry could do better?"

"I don't know."

"Well, I do. The innovators of industry would merely be replaced by unelected officials of state, who would be less enterprising and hopelessly inefficient. And, against all promises, the leaders of such a Utopian society would eventually carve for themselves the highest standard of living from their immovable bastions of power, allowing no means of challenge when it all goes horribly wrong; excess for the rulers and an iron-fist to the subjugated public. No, as things stand, the British people have the right to come and go as they please, to decide for themselves to whom they offer their labour. Only another revolution would oust the ideologists and they would hide behind the power of the Police and Army, whose very institutions do not allow for questioning of orders. It is far easier for an oppressive government to inflict harm than for a free government to defend itself against tyranny from within. No, foreign-inspired ideology is not for Britain. Our society is far from perfect, Mr Fairfax, but it is generally benevolent."

"Who are these agitators within our shores?"

"As I said, the most dangerous are foreign born persons, later settled in Britain, who have encouraged the public to become politicised in matters beyond the legitimate pursuit to better their daily lives. Our home-grown ideologists are quite different, of a more gentle nature and with generally philanthropic aims, usually preferring social change than the disintegration of democracy and capitalism as we know it. Believe me when I tell you, however, both varieties are capable of stirring up a great deal of anti-authority feelings on a mere whim. We are now discovering this to our peril. They are presently occupied disrupting industry and agriculture, but to some their greater goal is full-blown revolution, to turn Britain away from its traditions. You see, playing on the fears and anger of the poor can have the effect of rendering government, the military and industry quite ineffectual."

"Enemies to our way of life want to weaken us in whatever way they can," appended the Queen, "even though we do not ourselves seek to ban any religious or ideological beliefs as long as they are held personal to the individual and not dictated to all. As Queen and Empress, I strive to rule compassionately and task my Government with the same duty of care to all my subjects of whatever religion, but our trade and monarchy have to be protected from menace, whether of a home-grown or foreign-inspired nature."

"Thank you, Ma'am. So, Mr Fairfax, here is the rub. When considering whether we should, as a Government, encourage or dissuade certain new technologies, we have to respect not only the public purse, but address any wider political and military implications which could affect our way of life. And so, after much soul searching, we choose to preserve the military status quo, which is both politically and morally expedient. This avoids the possibility of harmful criticism and the accusation of warmongering, which in turn may hold the more extreme activists at bay. However, running alongside this policy is another to fully modernise the Navy with a new class of battleships. We are, as yet, unconvinced of the need to modernise the Army with machine-guns."

"I still fail to see what this has to do with me? If you are talking about my experiments in flying, I am only a novice wanting to produce something for pleasure," said Cornelius forcefully.

"But, who knows where such experiments might lead? Something playful to you might be viewed with more sinister intentions by foreign agencies. No, we have to keep a lid on it."

"Politics have no role in my life," added Cornelius.

"Politics have a role in *everybody's* lives, and can have more effect than a regiment of infantry when used to divert Government thinking. Why, political considerations can force weak Ministers into making totally incorrect decisions."

"I don't understand. You contradict yourself. A moment ago you said how frightened you were to have the public politicised."

"There is a world of difference between politicising the public and acknowledging how politics play a part in everyone's lives."

"Well said, Sir Benjamin. So, you see, dear Mr Fairfax, this explains why we are determined not to cause, what might be termed, an arms' race, which would be costly to win, militarily dangerous and politically suicidal."

"I now understand that, Ma'am, but not my part in it."

"You are scratching the surface of what could become a very deep and expensive problem, and a dangerous one for the Royal Navy if it became vulnerable to air attack," said Sir Benjamin as a knock at the door heralded the passing of a note, which he hurriedly read and folded into his pocket. He turned for the window. "It seems our escort has arrived, Ma'am. We are being encouraged to conclude our business within the hour and make our way to the coast."

"Then, progress quickly, Sir Benjamin."

"As your Majesty requests. Anyway, Mr Fairfax, returning to matters immediate to us, we now come to the conundrum of the situation. Despite the moral and political stance Her Majesty and Government are pursuing over flying machines and sub-mariner boats, Her Majesty believes the nation cannot be allowed to fall behind in such technologies, just in case, you understand. We have already touched on this and, once again, it's a situation of . . . damned if we do and damned if we don't. Clearly, we would be foolish to believe some foreigners are not attempting to master the air. In fact, we know they are and you have brought us further proof. We just don't want to help or encourage them, and the best way of achieving this is not to be seen doing it ourselves."

"It is a dangerous tightrope to walk, Mr Fairfax. Morality and maintaining peace, while keeping the nation safe from political unrest and foreign-inspired harm, has its price," added the Queen.

"Critical to this dual approach," continued Sir Benjamin, "is to ensure no British subject innocently or otherwise transfers technical knowledge beneficial to another nation. It has happened before, much to Her Majesty's Government's displeasure. However, to make this passive approach work, it becomes a matter of the gravest importance to know exactly what the other side is doing, enabling us to secretly match that expertise on paper without actually building anything of our own. It's also the cheap option. Preparedness is the watchword, without triggering a costly and damaging 'arms' race'. The English Channel is our greatest defence, a moat which has thwarted both the Spanish and French. To bridge our moat by air, or to put the guns of the Royal Navy at risk from air or underwater attack, would be intolerable."

"May I say. . ?"

"No, you may not, Mr Fairfax, until such time as I have told you the rest. We must hurry along."

Cornelius looked across at the Queen, who studied her lap, yet hung diligently upon every word spoken.

"By the way, when we talk of 'the air', we mean wood and fabric flying machines with engines and not gas-filled balloons and airships. We know what the French and Germans are up to with airships and have no concern whatsoever. Indeed, the British Army has a balloon detachment on its way to Cape Town as we speak, which should arrive around mid-December. No, such craft as they are, being subject to the vagaries of the wind, are not considered at all dangerous to human life, other than to their occupants, one might say. The British Government, therefore, has permitted itself to fall behind in the development of lighter-than-air craft for Army and Navy use, much to the chagrin of our generals and admirals, I might add. But, this is of little importance to the Government, which believes it acts out of respect for the public purse."

"You waste too much time, Sir Benjamin. Please proceed more rapidly to other important matters," demanded the Queen.

"As you please, Ma'am. And so, Mr Fairfax, this brings us to yet another aspect of the equation, one of monarchy. As I have already implied, if Britain is viewed as weak compared to foreign forces, it could be the flash that ignites Europe into war. The German Empire is high on the list of likely aggressors. If the worse of all scenarios happened and we found ourselves at war with the Germans, the British public could be stirred up by the same political activists into looking extremely harshly at our Royal Family. They would see it as another means to revolution. Your pardon, Ma'am, for putting it so crudely."

"Press on, Sir Benjamin."

"The old fighting Prussians, now part of the German Empire since '71, and others in Europe are champing at the bit to vent their traditional grudges, and it is our belief that only the strong but benign British armed forces here at home and on the high seas hold their excessive territorial ambitions at bay. But, if this policy failed, the catastrophe of widespread European war could, then, potentially threaten not only our liberty but the long-term prospects for the British Crown itself, even in victory. This is why Her Majesty has taken such personal interest and has come in secrecy to this place."

"It is a most unusual situation, and not without its risks," the Queen added succinctly. "A small naval vessel awaits us off the coast for our rapid departure to England. We have a long overnight journey to get there, so the issue must be resolved without delay. You understand, Mr Fairfax?"

"Not entirely."

"I shall continue apace," said Sir Benjamin, "but please try harder to keep up. Such concerns Her Majesty harbours involve the birthplace of the Queen's beloved and much missed Albert of Saxe-Coburg-Gotha, Prince Consort, the late Prince Albert. That birthplace was, of course, the German Empire. Consequently, everyone knows the Royal Family has German blood mixed in its veins, allowing the false perception of split loyalties to be levied if war with Germany broke out."

The Queen raised her stare. "My husband's own words at our betrothal were *'my future position will have its dark sides'*. He was right and there were times when the quite unnecessary mockery of his birthplace by British cartoonists made our royal blood boil."

"Quite right, Ma'am. If I may continue? Prince Albert won the nation's respect by his hard work for the national good and philanthropic care for the working masses of our nation. But, inevitably, his lack of Britishness meant *'he neither liked nor was liked'*, to quote Florence Nightingale. In truth, few people even now have any real understanding of what he did for us. Would you now wish to comment, Mr Fairfax?"

"I am bewildered. I reserve my thoughts."

"Well said, young man," offered the Queen, noticeably brightened. "We will make a diplomat of you, I feel sure."

Sir Benjamin coughed. "I will now attempt to bring together the various strands of our argument. Now, let me see. Ten years after the Prince Consort's death came the Franco-Prussian War of 1870-71. The Prussian Army was assisted by an Englishman, Henry Coxwell, who knowingly or unknowingly put the Prussians into an advantageous position just prior to hostilities by helping with the creation of two Luftschiffer detachments or, as we would now call them, airship units. This so-called air supremacy was, however, countered by the gallant defenders of Paris, when the city was in grave peril of being strangled into submission by surrounding Prussian forces. You see, French civilians and sailors in Paris used the few existing balloons and manufactured many more within the besieged city to fly out more than one hundred people and three million letters, plus carrier pigeons to be used to bring back messages using the newly invented process of microphotography. That, by the way, is a process of miniaturising photographs, allowing many impressions to be carried by a single bird. To continue, only two balloons were actually shot down by Prussian ground-fire, although others went astray due to the conditions of the prevailing wind."

"I knew it!" exclaimed Cornelius.

"What do you know, Mr Fairfax?"

"Balloons are of unpredictable nature, even in dire times."

"Just so. On the wider issue, do you see where I am going, Mr Fairfax?"

"I am equally blown away, Sir."

"Do I still not make myself clear enough, Mr Fairfax? You really must try to keep up with my arguments. The nation. . ."

"Please, Sir Benjamin," beseeched the Queen, "I will speak to Mr Fairfax alone for a few moments. I believe he is confused by you and the great amount already said."

"With respect, Ma'am, I most sincerely protest."

"Then protest quietly in the hall, if you must. My mind is not for changing. I have not journeyed this distance as a thief in the night to leave any door unopened."

The two government men left in agitated mood, leaving the

Queen and Cornelius quite alone except for the armed Naval rating standing by the doors.

"You look nervous, Mr Fairfax."

"I am, Ma'am, if I am allowed to say so in your presence?"

"You are, Mr Fairfax, and more. All this pomp and ceremony gets in the way of plain talking, and of seeing me as someone who can be approached. I am your Queen, Mr Fairfax, but I am also a mother with family concerns. In my case, I mother not only my own children, but also the great British people."

"Yes, Ma'am."

"Come, let me settle your anguish. I am old enough to be your mother, indeed your grandmother, and nobody quakes at a grandparent. Sit closer, so we may be more comfortable in each other's company and talk more freely. This is an impromptu meeting, after all, away from ceremony and confounded repeats of the National Anthem which, I say in private, is a tune during which I sing other songs inside my head to break the repetitiousness. I rather like Gilbert and Sullivan! Their new Mikado has been previewed to me. It has a catchy little tune which has caught our fancy. It's called The Lord High Executioner's song or something of the sort."

"Seems appropriate to my present situation!" remarked Cornelius lightly.

"There, we can be friends. Come, join me."

"In singing, Ma'am?"

"Hardly the time, Mr Fairfax. I meant, come closer."

Cornelius walked with caution the few feet to where the Queen sat. He stood until told to sit on a chair provided by the guard.

"It may not be well known, but I am somewhat partial to the company of men. I married young and have always treasured the support of the male gender. I have even heard it said at court, whispered of course and much to one's annoyance, that I crave a father figure. So much idle tongue wagging is the burden of position."

"The monarchy would have severed their heads for less in Elizabethan times" suggested Cornelius.

"Very probably true, my dear Fairfax. And, I have heard worse from behind doors left partially open. Why, I even heard a Lady in Waiting ask another if 'John Brown has had her yet?' I cannot tell you how much I boiled with pent anger, craving the reintroduction of Traitor's Gate."

"Goodness!"

"I probably shouldn't have told you that. Doubtless, I shock you."

"I admit to surprise, Ma'am."

"That the words come from the mouth of your Queen, or were spoken at all?"

"Both, Ma'am."

"Then, their ill-advised comments shall not be repeated. To continue, having heard all that the Ladies in Waiting murmured privately, I angered myself still further by finding myself deliberately avoiding John Brown's company at court, as if *I* needed to prove our innocence. I left him standing in the courtyard garden on many occasions, holding my horse's bridle and often soaked through, while I shrank from his company. Still he would not abandon me. It was his way of showing selfless devotion. My forbearance towards him made people think I was afraid to be seen outside the Palace, that memories of Albert held me prisoner. But it was not so by that time, although it had been before John rescued me from sorrow. It was only when I heard the same women later say 'the only way to get over unrequited love is to whore with another', I finally realised quite how stupid I had been to fall for their ridiculous aspersions. I was not amused. Consequently, we rode out together regularly after that time, and a great deal of good it did me to feel the fresh breeze on my face. Do you have nothing to say in return?"

"What am I to say, Ma'am? I listen and agree."

"And that is plenty. Thank you, Mr Fairfax. Anyway, the truth about 'craving a father figure' is far less headlining. I merely accept the advice of men as being part of the natural order of things, which somewhat flies in the face of my commitments as sovereign head of the Nation and Empire. Giving me advice was a role well suited to dear Albert and a burden accepted by John Brown, although dear John had no comments to offer on international affairs. They were both real men, while for amusement I have rather enjoyed the company of the dandy Disraeli, who many times made light with poetry and jokes. Alas, though, despite these diversions, the duties of the Queen are equal to those of any king. No allowances are made thereupon. And so, as for Queen Elizabeth centuries ago, I have had to find the courage of a man in the body of a woman, despite any misgivings. I might even have been called Elizabeth, had the name of any past queen not been forbidden to me at birth in an attempt to distance me from succession to the throne. I, therefore, became the first person in England to be called Victoria. Did you know that?"

"No, Ma'am."

"And why should you? It is merely a passage of my rather lonely life recorded in my personal diary. Now, isn't this better, talking in an atmosphere of ease?"

"It is, Ma'am."

"So, before I call Sir Benjamin back, I want to say something quite personal for your ears only. It is nothing Sir Benjamin does not already know, but, he has such a pompous way with words I doubt if you would ever comprehend his meaning. But understand you must."

"I am grateful, Ma'am."

"Your gratitude is duly noted. Mr Fairfax, it is a fact that our Royal Family will one day cast its benevolence over much of the Continent, as Sovereign rulers through marriage or as heads of state, as you must be aware. It is my sincere expectation that such a bond of royal blood will keep Europe generally safe from conflict. I think you will agree this is a reasonable assumption."

"Yes, Ma'am."

"However, whilst I worry little if the republican French

become entangled in armed struggle again with the Germanic races, as appears to be a regular occurrence, I do care if my expectations for general peace by the spread of our Royal Family does not stand up to events, particularly if hostilities ever bring us into direct conflict with the German Empire. I do not question the ability of our armed forces to win the day, but I have grave concern should accusations of 'split loyalties' ever be levied at the Crown from our own subjects if such a catastrophe happened. We have already touched on this when Sir Benjamin was present, but it does no harm to reaffirm the problem."

"No, Ma'am."

"Quite right. Under such dreadful circumstances, our people would be balefully reminded of my Albert's lineage and that of earlier British monarchs, and this would reflect badly on my children and their cousins both at home and abroad. Any new anti-German hatred would do immeasurable harm to the Monarchy and its future, and could give encouragement to those political activists within our shores who would gladly and maliciously foster such accusations in an attempt to rally the mob and destroy the Royal Family for good, in accordance with their own political doctrine."

"Destroy, Ma'am?"

"Come, Mr Fairfax, you must know what I mean. Other great nations have succumbed to the frenzied mob. Although Chartism was defeated a generation ago, the reformists are alarmingly ready to reappear. It was with some disquiet to us when Karl Marx settled in London in 1849, after being exiled from Paris, Brussels and the German Empire for his radical thoughts and occupations. I have to say, Mr Fairfax, it was with equal relief to my Government when he passed away last year. Did you know he was born of Jewish parents in the Rhineland, although they converted to Christianity, not that he cared much for religion, as it seems?"

"No, Ma'am, I did not. I am not familiar with the gentleman."

"Why, yes, he was. Yet, it appears he was fast to forget. Do you know what he said about Ramsgate?"

"No, Ma'am, I do not."

"That it was full of fleas and Jews. What do you make of that?"

"Not much, Ma'am."

"Well said again, Mr Fairfax. Nor do we. Anyway, we at the Palace made it our duty to become fully aware of the contents of his Communist Manifesto, produced with a certain Friedrich Engels. Marx saw class hatred as an instrument of revolution. Your Queen thinks nothing for revolutionaries in particular, Mr Fairfax, but cares deeply for all her subjects, whatever their standing. As it happens, my Albert worried about the poor more than most others, but that is a different matter for a different time. Society will be changed, Mr Fairfax, but not by the expropriation of property or the abolition of the right of inheritance, nor for that matter by cataclysm, but by the law of the land established and constantly reformed by free-thinking representatives of a just and elected government. Autocracy has no place in British Society."

"Yes, Ma'am. I mean, no, Ma'am"

"I have a mind to say more, Mr Fairfax, if you can bear it."

"I can, Ma'am, if there is time."

"Britain is, and always has been, a cosmopolitan mix. But, the immigration to our sacred shores of politically active refugees with socialist views from the sacked Paris Commune poured further fuel on the discontent of the poor. Yet, it was merely the tip of the iceberg. More recently, a former stockbroker by the name of Hyndman has founded The Social Democratic Federation, which could lead to further unease because of its published extremist views. Such an organisation might even question the future role of the Monarchy. And yet, even that is not the whole of it. Now William Morris, the famous poet and artist and a person in whom we take much pride in all except his politics, has left the Federation to establish his own Socialist League, while earlier this year my advisors tell me a Fabian Society has been founded to promote socialism. Where will it all end, we ask? Which can our Empire do without, its Monarchy or socialism? From what I have read, which is much, I see little chance of the two comfortably coexisting, judging by all so far professed. Where do you stand on such issues, Mr Fairfax?"

"Ma'am?"

"Are you a socialist by nature?"

"I believe I am not, Ma'am. Actually, if I may be so bold, I should admit to knowing little about socialism and care even less for politics in general. I hope I do not talk out of turn."

"I accept any truth as being fair comment, Mr Fairfax. Then, as this is understood, we must leave politics aside and deal with the pressing issue that brought us closer together. But first, I ask this of you as an ordinary man, to settle my curiosity. Do you not see that, in such difficult times for the Crown as a war, to have the Monarchy linked in any way to the enemy could, itself, lead to fatal accusations of split loyalties, even if we made our position public?"

"Yes, Ma'am. I see it could."

"An honest answer, in keeping with my own assessment. One might suppose such accusations, if backed by proof of genealogy, could be the very spark igniting revolution. Mr Fairfax, war must be avoided for generations to come, to avoid such accusations coming to the forefront, at least until our royal blood has less German flowing through it. Separately, we must hold all revolutionaries at bay." She took a moment's silence by playing with the simple gold ring on her finger. "I feel it is all too much for a woman to bear alone. I wish my Albert was here to advise me, or John."

"If I may enquire of your Majesty, is there likely to be war with Germany?"

"I trust not, my gentle Mr Fairfax. But it is as well to see ahead. I sometimes wonder at the antics of Crown Prince Frederick. I have more hope in Willy, who is next in line. It is my conviction little Willy will show more compassion and harbour fewer typical German militaristic attitudes because of his handicap. Do you understand?"

"Yes, Ma'am, I think I do. Only, where do I fit into this?"

"Why, to help prevent the possibility of war by providing us with intelligence on what others abroad are up to with flying machines, of course. To level the playing field if we are mistaken in not pursuing our own vigorous programme on flying machines. Britain is mighty at sea, but our army is small. It has always been British policy to pay foreign armies to do the fighting for us when away from our own shores, under our generalship, or make best use of the indigenous forces to swell our limited ranks. This strategy was used well when we expanded the Empire. We began with the gunboat and sword, Mr Fairfax, but the immense benefits we brought to backward countries were soon evident to all who lived there under the protection of the Union Flag, to their industrial and agricultural production, transport, health, local government and much more. It allowed us to win the hearts of those who became the subject of British rule and British law. Mark my words, Mr Fairfax, if ever Britain withdraws from its most glittering jewels of Empire, it will be to those countries' detriment and they would suffer most from disengagement, for in the long term and within broader issues we give immeasurably more than we take. This is also why we need only small standing armies to maintain law and order in the far flung reaches of Empire. Similarly, but more urgently, the Royal Navy must not become vulnerable to air or underwater attack. We are a sea-faring nation, with most of our national wealth brought across the oceans of the world. The Navy is our lifeblood and the protector of our trade. To sum up, Mr Fairfax, learn all from others in your travels but give nothing whatsoever away."

"You want me to spy? My apologies, Ma'am. *Me?*"

"Good! Good! So, what you must bear in mind when you listen to more of what Sir Benjamin tells you is that I do not want any situation to arise which could generate anti-Germanic feelings among the British population. You could be very useful in this. Now, be a good man and fetch Sir Benjamin back in."

"As you wish, Ma'am, but can I ask one further question?"

"If you are brief, Mr Fairfax," was the Queen's testy reply.

"Am I safe, both at home and abroad? Have I put myself at risk from both sides?"

"We are not in the habit of punishing our own, Mr Fairfax."

His anguished expression remained steadfast.

"You are unconvinced? What we have asked of you is a bitter pill to swallow. I, too, would be hesitant in your position. But, there is no need, I assure you. However, as time is short and I need to prevail upon your complete trust, I will tell you a terrible secret of the Crown to hold sway over your fears. In the circumstances, I hold no fear in telling you something which my ministers of government would thoroughly disapprove of."

"Gosh!"

"All my life, Mr Fairfax, I have had to fight my corner. As a young woman I battled against my own mother, who sought to arrest my freedoms and gain a degree of political power for herself. The old King held onto his life at the end for one purpose only, to see me turn eighteen before he died. My coming of age gave me the power to break free of her. And, believe me, what a relief it was. So, by telling you such a secret of state, we each now hold sway over the other, Mr Fairfax, and in such a manner guarantee each other's freedoms."

"That is too much to take, Ma'am."

"No, Mr Fairfax, it is no more than the situation demands. I may be Queen of England and Empress of India, Mr Fairfax, but even now much of my life is not my own. Despite my exulted position, I have to abide by state rules and listen to advisors who, contrary to their title, do not so much advise as coerce the Monarchy. In Britain, the head of state remains secondary to the will of the people expressed through the elected Parliament, which means in turn the will of the inner Cabinet of whatever political party is in power at the time, which means the will of the Prime Minister. So you see, one man, advised by others that he alone selects to office, holds swathe over me."

"Really, Ma'am?"

"In this way of things, brought about by the severed head of King Charles and born of Parliament's dictates, I too am no more totally at liberty to do as I might wish as you are, Mr Fairfax. I am your Queen, but I sometimes have to baulk the very nature of British democracy to have my way over matters of an entirely personal nature that are too dear to me to be the subject of governmental browbeating. In this, I am now thinking of my dear companion, John Brown, who saved my sanity after the loss of my greatest love, my dearest of all, Albert." The Queen hesitated at his name. She continued in softer tone. "I am a woman, Mr Fairfax, with a woman's needs to be comforted and cherished. Mr Brown recovered my life when all seemed dark and lost." She again paused. "No, what I said before about my mother is not much of a state secret to hold as guarantee of your freedoms. I am much warmed to you by your common sense, Mr Fairfax, and so I intend to entrust something to your hearing that is beyond imagination, yet is true, something I have longed to announce to another soul. Come to me, here, by my side, Mr Fairfax."

He did so. She took his hand, not lovingly but as an umbilical cord of trust. He stared at her old hand holding his, paralysed by the moment, a plain gold ring visible on her wedding finger.

"Before John Brown's death we married."

"Ma'am?"

"Don't you understand? I became Mrs Brown, but so named only to John himself. You see, there was nothing shameful in our unity, making a liar of anyone who suggested I was a courtesan in my own palace. This is the greatest state secret of my reign, and you are not told lightly. I wear his mother's ring, as you see." She held up the finger on her left hand. Her hand fell back on his. "I shall be buried with it, alongside a lock of his hair and a cast of Albert's beloved hand that I keep close by my side in the bedchamber. You see, I have imparted a shocking state secret, Mr Fairfax, which I am constitutionally unable to reveal to a single well-wisher outside the inner circles of government. The secret will accompany me to the grave. I tell you this in the strictest

confidence because I care more for the continuation of the
monarchy than fear any amount of newsmongering which would
follow its public revelation. Is this guarantee enough as an
expression of my faith and trust in you, and of your personal
safety at Government hands?"

"Yes, Ma'am, it is and I thank you for the trust. May I also
admit to immense shock? I am in a haze of general disbelief at
everything that has happen today. I may take a little time to come
to terms with it. In the meantime, if all this is not a dream, may I
congratulate your Majesty on your second wedding as no other
commoner can have?"

"You may, Mr Fairfax, although I am again a widow since John
died. But, yes, you may indeed. And, I understand your dubiety.
I felt much the same when I was first told as a young girl just
turned eighteen that the King had died. It took some time to
become real in my mind. Now, you must become settled in
yours."

"I will, Ma'am, yet I remain bewildered. Am I ordered to stop
my own private work on flying machines or merely spy on. . ."

"Mr Fairfax, please do as I have asked!"

Cornelius hurried from the room, jerking his head towards the
guards on both sides of the door in the hope of passing without
being stopped. He approached Sir Benjamin, who was occupied
in reading, paperwork resting on his knees. The message was
given and the papers were bundled into a case.

They re-entered, Cornelius quite deliberately taking back his
seat by the Queen's side, leaving Sir Benjamin surprised by the
informality. He stood, long faced and hunched, with his back to
the fireplace and his eyes half closed. He adopted all the bearing
of a castrated animal, hurt by his master and fearful of any further
approach. How easy it had been, he thought, for the Queen to
dismiss him and make him look quite foolish to the boy.

A ray of sunshine pierced the window panes, striking the
Queen's face. She turned to one side, causing hesitation in her

pleasant remarks to Cornelius. More low rays, now fully peering from behind the moving cloud and of greater intensity, also caught Cornelius's eye. He jumped. It was the opportunity Sir Benjamin's needed to regain control.

"Mr Fairfax, please pull the curtain against the brightness and sit back where you began today," he barked, straightening his posture.

Cornelius did so.

With her hands now away from her eyes, the Queen ordered Sir Benjamin to take back authority over the meeting and conclude the address hurriedly, in his own way. He needed no second telling.

Thus, for the next twenty minutes, Cornelius was lectured fiercely by Sir Benjamin. By the close, Cornelius felt his destiny was not his to determine. The Queen unexpectedly rose and the room fell into silence. She left the building, escorted by a dozen armed sailors, leaving only Sir Benjamin and Cornelius to take tea in an atmosphere finally lifted of rigid tension.

"Tea is so civilizing, don't you think?"

"I'm not sure what civilized means any longer."

"How come, young man?"

"I came to France in happy anticipation and with an open mind. I had no preconceptions of what I might find, but the prospect of advancing my theories on heavy flying was exciting. Now I feel like some shady sleuth of fiction, except this is real. I'm not at all sure I want the role. Can I return home to my parents instead?"

"I have no jurisdiction to keep you abroad, Mr Fairfax. I can only request your co-operation."

"Is there nobody else you can approach?"

"There are one or two persons with aeronautical knowledge whom we could call upon, but they are already published and are, therefore, better known than you. That makes them vulnerable. I also know they are barking up the wrong tree, so their experiments do not concern us. No, your knowledge and obscurity are of great advantage."

"Am I now at risk?"

"No more so than before we met. You were happy enough to gather knowledge then. What in essence has changed?"

"Nothing, I suppose, other than I am to be used as a conduit of deceit against foreign persons who might freely take me into their confidence for the benefit of science alone."

"Well then? Just do your stuff and see me in London afterwards. Do you need money?"

"Definitely not. If I am to seem as before, I must continue to travel publicly and lodge cheaply."

"So be it." Sir Benjamin rose to his feet. "I must rush along if I am to meet the boat."

"Before you go, tell me one more thing. Her Majesty talks of prohibiting sub-mariner ships and flying machines, but expresses vulnerability from other nations who could secretly develop them. Similarly, if I understand correctly, she feels socialists and activists could bring down the Royal Family by stirring up public unrest if war ever broke out with the German Empire because of our lack of preparedness. It seems to me to be an impossible position to hold. Surely inactivity against either event is a recipe for disaster?"

"Not impossible, Mr Fairfax, just very hard for those of us who have the awkward job of squaring a circle."

"Then, let me ask one thing more, if I may. You implied Her Majesty influences Government thinking, even when you might not entirely concur with her views. Is that so?"

"You question Her Majesty's integrity?"

"No, of course not. It's the integrity of politicians I question."

"I see. Then let me be equally frank with you, as we rely on each other. The Crown has many duties, but to Government it remains purely advisory within the process of decision making. Such is modern democracy. We concur with Her Majesty's expectations, but in practical terms the War Office even now independently allocates funding for various highly secret air experiments at Farnborough in Hampshire."

"Good heavens! Isn't that treasonable?"

"Not in today's Britain. My head will stay firmly attached to my shoulders. As to Farnborough, yes, rudimentary, but true. Funding comes from estimates for the Army, without any specific allocations put in writing. You see, we follow Her Majesty's wishes, but we have the mandate and duty to take wider opinion. Believe me, Mr Fairfax, sub-mariner boats and flying machines will come one day, whether we are ready for them or not, and war with the German Empire is not as unlikely as Her Majesty likes to believe. Trust me. In international politics, royal ties mean absolutely nothing. The German Empire is led by its generals and the nation's massive steel industry that fills the German Army with breechloaders, supplies armour for its Navy's ironclads and offers cannon to anyone with the cash to buy, while its railway equipment has no borders and provides for the rapid movement of troops. Germanic generals view war as a proud tradition and character building for the nation. Industry merely supplies the means, mostly I suspect for commercial gain. Still, don't fret. You should see the new battleships we have in design. They make everything currently afloat look like obsolete toys. We will not be Trafalgared by an enemy in my lifetime! Good-day, Mr Fairfax, and good luck with your spying . . . I mean your observations."

Cornelius, out of his depth and terrified, decided to leave France with all haste. And so, the very next morning, he gathered his few possessions and travelled north. The following day he bought an early cross-Channel boat ticket for England. The water was calm and he was home before the night had properly set in. He was having none of it!

Several days later Cornelius took the talisman to Cadbury fort where, having looked for one last time at the image of a creature with four wings resting at the foot of a hill, he threw it with great force. It rebounded off a stone and glanced against the trunk of the rowan tree, where it stayed until prolonged rainfall washed it down the bank, only stopping as it entangled itself amongst the rowan's roots.

Now, Cornelius needed to be untraceable for a time. He would look for inconspicuous employment away from the district.

***

Epilogue to the talisman – thirty years later

The talisman possessed the enchantment to fall only into the grasp of men destined for terrifying experiences. Whether it was as a warning or as a prediction, nobody could tell, for few survived the encounter.

As the years passed and more soil washed down to the rowan's roots, the talisman again embedded itself deeply into the chamber walls, its glint returning for another generation. Only its images mysteriously changed. The grassy hill with a winged creature at the foot, as previously depicted while the talisman remained in Cornelius's possession, became a jagged stump beside a creature whose wings were on fire. The reverse side regenerated to show wasteland where poppies grew, while above floated winged apparitions in long robes.

A British soldier from Wessex, barely more than a boy in uniform, felt in his pocket for a charm he had found in Cadbury a little time before shipping out to France in August 1914. He had carried it to war as a good-luck reminder of home. Now standing amongst his bedraggled and retreat-weary colleagues, lucky to be among the survivors to have escaped to Mons and luckier still that the enemy had halted its advance, he looked at it with amazement, for the foreign soil must have turned it dull.

Two months later, after receiving tragic news of his childhood friend who had been shot down during an epic mid-air struggle between his unarmed and outdated two-seat biplane and a vastly superior armed German aircraft, the boy soldier returned to Wessex on leave. Standing on the rim of Cadbury hill fort, he threw the talisman with all his might. The rain did the rest.

* * *

Historical Fact

On 26th August 1914, the exhausted British Expeditionary Force retreated to Mons, closely pursued by overwhelming German forces. For no apparent reason beyond mass hallucination caused by a brilliant light in the sky which shone upon three hovering spectres, the German army refused to press home its attack.

CHAPTER 8

Returning to 1884 — Rutting in the midden

With just one night to go before Emmie's arrival, John Madden remained uneasy. The waiting was worst, fearful of the thought of seeing her skittish figure restively appear through the gates and walk towards the door, where she would descend upon the quietness of his lonely house like a rampaging bull. He imagined her every first step, every first conversation, the first irritation to his even temper.

He tried to sleep, but found it more difficult to lie on his bed than while away the hours on a comfortable chair covered by a blanket, staring into the dying fire or trying to read Dickens by the white glow of the lamp. He longed for dawn, when he could go outside and use physical occupation to speed away the time before she came, dispersing such negative thoughts.

When first light came, it fell upon him gently through the drawing room windows. The book from the night lay open on the floor, where it had fallen from his hand during a snatched hour of sleep. The open pages, now creased at the corners, began *"Hush!" said Mr Jingle, in a stage-whisper — "large boy — dumpling face — round eyes — rascal!"*

He walked to the kitchen, where the stove was lit and a pot of tea brewed. A slice was cut from a thick farmhouse loaf. Resting both the cup and the plate on the arms of the seat, he slumped down again, rubbing his eyes and feeling the whiskers around his jaw. The drawing room was cold, as uninviting as the grey ash remaining at the bottom of the grate. He heard steps, sending his pulse racing. A milkmaid passed the window on her way towards the cowshed, her buckets swinging on chains suspended from a wooden yoke around her shoulders. He settled back, biting into the bread and washing it down with a gulp from the cup.

Revived but not rested, he took a pan of hot water up the stairs, pouring it into a thick china bowl. Whiskers were softened with soap and a cut-throat razor was applied to his face and neck, leaving tiny blood spots that stained the towel. A set of clean working clothes and a little lavender oil at last lifted him from the lowest ebb of dejection.

Outside in the cool air of early morning, he soon appeared to be fully occupied, even cheerful, erecting a short line of thatched hurdles on each side of the entrance to the house as protection against the unusually severe Winter weather. He began to sing, but only because the solitude of the dull and easy work gave him all the time he needed to replay over and over again in his mind the concerns of the night before. Singing every music hall song he knew provided temporarily freedom from such repetitious torment, giving the impression to any passer-by of a man enjoying every blow of the hammer. But, as if visible proof was needed of dark thoughts lurking under the surface, every so often he stopped singing and took from his jacket the letter Emmie had sent while at the Holman Clavel. Reading the same lines again girded his loins to face his moral duty to help Emmie start a new life in safe surroundings. Yet, the very moment the letter was returned purposefully to his pocket and the singing resumed, the same doubts magically re-emerged, crushing the accord and sending a cold rush through his body at his anxious wish not to reflect on relationships past.

And so, this carousel of duty and doubt circled in his mind

without remission. When the last post had been driven into the ground, the last hurdle nailed and his tools gathered together, the final decision was made to stop such pointless worrying. It was morally irreversible, but still left him questioning the wisdom. He re-entered the house, realising that he had taken far longer to finish the task than anticipated and, thereby, she was in all probability close at hand.

While recovering from his exertions with another pot of tea, he again heard footsteps crunching along the loose gravel, this time unmistakably approaching the house. It had to be her. Taking a deep breath, he opened the door. There stood Emmie, a large bag in her hands and her bonnet and dress blowing wildly. The gusty wind bit coldly into her face. He looked past to where the hurdles had already blown down and were now scattering along the drive.

With a deep sigh of resignation at his wasted efforts, he beckoned her inside, forcing the door closed against the head-on wind. Dead leaves that had swirled through the entrance dropped to the floor as the noise of the outside abated. Only the hiss of damp wood as it burned in the kitchen stove could now be heard, as welcoming as the warmth it provided.

Emmie grinned with all the joy of youth as she was shown into the kitchen.

"Shall I be here for Christmas or will I be expected to go home?"

"What?" was John's bemused reply, her question having come without any initial greeting or expression of gratitude.

"Christmas, it's only a few weeks away. Where will I be? I should let my parents know."

John thought for a moment. "Here, I suppose."

"Just wondered, that's all."

He felt strangely displaced, but expected it would pass now that she had arrived and the waiting was over.

"Well, here we are, Emmie. This, as you see, is the kitchen, which we will share." He followed her eyes as she looked around the room. "I know what you're thinking. It's a bit untidy at present, but I'm sure you can deal with the mess quick enough. Next, I'll show you your accommodation."

"Where will I be, inside or out?"

"Sorry?"

"Am I to be with the indoor servants or with the outdoor labourers?"

"I don't keep servants, Emmie, in name or deed. Those who work for me are free, honest men and women to whom I pay all due respect. As for inside staff, when my mother was alive she did most of the household duties herself, with the help of a certain Mrs Jobbins from the village. Recently, I ended the arrangement. But, the domestic never lived in. It would be improper for any woman to stay here who wasn't family, for the sake of propriety, you understand."

"So, I'll be outside in the workers' dormitory?"

"No." He thought for a moment. "Yes. I mean, no. Oh hell, I haven't thought it through properly. I have a room aired for you upstairs."

Her stare lifted towards the ceiling, her lips curling. Any considerations to be proper in thought and deed vanished. "It will do very nicely."

Although the day was young, the upstairs remained poorly lit and dark. The same matt-brown wallpaper hung on the walls as when Christabel had stayed with the family, the only real change being the loss of one of the occasional tables that narrowed the landing at regular intervals. Emmie had never been upstairs, but the gap made by the absence of a table was noticeable even to a stranger.

"I broke it," he said with reserve.

"I expect you couldn't help walking into it. The light is just dreadful."

He shook his head. "Actually, I was so annoyed the day when. . ." He stopped abruptly. "Christabel. Everything always comes back to her, even now, after all this time."

"Oh, John." She dropped her bag and stepped towards him,

hesitantly placing an arm on his shoulder. "It's alright to think of her. I do all the time. I miss her too, more so since I lost her ring."

"You lost that precious thing?"

"Actually, it was taken from me."

"And her shawl?"

"Oh, I still have that. Charlotte Elvington stole the ring from me."

"My God! That bloody family again."

"You know them?"

"I had run-ins with Edmond Elvington, the son. I'm glad to say we have since buried the hatchet and become tolerably friendly."

"I, too, know who he is," replied Emmie sheepishly.

He decided to let the subject of the Elvingtons drop. "You asked about the table. I broke it with my bare hands the day Christabel left Nether Bow. I should have seen her off properly, but I was a coward, trapped into retreating behind an upstairs window where she couldn't see me and I could hide my true feelings. For a moment after, I went quite mad."

Emmie bent for her bag. "Is this my room?" she asked, pointing to the next closed door.

"No!" John shouted, startling Emmie. "Not that one. You must never go in there."

He led her to the furthest room along the landing, which overlooked the rear of the property. It was pretty enough, with solid furniture and an old but serviceable rug covering most of the floorboards. A lamp stood on a small dressing table. Opposite was a marble wash stand with bowl and jug, a pleated curtain beneath concealing two empty shelves, while a heavy hanging cupboard and bed completed the fixtures.

"Will it do?"

"Nicely, thank you."

"Good. The whole house tends to be a little cold, but you may take as many logs as you wish from the storehouse out back to stoke the grate. The top wood is recently cut and remains a trifle damp, but if you use some of the older dry stuff from the bottom it will get the fire going nicely. Matches, tinder and paper can be found in there." He pointed to a small wooden box with a scrolled lid held on the wall by a single nail. "Oh, and the usual offices are under the bed and in the little brick-built room outside the back door. There is a washroom on this floor, but I alone use it. The lock is broken, so please don't forget that it's private."

She nodded.

"Good. Then I leave you to unpack. We will lunch at midday in the kitchen, if you don't mind getting straight down to things."

"Where will I wash my clothes and the like, John?"

"Use the laundry room, next to the kitchen. You may use anything in there. Only, if you have private items to dry, please pull the curtain across to save my blushes."

"And, what are my duties?"

"Goodness knows. I haven't got that far. No doubt you will have some uses." He pulled the door closed.

Emmie sat on the edge of the bed, looking at her surroundings. It was considerably better than the dormitory at Westkings and a little larger than her room at her parents' terrace in Stirminster Oak. Yet, she felt subdued by the reality and alone. The welcome had not been as warm as she had expected, not by a long way, and for once she felt almost trapped. What had seemed likely to be an adventure, sweet and sensual, was now overcast with apprehension and unfamiliarity.

"What have I done?" she asked herself, feeling her wanderlust returning.

She had only just begun unpacking when voices were heard outside. She pulled back the lace curtain to see a young man walking arm in arm with his lover across the grass. Their conversation was bright and unguarded, unconcerned others might overhear. Although the cold weather necessitated warm clothing and a covered head, from the distance Emmie fancied she recognised the woman under the wrap as none other than her old friend Louise from the Elvington estate. Jubilant, she rushed down the stairs and out to greet her. The couple stared as she approached at speed. Emmie pulled to a sudden and embarrassing halt. She nodded graciously, realising her mistake. The couple walked away, laughing, eventually climbing the wooden open-tread stairs leading to the workers' dormitory to the side of the main house. At the top of the steps the man stopped and turned towards Emmie. He gave a slight wave before the call of his lover turned his attention to other things.

As planned, at midday John sat at the kitchen table. He was muddy from working with the animals. Emmie joined him a few minutes later, now also dressed for work. He laughed.

"So, you are assuming my mind is already made up?"

"Sorry?"

"You, dressed as a housekeeper."

She looked down at her clothes, which seemed entirely appropriate for the occasion. "I didn't know what to wear. Have I done wrong?"

He smiled richly. "Far from it, little Emmeline, far from it. Indeed, you have made my day."

"How so?" was her suspicious reply, adopting a perverse look.

"I thought you being here could be a problem. That having you around me would be a constant reminder of Christabel. But, now I face you properly, in clothes similar to those she wore, I see you are nothing like her and never could be, nor do you remind me of her. She made even working clothes look gracious and appealing."

Emmie swallowed with disappointment. "Am I so ugly?"

"No, of course not, not ugly," he returned in apologetic tone. "No man could say that. But you are generally plain, as you must know yourself."

"So, nobody could be attracted to me?"

"We both know that isn't the case. Why, you rutted in the midden with the Lieutenant, and I doubt it began or ended there."

"It was romance with Longborne. Rutting sounds so bestial."

"It was lust, with no feelings of greater tenderness towards you on his part, I promise you."

"How can you say such things, when you know nothing of the circumstances?"

"Did he stay after I gave him twenty pounds to marry you?"

"Did you? When?"

"In Dorchester, when I discovered you in a dreadful rented room. I was willing to take you away to safety, if you recall, but he put on a puppy-dog expression and you fell for it again. More fool you."

"For a while it seemed so perfect."

"Poppycock! Repetition turns a hobby into an art, and I'll be bound the Lieutenant knew exactly how to get around you. Take my word for it, Emmie. For good men, having the admiration of various different women doesn't alter the lone nature of passion, it simply adds fuel to the flames. For bad men, and I count the Lieutenant among these, such dalliances are merely stepping stones to relieve animal desires and improve their situation. They merely trample one to get to another. I would venture you had something he wanted."

"Of course I did."

"I am talking of material things, Emmie, not physical!"

"You talk to me as if I'm a trollop. I'm not."

"I imply nothing of the kind. Love is a one-off exposure to sudden madness, as singular in energy as it seems everlasting at the time. The secret of a happy life for the Lieutenant is to duplicate that occurrence as regularly as possible with whomsoever he can entice."

"Despite being destroyed by rejection? I'm sure he must have been spurned sometimes. It is a feeling I know all too well and it hurts."

"Particularly then. For, when having fallen off a horse, it's best to get straight back on the mount."

"Sir!"

"Sir, nothing. But, damn the unfamiliarity, Emmie. Call me John, or Mr Madden at the very least. We are old friends."

"I'm not sure I should, or want to, now."

"You did in those earlier times. And you did so earlier today. I heard you. Yes, you must call me John."

"If you insist, Sir . . . John."

"What! Am I knighted at last? Yes, it fits me well to be Sir John, but, alas, I am yet to feel the Queen's sword upon my shoulder. Just plain John, if you please."

"Plain John and plainer Emmeline."

"Separate us. We are not a couple."

"Whatever pleases you, Sir John." She smiled wickedly, the repression of his harsh words already forgotten. "But, you still refuse to tell me what I'm supposed to do."

"Whatever I decide. At present I think you should look after my indoor needs."

"I thought I would be an outsider, perhaps looking after the milkers, hens, ducks and horses. I'm good with dairy cows and soon find they have a liking for my pair of steady hands. I've never had a cow kick over a bucket in anger."

"I keep many cattle and sheep, but these are already well attended. As to my horses and ducks, I take care of both, just as Christabel did before me. There, I have mentioned her again. I warn you, Emmie, make this the last time you trap me into mentioning her name. She belongs in my thoughts and nowhere else. Do you understand?"

She nodded in agreement, uncertain how to meet his demand in the course of normal conversation.

So it was that November slipped rawly towards its conclusion. Emmie took her place within the working farm, bringing an unexpected cheer to the house by her light-headed nature and unpredictable ways. And, just as the weeping willows finally let go of their leaves to fall on the littered ground already carpeted by ash, beech, oak and finally the elm, so John began to let go of

Christabel's memory, once again seeing life as a more pleasurable pursuit. He was no longer tormented without rest, although, when she did come to mind, his heart broke as completely as before.

The weeping willows grew in a single, small patch close to the river that ran alongside the farm, a particularly pretty spot where bulrushes abundant with seeds still doggedly clung onto their heads, ready for release before Spring. It was a favourite place of contemplation for John, who enjoyed Winter walks to spot migrant waxwings of grey, scarlet and yellow, graciously wearing their heady crests as they searched for rose hips or the fruit from berry-bearing evergreens closely associated with Christmas, particularly those of the holly, mistletoe and juniper. Elsewhere in the woodland, trees bore tell-tale scars from deer nibbling at the bark, or rabbits, hares and voles looking for food once the softer herbage became frozen, while at night moths flitted among the oaks. Furrowed holes revealed badger setts, with leaves and other materials which had lined the inside now spilling out of the hitherto secret places. In essence, while some creatures slept and nature retreated, others gave the month the energy of defiance.

"Grab your shawl," cried John in delight one late afternoon, seizing the brush from Emmie's hand and pulling her to the window. "Look out there. What's the date?"

"I think it's the thirtieth."

"Of course it is. Excellent!"

"Where are those people going with their lanterns?" she asked, watching the labourers disappear along the lane in festive mood.

"I'll explain on the way. There's no time now. Come on!"

Emmie rushed up to her room to wrap herself warmly. She met John in the hall, where he waited impatiently holding two bags of clothes.

"No, no, no, Emmie. You can't wear those shoes. Put your boots on."

"Why?"

"Just do as I say . . . Please"

She bounded back up the stairs, returning wearing her outside working boots.

"That's better. We'll have to take the quick way into Mangstone or we'll be late. It'll be muddy. Fancy me forgetting what day it is."

Grabbing her by the hand, he led her past the small church that stood within the farm estate and on to a kissing gate, leading to the riverside bridleway. After a short walk, they emerged in the village between the tiny inn and the watermill. She had heard singing and shouting from some way back, but, now they stood in the centre of events, the scene became riotous. Feasting and drinking was in full fervour and, despite the evening being young, several of the partygoers were already unable to stand.

"What's going on," asked Emmie, fully ready to join in the merriment, whatever the occasion.

"It's Saint Andrew's Day. Some places celebrate it on the eleventh day of December, the old traditional day, but we are progressive and have it in November. What fun! If we were at school, we would lock the teachers out for a few hours, while some people like to head for the woods to hunt squirrels."

"What are *we* expected to do?" she shouted through the noise.

"Enjoy ourselves in whatever way pleasures us, of course. Oh, and wear these."

He passed her a bag of clothes. She looked inside.

"You've given me the wrong bag. This is full of men's clothes."

"That's right!"

"What do I do with them?"

"I'll tell you later, after you've had a bit to drink."

With food from tables and cider from barrels being freely provided in abundance, the atmosphere became charged. Groups gathered around glowing braziers radiating light and warmth, while elsewhere men and women staggered about with tankards waving recklessly above their heads.

By mid evening only half the revellers were still standing, but those who could remain upright began dancing to the music of three fiddles and an accordion.

"Isn't this great," shouted John, his arm around Emmie's neck. "It's the only time of the year I allow myself to have one drink too many."

Emmie held John tightly around his waist, enjoying the occasion as fully as any villager. "You passed that point several drinks back," she replied through a laugh. "I think I should get you home."

"I'll have no defeatist talk," he cried, slapping her on the bottom. "There's more to the evening yet." He pointed to the bags, which had been left in a doorway. "Come on, it's time."

Obediently, she took her bag and together they entered the tiny inn where two temporary curtains already hung, dividing the space into three.

"Off you go with the other woman. Return as a man!"

Emmie disappeared behind the curtain, where other country girls were in various stages of undress. She turned her back as she slipped on clothes that swamped her small frame, re-emerging a changed person.

"My goodness," convulsed John, "you look horrible."

Emmie grabbed the curtain.

"No, no," blasted John above the gaiety. "Stop! You have me wrong. You look just right. Perfect, in fact."

She stood expressionless, feeling the only fool in the room despite the other women being similarly dressed. John knelt and turned up her trouser legs. He repeated the exercise on the shirt sleeves. Finally, he twisted her hair and forced it up and under a cap.

"There," he offered, standing back to look. "You look a proper gent and no mistake. Now it's my turn".

John pulled at the second curtain and walked behind. After much pulling and grunting, he made his grand entrance. The laughter reached fever pitch. He performed a twirl, his straw-filled bosoms being of such excessive proportions that they lifted the hem of his dress, where his muddy boots peeped out.

"Well, I don't fancy 'ee one little bit," exclaimed another man yet to change.

"Not even for a sixpence," returned John in high pitch, wiggling his hips.

"Not even if me life depended on it," said the first. "You're the ugliest woman I've ever seen."

"More ugly than me?" whispered Emmie into John's ear.

John stopped laughing. "I'm sorry, Emmie. I was rude when there was no reason to be. I cannot make excuses for my behaviour, beyond saying it was the result of the relief I felt when I realised I could be in your company without thinking of. . ."

"Stop!" she demanded. "I'm not going to be the cause of you saying her name again. Remember?"

He placed his hand on her cheek. It glowed with warmth. "Friends, Emmie?"

"Friends always," she replied, "but, what next?"

"The masquerade. We knock at the cottages, where we will be given hot eldern wine."

She looked at John and John stared back. "Must we?" she pleaded. "I do feel particularly stupid."

He looked down as straw fell from his dress, leaving him with only one gigantic bosom. "Maybe not."

CHAPTER 9

Elizabeth Grant

*E*lizabeth had taken Maria Trimby's censure to heart. The nurse clearly worried for the long-term future of the hospital and she had no right to put the place in jeopardy. Elizabeth had to respect her genuine concerns.

It had been far too easy for Elizabeth to hide in Glastonbury while learning how to be a mother without the proper support of her parents or, indeed, a husband. But learn she did, although no menial task came easily to a young woman used to being idle among the best society. Daily, she battled against her natural instinct to leave chores to those born to such small tasks, but in this Maria Trimby understood Elizabeth's nature well and refused to help with Unity's needs other than in a supervisory manner. More than any other action, this brought home to Elizabeth a stark reality. The day to leave was approaching with awful certainty.

With this decided, and with a good grounding in motherhood, Elizabeth had a mind to return home without unnecessary delay, to face any reprimand awaiting her. Surely there were friends and distant relations who already enquired after her whereabouts, making the truth the best explanation of the situation. Then, if she was to be cast away once more, it would be irreversible. At least there was a small chance of reconciliation once her parents looked upon the trusting eyes of little Unity Grant, their own flesh and blood.

So it was that within a week a covered carriage pulled up to the main entrance of the tiny hospital in the first light of morning, where the driver waited with some impatience as Elizabeth tried on one gown after another until she was happy that she looked suitably elegant, yet contrite. Yet, the mirror also acknowledged her worse fear. Her tiny waistline had gone.

She lifted Unity from the austere wooden cot and carried her carefully down the stairs.

"Bless the little thing," said Trimby, pulling back the covers to look once more on the baby's tiny features. "Does she have any of her father's looks?"

"I believe she does," was the reply, "although I hear it said most babies do, to make the father know the child is his."

"Complete rubbish, Lizzy. If she takes after her father, then it is the natural order of things. Handsome, is he?"

"John? Why, I do believe he is, in a mature way."

"The best kind, in my experience." She rearranged the covers to provide maximum protection against the outside elements. "I suppose the payments will stop?"

"That's not for me to say." She turned for the door, looking back as she prepared to push it shut. "Goodbye and thank you. I shall not return."

The very long journey back to her parent's elegant house began at a creeping pace, passing town houses marking the juncture between Glastonbury and the open countryside beyond. Maria Trimby had watched her go from a window, half expecting the carriage to stop and Elizabeth to coming running back, pleading to stay a while longer. But, Elizabeth did not waiver, and instead sat inside in an anxious faint. She travelled with a blanket placed over her legs to keep some of the bitter cold from her bones and another as a general wrap that also engulfed Unity in several layers, ensuring the ride would be comfortable.

No conversation passed between driver and passenger for the first part of the journey, as if observing the usual social divide. But, as mile followed mile, now at a reasonable speed to make sensible progress, words began to be exchanged.

"I will have to feed the baby soon," mumbled Elizabeth shyly, "but there is no need to stop. Just keep your eyes ahead until I say you can turn. I have been looking and we are quite alone on the road."

"As you wish, Ma'am, but I could find a stopping place if it helps. I don't like the stuff, but I know of a fine ale house just up the road a bit."

"No, thank you. I want the journey over as soon as possible. I can manage where I am, if the pace is kept steady."

After unbuttoning her coat and the top of her dress, and bringing Unity close, she raised the edge of the blanket to fully cover the gap.

"Is this pace to your liking, Ma'am? I could rein-in the beasts to a walk."

"No, carry on as we are," she replied. "Tell me, where do you live, my good man?" using small talk to cover any embarrassment.

"Oh, nowhere worth knowing. 'Tis little bit of a place called Bere-sub-Nettlebury, only a few miles from our destination but merely a blot on the landscape. It's known to nobody who doesn't live in those parts. Six cottages and an inn, and nothing more until the church at Winchberry a mile and a half north. I visit the inn on my return from church, where I often buys a quart for the vicar. 'E likes his ale on a Sunday, does 'e, especially if taken behind locked doors. Says 'tis all part of God's rich bounty. I join him in this celebration, just to be God fearing, you understand. Gor, I have to force the stuff down me throat to keep his company, and consequently feel so much the better for observing God's grace that I down four more in devotion before returning to the wife."

"So you know the area well?"

"That I do. I'm much called upon around there."

"What news of the place? Any gossip?"

"Nothing much happens. Just life and grind, and life and death. The countryside seems to be dead compared to the fast changes taking place in towns. I did hear, though, there was quite a rumpus over a family of landed toffs mislaying their grown daughter. Fancy that. Careless I call it. Apparently, people in the village became mighty anxious at not seeing her for months, and their friendly enquiries at the big house got them the door slammed in their faces. Blow me down with a feather if someone didn't call in the police, thinking something suspicious might have become her. But no, it appears she had taken off to London or some other elegant place and was not expected back for years. Mind, some other busybody who asked a visitor to the house if he knew her whereabouts was told she nursed at a charity hospital, a story backed up by the young master of the establishment, her brother, no less. Of course, nobody believed that, her being so high and mighty. But, the law was satisfied all was well, so the rumpus quietened down to a whisper. Now, nobody talks about her anymore."

Hearing this, and knowing all too well it was her own family at the centre of this ridicule, Elizabeth became sad. She had not only become invisible to everyone she had ever known, but had caused a great deal of trouble to the family as a whole, even by her absence. Yet, she assuaged this regret by remembering how it had been her parents who had forced her away in the first place. At least she would arrive late afternoon or early evening, when the light would be fading and she would be disguised from the village. It would be shock enough to her family that she was back in Matchcomb Magna without adding renewed gossip, when they supposed her to be far away and out of their lives.

Allowance was made in the itinerary for a single stop in the pretty town of Sherborne, where Unity was to be fed once again and her clothes changed. Elizabeth had always admired Sherborne as a place of romance and fashionable shopping. It was huge when compared to her home village of Matchcomb Magna and those other villages and hamlets surrounded it that were little more than tiny populated islands within the open countryside, although clearly bigger than Bere-sub-Nettlebury, whose very name was new to her.

The carriage eventually entered Sherborne from the northern end, working its way along the many twists and turns, rises and falls in the narrow road. Neat terraces of tightly packed brick or stone cottages closely guarded the route. At an island junction, where a fine large building stood magnificently opposite bearing the inscription *Licensed to let Post Horses*, the road divided into two. Here marked a contrast in building styles. To the right, alongside three-storey, brick-built Georgian houses with wooden bow windows, were in-filled two-storey stone cottages made special in their appearance by the setting of impressive mullions.

"We be here," shouted the driver through the brisk wind that softened even the harshest spoken word.

"I saw a place with an inscription over the door. What is it?"

"'Tis a school for fine young ladies."

"Licensed to let horses?"

"Bless you, no. Before becoming a school, 'twas The Angel Inn, and a right goodly place it was, too. Being on the crossroads for coaches making long journeys to and from the coast, 'twas well suited to offering post horses with careful drivers, as well as having superior Clarences and Broughams for hire, neat wines and foreign spirituous liquors for thirsty passengers. Oh, and stall stabling for the beasts of burden."

"Quite a business by the sounds of it."

"And aired beds. It offered aired beds for the travellers. Still, 'tis no more, and fancy liquors have given way to pretty dresses. What a shame for those with the discomfort of a dry throat, not that I like spirits or ales, you understand. Still, Sherborne isn't short of other places. I'll take the carriage past a few still in the business of hospitality. Then, you may pick a watering hole. For my part, I'm off for a bite and a beer at the Blue Compass Inn. I know of a ready welcome there. But it might not suit you to mix with the likes of me, especially with a child. Now, which place we pass do you fancy?"

Elizabeth looked at the choices as they passed at a slow trot. Not being too far away from Matchcomb Magna she had shopped in Sherborne on many occasions, but had never been there long enough to require the services of an inn or hotel. Anyway, her father, her grandfather and his father before him had always received a warm invitation for lunch at the Bannerman House, a small stately home in magnificent grounds that had, despite its name, been purchased from the Bannerman family in the 1780s by Rear-Admiral Mayhew, son of a local Earl, taking ownership from a gentleman of Army personage to a gentleman of the Navy. It had remained the principal residence of that family ever since, through successive generations. Still, it was Elizabeth's father who knew the Mayhews well and she had no reason to expect uninvited kindness, less so with Unity in her arms, the revelation of which to the Mayhews would cause her family great distress.

But how things had changed since the Rear-Admiral had taken on Bannerman House, for good and ill. For, having found the parkland to be of little scenic interest, a descendant had employed none other than Capability Brown to give the grounds the character it so richly deserved. With much new planting and landscaping, and azaleas aplenty nestling by lakes and waterfalls, it had been transformed into one of the great parks of England. Even rhododendrons now played a part in the changed horticulture, a more recent addition brought back from the Himalayas. Yet, in contrast, Bannerman House itself was now riddled with rot and was likely to be pulled down in the not too distant future, the cost of repairs being almost as great as the cost of rebuilding in a more comfortable style.

"The Volunteer looks nice," Elizabeth said in questioning tone, "and so does The New Inn."

"And so they are," returned the driver. "But, if I was asked what might suit you best, I would suggest The Noble Hind, which is just up there a pace." He pointed. There was no mistaking the place, its name in large letters carried beneath an impressive bowed window projecting over the main entrance. "To my way of thinking, it be a hotel more than an inn, which a refined lady as yourself might prefer. I be told 'tis one hundred years old or more, built on the site of The Old Boat. Only been inside the place once, to collect a fare. 'Tis monstrous big and of great wonder. I don't know if 'twas The Noble Hind or Boat they spoke about when they described the place in olden times as having two large parlours with French-style plaster ceilings, two bars, and two dozen bed chambers on the second and third floors, all richly ornamented with good coloured paper, plus nine more upper chambers. Imagine that. Fair turns me head to think how some people live. More to my liking was its brew-house, with four vaults for 160 hogsheads, and bottle houses for beer and wine." He pulled the horse to a halt in Cheap Street, so called because of its accommodation for local textile workers. "If you're decided, Ma'am, I'll drive back around the streets."

The carriage came to rest outside The Noble Hind. Elizabeth was helped out, the driver doffing his hat in the hope of an early tip to cover the cost of his lunch. She removed a shilling from her purse, which he received with civility.

"We shall need to be on our way in an hour, to beat the dark. Is that convenient, Ma'am?"

She nodded that it was. "By and by," she added, as she lifted her hem from the ground before climbing the first step, "do you know what is best on the menu?"

"Oh, yes, Ma'am, but only by reputation from paying passengers. I be told a plate of boiled lamb is supposed to be excellent, with honeyed pork on the side and sweet pickles, followed by a tart." She walked away carrying Unity. He folded the blankets and placed them neatly on the seats before leading the horse to the rear. "I, too, likes a good tart," he muttered to himself. "I knows full well what goes on at that hospital."

The stop was all too brief and soon the carriage began to wear away the remaining miles, interrupted only by a slight detour when the driver delivered a small parcel of lace to his sister in Muchly Cerne, purchased the previous day from a drapery in Glastonbury High Street. The short stop gave Elizabeth time to re-engage in small talk, having settled back into the routine of the journey and the now familiar scenery.

"Tell me, my good fellow, were you well served at the Blue Compass?"

"Bless you, Ma'am, indeed I was. Thanking you for asking. It's a grand place and no mistake. The food was aplenty and I had a beer forced down me gullet by the jolly landlord. I swallowed only to be sociable. Plenty of good company, too. And you, Ma'am?"

"They were very helpful."

"The food?"

"First rate, as it happens. I ordered the meal you suggested."

"And what for the baby?"

"Please!" she replied with an abruptness that took her normally pastel voice into something almost physical.

He jumped at his stupidity, the heat of rebuke going straight to his cheeks, which flushed a patchy red. She almost felt the change in his visage and regretted the harshness of the censure.

"You must know this road like the back of your hand," she said in her old tone, hoping to re-engage his fellowship.

"That I do, and I pick up many interesting facts to tell those wishing to know. 'Tis all part of me job and expected by most newcomers."

"And earns you not only their respect but an extra sixpence, I shouldn't wonder, for helping pass the time pleasantly?"

"You could say that, although I talk willingly for free. My mouth moves of its own accord, being host to such a lonely occupation as mine."

"So, what can you tell me about Sherborne that I won't already know, anything that might encourage me to part with a penny?"

"A penny's worth? Well now, here lies a pretty story and no mistake. In olden times, July 1616 to be exact, a party of men escorting Sir Water Raleigh stayed in the town overnight. The poor bugger – begging your pardon Ma'am – was under arrest at the time, being taken under guard from Plymouth to London. It seems Englishmen don't always show proper loyalty to their heroes."

"What happened?"

"Let's say his natural cheerfulness was at odds with the situation and didn't quite succeed in saving him from later despair."

"Sorry?"

"He was beheaded a couple of years later, Ma'am, his head needing two strikes of the axe to sever clean off."

"My Lord, how horrid!"

"For him, it was."

"What was his crime?"

"Trumped up, I think. Wasn't he arrested because he tried to take gold from the Spanish? I think that's how it went. The Spanish king demanded King James should execute him and he obliged the foreign gent. Never would've happened in good Queen Elizabeth's time. She turned a blind eye to a little piracy in return for swelling the Crown's coffers. In the end, he was supposedly taken to the block for plotting against James. As I said, trumped up – bastards. Oh, beg your pardon."

"No, you're right . . . bastards."

He smiled, but only inside. Elizabeth felt uneasy at having let the word pass her lips, even to a stranger, for now it had new meaning, a quite distressing one.

Matchcomb Magna was approached through a gentle cutting, with high banks peaked by trees. Elizabeth was now only two miles from Cerne Abbas and not much further from John Madden at Nether Bow.

Saint Andrew's church appeared on the left, its square tower of no particular height topped by ten small spires that reminded her of pine trees. An abundance of crosses adorned all other parts of this quaint structure which abutted the road. Its bells rang out in crisp air, the sound rising and falling as gentle waves over the countryside.

Next to the church was the impressive entrance to a grand estate, while all about stood quality stone dwellings of various periods and styles, all in harmony despite their architectural differences.

In general, it was a village of aquatint at this time of year, its colour soft, neither spoiled nor hurried through by those journeying to larger towns along the road that cut a swathe through its centre. It was neither of the past nor of progress, but perpetual in character, carrying the laughter of children and the groan of workers spanning centuries.

The carriage took the small rise in the road with ease and moments later, at Elizabeth's direction, turned into a long drive marking the entrance to the Grant family home. It was the end of the journey and the driver lifted in vigour, although he looked about suspiciously at its general resemblance to the landed house of his earlier story. It was a building of appreciable antiquity, not so large as to be awe-inspiring, but, nevertheless, of breathtaking aspect, framed by neat gardens which had been planted low to take none of the elegance from the building's façade.

In marked contrast to the driver, Elizabeth felt her stomach churn with anticipation. She felt like a spirit, neither real nor seen, expected by nobody and wanted by nobody. The sound of turning wheel and trotting hooves in an otherwise silent landscape only reinforced that feeling of isolation. She was, in all respects, entirely alone as an adult in a new world she had created.

The house begged for a handsome heir of fiction to be standing powerfully in the doorway, back-lit by a thousand lamps and with an obedient hound at his feet, a string orchestra playing an uplifting melody as the carriage approached. But, that was romantic fiction. Instead, as she approached the house, and to her horror, her father and mother appeared from the front entrance and stood expectantly under the elaborate portico, a stone-built shelter of sufficiently large size to allow carriages to pull-up under its roof as protection against bad weather. As they held lamps, Elizabeth had no difficulty seeing their faces; they struggled to recognise her.

Elizabeth gaped. Her parents stared back, turning grim faced at finally recognising the fare. It was the greeting Elizabeth feared most, but had hoped was an unwarranted apprehension.

"Yes, Mother, it's me," she said from the confine of the carriage to soften the moment.

"I thought you were gone from here for good," barked her father.

"I have come back."

"Not as you were, I suppose?"

"That is a dreadful thing to say."

"You are not alone, then?"

"How could I be?"

"By leaving the foundling behind, of course."

"No, not alone."

"You'd better come in, I suppose," said her father in besieged voice, paying the driver and walking ahead. There was no tip.

"Would you like me to wait, Miss?" called the driver to Elizabeth, concerned for her wellbeing and now certain it was the place in his story.

"Be away, damn you," bawled her father. "This is private and you are on my land."

The carriage remained motionless as the question was repeated.

Elizabeth looked between the driver and her father, both at odds. "It is alright, thank you. Please leave," she said, giving the driver a shilling.

"If you need me, you knows where I can be found."

"Thank you," she repeated, aware he now called her Miss instead of Ma'am.

The carriage made a sweeping turn and was soon out of sight.

The group retreated to the drawing room, where Elizabeth sat with the baby by a roaring fire that warmed them quickly. Her mother sat opposite, leaving her husband to stand alone with his hands grasped tightly behind his back, forcing his long jacket to ride up into a bustle.

"This is Unity, your granddaughter," said Elizabeth brightly, holding her high. She expected nothing in return, which is exactly the response she received.

Her father glanced between mother and daughter, his taciturnity a sure sign of displeasure.

"Mother? What do you think of my child?"

"It's a baby, alright."

Elizabeth lowered Unity, offering a gentle, close-up smile as recompense for the lost love of her grandparents. As moments passed in awkward silence, Mrs Grant could stand the tension no longer. She lunged for the bell-pull and the solace of tea.

"Now we're in for it," rebuked Mr Grant. "Could you not have waited until a plan had been formulated? Really, that was a most irrational thing to do. What do we do now?"

"Shall I hide Unity from the maid?" suggested Elizabeth in crushed voice, not wanting to make her mother's position worse.

"Now you strike at the root of the problem," scolded her father.

"Jeremiah!"

He turned, as if betrayed. "What now, woman?"

His wife nodded towards the young mother and child, so elegant, so homely and so unwanted.

"What?" he repeated harshly.

"For months we've sat scarcely talking, yet knowing exactly what the other was thinking. Look at them, husband. What has been the use of it?"

"The use?" he demanded.

"Yes, the use. We both knew ignoring the issue wouldn't change a thing, but we could not force ourselves into breaking the circle of anger."

"Don't speak for me, Harriet. There was good reason for reflection. Nothing has altered by Elizabeth coming back with her arms full that I can see. I will not be compelled to accept a situation thrust indifferently in my face."

But Harriet was not to be diverted; the joy of seeing Elizabeth again after so long away played a part, just as Elizabeth had hoped but was yet to know. Since the initial shock of Elizabeth's return, just moments before, Harriet had quickly come to realise the importance of consideration, rather than ill temper. After all, consideration had led to a solution being found to the original problem, so shockingly presented to them in April, one that had avoided destitution for their daughter. The same common sense had to be rediscovered.

"Now I look back," said she, "it was completely ridiculous to mull over in our heads a situation which could not possibly be put into practice months down the line. It was a lazy attitude to adopt, and hurtful to all parties, where dissatisfaction and inadequacy were the only likely outcomes. No, the way I see it, only Elizabeth has acted with any rationality, for she stayed quietly in hospital without fretting for the future as we sat opposite each other at the table, blinded to the truth while tucking heartily into so much meat and gravy."

"I can see no virtue in that," blustered Jeremiah, now pacing the floor. "And no contrition either."

"It's not true," interrupted Elizabeth in her softest voice.

"What's not?" he boomed.

"That I have not fretted. I have, and worried, and regretted. That is, until Unity was born. Then everything changed. All regret disappeared."

"There you are," bellowed Jeremiah, "out of the mouths of babes. See, she no longer regrets."

"Do you regret, Mother?" asked Elizabeth, holding Unity towards her.

Harriet glanced towards Jeremiah, who was clearly irritated at the ill-timed betrayal of their solidarity. "I'm unsure what to think," was her reply, enunciated rather than spoken with sincerity. "I do know Collins will soon be here with the tea. Should Elizabeth take Unity elsewhere, Jeremiah?"

"No damned point! It was obvious to the entire household what was going on well before she took flight to Glastonbury. If secrecy was wanted, she should've gone earlier. I merely hoped to save us from the censure of our friends and the wider family."

"But, I don't," interrupted Elizabeth, now almost weeping, for the apprehension of the past few days had passed, allowing her emotions to be released. "I'm not ashamed of my daughter. I would be proud to introduce her to the world."

"Would you? Well, that tells a lot of what you think of us."

"I love you both, as much as ever. You know I do. But I have Unity to consider now. She is a Grant, whether you like it or not."

"Not, would be good!" was his austere reply.

"Mother?" pleaded Elizabeth.

"Don't try to get around your mother. She stands full-square with me on this one. Don't you, Mother?"

Wincing, she nodded weakly.

"What needs to be worked out is just what you expect from us, now you've so kindly brought your problem back here," he added firmly. "I really didn't think you would ever have the affront to return, after we expressly forbade it."

His strong words caused the room to fall once more into stunned shock. Elizabeth removed a layer of wrapping from Unity, the heat from the fire now enveloping them both. She dried her eyes on a corner.

A single hard knock rattled the door and the tea was wheeled in on a trolley, together with buttered bread and a selection of cakes. Jeremiah fidgeted, watching the maid's reaction. Much to the annoyance of the elders, the maid was barely able to contain her enthusiasm for the baby, having seen them arrive from an upstairs window.

"That will be all, Collins," bellowed Jeremiah, unexpectedly cutting off her route to the door. He put his mouth close to her ear and whispered. The maid curtsied, smiling back at Elizabeth through the closing gap in the doorway.

"The news will be around the servant's hall within five minutes," he snapped as he took a delicate cup of steaming tea from Harriet's outstretched hand. "Blowed if I'll be able to stop their tongues wagging."

"But, dear," his wife added with civility, "if you are so certain they already knew of our little misfortune, didn't you tell them the first time around what would happen if they blabbed about our business outside the house, or discussed it among themselves for that matter?"

"Goodness, Harriet, are you really that vacuous? Is that where our daughter gets her featherbrains? Some secrets are just too scandalous to be kept away from eager ears. It's like giving someone a million pounds on the condition they don't spend any of it."

"Oh!"

"Oh, is right! I gave warning months ago to fear for their employment, but I hadn't the slightest doubt I had as much chance of containing the family secret as stopping the sea tide with a bucket!"

"Then why did you bother?"

"For pity's sake, Harriet, isn't that obvious even to you? We had to try to preserve our good name, however fruitless. And I mean it. Should one or all of the servants so much as mention the fatherless child in our company or spread gossip, he, she or all will be kicked out without notice and without a reference to boot. Do I make myself absolutely clear?"

"Yes, Jeremiah, you do," uttered his wife obediently.

"Good, then we will hear no more on the subject at present, while I think. Please pass me a cake."

Having done his angry bidding, Harriet filled a second plate with delicious treats and placed them on a small occasional table next to Elizabeth's chair.

Elizabeth took a bite, but the trauma of the reunion had taken away her appetite.

"How is it you knew we were coming?" asked Elizabeth casually.

"We didn't. We heard the carriage and thought it. . ."

"Stop!" blasted Jeremiah. "Consider what you say."

"Mother?" enquired Elizabeth, with more curiosity than concern.

Harriet froze. "Address all questions to your father, dear. He must answer for us both."

"Father?"

He cleared his mouth. "We thought it was your brother approaching."

"Daniel? Is he coming in soon? How glorious to see him."

"We are expecting him at any moment, in the company of a friend. The cakes were baked for them."

"Not. . ."

"Yes, John Madden."

Elizabeth jumped in disbelief, hardly able to take in the ramifications of the prospect. Even the pain of her parents' lack of interest in Unity could not displace the frightening thought of seeing John without due preparation. He knew nothing of Unity, his daughter by default. Suddenly her mind was set against remaining in the parental home, and she said as much.

"That would be foolish beyond measure. There is no time for such an escape," interrupted Harriet.

"What do I do, then? Where shall I hide? We can't meet like this. Father, Mother, help me."

"Jeremiah?"

"Keep calm. Do you think the same thought hadn't already crossed my mind? As it happens, I've seen to it. Now, sit and finish your tea."

The ladies sat in anxious trepidation, nibbling but not properly consuming the treats. Jeremiah held the moment, knowing he had played a trump card. "I've instructed Collins to stop them at the gate," he said presently.

"How?"

"Easy. I've given instructions for Daniel to go straight back to Cerne, to pick up some papers from Cubit's solicitors. I know Daniel won't miss the opportunity."

"Opportunity?" enquired Elizabeth.

"Your mother and I bought him a fancy gig for his birthday. It arrived the day before yesterday and he can't stop admiring himself in it. Until the novelty wears off, he'll drive anybody anywhere just to show off. It has brass lamps, fancy paintwork and everything. He says it's the fastest vehicle on the road and now does the miles to prove it. He'll kill himself if he's not more careful."

"And John with him!" exclaimed Elizabeth.

"That would solve a problem or two," remarked Jeremiah glibly.

"What are you saying, husband? Surely we hope Elizabeth and John will marry?"

"Mother!" pleaded her daughter with indignation. "Who I marry, and when, will be my decision alone. Please don't attempt to force on him a wife he doesn't want."

"He wanted you enough to. . ."

"Stop that at once! I respect you both as my parents, but I draw a line at this conversation which is not suitable between us. Anyway, I'm surprised you two have let John into the house after what he's done."

"How could we stop him? He's been coming here for years to spend time with Daniel and sometimes you. He doesn't know we know he's done wrong, even if we *do* know what he doesn't know, if you see what I mean."

Harriet's eyes rolled in confusion.

"And nor does *he?*" proclaimed Elizabeth with some force of attitude.

"Sorry?"

"Father, I have a terrible confession, which proves John's fine character."

"I doubt it, but go on if you must."

She hesitated, the words being difficult to express. "How can I say what needs to be said. You are my parents. It's not easy to talk about such personal things."

"Then tell your mother and keep it among women. She can fill me in later."

With this advice accepted, he left the room for the garden.

"At last! Now we can talk. Can I hold Unity?"

Surprise, mixed with inexpressible pleasure, Elizabeth passed the baby into Harriet's expectant arms.

"She is a complete delight. Can I kiss her?"

"Of course," agreed Elizabeth with tearful eyes. "Unity darling, this is your grandmother."

A tiny finger touched Harriet's nose, causing the slightest smile.

"She's an absolute sweetheart, a complete treasure. Here, have her back in case your father returns. Now, what was it you wanted to say?"

The difficulty of the story to be told showed on Elizabeth's face. She suggested they both sit again, as the words required much reflection.

"It's like this. It was February when Unity was conceived, but conception was not as you might imagine."

"I have tried not to picture it at all!"

"I should hope not! Anyway, it happened when General Gordon saved Khartoum. The entire nation was in raptures. John celebrated more than most. While everyone was having a great time, I took care not to drink too much myself. In due course I took John back to Nether Bow. He could hardly stand. I think the best way of saying what followed is how I described it to my nurse. His enthusiasm for the evening spilled over into more drinking and I became a willing participant to his merry making. He became passionate towards me without really knowing what he was doing, and I didn't resist. It was as simple as that. Am I completely shameful?"

The collapse of her daughter's morals, explained in such a

matter of fact way, caused gloom and resentment within Harriet. For, the explanation revealed not only that her daughter was the single guilty party, but that she had played a physically active role in her own downfall, the reasons for which were not only selfish but ambitious.

"I'm afraid you are," was Harriet's testy reply. "Oh, we all know such things happen frequently among poor country girls. They are born and bred to mimic the animals they tend. Well, not all, you understand, but a fair number. But, those of us of the better classes are supposed to have an incorruptible superiority, thereby setting the standard to which all should aspire. Young men love the company of bad girls, the loud popular ones in particular, but they never, ever marry them. It is a gospel truth as old as history itself. Think of any girl of your age who knew men and I guarantee you will find a long-term spinster. It is a fact that an ugly girl has more chance of marriage than a gameful one."

"Then, I'm done for!"

"I fear you may well be, and there is nothing any of us can do to help. Fidelity to virtuous womanhood is, in a man's eyes, like a bank. Withdraw the savings and deposit them elsewhere and the bank will foreclose."

"Oh, my God, I am ruined!"

"Indeed, you need not only His help but His forgiveness. Have you prayed?"

"Yes, Mother."

"May I ask what for?"

"For forgiveness, as you said."

"Anything else?"

"That John should see me in good light and accept Unity as his own."

"You ask for much, which may be beyond even divine intervention. But your contrition is admirable, if not rather late. I will relay this to your father when he is more settled."

"I wish to say more, Mother, but I hardly want the words in my heart to be spoken."

"Just say them as they come into your thoughts, Lizzy. Do not try to re-arrange them into clever phrases, but speak as your feelings dictate. It is the only way I will properly understand, and the only way I can judge your sincerity."

"It's just this, Mother. How easily I am attracted to an unsuitable man, when others crave my company and I ignore them."

"You mean John?"

"Yes."

"But, he's the most suitable man in the district."

"Not to me. Why do I feel this? Because I know he doesn't return my affection, yet I convince myself one day he will. Every time he smiles my way, my heart jumps and my pulse races. If he then abandons me, I hurt until I see him again, when I completely forgive him for his absence and convince myself I will win him with patience. And so it goes on year after year, pretence after pretence, farce after farce."

"Lie after lie?"

"No, Mother, never that, not on his part at least. He only tells the truth of the situation, even when he doesn't speak."

"How can that be?"

"It can be seen so easily in his body language, his demeanour. They never lie to me. He never tries to hide behind false promises or false actions. It is his honesty that occasionally gives me hope, but more often crushes me completely. I know how it is to feel as insignificant as mortally possible, to ache so wretchedly that it takes on a sweetness of its own, as if love demands suffering and the more one suffers the greater the expectation of love. Does that make any sense?"

"Unfortunately it does, my dear child. Few people escape it before finding their true partner in life. But, eventually, it passes."

"How? Please tell me."

"It ends sometime after final rejection, but you will only know when you can meet the man you desired without suffering pain. Then, and only then, can you move on."

"Do you talk from experience, Mother?"

"That is my secret, dear."

"And, in the meantime, while I await this release, what do I do with Unity? Where do we stay?"

"In your old room, I suggest. The baby can be put in an open drawer for the time being. But, first, you should complete the story, for I have more questions requiring answers."

"What of Daniel and John if they return together?"

"Clearly, Daniel must be told. John can wait. Hopefully, he may not choose to come back here after all, now that your father has sent them back to Cerne. Anyway, according to Daniel, John is a bit preoccupied at the moment with a new girl he's taken into employment. That, alone, might colour his plans."

"Not again!" cried Elizabeth, the image of Christabel in her mind.

CHAPTER 10

To save a soul

*H*arriet's curiosity to know even more than Elizabeth had so far divulged led her into a journey through the ins and outs of her daughter's strange relationship with John Madden, in words that were often hard to bear. With so much to hear and absorb, she wished it was earlier in the day, allowing more time to carefully consider everything and weigh up all the likely repercussions before coming to a judgement. Yet, as time passed in conversation that was never heated and often emotional, the explanations and counter-claims provided a general understanding of why Elizabeth had returned to Matchcomb unannounced. And so, after all had been said that could be said, it seemed clear to Harriet what she had to do.

For the first time in her married life, Harriet realised the necessity of not allowing herself to be bridled as a dutiful wife while in conversation with her husband. The consequences of failing to get her views across were just too great. This time *he* was going to have to listen, whether he liked it or not. She rather feared he 'would not'. Yet, as events would show, the novelty of being talked at could not altogether displace for Jeremiah Grant his proud concern for family reputation.

She knocked on his study door and entered to find him reading.

He returned the book to its usual space on a shelf and sat, listening to all she had to say. Throughout, his blank expression gave no visible signs for interpretation. She continued.

"That's why she came home in such a flurry. It was leave now or cause harm to the very institution she had relied upon."

"My money paid for that place. I have given extremely generously."

"There's no denying that, good husband. But, we must face the truth. The money was given to assuage our conscience for abandoning our daughter. We both know it, yet both deny it to ourselves and each other."

"What are you suggesting? That we should've been present before and after the birth?"

"Would that have been so terrible?"

"Yes, frankly it would. I feel very strongly on that point. I gained comfort in my pain from Corinthians, 5: 3, taken out of context, but appropriate to my inner thoughts. *Absent in body, but present in spirit*. But now that it's done, and knowing all too clearly which side of the fence you stand, I may be persuaded to be a little more flexible in my actions over Elizabeth and the bast. . ."

"Unity. Her name is Unity."

"As you wish . . . Unity." He looked perplexed. "This is mighty strange. Having said her name just once, I feel quite differently towards her. How is that possible?"

"It's called unconditional love, husband. You have, at last, recognised her as a real person in her own right and a fully paid-up member of the Grant family."

"Was this a trick contrived between yourself and Lizzy, to turn my head?"

"No, dear, I have been as surprised by everything as you."

"Then, as we are decided, we must devise a plan to trap John into accepting his responsibilities."

"Persuade him would be better."

"Of course, we must play semantics. After all, family reputation is family reputation. But, and understand me well, we will not be able to hold our heads up in good society if we don't manage to get Elizabeth and John wed. That's the top and the bottom of the matter, the sooner the better, in fact. If it can be hurried through, as a private ceremony for close family only, we may even now be able to make it seem as though the wedding and child came in the natural order of things and not the perverse way around. To achieve this, it might help if we send them away after the ceremony for a very long honeymoon. A tour of France and Italy might serve our purpose, by way of a wedding gift."

"A costly present on top of your payments to the hospital, don't you think?"

"You are right! Let's not get ahead of ourselves. A long stay in the Lake District should do equally nicely. Oh, and I shall send no more payments to Glastonbury. I think that is best. Cut off all connections and traceable lines."

"But how are we to exercise such a plan?"

"Confront John with the facts, of course. The question is, who is best placed, me as head of the family or Lizzy?"

"What if he can't remember the night of the celebrations? He may have no recollection. Would Lizzy's word be enough authority? From what I know of John's practicalities, I'm not so sure it would. To form a life-long attachment to a woman he has never wanted to woo in the first place, on the slim chance the child she has produced after leaving the district for so many months is his, may be expecting far too much. Yet, for the plan to work, he has to be ready to commit the first time he is approached. Once he agrees – if he agrees – even in haste, he would be as good as his word."

"There's a complication."

"What?"

"The new worker at Wheat Sheaf Farm. . . Emmeline something or other."

"He wouldn't want her, not a woman from the dairy. She would embarrass a man of his position. No, she's nothing more to him than a skivvy."

"As was Christabel Mere? Don't you remember how he used to describe her when he came to play cards of an evening? He called her a virtuous maid with a full, roundly figure, not gangly tall, with porcelain skin made ruddy about her high cheeks by the outdoors, eyes framed by dark lashes and lips as naturally rich as roses and shaped like a seraphic bow."

"My goodness, what a memory you have! Yes, you may be right."

"It was hard to forget such a goddess once described. No, face it, our Mr Madden seems to have a liking for the rough side of the sheets. That surely throws a spanner into the works."

"Not necessarily, if we are cunning for the good of our daughter."

"And for John's good, too, if we save him from himself. We mustn't lose sight of that. No, we must view our plan as his salvation also."

"Yes, quite right. That's how to look at it. We must lure this Emmeline wench away from his company. But how, my husband?"

He took a Bible from the shelf, blowing dust from the spine. "I am reminded of Ezekiel 27. I shall read. *When the wicked man turneth away from his wickedness that he hath committed, and doeth that which is lawful and right, he shall save his soul alive.*" He slammed the book shut. "There, the Bible guides us towards our actions. John must be made to face his wickedness."

"And do what is lawful and right."

"And in this we show circumspection, for we save his soul."

"And our skins!"

"A consequence, my dear, merely a consequence of our moral duty towards him."

That same evening Daniel was told of all that had befallen the family, with emphasis on John's part. He was truly shocked, for he knew nothing of Elizabeth's original condition and had accepted blindly his selfish sister's uncharacteristic wish to do some charitable work. The hammer blow of truth meant more than his sister's disgrace. Shame would be heaped generously upon all the Grants, innocent or otherwise, an affliction to their reputation which would continue in the district even after he inherited the house and its income.

"So you see, Daniel, we have a bit of a dilemma on our hands."

Daniel rose and paced the floor, finally stopping by the fire, where he lit a cigarette.

"I think you understate the problems, Father," he replied through a cloud of expelled smoke. "Do you actually believe Elizabeth's fanciful story?"

"Of course," said Harriet without hesitation, not wanting to chance Jeremiah's response.

"Because it's true or because it's convenient to the family to want to believe it?"

"Daniel, remember who you talk to," demanded his father.

"Father, Mother, I respect you both, but I cannot help wonder whether you are being just a touch blinkered. I have never had the slightest reason to doubt John Madden's sincerity as an honest man over any issue. To my observation, in matters of the heart he has been true in word and deed towards his friendship with Elizabeth and his love for Christabel Mere. If ever a man held a torch for a single creature, that person is John and his devotion to the dairymaid."

Poor Elizabeth heard all that was spoken, having kept the bedroom door open with a wedge, relying on the large lime plastered rooms to echo the voices to within her reach. She could endure no more, but could do nothing to stop herself listening.

"But, she is dead," exclaimed Jeremiah. "The dairymaid is laid six feet in the ground."

"And so she is, but that fact has not given him a single night of peace, even after the fullness of time. I would not be speaking out of turn to say, I believe he loves her as much now as he ever did. She haunts his very soul. He would not be ready to love another. I just know it."

"You may be right," said his father in languid voice, "but that may not be the whole of it. You are not a worldly young man, yet I shall not let such trifles stop me from talking plain to you. Where passion is concerned, there is not a world of difference between love and lust. Whilst I will accept John does not love Elizabeth. . ."

"And never has," interrupted Daniel.

"Just so," was the reply, "he, nevertheless, is capable of expressing a man's impulse towards a beautiful woman. On this occasion, such expression has been turned towards your sister, with the most undesired consequence."

"Jeremiah," exclaimed Harriet, "you said you were comfortable with Unity. I hope you do not change your mind."

"I do not," was his brusque reply, "but Unity is the happy conclusion of a situation that has no other virtues of its own."

"Nevertheless, Father, I do not feel John is rationally capable of what is claimed and I shall not alter my opinion."

"Then you accuse your sister of knowing other men, of prostituting herself."

"I do nothing of the sort! John could be the father, but only if he was disabled at the time by alcohol. If this was the case, and it is the only scenario I am willing to believe, I suppose it would still make him responsible for the outcome of his actions, even without remembering what those actions actually were. But, and I mean this strongly, he deserves no rebuke and no schemes made against him."

"Implying, Elizabeth took full advantage of him?"

"It could happen."

"For heaven sake, man, think what you accuse her of."

"Think what you accuse John of doing. Should we so readily apportion blame on one party for no better reason than he is not family?"

The door swung fully open with the creak of dry hinges, and in the light of the hallway the silhouette of Elizabeth filled the space. All turned in silence. She was crying.

"Listen to Daniel, please," she spoke shyly, wiping away her tears. "I told you I was to blame. It is not right to alter my account to suit your aspirations."

"How long have you been there?" asked Daniel.

"Long enough to realise what you all think of me."

"Oh!"

The following morning was crisp and cold. Fires were lit early in every occupied room and breakfast was taken at eight o'clock. Daniel, who was the third to sit at table, had only just begun to tuck into a substantial plate of eggs and ham when Elizabeth entered. She carried Unity. He was visibly embarrassed, feeling her to be a stranger in his midst.

Returning his cutlery to the plate, Daniel advanced gingerly towards his sister, as if stepping ever closer to the edge of an abyss. Unity's eyes were bright and her fingers played in the air. He placed a finger in her palm.

"By George, she has a grasp. You know, she does have the look of John."

"As we told you," said Harriet.

"Is he truly the father, Lizzy?" His open expression demanded the truth.

"He is."

"I quite see it. And living in this God-forsaken wilderness of a place for all your years, naturally you have seldom had any other man court you?"

"Seldom."

"My God!"

"Stop saying that, Daniel," demanded his mother. "I have told you not to use that expression."

"It's of little consequence, given the circumstances of the day," he replied dismissively. He was spellbound and looked again upon Unity's face. "Yes, well. . . Heavens. . . My God!"

"Do you want to hold her?" responded Elizabeth, raising the small bundle towards him.

"Yes, I jolly well believe I do."

Jeremiah glanced sideways at Harriet and winked. He turned to Daniel.

"Now, my boy, we have formulated a little plan which requires your help."

CHAPTER 11

Third love

Whatever revelations were coming to the forefront at the home of the Grants, at Wheat Sheaf Farm it was business as usual. A routine had been quickly established between John and Emmie over the short period of her employment which seemed to work with amazing smoothness. Each had their tasks, and John was not any longer in the slightest bit disturbed by Emmie's constant presence. Indeed, he often invited her to join him for impromptu breaks and occasional suppers, when otherwise she would have nipped across to the labourers' dormitory after preparing John's meals, where she would eat with the other workers. She was unsure which she preferred and took either invitation as they came without favour.

This lack of preference at mealtimes was not to suggest her heart was settled. Far from it. Whilst Emmie enjoyed the company of a group, where she could have fun and flirt freely, she looked upon John as a most likely lover, as and when he realised for himself that it was she he wanted and she who most resembled his beloved Christabel through shared experiences on the poorer side of life. Not that Emmie was in love. She fancied John, a feeling bordering on affection but more closely akin to desire, but her thoughts never drifted far from the obvious advancements he would offer as a husband. Then, with her future secure, the odd dalliance with the field-hands to satisfy other needs would do nobody much harm. It was the way of the countryside.

Thus, Emmie was ready to play the long game, slowly wearing away John's resistance to see her as anything other than a friend in need. She had even begun to adopt some of Christabel's ways as a role model, showing slight hesitation when accepting compliments, companionship or treats, against her natural exuberance to say an immediate 'yes'. It felt good to be asked, rather than do the suggesting. Indeed, slowly, but surely, she came to understand the advantages such behaviour held, remembering with a shiver the stormy relationships she had had with Edmond Elvington and the consequent rebound affair with Lieutenant Charles, both proving to be an absolute disaster in her haste to get a wedding ring on her finger. Her third love would need to be coerced into her arms, rather than browbeaten or tempted by womanly guiles. John and the farm were prizes worthy of the hunt and, once won, she could take her time to fall in love properly.

In the solitude of her room at night, she taunted herself for her stupidity during the Saint Andrew's Day masquerade, when, with a little more deliberation, she could have got him thoroughly drunk on hot eldern wine, releasing his inhibitions. Still, there was plenty of time to exploit opportunities, especially with Christmas so close.

Emmie had struck up particular friendships with Fanny Smart and Abel Tucker, the two she had mistakenly approached as old friends on the day of her arrival. Abel, who had been affable from the outset, needed no encouragement and greatly liked Emmie's silly ways. Noticing their companionship, Fanny had been quick to add her friendship to theirs as a means of keeping both under strict observation.

As it happened, Abel Tucker was better educated than Emmie and fully capable of spelling words she merely guessed at, but spoke in a manner that was becoming outdated, even in the countryside. To Emmie's delight, he expressed no hesitation at being asked to pen a personal letter intended for her parents, glad to be trusted to deal sensitively with matters of a private nature. Fanny watched over his shoulder as Emmie dictated the first lines and they appeared on paper, but quickly became bored and left them to continue alone. Then, when she had gone, Emmie asked Abel to screw up the first letter and start again, now feeling free to express her inner thoughts without ridicule. Indeed, relating such matters in front of Abel felt very much like flirting, without the embarrassment of censure. The letter was addressed to Mr and Mrs Sturry, Stirminster Oak, Wessex.

Dear Mother and Father

I hope you are both well. I am well. I am settled at Nether Bow and I like the work, which is mostly domestic. I am well fed and well warmed. I live in the house with John. I have my own nice room. I have made a few friends. Abel Tucker is writing this letter for me and he will read to me any letters you send back, so please do not say anything too much of a personal nature. Abel is smiling at me now for asking him to write that. I expect I will hit him once he has finished (he has written that, too).

John Madden is very kind and I quite often share meals with him. I think he likes me most of anybody on the farm except for Abel, who he relies on. John shows this by his kindnesses to me. I think John is a lonely man. He has his own friend called Daniel Grant, but most of his spare time is spent wandering about the place and sitting by the river. I am sure he thinks a lot, and often looks sad. Sometimes I think I should sit with him, but his sadness is of a dreamy kind which needs no company.

Not long ago he took me to Mangstone. We had a lot of fun and it stopped his melancholy for a short time. He

dressed as a woman, but looked exceeding ugly. Funny that,
as he is a nice looking man.

I hope to have some good news soon. I expect to be here for
Christmas and I would like a new dress if you want to make
me one.

> *Your daughter*
> *Emmeline*

Two days later, John came rushing up.

"You have a letter come by second post, Emmie. It could be from your parents. Shall I read it to you?"

"By all means, no," she replied, taking it quickly and thrusting it into her apron pocket. "It can wait."

That evening, after having supper with John, who enquired about the communication, Emmie left the house for the dormitory where she found Fanny sitting on Abel's lap.

"What's all the excitement?" he asked as she approached.

"I have a letter."

"And 'ee wants me to read it?" he replied, forcing Fanny to stand.

"You don't mind, do you Fanny?" she said in friendly but knowing tone, as if exercising power over him.

"Can't you read it yourself?" replied Fanny. "Everyone can read a bit and you speaks well enough for your station."

"Abel?" begged Emmie.

He saw a situation brewing. "It's not that Emmie can't read, me love, but she's been lazy in her education and finds reading and spelling harder than most. I be sure we can show a little charity and help her now, can't we?"

Fanny did not reply, but merely stomped into a corner.

"Now, let me see. Oh, yes, 'tis from 'ee parents alright. It says:

My darling Emmeline

We received your letter with pleasure. Yes, we are
exceeding well except for light colds which we contracted

while delivering pasties and other comforts to the arsenic miners, thanks be to God. I would not let your father go alone, as he recently suffered palpitations at news of your brother in Australia, but has since fully recovered. It was bitterly cold down the shafts and I fear many men will not survive the Winter if they stay in such damp conditions overnight to save the inconvenience of the long walk to their shabby little homes and back again for an early shift. Much to our disappointment, the mine managers will not stop double-shifts if the men volunteer. Such temptations put the miners at grave danger from tiredness while operating the hydraulic machinery and their health is at constant risk. I am collecting clothing for the miners' families as it is nearing Christmas, which may be of some comfort, should any of the men freeze to death or be injured.

We are very happy to hear you are settling in nicely and are well housed. You say you are sharing the house with John. Are there any others living in? I am sure John is a true gentleman, but we would be happier to know you two are not residing alone.

Is John well? We are concerned he wears women's clothes and perhaps you might fully explain this in your next letter. If he is of a melancholy disposition, I fancy he should purchase Doctor King's Dandelion and Quinine Lover Pills that come in boxes of various sizes from 1½d to 11 shillings. We get ours by post from London, where they are made, but every respectable chemist should stock them. For goodness sake do not let him take Blue Pills, which contain mercury and tend to destroy the constitution. Doctor King's pills offer relief from bile, indigestion, headaches, loss of appetite, giddiness, spasms, heartburn, flatulency, nervousness, gout and disorders of the stomach and bowels. Indeed, it is hard to think of any ailment they do not work against for the good.

We await with eagerness your expected good news and answers to our concerns.

Your affectionate mother
Rachel

PS. We will see about a dress for you. No promises.

Abel lowered the letter to his lap. "'Ee mother writes very well, but signs herself Rachel. I find that strange. Are they strict?"

"They like to think so."

"And rich?"

"Not a bit of it! But, they are more shop class than manual. Shame none of it rubbed off on me. I couldn't be bothered to listen at school and left as early as I could to become a dairymaid. I spent hours in the classroom staring through the windows at the hills beyond, longing to be out there. I was a fool, but a very young and happy fool. In the end, my teacher ignored me, preferring to concentrate her efforts on the children who paid some attention."

"What's that about the master wearing women's clothes?"

She hit him, as promised. "You clot, Abel. It was during the Saint Andrew's Day masquerade."

"Of course, I knew that," he teased, receiving another clip around the ear.

"They say I should get John to buy Lover pills. Will it improve my chances?"

"I think 'twas a spelling mistake, Emmie. 'Ee parents meant *Liver* pills. Doctor King makes Liver pills."

"Oh!" she responded, "that's a shame."

"Don't fancy him, do 'ee? Mr Madden I mean."

"No! He's far too old. By and by, Abel, what's flatulency? I think I may suffer that myself."

"Farting. It be farting and 'ee do suffer it from time to time. I have heard 'ee . . . and worse besides." He laughed. She hit him again.

* * *

Among his duties, Abel Tucker was entrusted with the general maintenance of the main house. It was during such a time, a few days later, that he met Emmie walking along the landing. He grabbed her waist, playfully.

"Dear mercy, Abel, you gave me a fair fright, creeping up on me in the dark."

"Dark says 'ee, Emmeline, and it being the fullness of midday."

"Not up here it's not. Have you ever seen such a gloomy place? Why, I'd go crazy if I had to remain inside as an invalid."

"Then we must pray 'ee stays good and healthy and take regular supplies of Lover pills."

"What are you doing here, anyway, young Abel, other than pestering the life out of me? You'll catch it if Fanny sees you trifling with my waist."

"Don't pay her any heed. I do as I want, when I please."

"And are you pleased to see me, alone, up here, Abel Tucker?" she asked, twisting seductively with his hands resting on her hips.

"Now stop that before 'ee be seen."

"So, you are afraid."

"No, I not be! Anyway, I've got to be quick. I have a deal of lime burning to get on with. But, first, I have a door handle to mend." He held up a large bunch of keys suspended from an iron ring.

"Cluck, cluck, cluck," she replied, a broad smile on her face.

"Now stop that. 'Ee be a wicked woman and no mistake."

"And if I am, what do you want to do about it?"

"I'll take the flat of me hand to 'ee, that's what."

"And if I like it?"

"What's to like? No, let me be."

"Cluck, cluck, cluck."

"I'm no chicken. Stop pretending I be."

"Prove it, Abel Tucker."

"What?"

"Now!"

"How?"

Emmie looked about her. "That room, there." She pointed. "Let's go in and have a look around."

"Oh, no," he returned with unease. "Going in there i'nt allowed by anyone."

"Have you never wanted a peep?"

"No, never."

"Not even a bit, to satisfy your curiosity?"

"No. It's the master's business and I respect it."

"Cluck, cluck, cluck."

"Stop it!"

"I'll give you a kiss if you open the door. Two kisses if you look inside."

"I don't know, Emmie. Much as I would like to be kissed, I'm afraid we might be dismissed by the master."

"Cluck, cluck. . ."

"Alright, but only after I've had my first kiss. If it's not worth the trouble, the door will stay locked."

In an instant Emmie pressed him against the wall, standing on tip-toes to kiss him full-square on the mouth.

"There, and there's another once you've looked inside."

He licked his lips.

"You're wiping it away?"

"Not likely. I be tasting every drop."

He fumbled for the key. Looking right and left to ensure the coast was clear, he turned the key in the lock, twisted the handle and pushed the door open to peer through the emerging crack. Before he had time to think, Emmie barged through, taking him forward in her wake.

She stood, motionless, bewildered at what she saw. "Lord, what a state!"

"What be all this stuff?"

"Piles of old cottage furniture, stacked in with the good bits. I wonder what this is?" She grabbed a parcel wrapped in brown paper and secured with string.

"Here," said Abel, taking a knife from his pocket.

The string was cut and the paper ripped away, discarded carelessly on the floor.

"It's an old mirror." She propped it against a wall. "Look at the rest of the things. The windowsill, mantel, picture frames and the good furniture are thick with dust, yet this old cupboard and the rest of the rubbish are as clean as a whistle and smell of fresh polish. What does it mean?"

"It means," bawled John from the doorway, "that you are trespassing in my private space. Get out at once, both of you."

Emmie looked up meekly as she squeezed past John, who remained fierce but strangely thoughtful, almost wounded. As Abel left, and in an impulse, John grabbed the keys from his hand and pushed him roughly along the corridor, an action so perverse from his accustomed manner of dealing with problems that it had twice the effect. He then turned back into the room, surveying its contents. Only when he was sure nothing was missing, he stepped inside.

"You must not, you must not," John repeated fearfully. "This is mine and hers."

For a few seconds John stood motionless among the jumbled furniture. It was as if a time and place long since dismissed as the past had been reawakened, like a favourite book gathering dust had suddenly and unexpectedly been rediscovered, its characters reacquainted in the mind of the reader. Seeing the mirror unwrapped and naked as the day it had been brought to the house broke a spell of stillness and ageless slumbering that all his frequent polishing of selected pieces of furniture had never done.

At last the lock was tripped and the room returned to silence, its possessions conserved. Fear, or was it regret, now furled John's brow, for he could not afford the tingling burden of Christabel's memory being reawakened, when he struggled so hard to live without her.

"Are 'ee alright, Sir?" begged Abel earnestly, shrunk in fear and aware the moment held significance to his master that was shared with nobody. "Only, 'ee look queer like."

John pulled the key from the lock and the umbilical cord between the present and the past was cut.

"I'm surprised at you, Abel Tucker," he wailed, in a tone so strange that it was neither a shout nor a whimper, but the voice of hurt. "It's so unlike you to behave irrationally. What have you to say for yourself?"

Abel hung his head in shame. "Everything be the fault of I. It was me trusted with the keys and I failed 'ee."

"And, as for you, Emmeline, I shall have to think what will become of you. I told you that room was to be kept private. I made a point of demanding that from the outset. You have deliberately disobeyed me. What did you disturb, other than the mirror?"

"Nothing," she replied. "We only undid the parcel because we were curious to know what was inside."

"It was Christabel's mirror, not any old mirror."

"Oh, Sir, I had no idea."

"How dare you. Of all the things in there, you interfered with that. My mother covered it when Chrissy first came here. She would not allow any mirrors in the house, except mine. It has remained wrapped ever since that day. Now you have violated it."

"I didn't know," she stammered.

"Why the hell should you? It wasn't yours to touch."

"I'm so sorry."

"Apologies, be damned. You're most sorry for having been caught. Am I not right?"

She nodded absently.

"If I was to hold just one of you guilty of breaking my trust, who would it be? Who was led by the other?" he asked with a chillness that took no account of the recipients' gender.

Emmie raised her head towards Abel, offering a fragile look and playing the very trick John had avoided.

"Me, Sir," replied Abel in self-sacrificing tone. "'Ee must blame me."

"Is it so, Emmeline?"

After the briefest deliberation she repeated her nod, looking askance to see Abel's reaction. She feared he would now tell the truth, after such betrayal. But his look was benign. He merely shook his head slightly, wounded by her treachery.

"By your own lips you condemn yourself. It is with very much regret, Abel, I give you notice to leave the farm. You have served me well and I will say as much in a reference to another employer."

"Obliged, Sir," were his plain words, gently spoken. Humiliated, he walked away.

"This isn't right," exclaimed Emmie at last. "Don't speak to Abel like that. He's such a good man."

"I know it," replied John.

"Then, stop him, Sir."

"And hold you guilty instead?"

"I don't want to go either."

"Then hold your backchat!" rebuked John, pressing a hand to her mouth. "Just don't say another word. We both know poor Abel was led on by your foolishness, and by his chivalry he has reproached himself to save you. I fear he has acted unwisely because he is a man, and as a man he must now take the punishment prescribed upon himself. I shall not change my mind. It is a matter of integrity. You have ruined another good person, Emmie. Remember that when you try to sleep, and feel pity for his unknown future."

That evening Emmie stayed away from the dormitory, preferring to take supper in her own room, away from angry faces. Across the yard Abel could not eat, afraid of the poor prospect of finding new employment until farmers released animals into the fields in Spring. He had saved a few pounds, but this would not sustain him throughout the long Winter months. He turned face down into the bedding, although the evening was still young.

Fanny, who had been outside and had now climbed the wooden stairs to the dormitory while wearing the netting of a bee-keeper as a veil, made straight for the male lodgings and, in particular, Abel's bed. She removed a small bag to sit on the edge and began to rub his shoulders.

"I've heard, poor love. Why go so soon? The master be bound to give you a week's notice, maybe more. Answer me, Abel."

He turned, wiping a sleeve across his eyes and sniffing hard.

"'Tis that you, Fanny?"

"Who else would touch you so tenderly?"

"Indeed, nobody. Can 'ee not show me your face?"

"I dare not, for looking so draggletailed. Old Mrs Hooper has died and I be asked to tell her bees. But, look as I might, I could find no hives or wicker skeps. Yet, there was a rotted tree out back, which I be told is sometimes used by bees as a natural labyrinth. So I did the right thing by her. I knocked three times on the stump with an iron key and said *the mistress be gone*. Then I tied black ribbon around it, to show the bees were in mourning."

Abel sat up. He lifted the netting where it covered her face and gazed into her large, dark eyes. "'Tis just that 'ee has such a pretty face. Please, take the thing off. 'Ee don't need it. Not now."

She obliged, smiling as he ruffled her flattened waves of natural brown.

"Answer me, me lad. Why must you leave? Give the master time to change his mind."

"'Tis me duty to go. I try to live as an honourable man. I just cannot face censure from a master I respect. How can I look him in the eyes without feeling shamefaced?"

"It's that bloody woman's fault. I knew trouble would follow her around as soon as I clapped eyes on her. I notice she's kept away tonight."

He smiled tender-heartedly, but remained subdued. "I rather think it was 'ee she couldn't face, Fanny."

"She's in love with him, that's why she's desperate to stay."

"Yesterday it was me she loved, so 'ee said."

"I could give her what for!"

"Hush yourself, girl. 'Ee don't want to be thrown out as well. I can live rough for a while, but a woman needs more than the shelter of an unlocked barn."

Across the yard in the big house, with her supper mostly eaten and the plate left carelessly on the floor, Emmie lay in deep sleep. It had been a long day.

CHAPTER 12

Revelations

The night was uncommonly sober at the farm. The usual chattering voices that came from the dormitory until lights were extinguished had fallen silent, the workers finding no reason to be jolly.

Fanny had joined Abel in his bed, offering the warmth of her body as comfort as she soothed him without intimacy, fearing he had many nights ahead that would be riven by cold in some pigsty or other. In this manner, she protected him until his eyelids finally released themselves and she could feel his breathing becoming slower and more rhythmical. Only once did he wake, and such was her devotion that she was already alert and ready to listen to his dream.

"I dreamt 'ee followed me from here and somehow strayed to the east of England, where 'ee found 'eeself burning faggots of green ash in a village churchyard. Then, suddenly, a great boom was heard and the earth heaved, gravestones toppled and buildings began to crumble all around. Workers in the fields stood paralysed as ripples crossed the fields, sure it was judgement day. The ripples ended at the sea, where the water pitched into a great hollow, into which 'ee were swept. I tried to rescue 'ee, but I was running in slow motion and I had to watch as the waves, now nine feet tall, came crashing down. Please, Fanny, promise me 'ee will not fulfil my dream. Stay here until I can fetch 'ee properly."

She placed her arm back over his shoulders and snuggled close. "I promise," she whispered sincerely, "but you must promise me in return that you will stay close by for one night, so I might know your whereabouts and fetch you by gig if the master sees fit to change his mind. Make it Iverham. I could find you in such a bit of a place as that. Do you agree, Abel?"

He said he did. Her head touched his pillow and at last she fell asleep.

In the big house, John had also retired early from the stress of a dreadful day. But, while a few doors along the landing Emmie hibernated, curled and warm in her bed, John remained restless. He felt deep loss at the prospect of losing Abel, his right-hand man and the most trusted worker on the farm, and so for most of the night he re-enacted the scene, going over the events time and time again in the hope of finding a reason to change his mind without losing authority. In this unease, whichever way he laid his neck, arms and legs, they fought back for a more comfortable position. Every so often he felt for his Hunter watch, flicking open the silver cover to count down the hours until he would have to face the next day. And so the minutes dragged by.

By the light of morning, with his head aching and eyes half-shut from no more than two hours of disturbed sleep, John fell out of bed. He again reached for his watch, trying to focus on the hands.

"Good grief! Why didn't someone wake me?"

Throwing open the bedroom door, he screamed for Emmie, who came running up the stairs with a mop and bucket in her hands, her hair tied untidily under a cap and falling indifferently over her face. She wiped her nose on her sleeve.

"Fetch Abel Tucker at once!"

"Are you still angry with me?"

"Shut up, Emmie, and do as I say."

She conjured the horror of entering the dormitory and facing the hostility of Abel and his friends.

"Me?" she replied weakly. "I don't know if I can."

"Who else is here to do it, silly girl? I have no shirt on my back. Hurry yourself before it's too late."

Emmie scurried off, returning minutes later.

"Nobody in the dormitory will talk to me. They turned their backs."

"Did you tell them I sent you?"

"I did. They took no notice of that, either."

"Did you mention Abel?"

"I wasn't given the chance."

"Was he there?"

"I could see his bed through an open door. It was stripped, which makes me think he wasn't."

"Damn!"

John slammed the door indifferently and rushed to the window. Nobody could be seen. Abel had gone.

With no gain to be made from indolence, Abel was already more than two miles from Nether Bow, climbing the small, grassy hills punctuated by outcrops of trees and gorse. He was on his way to Iverham, where he would stay out of everyone's way for the rest of the day, thereafter making for Piddletrentide and Matchcomb Pava, where he hoped his skill at lime burning might find him work.

"Well," said Fanny to the others in the dormitory as they returned from early morning chores, "should we remain quiet at what be heaped so unfairly on poor Abel?"

"What can we do?" asked another in simple tone. "He's gone now."

"I've been pondering that. Happening to remember Abel reading a paper, I found this small advertisement for a lawyer."

"Lawyer?" he replied, laughing. "Such matters are not for the likes of us."

"I think you be wrong, Mark Gladtide. On the face of it, he doesn't seem to be a very prominent lawyer with a name worth half-a-crown a letter before he speaks. Will you shake a hand and give a shilling from this week's pay on me enquiring?"

He offered his hand with stiffness, but withdrew before palms touched.

"No, this is daft. We can't be doing with lawyers, not on what we earn."

"Didn't you like Abel Tucker and wish him back?" said Fanny, daring him to show no regard.

"I like Abel as much as you! Well, perhaps not quite as much as you. But I can see no good coming from giving away hard-earned money to a lawyer. He would take a month's pay from us just to say the master has every right to dismiss Abel if he wants to. I've never heard such a foolish undertaking. What do you others think?"

They all agreed a lawyer was a truly bad idea.

"Then, Abel be lost to us."

They said he probably was.

"And does that poisonous Emmeline Sturry get away with it?"

"Ah! Now that's a different matter," snarled Mark. "I vote we teach 'er a good lesson she won't quickly forget."

"If she makes an appearance here, I shall insult her, just see if I don't."

"Come, come, Harry Potts, that's not fair.

"No? But I thought. . ."

"No, not by a half measure. We should unpretty her face at the very least!"

While Fanny schemed, Emmie walked up and down the hallway, mopping the floor and looking remarkably pale. She knew by John's desperate actions to talk to Abel that it was unlikely the matter and consequences of the private room had ended with his dismissal, but remained a festering wound. She worried for what was to come. She did not have long to wait.

John reappeared fully dressed, except for footwear. As a gesture of submission, she asked if he was ready for a full breakfast.

"I suppose I would be, if I wasn't so damnably sure a grave injustice has been done," he replied in languid tone. "It cuts my appetite to the quick. And you, young lady, were at the heart of it."

Emmie rested the mop against the wall and turned shamefaced.

"I'm truly sorry, Sir. What more can I say to make up for my foolishness? I can only offer my good resolutions for the New Year."

"A clean slate? This is pure vanity, a cheque drawn against an already empty bank."

"Yet, it is said with honesty, Sir," she muttered in hope.

"The trouble with resolutions is that they come only after a terrible deed has been done, and in so doing have no chance of making better anything already passed." John noticed her chastened look as he sat to pull on his boots. "Good grief, my bloody socks are soaking."

"I've only just mopped the floor, Sir, and it has yet to dry."

"Admirable, but it doesn't get me going. Run to my room and fetch another pair at once."

She returned quickly, kneeling at his feet.

"Just give me them and get up." The damp socks were left on the seat when he stood, pressing his toes to the end of tight boots. "You are heartless, Emmie. You have done a great many bad things in your life which have impacted to the detriment of others. I think now of Christabel, as well as Abel, and I can well imagine there are others I know nothing about. And, when considering myself, we both know I have ridden half the length of the countryside on more than one occasion to save your hide, not always successfully I might add. Yet, has any of this caused the

slightest variation in your character, the slightest genuine and
long-lasting remorse? I think we both know the answer. You
seem to believe you can be forgiven any misadventure as your
right of self-discovery, no matter the consequence, and that some
poor fellow will go down on his hands and knees to gather the
pieces you scatter so irresponsibly. Well, it's not true, not before,
not now and certainly not in the future, at least as far as I am
concerned. Your train has met its buffers."

"You are too harsh, Sir," was her listless reply. "If I am capable
of bad things, they come so separated in my life that I fail to
believe my character is generally flawed."

"Perhaps you do believe that. It matters nothing to me. You
are not without intelligence, Emmie, your answer indicates that
even if the words spoken were not entirely sincere. However, a
clever tongue is not enough any longer."

"But, it is always the circumstances I face which cause so many
misjudgements. The poor have fewer choices than the rich."

"That's not true, either," he scolded, repugnance showing on
his features, "and certainly has no bearing on your wilful intrusion
into my private space. Christabel lived an impoverished life, yet
remained faithful to her conscience and natural good ways. In her
case, my wish to help drove her away, because she asked for
nothing she hadn't earned by the sweat of her own brow."

"I try hard to be more like her, I honestly do."

"Then stop. You are not at all like her and never could be. It
would be deception to imagine there could be any similarity
between you, and I treat the suggestion with all the disaffection it
deserves."

"Please don't say such things. It's so cruel."

"I'm afraid a cruel tongue often follows a cruel act. There is a
primitive instinct in us all to lash out when hurt, but it is often the
only time certain truths are spoken. We don't all have a cast-iron
constitution which enjoys giving pain by word or deed, or can
deflect censure without some of it sticking. The secret to a cruel
response lies in the measure."

"An eye for an eye, tooth for a tooth?"

"No, Emmie, you don't listen. A blinded man is not cured of his affliction by inflicting identical retribution. Indeed, a perpetrator may endure more pain through regret suffered over a long sentence to consider his brutal act than by bearing the same quick fate visited upon his victim. The blow has been struck, and so it is right that a suitable punishment is sought, but it has to be measured to be effective."

"If I am not to be sacked, like Abel, will I take a punishment at all?"

"Good Lord, woman! Do you only think of yourself and not see the harm you have done, not only to a good man but to the efficient running of the farm?"

"Yes, Sir, I do and I am very sad about it."

"Well, that's a start at least, and the only words you have spoken to date I actually believe. But, remember this. Harsh condemnation is not enough when other peoples' lives are affected. So, expect a consequence for your actions." John walked away, grabbing a walking cane as he headed towards the front door. "As to breakfast, I want nothing. I may be away for the remainder of the day. In the meantime, have my evening suit pressed, ready for tomorrow. I have received an invitation to party with the Grants and look forward to it greatly. I intend to go despite my mood. Indeed, I hope it will take me out of myself for a while. But, be warned. It has only been that happy expectation that has prevented me from dealing with you severely, as you so richly deserve. Now, I have more important things to do than banter with you."

"Are you searching for Abel Tucker? If so, I would like to help."

"I think not, on either count. Shamefully, I'm off to poach a bailiff from another estate, under the guise of Christmas fellowship. You see, your actions have now forced me into unchristian deception. Pass me that parcel."

She looked surprised, but managed a slight smile as she handed over a large box.

"Now anyway with you, Emmie!" he demanded. "You may think yourself lucky to have remained here, but I can assure you the roses have been removed, leaving only thorns. And I warn you further not to use my lack of propriety now to influence your future dealings. Needs must when the devil calls, or drives, or however the expression goes. I know the devil features in it somewhere."

"I thought I was the devil?"

"Be quiet, wretched girl, and get about your business. Leave me to mine."

By ten o'clock that evening John had still not returned. Emmie had waited up, wanting to serve a mutton stew she had carefully prepared, but, because it had stayed in the range so long, the rich brown gravy had turned toffee-like around the edges of the dish and the chunks of meat had become dark and dry. The stew was discarded and any remaining fat after such a baking was left to congeal as it cooled. After inspecting the jars of pheasant and chestnut pâté made earlier, checking the melted lard formed air-tight seals and the stretched pigs' bladders were still held tightly in place by lengths of hessian cut into strips and knotted, she turned down the wick of the lamp and pulled the kitchen door shut, leaving a single place setting and a wine glass unused on the table.

Emmie's plan to reach the man through his stomach had not taken into account John's deep depression, made worse by his failure to obtain the services of a new bailiff. The failed mission had taken him south to Wintercompton, a journey of eight miles or so and, thus, finding himself mid-way between Cerne and Lyme Regis, he had decided to press on and take the salt air of that coastal resort. Later, he would send a telegram home to convey his whereabouts and then purchase a few necessary items in town for an overnight stay.

Lyme Regis was a place of fashion and respectability, emerging from Jurassic cliffs as a splendid jewel of regal amusement, its coastline of antiquity shared by parades of small shops built on the many steep rises and falls in the natural landscape. Formal garden terraces, planted groves, magnificent hotels, the River Lim and its estuary, the Buddel flowing low between tall walls and the cupola of the Guildhall, and even an old fossil store, gave Lyme Regis a character as uniquely individual as any resort along the entire south coast of England.

Broad Street, in which John would make his purchases, was of particular length and steep to descend, and guided visitors to the sea itself. There, a promenade was provided as The Walk, where the sea was not invasive to those strolling between the sand and the private residences defining its northern edge. Most particularly, it was from The Walk that the glorious Cobb came into view, a man-made edifice of stone curving out into Lyme Bay to form a harbour for the many rigged ships seeking a safe mooring. Waves would crash against its solid sides and spray over the broad top during the worst storms. A new lifeboat station had just been completed nearby to rescue those caught on the wrong side.

The town also had another claim to fame. It was here the Duke of Monmouth had raised his standard during the 1685 West-Country Rebellion. It failed and led to the execution by hanging of twelve locals, having been found guilty of the charges at the Bloody Assize, so brutally administered by the famous hanging judge, Jeffreys. It was rumoured Jeffreys' ghost still haunted parts of Broad Street, where he could be seen chewing a bloodied bone.

John had been to Lyme Regis on many occasions and had often sat on 'Granny's Teeth', a series of cantilevered stone steps projecting from the side of the Cobb before it reached the sea. And it was here he could be found once again, having bought what he needed, checked into a hotel and eaten supper. The steps were cold and carried a frosty glint, but he was well wrapped and, with his coat collar turned up and a scarf wound several times around his neck, he returned to a measure of mental calm.

He stared ahead into nothingness, for the water had taken the colour of the sky, while towards the town the roofs and spires of the tallest buildings were silhouetted against the stars, giving them a prominence not to be noticed during daylight. In all things the peace was infectious, the only sounds coming from lapping water and a few feral creatures roaming the dark alleys, the street lamps bathing in haloed glows casting little downward light on their secretive movements.

The hour now being late, John pulled himself up and casually strolled back towards his lodgings, passing the post office to his left. Only then did he remember the telegram. He kicked himself for his stupidity, arresting the tranquillity so recently gained. For no particular reason, and certainly for no immediate benefit, he quickened his step and was soon within to the hotel grounds.

Meanwhile, in Nether Bow, Fanny had stood at John's front door ever since she had seen him ride away, in the hope he would return quickly. She cursed her bad timing, having noticed him saddle up from a window high above the courtyard and rushed down the dormitory steps to prevent his leaving, only to see him trot past before she had come into view. And so, since that time, she had braved the cold to stand guard. Emmie had seen her lonely vigil and in better times might have invited her into the house, but their present strained relationship forbade such contact. Anyway, she also had no idea when John would return. Had she received the telegram, she would have used it to build bridges with those in the dormitory, and particularly Fanny. But, unfortunately, she had not.

That evening, noticing the kitchen lights go out and the house plunge into general blackness, Fanny walked sullenly back to her room, knowing all chances for saving Abel had vanished with the night. All about was silence, the others having slipped away to an illegal cock-fight. How quickly Abel's friends had forgotten him languishing alone at Iverham, lamented Fanny as she climbed the dormitory stairs.

CHAPTER 13

The cock fight

As Fanny huddled in her cold bed, her thoughts dark and her body lonely, Mark and the others were making merry, drinking, smoking and shouting around the edges of a circular cock pit, in the company of all classes of society who collectively chose to break an old law they viewed as 'unnatural to the countryside'.

A local squire arrived and the crowd erupted into more cheering and clapping as he inspected the progress of killing, taking an elevated view from the top of a pile of straw bales where the scene was prime. He wore a slight mask, as would a highwayman of old, for he was a magistrate and was not to be recognised, although everyone present knew his identity, many having stood before him in the dock. No such disguises hid their faces, for they knew their sentences for small misdemeanours would be light if they were recognised as companions in wrongdoing.

"'Tis the nature of cock birds to fight," said Mark, as he waved to the magistrate he had stood before on several inauspicious occasions.

Harry, attending his first event, was less sure of the sport's merit and said so, as the carcass of the loser from the last round was grabbed thoughtlessly by its lifeless neck. The bloodied victor fared little better, it head raw and swollen, its beak torn from the flesh and hanging loose to one side. Its owner, normally so caring for his best birds but now sure this one could neither fight nor eat, pulled its neck until it cracked, throwing the remains into a canvas sack once its metal spurs had been removed. The spurs, curved and pointed, would be fitted to a new fighting cock after its natural spurs had been brutally cut away.

To general delight, two more birds promptly arrived, their heads hooded, crowned by coloured plumes. These were the best of the prize fighters, held firmly between their owners' hands. The hoods were pulled free and the birds were brought together, still held in vice-like grips. This closeness taunted the fighting cocks into frenzy, their beaks pecking and their feet slashing at free air. The crowd, sitting on long benches, rose to their feet, roaring approval and shouting for bets to be taken. Money was snatched from the outstretched hands of eager gamblers as the birds struggled to be released.

Suddenly, and with much flapping, the birds were thrown into the fray of red-spattered dust. One immediately stabbed forward in a barbarous attack, but was repulsed by a bloody slash from its opponent's rough, inward-facing spur. The aggressor, its crooked beak now held low and its tail high, stalked the other, whose small head and large eyes were held proud and upright. A further cheer went up.

Harry sat gasping as the gladiators circled and then, with the spreading of its wings, the aggressor jumped, ripping at its adversary's head. It drew blood from around the eye. The strutting was over. The other bird, now also with its head down, thrust forward, tearing feathers until the victim fell back. With little care, the handler grabbed it, checking it was still alive before throwing it back into the centre of the ring, where the other bird waited. The mauling continued. The crowd laughed at the one-sided contest. Again the handler grabbed the bird. One leg was now broken, dangling limply in whichever direction was downward. Hearing the jeers, the handler again launched the beaten bird into the ring, hoping to catch the other with its spur as it landed in a heap of noise and feathers. Almost at once both birds recovered their fighting instinct, despite grievous wounds.

Still with aggression in its brain, the broken bird tried desperately to stand. It could not and fell to one side. The other began to close in, surprisingly cautious in its approach. The downed bird was again slashed and then once more, taking savage pecking around the eyes, no mercy given or expected. Still it fought back, jabbing its sharp beak where its eyes could no longer see. Then, taking another wound to the breast, feathers scattering to the wind, it finally stopped fighting and fell motionless. The crowd held its breath, wagers won or lost. The loser, now obviously dead or dying, was thrown unceremoniously onto the dirt floor and kicked in the direction of the sack; the scarred winner, dripping blood, was held high.

John rode back to the farm in the late afternoon of the following day. Having stabled the horse, he entered the house. Emmie looked at him steadfastly, hoping to judge his success at engaging a bailiff without asking the question. But, there was no clue in John's demeanour and she thought it wisest not to enquire. The package had clearly been delivered, whatever that meant.

Emmie picked up the cane, hat and coat thrown carelessly onto a chair and watched his quick footsteps as he bounded up the stairs. An hour later he re-emerged, properly attired for a candlelight party in gracious company.

The exquisite attire, and the difference being well groomed and handsomely dressed made to John's mood, was astonishing. At last he smiled. Emmie was shocked by the cut of his appearance, which was little short of breathtaking. She was used to seeing him in casual clothes, suited to walking, riding and working around the farm. Now, he was dressed for fine company and would, in her opinion, outshine any woman hoping to take centre stage for merely corporeal attraction. At once, she began to feel physical attraction for a man she had only previously admired for his position and kindness. It was almost a noble feeling, an empathy that seemed likely to continue even after the sense of surprise tired.

"Do I look alright?" he asked apathetically, for he still failed to understand the need to be trussed as a peacock.

"Yes, Sir, very much so."

"Then I will do as I am. All this dressing-up nonsense is an annoying waste of time. Imagine hosting a Christmas gathering half-way through the month, when the thought of Christ's birth has yet to loom large in anyone's mind. Still, we do as is expected of us. I have ordered a coach to take me to the Grants' home, as Tucker isn't around to drive me."

"No, Sir. I mean, yes, Sir."

"Quite." He took out his Hunter. "I see I have made good progress and have all of an hour to waste. I will take port wine in the drawing room."

She returned with a glass. "May I take the rest of the evening off?"

He turned towards her, offering a look that could be taken equally as rebuke or agreement.

"Is that a 'yes', Sir?"

"It is. Do as you wish, but do it with dignity, please. You know what I mean?"

"I do. Thank you."

"Do you have plans?"

"Of an unexpected kind, Sir."

"Oh, yes? And stop calling me 'Sir' all the time. Keep it for when you're in deep trouble, which, I suppose, means you are likely to wear the title thin. Is 'John' too much to ask for at this moment?"

"As I feel at present, I think it is, Mr Madden."

"As you wish, silly girl. Where are you going, if you don't mind me enquiring?"

"I've been invited to the dormitory for a few pre-Christmas games."

He winced with grave concern. "Are you sure? I thought you were unpopular over there?"

"Just shows how people can be misjudged. It seems I was mistaken."

"Be careful, that's all I ask."

"You worry too much. I can look after myself."

His sniff was one of castigation.

As soon as John settled in his seat with the port wine, Emmie raced up to her room to clean up for the dormitory party. She had only one suitable dress, still mud stained from her time at the Holman Clavel, but it was adequate for the occasion. Fifteen minutes later she was back down, deliberately parading herself in front of John.

"Well, well," he commented. "You are a picture and no mistake. I am quite jealous you go elsewhere for the evening."

She brightened noticeably. "Are you really, John?"

"It was a joke, Emmie, nothing more. Off you trot."

She left without further comment.

In the dormitory, the doors to the sleeping areas had been closed and the furniture stacked, leaving a large and well-defined open space. A small barrel of cider stood on the floor, held by chocks, rather too small for a long evening of revelry among folk used to drinking several pints a day in the normal way of life, but, nevertheless, a welcome addition to the festivities.

Emmie climbed the wooden open-tread stairs and peered meekly around the door before entering. Everyone had gathered at the far end of the room. The creak of the hinges and the appearance of her face brought an abrupt end to the chattering.

"So, you be here," observed Fanny, causing the others to stare her way. "We wondered if you would come."

"I was invited."

"And so you were," replied Mark, beckoning her inside.

Emmie walked forward cautiously, curious of an atmosphere that was far from convivial for a party.

"Was I meant to bring something?" she asked, unable to understand the tension.

"Only yourself, that's all we want," replied Fanny through a half-smile.

"Is something up?" retorted Emmie, now feeling markedly uncomfortable as the others approached as a mass of bodies.

"Up? Absolutely not. No, if anything, it's what's going down," mocked Mark. "Grab her!"

In a thrice, Emmie was manhandled to the floor and pinned down by their combined weight, leaving Fanny to simper above as she looked down on the frightened girl.

"This be where the party begins."

"Leave me be. You're hurting me," screamed Emmie, genuine fear in her voice.

"Shout all you like. The master has gone out for the evening."

"Get the barrel ready, Mark."

Two men jumped down from the dormitory and heaved a large cooper's barrel to the bottom of the stairs. The lid was pulled free and tossed casually to one side.

"Right, get her down."

With much pulling and clutching, Emmie was carried head-first down the stairs to the barrel, where she struggled hard to stop them forcing her inside. But, her small size combined with their overpowering strength made resistance impossible.

"Please, leave me alone," she yelled, her hands pressing hard against the inside curves of the barrel as she twisted to gain an upright posture, her eyes staring wide from the opening. "What are you doing? I can't stand small spaces. Help me, someone!"

With a final shove, she disappeared fully inside and the lid was banged closed, secured by the taps of a mallet. Emmie's plaintive, but now muffled, cries were ignored as the barrel was tipped onto its side and rolled towards the lawn, where a small incline led to the river. They could hear her body thumping unchecked against the sides as she fell about limply with each rotation.

"One, two, three, go!"

The barrel was released from their hands, gathering impressive speed from the outset.

"'Tis going far too quickly," remarked Mark in panic, watching it roll out of control.

"Who gives a damn if she be hurt?" laughed Fanny to a stunned audience. "We don't care, do we?"

But Mark and the other men saw danger, taking off after the barrel in a sprint. Despite burning the skin of their hands against the rough wood, they were unable to retard its progress. And so the barrel continued to gather speed, unaffected by anything they could do.

"She's going to be killed!" screamed another girl, holding her hand over her eyes. "We'll all be hanged for murder. For pity's sake, do something".

"We're trying," bellowed Harry in panicked tone, as he scrambled to divert the barrel from the river, "but the bloody thing is unstoppable."

"I'm off," exclaimed the girl resolutely, as she turned to flee. "You're a murderer, Fanny Smart. None of this was my doing and I want no part of it."

Fanny stared wide-eyed at the unfolding tragedy.

"Please, Mark, please, please, please!" Fanny screeched. "Oh, Lord, help me."

At the water's edge, where the river now flowed higher and faster than usual because of recent heavy rainfalls, one side of the barrel struck the trunk of a willow tree, almost climbing a few inches before causing the barrel to spin wildly. It gave Mark time to jump on top, bringing the barrel to a stop by spreading his legs as an anchor, his heels ploughing into the soft turf. The abruptness of the collision with the tree had caused the lid to fly off and roll into the river, where it now bobbed rapidly from sight. Mark crouched to peer inside, too exhausted to speak.

"Be she dead?" shouted Fanny from a distance, frozen with fear.

"I think she is," cried another as he reached Mark.

"Oh, no, please, no!"

A murmur came from inside.

"No, I'm wrong. She's alive."

Mark forced his head and shoulders into the opening, cupping his arms around Emmie. "I can hear her moving".

"Get her out," demanded Harry, trying to help but unable to get his own grip within the confined space.

"Is that you, Edmond?" came a confused voice from the inside.

"'Tis me . . . Mark. We'll soon have you free."

With Emmie now able to push unsteadily against the bottom of the barrel, she was soon pulled clear. Mark placed his jacket on the cold ground, where Emmie collapsed with a manic spinning sensation ringing in her head. Her eyes were screwed shut, her throat swallowing hard against a retching need to be sick.

Only slowly, as everyone stared at her in continuing alarm, did Emmie focus on those above, giddy to look upwards.

"That was fun," said mumbled unconvincingly, "but I don't want another go?"

"I think the party's over," offered Mark as he helped Emmie to her feet. "Are you steady?"

"I will be, I think. Do you mind if I go home?"

"Of course not, but you must take it easy. We'll help you. We don't want the master thinking you're drunk. Would you like a bowl of arrowroot for your head, to make a compress?"

"I don't think so. I can't feel my head at all."

The slow walk back to the house gave Emmie time to recover a little. At the door, Mark and the other men ran off, forgetting nobody was expected to be inside. It had all gone horribly wrong and they were blissfully thankful she had survived the prank. Emmie reached for the bell-pull.

Contrary to expectations, John answered. The carriage had still not arrived to whisk him away. She collapsed into his arms.

"What have the blighters done to you?" he enquired aggressively, looking for signs of misdeed.

"It's alright, Sir, just a harmless game. But, I don't think I want to play anymore. Can I come home early?"

"You're not going to be sick on my suit, are you Emmie?"
"Probably!"

Despite the appearance of the long-awaited carriage and the late hour for leaving, John ordered the driver to wait outside while he attended the needy.

Emmie lined an enamel bucket with the partially digested remains of her lunch, which John removed to the yard at arm's length. He hated the very smell of vomit, so reminiscent of childhood.

"Feeling any better?"
"Dizzy!"
"Are you going to be sick again?" he asked with alarm. "I've left the bucket outside. Shall I get it?"
"I'm alright, I think."
"You look as pale as a ghost."
"Fashionably pale or ill pale," she groaned.
"I would say . . . sickly."
"Oh, don't mention that word. I'm struggling here."
"Take a drop of this," said John, reaching to the table, "it'll calm you."

She spluttered as the port wine burned her sore throat. "Can I have water?"

"Avoid the stuff myself. Still, if you're feeling steady enough, I'll fetch some. Or would you prefer milk? That's good for throats. It's from Betsy. That cow produces more milk than animals half her age and none goes up to her horns in temper. She's like a favourite great aunt to the others, bless her udders."

"Milk? Oh, the very thought makes me feel bilious."

"Then, forget I said it. We must save my clothes. Pure Adam's Ale it is."

CHAPTER 14

The party

$\mathcal{A}$t the Grants' lavish home, everything was complete for an evening event that was as contrived in its aims as wicked in its expectations. The invitation sent to John gave the impression of a large pre-Christmas gathering, while in truth the only outside guest was to be John himself. The scandal that was to pass as polite conversation was most certainly to be kept from the ears of anyone not directly involved in the plot.

> *"Is it a party in a parlour?*
> *Crammed just as they on earth were crammed,*
> *Some sipping punch, some sipping tea,*
> *But, as you by their faces see,*
> *All silent and all damned."*

"Shut up, Daniel, you fool, and get yourself ready."

"I am ready, Lizzy. Now I read Wordsworth to while away the time."

"Tell cook the hour is approaching," commanded Harriet from afar. "Make sure she has everything at hand. We want no slip-ups."

"Who's she bawling at? Me or you?" asked Daniel, poking

Elizabeth with the end of a tennis racquet he used to strike dramatic pose while reciting.

"You, you damned idiot."

> *"We may live without poetry, music and art;*
> *we may live without conscience, and live without heart;*
> *we may live without friends, we may live without books;*
> *but civilized man cannot live without cooks."*

"Are you still here, Daniel?"

"He's annoying me, Mother, spouting Wordsworth all over the place instead of doing anything useful."

"Goodness, Lizzy, you are so ignorant. That was Ellis Meredith, written a couple of decades ago."

"Then follow his advice and chivvy up the cook, as Mother asks."

By eight o'clock, the Grants were beginning to feel abandoned. All was elegance, the table in the next room laid for a fine meal that was starting to overcook. As the clock chimed the hour, the women looked at each another in dismay.

"It's not my fault, Ma'am," said the cook, bypassing Collins. "You said seven for half-past. It's now well past that time. The pheasants are roasting dry and the iced-cream is beginning to run. I'll pack some more ice around the bowl, but I won't be responsible if I can't serve soon. Any longer and the ice cream will have to be drunk from a cup."

"Not at a cost of twenty pounds a bowl to make, it won't," rebuked Jeremiah.

"What the devil's happened to the man? It's so unlike him," griped Harriet, looking from the window and seeing no coach lamps approaching in the blackness.

"Be patient, Mother," offered Daniel in conciliatory tone. "John won't let us down. Shall I read a bit of Byron, appropriate to the moment? '*So, we'll go no more a roving, so late into the night, though the heart...*'"

"I hope he hasn't got wind of our little plan, Harriet," said Jeremiah, the earnestness of his tone putting an end to Daniel's boyish pranks.

"How could he? No, we can relax on that at least."

"Relax, when you consider the importance of tonight. You stand there, feebly staring through the panes, and glibly tell *me* to relax. Gracious, woman, it's obvious to all that you can't relax any more than me! And, Elizabeth is at her nerve's end. Only Daniel isn't in a kerfuffle, although why he should be spared is a grave injustice to family unity. If one of us is in panic, we all should be."

Daniel laughed, but said nothing. Jeremiah joined his wife at the window, placing a reassuring hand on her shoulder, which she brushed aside in case it creased her sleeve.

"Why," said he, returning to his seat, "I'd rather be chased by a lion while carrying a loin steak in my mouth than be the bait here. Because, like it or not, we are all bait to catch a mackerel."

"Actually," interjected Daniel, pulling at his cuffs, "I rather see John as a shark."

"No, surely a horse?" added Harriet, turning her back on the window. "Proud, yet obedient."

"A horse isn't a sea creature, Mother."

"Alright!" she reproved. "I meant a seahorse, anyway."

"Of course you did, Mother, and the likeness is so strikingly apparent it requires no explanation."

"Stop it," rebuked Elizabeth as she re-entered the room. "It's entirely obvious that I'm the sprat to catch the. . ."

"Mackerel," shouted Jeremiah. "So, I was right all along. Hurrah!"

"Where is Unity?" enquired Harriet sternly, wanting nothing more to go wrong.

"In my room. Collins can pop in now and again to keep an eye on her."

"See that she does, and often. We don't want the child crying before John is told of his responsibilities."

"Don't be concerned. I've just fed her and now she'll sleep into the early hours. I was pleased to do it, too, to get away from Daniel."

"Quite," blustered Jeremiah, changing the subject.

"There's nothing wrong in talking about lactation, Father," chirped Elizabeth. "Nursing a baby is as natural as nature itself. Mother did it for us."

"Food of life, one might say," added Daniel through a broad grin. "Why, I've seen many nursing mothers take their babies to the breast and it is a scene of the greatest tenderness."

"When?"

"When what, Mother?"

"Have you seen such a private thing?"

"I get around. I get around. Country girls in the fields and so forth. Such girls are hardly circumspect, when often they're not allowed to leave their jobs for a second. Even a quick pee is sometimes had standing in the open. Their babies are merely brought to them, to keep them working."

"Is that true, Jeremiah?"

"It happens in some starve-acre places. Mostly to the west of the county, but much depends on whether work is overseen by a good bailiff who is permanently employed on a farm or by a gang-master hired for a fixed fee to do a particular job. Gang-masters can be quite brutal in their lust to maximise profits, often picking up the most desperate workers at mop fairs, those left behind after the majority of hiring has been done and are willing to accept starvation wages for long hours."

"You've seen such dreadful things, Daniel?"

"Of course. You should get out of the carriage sometimes, Mother, and look for yourself. Anyway, brandy anyone? Or a glass of milk, perhaps, for the ladies?" he added fiendishly.

Just in time to save a clip around the ear, the door bell rang.

"Quick everyone, this is it. To your places."

John arrived wearing a rich smile. The Grants returned the compliment, until their faces suddenly dropped with the unexpected presence of another person entering the room. She walked timidly a pace to his rear. The uninvited guest curtseyed politely.

"What is this?" bellowed Harriet, staring intently at the woman.

"Not 'what', Mother, but who. Why, I know this little creature. She is Emmeline Sturry, John's new housekeeper. We have talked of her before."

"What's the meaning of this, John?" Harriet returned rigidly, looking fiercely towards the intruder.

"Your pardon for my lateness Sir Jeremiah and Lady Grant, Elizabeth, Daniel," he said, nodding to each as their names were called, "but we had a bit of an affray at home and this poor thing was the guiltless victim. For her own safety I thought it best to bring her along, to protect her, as it were. The only alternative was to cancel, but, I have been looking forward to coming so much, I considered that option to be unacceptable, particularly as Elizabeth is here with us after so long away. I used my initiative in the matter."

"Quite right," chivvied Jeremiah, glancing across to his wife as a warning not to take further offence.

"I knew your generosity has no bounds," added John quickly, "so I brought her without the slightest fear of upsetting you. Am I not right to do so?"

"You are quite right," laughed Daniel, holding out his arm to shake John's hand and then moving to Emmie, who he kissed rather too warmly. He took her wrap. "I would like her to sit next to me at the table. See to it, Collins." He turned to his family, a broad grin still across his face. "Well, this is turning out to be an eventful evening. I can't wait to see what comes next!"

The maid left, slipping Emmie a sideways look of distain.

Elizabeth strolled graciously to Emmie, offering her outstretched hand, which Emmie took and kissed.

"No, child, you are our unforeseen guest tonight. A light touch of the fingertips will suffice."

"Thank you, er?"

"Elizabeth. Call her Elizabeth," said John, a suggestion met with general, but mute, disapproval. "Come, come, everyone, we don't all live in cowcumber houses," the light-hearted rebuke masked within his smile. "We can all take the occasional knock to our sensitivities."

"I agree," added Elizabeth, at last seeing advantage in the situation. "A little generosity of spirit is now called for, especially at this time of year, and I, for one, intend to make the most of the moment." She took Emmie to one side, surveying her from head to foot. "Tell me, where did you get that gown? It is all elegance and, yet, if I may be so bold, a tiny bit out of fashion and an infinitesimal bit large about the shoulders and length."

Startled, Emmie looked up at John, seeking permission to speak. He nodded encouragingly.

"Thank you, miss . . . I mean Elizabeth. It is not mine. I have nothing suitable for such company. It was loaned to me by John."

"Ah," scoffed Daniel, "one of John's infamous masquerade dresses. That makes sense."

"Oh, no," replied Emmie quickly, a touch embarrassed. "It was one of his mother's best."

"Of course it is," offered Elizabeth, running her slim fingers under the lace of the collar. "Now I recognise it. Isobel was a diminutive lady too. It was her age, I believe, that made her small. Why are you so small, Emmeline?"

"Don't rightly know. I just am."

"And very well proportioned you are," threw in Daniel, still grinning at everything. "I like her, John. I like her much. Come, Emmeline, take my arm for supper."

"My hat. Where do I leave it?"

Elizabeth sniggered. "Give it to me, Emmeline, dear. Such a lovely straw hat decorated with fruit. Look everyone, it has cherries and miniature apples and berries. Such a basketful of flavours and colours. I don't think this ever was Isobel's. Am I right or wrong?"

"You are right. It's mine. It's my Sunday best."

"Of course it is," petitioned Daniel, "charming to the core."

As the hat was given to Collins and all eyes were elsewhere, Emmie took a discreet step backwards and whispered judiciously into John's receptive ear. "I'm really not hungry, honest. My belly is still turning with the barrel. What are we having for dinner?"

"The Grants, I think!"

With social divisions embarrassingly lowered, Emmie took Daniel's proffered arm, unsure what to do next. Again, she gave a quick backward glance towards John for reassurance. But he was distracted. Elizabeth had seized him, fondly taking his upper arm in both hands and dragging him into line behind her parents.

In this formation, the party entered the dining room, where six candles burned softly in each of three gilt candelabra, bathing the room in a translucent glow, while suspended cut glass drops added festive sparkle. Emmie was dazzled by the elegance. Daniel dragged a chair away from the table and Emmie slipped nervously into the vacant space. He bent over as he pushed it forward to meet her legs, nestling his cheek against hers.

"Don't be frightened at all the knives, forks and spoons," he whispered, his spoken breath tickling her ear. "Just do as I do. Start from the outside and work inwards as the courses arrive."

"Will there be a lot of food?"

"I hope so, mountains of the stuff. I'm ravenous. But don't worry, it's normal for young ladies to leave some on their plates. Only older, fat women don't. You watch my mother as an example of someone who steams through everything. Oh, and by the way, watch out for my sister. She has a nasty bite. She's quick to make a fool of anyone who steps out of rank."

"I think I've already experienced her arrogance tonight."

"She comes from an arrogant family, dear Emmeline. Still, maybe now she has less reason to be so."

"Meaning?"

"You ask too much of me. Be forewarned. That is enough for the present."

"Thank you, Sir."

"Thank you, Daniel," he replied, before taking his seat at the table. "This really has turned out to be a jolly occasion. Let's see how Elizabeth and Mother get out of this one!"

"I don't understand?" said Emmie.

"You don't have to. Just watch and enjoy. Ah, the soup has arrived!"

And so the dinner party got underway, the usual casual attitude to light conversation faltering with the awkwardness of the group gathered and the purpose yet to be revealed. Only Daniel revelled in every difficult pause.

Emmie, too, was thoughtfully engaged, although her plan was less complicated. She merely wanted to show John that she could conduct herself correctly in such eminent company and not disgrace him. If this meant forcing food down her throat, she would at least try. Daniel taking a shine to her was a boost to her confidence, and perhaps with a little flirting she might even make John jealous. In this, Daniel unknowingly obliged.

"I may be talking out of character, and I pray forgiveness if I tread on anyone's toes, but I am of the opinion that there are many worse things than a simple wife. Not of mind, you understand, but of background. This, in my judgement, is doubly true if the gentleman is lacking a fortune, for a simple girl would think nothing of lending a hand with the domestic side of running a home or a farm, for example, which not only occupies her but adds to the family purse. A woman unoccupied is a woman set on spending. Do you not agree, Mother? Shall we debate it, everyone?"

Harriet choked on her fish.

"In your own time," added Daniel with delight, knowing he had displeased her.

She raised a napkin to her mouth. "There are worse things, I don't doubt, but a gentleman with no need to penny-pinch has no use for a marital worker."

"Strange that," added John without first considering the consequence, "my mother thought similarly." Suddenly, the penny dropped.

"Well," interceded Daniel, "do carry on, old man. I can speak for everyone in saying, we are all ears."

John hesitated. "There's nothing much more to add. I only meant Isobel, my mother, said I wouldn't need a wife who could make cheese."

"Cheese?" gibed Daniel in jubilation.

"Silly, isn't it. She said I needed a wife knowledgeable in fashion, card games and organising a household of servants."

"And she was quite right," added Harriet with glee. "Of whom did she speak, this cheese-maker woman and the other, her preferred mate for you? Any women in particular?"

"Mother!" exclaimed Elizabeth, staring murderously.

He swallowed hard. "Well, her preferred choice was, of course, Elizabeth here. Naturally, Mother didn't understand the true nature of our relationship and took far too much for granted."

"Taking a Grant for granted! I like that," roared Daniel, alone in his merriment.

"The cheese-maker was Christabel Mere," John added in more sombre tone. "I have never uttered this before, but tonight I feel free among good friends enjoying such marvellous fellowship to say something secret to myself. I had a nickname for her, one I kept in my head."

"Cheddarbel, perhaps? That fits."

"No, Daniel, it was *Angel*, the only angel in Wessex. She was as close to being an angel as ever a mortal could be."

Elizabeth stared ferociously at Harriet, while Emmie bent her head in despair.

"Remove the plates at once, Collins, and stop dilly-dallying in bringing the meat course," shouted Harriet to mask her disappointment. "And make sure Emmeline gets extra of everything."

"More wine?" blustered Jeremiah, knowing the bottles on the library table would not be poured until Collins returned. The question met with silence.

"Interestingly," continued John, "at the time Christabel lived with us, she had a history capable of taking any degree of inquest. Thereby, I discovered something quite remarkable, a lesson for us all, perhaps. Being poor doesn't prevent a person from being noble. Later, sadly, Christabel was much misused and put upon, and died in defence of her honour." There followed a few second's reflection. "Anyway, we must put such despondency to one side. This is a dinner party and, as such, we have a duty to our hosts to be jolly. Yes, as I said, Elizabeth here was my mother's front runner."

Both Elizabeth and Harriet immediately perked up, as if told they had been short-listed for a great prize.

"Do you consider in hindsight that your mother was right?" asked Harriet before Elizabeth demeaned herself by enquiring of the same, sure of the reply.

"Oh, I've really given it very little thought. Please, don't let us embarrass Elizabeth further by such conversation. We all know mother had it in her head that Elizabeth and I would make a suitable match in marriage, and said so often."

Emmie's eyes flared.

"Your mother was a saint," said Harriet. "Why, what a kind thought for your sister, Daniel."

"And she was entirely correct," tittered Daniel.

"What do you mean by that, boy," exclaimed Jeremiah, a warning in his voice.

Daniel giggled weakly. "No, you have me all wrong. I only meant, my dear sister can't make cheese! She thinks it grows on a bush, ready wrapped in a brown paper leaf."

"I do not," quarrelled Elizabeth.

"Be silent," screamed Harriet, before assuming calm. "Siblings, John. What would you do with them?"

"It's of no matter. Daniel might have brotherly fun at Elizabeth's expense, but we all know Elizabeth has her own many virtues."

Elizabeth smiled sweetly.

"What are they?" asked Daniel. "Damned if I can think of any."

"Shut up!" commanded Jeremiah, stamping his foot on the floor. "I mean . . . I think this conversation has gone on long enough. Look, we are here for a Christmas evening, not an inquisition. Instead, we are embarrassing our guests. Let us be merry."

"Virtuousness!"

"Pardon, John?" enquired Emmie, speaking for the first time.

"That is the prime accomplishment of a woman."

"Well, you won't find a virtuous woman around here!" laughed Daniel, placing his hand on Emmie's leg under the cover of the table.

Jeremiah rose to his feet in anger. "Apologise for that remark, Sir! You speak entirely out of place."

Daniel shrank. "Yes, you are quite right. I spoke out of jest, meaning no harm. I apologise unreservedly to all, especially to you, Mother."

Emmie let out a shrill cry as he squeezed her knee, contradicting the apology. She grabbed a napkin to cover her quivering lips, leaving his hand where it rested, smiling in all directions as if innocent of any wrong-doing.

Jeremiah sat, straight faced. "Now, may we please be jolly!" he demanded gruffly.

The meat was brought in on a huge silver platter. It was placed at the head of the table, where Jeremiah removed the domed lid to reveal the pheasants.

"This is more like it," he proclaimed, taking a broad knife to the first backbone. "Lucky cook procured three brace."

Daniel leaned to Emmie. "Cook always buys more meat than we need. Father thinks it is clever planning. I know it's because she will have her own knife and fork ready in the servant's hall for the left-overs. You being here will scupper that."

The remainder of the meat course and the sweet course that followed were attended in the pleasant occupation of genuine small talk, during which the vacuous questions asked and answers given were of absolutely no interest to either party so engaged in conversation. A state of social balance had been restored and the pleasure boat of eloquent sufficiency, at last, steered an even course. In such an ambience of insignificance, bordering on the trifling, everyone fully engaged and, thus, remained smiling and giggling throughout. At the conclusion of the feast, when the cheese had been passed between guests without any disparaging remarks, even from Daniel, the port was poured.

"We should retire and leave the gentlemen to their cigars," proposed Harriet.

"Must we?" pleaded Elizabeth, nonplussed at letting John out of her sight. "I have been absent from the area for such a long time, and now every moment with John is as precious as a jewel. Father, may we stay?"

"Ah, yes, I see what you mean. Quite right." He caught his wife's eye and nodded slyly towards Emmie.

"Tell me, Emmeline," Harriet added abruptly, "have you ever seen such a grand house as this?"

"Yes, Ma'am, I have".

"Where?" challenged Harriet irritably.

"Why, at Westkings. It was there I first met . . . well, never mind that. The place was large by any standard."

"You saw it from outside or in?"

"Both, Ma'am. I was mostly occupied in the dairy, but for a brief time I became betrothed to Edmond Elvington, the son of the house, and it was then I visited the inside beyond the servants' places."

"I didn't know that," exclaimed John. "I thought Edmond's attentions were aimed squarely towards Christabel."

"Yes, they were, but after I had my turn. I was the unlucky victim of their romance."

"That's ripe. Really ripe, don't you think? Did I know it at the time, because I don't remember?"

"I think you might have."

"So, it is settled," said Elizabeth. "I am to stay and Mother is to show Emmeline the house."

"No, Elizabeth, I did not mean that. My place is here, with our guest. No, I believe it would be seemly for Collins to be the guide. That would occupy everyone who is not family."

"Except John. He's not family," offered Daniel. "Or, perhaps, maybe one day he might be."

"Be quiet, Daniel, you idiot!"

"It's all right, Elizabeth," John added amiably, "I ought to understand Daniel's godforsaken humour by now. Take no notice. I don't."

Emmie and Collins left the room and Daniel returned his hand to the table. The door was closed and the remaining guests looked at one another for inspiration.

"Shall I begin?"

"Begin what, Daniel?" asked his father.

"The fun and games, of course. I have an idea."

"I thought we. . ."

"A little jollity first may be in order, dear," interrupted Harriet. "We must preserve the atmosphere and work around to other things."

"Am I missing something?" asked John, looking between his hosts.

"Not a thing, dear friend," said Daniel. "Let's get on. Have you ever heard of a parlour game called *Consequences*?"

"Is that where we all write down on a piece of paper different answers to questions?"

"Almost, Mother. What we do is to think of a *girl's name* and scribble it down. Then, we fold the paper to keep the answer secret and pass it along to the person on our left. After that we write a *boy's name*. Then, *where they met*, followed by *he said something or other*, *she said something or other*, *he did something*, *she did something*, and finally *the consequences of this were?* At the conclusion, when we are all done, we pass the folded papers to one person, who reads them out. The results can be quite entertaining by their absurdity."

"Just the ticket, I would say." Jeremiah rose from the table and returned with five pieces of paper and a similar number of pencils, which he distributed.

Harriet moved places to take Emmie's vacant chair, putting herself between Jeremiah and Daniel.

"Right, if you are settled, dear, the first question is a girl's name? Oh, by the way, I suggest the people have to be famous, say kings and queens? It should avoid any chance of personal embarrassment."

"I have a further suggestion," added Daniel. The others looked on suspiciously. "No, listen to me. Even if the people are royalty, the circumstances can be anything at all. In fact, the less connected to the type of people they are, the funnier will be the outcome. Don't you agree? It is Christmas after all, or nearly."

"If we must," remarked Jeremiah, "but, be prudent in your amusement of us."

"Of course. Right, here goes. Everyone write the name of a queen."

They all scribbled, folded the paper and passed it on.

"Come on, Mother. Get working on the next question."

"Oh dear, my turn is it? Right, everyone, name a word that rhymes with dove which describes something a woman wears on her arm?"

"What! No, Mother, that isn't how to play the game at all. You don't make up a question. We all now write a king's name."

"Like Prince Albert?"

"Not quite, Mother, but it will do."

"But it goes so nicely with Victoria, my first answer." She wrote Albert and folded the paper.

"Now it gets more difficult. *Where they met.*"

They wrote answers, made them secret and passed them to the left, all, that is, except Harriet.

"Are you done, Mother?"

"I seem to have two sheets of paper."

"That's because you haven't passed on your earlier one." Daniel grabbed a sheet and gave it to his father. "Now, write something down for *he said.*"

The papers moved on.

"*She said.*"

Again the game progressed.

He did, was quickly followed by *she did*, the papers passing neatly to their respective recipients.

"Easy," said Elizabeth, having whispered into John's ear and made him giggle, before writing her own few words.

The papers finally reached their end destination.

"Right, this is the best part. We all have to think up a *consequence*. Make it funny, everyone."

"I'm at a total loss," said Harriet. "Having put Victoria for the queen, I don't want to be disrespectful in my consequence. Can I say the consequence was, she ruled happily?"

"You can put whatever you like, Harriet," remarked Jeremiah as he scribbled his own answer, wearing a broad grin across his face. He looked up, having folded his sheet. "Only, dear, the piece of paper with your queen written on it will be somewhere else by now, so you can put anything without the slightest concern for Her Majesty."

"It's only a game, anyway," remarked Elizabeth. "Leave it blank if you wish."

She thought and folded the paper.

"Has everyone finished?" asked Jeremiah. "Excellent. Pass them up here and I will read them aloud." Five folded papers gathered at the top of the table. "Do I need to remind us of the questions?"

"No, Father, just get on with it."

"Right, here goes. The first says: *Victoria* met *Richard III* at a *bath house*. He said *I like your cherries*, she said *I have five unmarried sisters*. He *rode his horse wildly*, she *ate so much she burst*, and the consequence was *he bought her a new hat*."

There was a round of polite laughter.

"Richard III was mine," Jeremiah added. "I think I played well. I like this. A first rate entertainment. Very well done, Daniel."

"And I said Victoria," smiled Harriet.

"We know, Mother. You told us."

"I knew somebody would say Queen Victoria," exclaimed Elizabeth. "That's why I put *she ate so much she burst*!"

John added his laughter to Elizabeth's, but they were alone.

"We'd better move on. Number two," said Jeremiah. "It says: *Queen Victoria*, again, met *Henry VIII* at *a butcher's shop*. He said *give me a pair of stockings*, she said *you smell of fish*. He *caught a cold and died*, she *slipped on a stone and fell into the river*, and the consequence was that *she became a Chinaman*."

The guffaw was hearty, with the opinion that the second was generally funnier than the first.

"Number three reads: *Mary Queen of Scots* met *Prince Albert* while *swimming the English Channel*. He said *you have a red nose*, she said *I like iced tea*. He *offered to take her arm*, she *opened a Christmas present early and found a monkey inside*, and the consequence was *they were shipwrecked on an island*. Shall I go straight on?"

It was agreed he should.

"Number four: *Boudica* met *Edward the Confessor* at *the top of a hay rick*. He said *I suffer from wind*, she said *my dress needs new ribbons*. He *showed her his new ladder* and she *dressed like a boy*."

"There's one answer missing. I counted only seven," complained Daniel in despair. "Where's the consequence? Without a consequence there's no point to the game."

"My fault," admitted Harriet. "My mind went absolutely blank."

"No matter, dear, we still have one more to go. It says: *Elizabeth the virgin queen* met *King John* at *a church barn dance*. He said *leave me alone*, she said *I like a man who is clean shaven*. He *kissed her passionately under an oak tree* and she *lifted her skirt to show her bloomers*. The consequence was, *they married and had twenty children*."

"How could you all be so beastly?" screamed Elizabeth, leaping from the table and running upstairs. "Why mock me in company?"

"I just knew something like this would happen," declared Jeremiah. "Games are so unpredictable. Why didn't we play cards instead? I said it was a mistake from the outset. You had better go to her, dear."

Harriet hurried off in a flutter.

"This is your fault, Daniel."

"Why me, Father?"

"Because, I just know you wrote *Elizabeth the virgin queen* and that bit about *showing her bloomers*. It has your mark all over it."

"I admit to the *bloomers* bit, but not the *virgin*. Anyway, I can prove it. With five of us playing and eight questions, and knowing I wrote bloomers, my other answer had to be *King John*. And it was."

"He's right," accepted John. "I put *Elizabeth the virgin queen*, because that's how she's remembered. It never occurred to me I could offend your daughter by it."

"Who put *kissed under the tree*?"

"That we me, too, I'm afraid," admitted John once more, now looking rather sheepish. "When playing the game, it all gets into such a jumble that it's far too easy to forget what was written on each piece of paper as they circulate. I'm so sorry."

"Actually, I rather think my sister was to blame. She probably encouraged him. I saw her whispering."

Jeremiah clipped Daniel's ear and sent him from the room. Embarrassed, he brushed past Emmie returning from the tour.

"Was it fun, whatever you did, John?"

"No, not in the least. We have one woman in tears and Daniel sent to bed." He closed towards her. "He's a bit old for such punishment. What a booby!"

"Shall we go home?"

John heaved. "I think we probably should."

"There's no consoling her," pronounced Harriet, striding back into the room and taking her seat at the table. "She won't even open the door to me."

"Is there anything I can do?" asked John after a few moments' pause, now loitering by the fireplace.

"Certainly not! You can't go up there, unaccompanied," snapped Jeremiah brusquely. "I really don't think it would help in the least, given *all* the circumstances."

Harriet dipped a finger into a small glass bowl filled with rose-water, pushing the floating flower idly around the edges. "Perhaps, Jeremiah, John's suggestion is the only way forward."

"I'm willing to try anything to make her feel better," replied John, looking between them, "as long as I don't run the risk of making matters worse."

"I doubt they could be," said Harriet glumly.

"I don't remember ever seeing her in such a state," John added. "Frankly, I can't help but wonder if there's more to it than *bloomers* and *virgin*, if I may say such words now the game is over. Tell me this, Harriet, as a friend. Has she become prone to sudden mood swings since being away? I notice a marked difference in her composure."

"You could say that, kind John, and more than you suppose. You are a thoroughly decent man and, I hope. . ."

"Not easily shocked," blurted Jeremiah punctiliously.

"Goodness, is she unwell?"

"No, not as such," was Harriet's downhearted reply. "Not as you might imagine, anyway. More accurate would be to say, she is not as she was. She is, well, indisposed. Look, I can divulge no more, but I can see no greater harm coming from you going upstairs to speak to her, alone, and with our blessing. So go, talk to her if you wish, but first remember that you will always be welcome in our house no matter what happens."

Puzzled, John left, leaving Emmie open-mouthed and awkward. He took two stairs at a time and knocked on her door.

"It's only me," he said in gentle voice. "I've called to see you before I go home."

There was no reply, or sound of any sort. Inside, Elizabeth crouched in dismal uncertainty, a women torn by knowing his secret when he was as yet to learn hers. He tapped again, positioning his face closer to the door.

"Please, I want to talk. We are old friends, Lizzy. You can tell me anything and I promise I won't repeat it to a living soul, including your own parents if you like. You can trust me completely to remain mute. Only, do tell me what upsets you. If I was the cause, I'm truly sorry."

Shortly after his impassioned speech, the handle turned and the door opened a few inches. The room that came into view was strange, almost child-like. Everything was broad blue and white stripes, from the centrally-pitched ceiling to the walls and carpeted floor. Even the window blinds were of matched material, leaving the decorations in perfect harmony throughout.

While John stared in amazement, Elizabeth's face appeared obliquely through the opening as if detached from her body, which remained hidden. Her eyes were red rimmed, her hair unroped from its formal style and falling long over her shoulders.

"Can't you leave me alone?" she admonished.

John reeled, but stayed calm. "I see you've decided not to join us again tonight."

"Yes," she replied, looking down to the floor.

"Lucky I've come to you, then."

She made no gesture to indicate reciprocal feelings.

"Can we speak?"

She raised her stare, so honest and clear behind a pale complexion which gradually grew richer in flushed hue as she looked into his face.

"Please don't force your way in. It would cause you considerable distress."

"Force, be damned. I'd no more push my way into your private room than break down the door. I'm a friend, Lizzy, not a bully. Just tell me to stay where I am, or go, and I will obey without question."

"I don't know."

He lifted a hand to her cheek, so slowly that his intention was understood, rubbing away a single tear with an outstretched thumb.

"Can anything be so terrible as to make an intruder of a friend? I'm certain it wasn't only the stupid game that has upset you. It has to be something else. It is, isn't it?"

She remained dumb-faced. Then, seeing he posed no threat, she took a half pace backwards, allowing the door to swing fully open. Unity laid cradled in her arms, her eyes closed and mouth curling.

"Haystacks, Elizabeth, you nurse someone's child!"

She smiled gently. "At least you understand anatomy."

"Whose is it?"

She hesitated before saying in a clear but mellow tone, "she is mine."

The words fell on John like a blacksmith's hammer glancing an anvil. "What!" he yelled. Then, noticing no change in her mood, he calmed, apologising for his raised voice that disturbed the baby's sleep. "Yours?" he repeated softly.

"*My* baby."

"Is this one of Daniel's jokes, a trick to catch me out as part of the Christmas fun?"

"Is a child something to jest about?"

"No, of course not. Forgive me. But, surely she can't be. Is she? Well, I'll be darned!"

Elizabeth rocked Unity with the compassion reserved for a new mother.

"Haystacks!"

"You've already said that. If you can't think of anything more sensible, perhaps you ought to go."

"Hay. . ." He stopped himself. "Gracious, no wonder you've been away for such a length of time. Now, it all makes sense. You weren't helping as a volunteer at that hospital at all. You've been lying low during your confinement."

"I was lying in both senses of the word. I used it as a nursing home. My parents insisted. Are you angry?"

He thought for a moment, but quickly looked up, captivated by the scene. He conceived no part of the revelation that affected him or his friendship and, thus, any condemnation on his part had no bearing on the matter one way or the other.

"Not in the slightest," he answered at last, "especially if you mean my donations. Why should I be angry? A good cause is still a good cause. The only thing I don't understand is why you felt the need to run away from your closest friends, those who could have offered you their support. I could have been trusted with your little secret."

"Not so little, as it happens. She was eight pounds at birth."

John touched the baby's nose with tenderness. "What's the child's name?"

"Unity Isobel."

"You named her after my mother?"

"Yes. Isobel is such a pretty name."

"Little Unity Isobel. She's beautiful. My mother would have appreciated the gesture, God rest her soul."

"Oh, John!" She fell on his shoulder and wept, one arm gripping him tightly. "What have I done? Have I ruined my life?"

His hand reached for her head, falling congenially on her hair, which he stroked. "Don't ask me. Ask yourself the same question, but only after you've looked again at Unity Isobel. By all that is great, you've performed a miracle and nothing less. A miracle can engender no regret of any kind." He gently pushed her to arm's length so that she could see the sincerity in his eyes. He nodded reassuringly.

"There is more to know."

"More?"

"Much more, but I cannot bear telling you this way."

"Oh?" he replied with little apprehension, drawing himself up. "Come, you should not hold back anything tormenting you. The train has left the station. I believe it would be harder to stop it now than let it run its course. Will there ever be a better time to tell me?"

"Probably not," she murmured, her nerves wearing thin.

"Well then, get it off your chest. Especially now you've made such a good start. Say the words: I was in love with . . . and could not control my passion."

"Stop!" she entreated. "It was nothing like that. My story is not one of passion or lust, but of long-lasting love that was too much one way held."

John took a deep breath, shook his head and settled back to listen, certain he would be indifferent to anything she had to say. She stared into his open face. It held no malice or blame. She paused and then invited him inside. He stepped forward. At once she detected a change in his disposition, his relaxed attitude changing to one of malaise. The truth was, John found the room immediately intimidating, its peculiar decorations adding a subtle atmosphere of dubiety to the strange situation. Mostly, he noticed how the languid glow from the oil lamps illuminated only part of her delicate skin, but fully cast a menacing shadow on the opposite wall. She was unaware of anything John could find in the least threatening and chose to continue assertively.

"Do you remember long ago, in February to be precise, when we celebrated General Gordon's success?"

"I remember the occasion. I don't remember much else, except for the raging headache that followed."

"And there hangs the rub."

"A curious comment," he replied innocently.

"Tailor-made for the occasion, I'm afraid."

She walked to the window, where the glow from the lamps

blackened any outside view. She tugged, one handed, at the curtains.

"Go on," encouraged John. "You keep me in too much suspense."

"Meaning, you and I got up to unspeakable things under the influence of heavy drink. There, you have it in a nutshell."

"I don't think so," he replied through a half-smile, which fell away once he noticed it engendered no similar response. "Anyway," he added more seriously, "I don't remember *you* drinking anything."

"Oh, but I did! I started late, that's all. That's why you won't remember," she added with the startled expression of a lie. "Why, I had nearly as much as you by the end."

"Alright, I drank too much and so did you. So what? It was a special occasion of national rejoicing. We can be forgiven that small indiscretion. It's hardly unspeakably terrible, except to our constitutions, which took a battering."

Her gaze remained grave. She tightened her hold on Unity, a gesture made so conspicuously that suddenly, powerfully, it finally dawned on John where the conversation headed, the realisation of which sent a shot searing through his body.

"Hang about! You're not saying we, you and I, did anything to be really ashamed of, in an intimate way, I mean?"

"There can be no doubt we did. I've already told you we did unspeakable things."

"Maybe, I can't comment, but there are unspeakable things and really bad unspeakable things. I assumed we belonged to the former. It's all a question of measure, surely?"

"No small measure this time," was her shattering reply, holding Unity forward.

He stepped back. "Stop it! I could never do that to. . ."

"To me? Is that what you were about to say? Am I not an attractive, unattached woman?"

"Of course you are. But, we are friends. I almost think of you as a sister."

"Good grief, John! You make me feel asinine, no, feculent."

"I have absolutely no idea what that means."

"Foul, if you prefer, depraved."

"No, you mustn't talk that way. Come what may, we are not related. However, you must understand, when I look at you, as beautiful as you are, my eyes see past the bloom and recognise only Daniel's sister."

"Then I am damned, both to you and to God."

"No, that's too much. You have me all wrong."

"I don't have you at all!"

"Stop that and listen. Face it, Lizzy, would you really wish me to say I view you as a lover, when the love so casually offered could never be beyond friendship?"

"I truly would, if there was any hope of more to come."

"I can give you no such hope. Don't you understand? I cannot believe I played any part in the child's making, because no degree of incapacity could make me see you in the light you wish to shine upon our relationship. That is the hard truth of the matter. Why trick me this way, especially when you are guaranteed my help as a trusted friend."

"Trick?"

"What other word fits? You have a child. Well, good on you. You have no husband. Not so meritorious. You want a father for Unity Isobel. I can understand that, too. But, any father, other than the real father, is by proxy, a freely acknowledged substitute. All this 'blame' business is unworthy, Lizzy, especially directed towards me. I can help, nay, I *will* help, as I have already done without knowing the true situation. But, that has to be the end of it, and the end of your accusations!"

"But, I love you!"

"Of course you do, because the situation demands those empty words to be spoken."

"No, John, I really do."

"Stop it, Lizzy. This is unbecoming and entirely wrong. Only one woman has ever loved me as a man should be loved."

"That blessed Christabel, you mean?"

"Of course Christabel. She *did* love me, and not only for what I could do for her. God knows she needed help, but her love was pure and unselfish. Can you say the same?"

Elizabeth froze, for his reasoning erected a barrier so high that even she was caught on the wrong side.

"How can I say anything and remain honest in your blinkered eyes. We both know she would've loved you forever, on earth and into eternity beyond. I can do no more."

"Then, it is said and done."

"But, John, as God is my witness, no living, breathing woman could promise you more than I. Don't you understand? I offer you the love of a woman made of flesh and blood, who will cherish you here and now. The alternative is for you to forsake such worldly pleasure and cast me adrift for an angel whose immortal soul has fled the grave where her mortal bones lie buried."

The austerity of her words cut him deeply, for he recognised the same truth as being real. Christabel had been his soul mate, a conjoining of hearts when she lived and a faithfulness of spirits that transcended the barrier of normal rationalities now that she was dead.

"Come, Elizabeth, this is hurting us both and getting us precisely nowhere. We are in danger of entering the realms of the fantastic, whereas we need to stick to the facts."

"The facts as you view them or the facts as they really are?"

"Facts are facts."

"Alright, so be it. Unity was born on the 14th of November. That is a fact, verified by documented registration."

"Agreed."

"We celebrated Chinese Gordon on the 18th of February. Please, John, use your fingers and toes to work out the period in between."

His face glazed as he counted. "No, something must be wrong. I don't know what, but something's amiss."

"The dates speak for themselves. As for the rest you have said against me, I forgive you."

He turned away, releasing by distance the burden of her accusation. Familiar, everyday things at once seemed strange, as if he was in a time and at a place far away from the world he knew and understood, her words repeating themselves as echoes in his thoughts.

Elizabeth thought of falling to her knees to beg forgiveness, to show sincerity. But, just as she might have, Unity gave the slightest involuntary sound that broadcast her presence, giving her mother the resolve to be strong for the child's sake and not weak for her own. In this turnabout, Elizabeth did nothing, waiting for John to react in his own way. When nothing came quickly, she sat.

"Oh, Lizzy, I just can't take it in. I can no longer be sure what is right and what is wrong. It's too much to coldly throw at me without warning." He began to shake as the ramifications came flooding to mind. There was only one alternative, which, in normal circumstances, he would not find it in himself to suggest. Yet, there was nothing normal about the present situation and barriers had to tumble. "I suppose you haven't. . ."

"Don't, John. Don't even think what you are about to suggest."

"But, you are Daniel's sister for goodness sake."

"What's that to do with the price of bread? For all that is good between us, John, take a look at Unity. Doesn't she have the appearance of anyone you know?"

"She doesn't look a bit like me!"

"Oh, but she does."

"No she doesn't. I have whiskers and . . . and wrinkles . . . and whiskers and. . ."

"A daughter."

"Jumping Jacks! Can it really be so? No, I can't believe it. Who else agrees with you? Who else have you told?"

"The entire family knows. Oh, and the nurse at the home, only she is of no consequence. Nobody else. Your reputation can be saved in wider circles if you walk away. My family will certainly never make an issue of it, for my sake and their dignity. Walk away if you have no stomach for fatherhood, and I'll never utter your name again inside or outside these walls."

His face displayed indecision, his movements expressing disbelief. He lowered his anxious eyes to hers. "Heavens, Lizzy, what am I to believe? If it's true, what must your family think of me? Ten minutes ago I was playing games with them in ignorance of any pent accusations, while all along they silently judged me across the table. It beggars belief. How can I now face any of them? I have been pre-judged as guilty."

"By facing down their dubiety and taking appropriate action. They want deeds, not excuses for past mistakes."

"Is all this really, honestly, completely true?" he asked again in very low pitch, his startled eyes turning once again to Unity, "or are you merely looking for a stand-in father? Because, I will tell you frankly, I might well have less trouble accepting the second possibility than the first. So tell me the truth, please, as if your life depends upon it."

"Unity Isobel *is* my life. She became the most precious thing to me the moment she was born." She rose and stepped forward, placing her hand on his. "I think it's time to let me allay your fears, John, while telling you a terrible sin. I do not demand that you feel any commitment towards me. The whole matter is one of error and drunkenness, in which you played no coherent part. As to the whole of this evening, I am ashamed to admit that it was contrived by my parents to entrap you, to introduce you to the idea of Unity. Foolishly, I went along with it, but when it became obvious that it wouldn't work, I felt cleansed, almost purged. Now this turnabout situation has arisen, the only unplanned event of the fateful evening. It has made me realise something important. Whilst it was my moral duty to tell you of Unity, I am a stronger woman than I imagined and can, if necessary, manage perfectly well without you. You see, Unity and I are bonded. Even you are an outsider to that."

"Then, you make my position impossible. Either way, I can do no right by you, Unity or your parents. I am an interloper if I stay and a Lothario if I go.

"I suppose."

"Quite a revelation, and quite a predicament for someone who only came tonight for a bottle of good claret and a few silly games."

"My parents aren't important."

"Maybe not, but their part in this charade is undeniable."

"You turn from embarrassment to blame."

"I try not to, but it comes quite naturally."

"They are not the issue. Unity is, and perhaps what might become of us."

He pulled a handkerchief absentmindedly from his jacket pocket and began to mop his brow, refolding it between sweating hands before stuffing it back into his pocket with equal indifference.

"What I have to decide is whether I should judge your family harshly for looking after your interests above mine? Frankly, I suppose I should not, although, being a straightforward sort of chap, I should've been given the facts of the matter in a proper manner and not by means of trickery."

Elizabeth looked up at John with curiosity, noticing how he refused to speak any longer without due care. Yet, he dwelled too much on the actions of others and not enough on her. He also spoke without love, holding caution foremost that incited none of the unselfishness of passion that often accompanies relationships.

"But, enough of me," he added at last, breaking free of confusion. "Forgive me, but I have to ask. How do you feel now strange and unforeseen circumstances have contrived to win you the day, to bring me to heel? Do you feel satisfaction?"

"Actually, I feel nothing but humiliation. I can't speak for the rest."

"Do you?"

"You doubt me again? See here, John, everything is not as it should be. Unity is my greatest joy and my most dreadful responsibility. I say that truthfully, not out of resentment for her, but out of love for all my family. I am, as yet, to discover whether having Unity will cause me to be abandoned by them." She shuddered at the lie. It went unnoticed. "Let there be no mistake, for I will not hold deception over Unity's life. The entire evening was a sham, but it was their sham, not mine. They didn't ever want me to come back to the village after she was born, but, in my weakness and ignorance of not knowing how to live without the support of others, I tried to force reconciliation upon them. It was that event that has led to tonight's fiasco."

"And this attitude persists?"

"I think it might," she added plaintively, knowing reconciliation had already begun.

"What can I do?" he petitioned.

"Do whatever you want. You are free to be the man you chose to be."

"As to that, I am uncertain who that fellow is anymore. I feel like a new-born babe, trying to comprehend an outside world so strangely and suddenly thrust upon it after the comfort of the womb. But, I know this much. I shall help in all ways with Unity, whether she is mine or not. It just depends on whether I do it as a father or as a friend to you."

She hung her head. "You still doubt my word?"

"Wiser men than me would have doubt. You are disarmingly beautiful, Elizabeth, so I would be wrong to believe no other gentlemen have noticed you. I, for my part, do not hold myself upon any such pedestal. Yet, the antithesis to this is that if I was a total mediocrity, your parents would not wish me upon you or Unity under any circumstances, father or not. And, without wishing to put words into your mouth, I rather feel you too would be of the same general opinion. And so, because I am not a mediocrity, I have to consider all things. Even if I take your account of that February evening as being faultless, I have to ask myself why you remember any more of it than I do, if, as you say, we were equal in drunkenness?"

"There is no reason I should," she replied sadly, "I just do. You have no proof of my virtue, beyond my solemn word. If that is not good enough, then we should end our conversation here and you should leave me as a licentious woman."

John reeled at the challenge.

"Look," she advanced, "it isn't something you can decide now, so stop beating yourself for an instant answer. Stop driving yourself to distraction. You are not having to choose between a pound of topside and a lamb chop from the butchers. This is life changing in more ways than you can ever imagine. I am not going anywhere, at least not at present, God and my parents willing. There is time enough for you to take it all in and be rational in your choices. I have had that time, nine months of it, in fact. Now, it is your turn. I shall stand by your decision, whatever that is, knowing you to be a good and fair man. If you abandon me, and I say *me* as I know you will always help Unity as a guardian, then no animosity will ever pass between us. If you take another view, I can promise you this. I will love you for the rest of my life, as I have already loved you for more years than I care to remember."

"Hang about. If I recall correctly, only a few moments ago you said that if I rejected fatherhood you would never speak my name inside or outside the house?"

"I lied!"

"Have you really loved me for so long?"

"For heaven's sake, John, are all men so obtuse, so wrapped in fast carriages, hounds and sport? Of course I have loved you, and still do. My recklessness in telling you this comes only from the terror I feel if, now, we never see each other again, even in friendship. Unity will grow to love you, too."

"If that is so, then I am the only star in the sky not ready to form a constellation. Strangely, I will gladly admit to warming to Unity Isobel already. Whether this is the result of her name or her little wrinkled face, I cannot say with any certainty. I suppose, now that there is a chance she is mine, I feel somewhat closer to her. But, that is entirely different from acceptance of fatherhood. If she is not mine, or I cannot believe it, I vow anyway to be her protector, for she may never have another to call upon."

"There is also another star in the heavens waiting to form a constellation with you, John."

"Another?"

"You really do put the horse before the hounds. Don't men ever see what stares them squarely in the face? It's Emmeline, you dope. She adores you."

"What absolute rot!"

"Is it? I speak as a woman about a woman. I despair of you, John. Are you so much out of touch with the fairer sex that you see nothing further away than the end of your nose? You have two women who crave your admiration. The question is, do you want either?"

With the unselfish words passing from her lips, Elizabeth turned away and busily attended to Unity's needs. The audience over, John closed the door quietly as he left.

Downstairs, the rest of the Grant family waited anxiously for news. Nobody spoke and yet, as the minutes passed, so their expectations began to grow. Dialogue meant progress, and progress might be indicative of understanding. The question on everyone's lips was, had Elizabeth the guile to judge John's mood correctly? Would he best respond to contrition or reproach?

At last, John's footsteps could be heard on the stairs.

As John's final duty of the evening was to collect Emmie, he walked determinedly into the dining room, already holding her wrap and hat. Harriet, Jeremiah and Daniel smiled invitingly, hoping for a summary of events just past. But, John gave no such account. Instead, he thanked each individually for a pleasant party and hurried away. The Grants sat back, bewildered.

Emmie struggled to keep pace as they stepped briskly towards the awaiting carriage, her arm held firmly. She could hardly believe the abruptness of their departure. The outside was bitter, bathed in a chilling mist. The carriage door was slammed shut and the driver clambered onboard. With the horses reined in and a flick of the whip, the carriage rattled away over the loose stones and down the long drive.

Straining to look back towards the house through the mist, Emmie expected to see the Grants forming a row of open mouths framed within a window. They were not and she sat back. Whatever had gone on within the walls, it was a secret to the outside world.

"Don't ask," said John with firmness as the carriage crunched its way along the drive.

"I didn't say anything!"

"You were about to."

"Ha!"

Emmie sneaked one last backwards glance as they turned the corner and moved onto the road. But, the house was lost to the weather.

"They didn't talk to me after you went upstairs," she grumbled as she settled. "Even Collins gave me a sour look."

"Not a glad eye from Daniel, either? I won't ask what he was doing under the table that bewitched you during dinner, but it was hard not to notice something was amiss. I think that's why you were sent on the tour."

Emmie blushed. "You would've thought he might've made a bit of an effort with me, but he was as preoccupied as the rest in whatever you were doing up there. It seemed you were gone for hours. Still," she added smugly, "I helped myself to all the dates, as nobody cared a fig about me. I took this, too." She handed him a small bunch of mistletoe that had been hanging above the dining room door. "Waste not, want not!" she exclaimed through a sardonic grin. "I'm sure we can find good use for it."

"What an evening!" said John without regard to Emmie's suggestive tones, holding the twigs indifferently.

Emmie gave up. "You said nothing about seeing them again before Christmas. I think everyone noticed."

John felt in his pocket for his travelling diary, a discreet little book no larger than a calling card holder. He opened it at Christmas week. The pages were empty. "I don't know if I can."

"Really? What's wrong? Something's up, I know. I can see it in your face. Can I help at all?"

"Yes, by remaining quiet and allowing my brain to think."

Nothing more was said until the carriage turned off the road and onto the drive descending to Wheat Sheaf Farm, where the driver opened the white gates by the light of the vehicle's oil lamps. A few yards further and the carriage came to a final halt. The driver leapt down to open the door and unfold the step. Money exchanged hands and the carriage pulled away.

Emmie hurried towards the house, but John stood motionless, looking up. All was dark, a blue-black of almost perfect uniformity, as uninviting as the air was raw. Yet, by straining he could see how the sky was bejewelled by a tiny number of perfectly defined stars defying the general blackout. Only the constellation of Orion was complete. John's eyes then fell onto the other houses in the locality, their chimneys wafting little clouds of grey smoke. And in the distance the carriage lamps could still be seen, incandescent glows with hazy halos, becoming ever smaller.

"Can we go inside, John, the cold is chilling my bones?"

"I'm sorry, Emmie, I was preoccupied. Fancy joining me in a mug of hot chocolate?"

"If the stove's still warm, I will. Otherwise, I'm for my bed and the comfort of thick blankets."

Remarkably, the stove still glowed with red embers and responded quickly to a few dry logs carefully stacked on top. John made the drinks and the two sat cosily together, cupping the mugs in their hands and enjoying the first waves of warmth.

"This takes me back a while," remembered John in good cheer, trying to push darker thoughts to the back of his mind that could wait for the clarity of morning.

"Really?"

"It does, to a time when my mother was still alive. I had been out in a cart with Christabel and we had a bit of a near accident."

"Oh!"

"No, let me complete my tale. She had grazed her hand on a wheel. After the wound was cleaned, we sat on this very spot listening to endless stories recounted by Mother, telling of when Jack Mere used to come to our home. She bored us both to death, bless her. I now look back at my impetuous ways and shudder."

"I remember Chrissy telling me that same story."

"Did she remember it as I do?"

"Pretty well. She told me you were a lovely man of low self esteem."

"She said that? How ridiculous."

"Maybe I'm mistaken in what she meant. She also said, you were so anxious not to leave a bad impression that night, you wouldn't let her go to bed."

He felt crushed by Emmie's words, although his own recollections were similar. He had hoped Christabel had viewed the episode differently. Clearly, she had not.

"I made a complete ass of myself."

Emmie put her warm hand on his in comfort. "No, John, you made her feel special for the first time in her life. Oh, she did think you were rather silly at first. She told me so. Especially when you tried to make out that you were well occupied in business, when all along you were idling in bed or riding out to see friends. Daniel and Elizabeth, I suppose. But, first impressions pass."

"Evidently she saw straight through that ruse too."

"Is it important? In the end she loved you. There can be no question of that. You did something right."

He looked into the stove. "*Remember me as a flame in your heart.*"

"Sorry?" replied Emmie.

"Oh, something and nothing. Take no notice of my ramblings."

"Then, I'm for my bed. Thank you for the evening."

"Was it fun?"

"*Strange* is the word I would use, remembering how it started and ended."

"You are feeling better now, aren't you? No ill-effects from the barrel?"

"None at all."

"I shall have a word with Fanny and the others tomorrow."

"Oh, please don't. It's cleared the air and I'd prefer to let sleeping dogs lie."

"As you wish."

Emmie hovered by the door indecisively.

"Anything else on your mind?" he enquired, not wanting to keep her.

"As a matter of fact there is. Can I ask what my punishment will be for going into the private room? Only, I won't sleep if I don't know."

"Maybe this once, Emmie, you have suffered enough. The matter is closed. Goodnight."

She left. John stayed by the stove until all flames had gone and the room became unbearably cold. Putting his coat around his shoulders for the quick dash up to the bedroom, he realised something quite shattering, which overcame any immediate discomfort. For the first time since Christabel died, he actually had a reason for living. It came in the little form of Unity Isobel Grant. Yet, life without Chistabel still struck terror into his heart, the room casting its own deep shadow of memories. But, perhaps, it really was time to let go, to let Unity fill his waking thoughts and take Elizabeth properly to his bed. Christabel had said in her crushed and wounded state that she welcomed release from this life in the sure knowledge that one day he would look for her in heaven. Since then he had only known hell. Would Christabel understand if he tried to love again, or should he die of a broken heart?

CHAPTER 15

·

New Year resolutions

For the next few days, John was rarely at home during daylight hours. He missed evening meals too, without any prior arrangement, and could be heard closing the front door quietly as he re-entered at a late hour. In this situation of mystery, meals prepared and fires set were invariably left to languish. On the few occasions their paths crossed, John was polite to Emmie but unwilling to stop and talk.

When completely sure she was alone, Emmie occasionally sneaked a look into his room, finding the bed straightened by his own hands or, perhaps, lying unused, a thick blanket cast carelessly on the occasional chair. The different ways the blanket laid across the arms indicated use. She also noticed the mistletoe lying abandoned on the table, its leaves drying and the berries showing the first signs of collapse.

On the morning of 18th December, slightly brighter and warmer than recently experienced, Emmie was outside beating dust from rugs when Fanny came rushing up. Emmie panicked, as the silent truce established between herself and the workers in the dormitory had made her existence at the farm a lonely one.

"Emmie," panted Fanny breathlessly, "I've come to ask if the master be back?"

Emmie replied that she never knew when he would be home and had no idea where he went.

"Only," Fanny continued, "there be rumours suggesting he be going backwards and forwards to Sherborne and Glastonbury and places between searching for my Abel."

"Why would he do that?"

"I don't know. Not usual behaviour."

The truth was somewhat different. John had been to all these places, riding hard and fast to cover ground quickly, but finding Abel working as a lime burner at Canal Wharf in Glastonbury had been a happy coincidence rather than the purpose for all the rushing about. Nevertheless, the unexpected meeting gave him the opportunity to address an injustice.

He had first caught sight of a white figure of familiar shape while walking his horse along a towpath. At the time, Abel was leaning against two stacks of wicker tubs, surrounded by various ladders and a large grading sieve. He was standing, but asleep.

"By heaven, Master Tucker," shouted John to wake him. "Is that really you or a ghost in my midst?"

"Oh, Mr Madden," he sighed, 'tis me alright, somewhere beneath all the powder."

John secured the horse to a railing and marched the short distance with his hand outstretched. Seeing him approaching, Abel removed the cap he had recently purchased in a sale, where a thousand hats and caps had been offered at half the maker's recommended price, but which already looked well-used.

"I'll not shake 'ee hand and make 'ee dirty," said Abel apologetically, "but we will assume it be done in fine fellowship."

"Are you well? Only, it's unusual to see people asleep half way through the working day."

"Never better, Sir. As to sleeping, I can't help myself. I'm so used to having a quick nap in the afternoon after starting early at the farm, I can't break the habit. Why, the other day Mister Ellis found me asleep when he brought down a large pork pie for dinner. It was accompanied by his usual griping, rather than any delicious sweet pickle of the type I used to enjoy at the farm. He poked me with the end of a broom handle to rouse me. Me jaded eyes saw the pork pie, so I swallowed a large lump and immediately fell over again. I don't rightly know what's happening to me. I've never been so lazy before."

"Drink plenty of water or beer, Abel, that's my advice."

"'Ee could be right, Sir. I can feel the heat sucking water from me body."

"Damn you Abel," came an angry yell from above. "Have you gone to sleep again, you bloody waster? The burner hasn't been lit."

"If 'ee will excuse me a moment, Sir, I need to light these twigs and push them in the eye."

"Whose eye?" John exclaimed with horror. "Not his, I hope?"

"A good joke, Sir," was his cheerful reply as he put a match to the bundle. "Why, the eye be the name given to the fire grate under this heavy iron door." He lifted the door and thrust the burning twigs inside, then sealed the gap to ensure slow burning. He wiped away any lime transferred from the handle to his hands, causing a white smear across his waistcoat.

"Is it done, you good-for-nothing malingerer?" the man called.

"Just done, Mister Ellis. 'Tis started nicely."

"Taken your time about it, you bloody idle ne'er-do-well." A head appeared from the loft wearing a tight-fitting hat, hanging upside down from the shoulders. "Now, get out of my sight, Abel, you slack-crooked, half-baked mooncalf." Noticing John he doffed his cap, which fell to the floor. "Begging your pardon, Sir, but business is business."

Abel turned casually to John, knowing the fire would catch quickly and no more would be said. "Don't mind him, Sir. That's how he speaks to everyone. He be a proper bald bastard and no mistake, who thinks he's higher and mightier then everyone else. He's right about the half-baked bit, though. 'Tis a mighty hot job, and a proper mucky one."

John, dressed in a fashionable tweed suit and high leather boots, provided as good a contrast in lifestyles as could be imagined. He looked around the inside of the works without moving.

"From the open air to this dreadful place, Abel. What are you thinking?"

"Needs must, Mr Madden, when the belly rumbles. 'Tis the only other trade I know, other than tushing. But, I couldn't find a farm with heavy horses wanting an extra hand to drag logs to the saw pit. There's no hiring at farms at present and probably won't be until the next Candlemas hiring fair in February. And even then, if I not be chosen straight away by a farmer or agent and given a fastening penny to seal the deal, it could be weeks later when I get employment at a runaway mop fair, along with all the other lame ducks."

"With a letter of recommendation, Abel, you'll be snapped up. You didn't wait for one. I could write it now."

"I suppose 'ee could and I will get a better job, but that's for later use and we be here and now."

"I don't like to see you reduced to this."

"No matter, Sir. 'Tis regular work and I be remarkably happy living in a town where there's a lot going on. That's been a big surprise, me being a country bumpkin born and bred."

"There was nothing else available?"

"A place making top hats had a vacancy. But the workers there are as mad as hatters."

"What do you mean?"

"Mad hatters, don't 'ee know the expression? They use mercury in hat making, which turns some of them barking crazy. No, I'm better off here. At least I keep me sanity, for what it's worth."

"Won't you accept my apologies and return to Nether Bow? We need you."

"I accept the goodwill with pleasure," he offered in peace, "but me mind be to stay here."

"Get about your work, Abel, if you don't want to feel the end of my fist again," bawled Ellis. "I'll dock you half a day for this."

"That's not how I treated you," said John, angrily.

"No, Sir, it isn't. A proper gent are 'ee to everyone."

"I didn't have to be harsh, Abel. Everyone knew their role and carried it out fairly and properly."

"That's me only concern about here, Sir. He be a terrible hard task master who now wants me to work on Sundays to meet high demand for the lime. He offers more money, right enough, but that's not really the point, be it?"

"Isn't it?" questioned John. "No, I suppose it can't be if he gives with one fist and takes it away with the other."

"'Ee don't understand, Sir. I'm no church-going man, as 'ee knows, but I hold the Christian faith hard in me soul. I don't believe in all that stuff about 'where two or three be gathered together'. I feel I can pray silently anywhere I wish and, if God be compassionate, I'll be heard. It means God and I can be proper strangers for weeks on end, but, when I feel the need to ask for His help or thank Him for me bounties, I'm sure I be forgiven any lapses. So, the question be, can I work in all faith on the Sabbath? What do 'ee think, Sir?"

"I'm entirely the wrong man to ask. You must look to your own conscience." He watched Abel in his silent composure and admired him greatly. "Anyway, tell me how this thing works, if you will."

"Oh, 'tis a simple enough process, Sir, as old as history itself. We just do it in grand scale. We heat limestone in the kiln. Simple. Shells also work well, believe it or not, but 'ee needs vast numbers of the slippery things to get a return and they be hard to shovel. The slow heat changes the composition, whatever that means, leaving the white powder behind that can be gathered up and used with horse hair to combine plaster and mortar. Of course, it has lots of other uses too, but around here most of the stuff be used for building. We can get eleven hundredweight of good quality lime from every ton of raw material after eight hours in the kiln. Takes an awful lot of shovelling to move it, I can tell 'ee, and we have to be extra careful not to get it in our eyes or throat. 'Tis not at all like the little bit of burning I did at home."

"You said *home*."

"I meant the farm, Sir. I still think of it that way."

"Goodness, Abel, listen to yourself. Is this really what you want? Only, I have apologised and you are welcome to return to the farm at any time. Fanny misses you, too."

"Nice try, Sir, but Fanny be only a distraction. I don't deep-down love her, although I like her an awful lot. No, I will stay 'ere a while at least, find me feet and decide what to do in the New Year."

"Does she know how you feel? I rather got the impression you two were very close."

"We are, Sir, and no mistake, but she has been too quick to see long-term in it. I'll get that sorted in the New Year, too."

"Another New Year resolution?"

"Sorry, Sir, but I don't know what 'ee means by that."

"You're a wicked man, Abel, leading her on."

"Actually, if I may be so bold, I think I'm a complete failure as a wicked man. Contrarywise, as to being a young man experiencing the sea when it laps over me feet of its own accord, well, that I'll admit to."

John added his laughter to Abel's while pulling on his gloves. "No matter," he said, slapping his back and causing a small cloud of dust to rise. He took a few silver coins from his pocket. "Here, you earned these."

Abel looked into his palm. "It's too much, Sir."

"I rather feel it isn't enough. Be well, Abel." He offered his hand.

"Better not, Sir. Remember the lime."

"Hang your concern, my friend. Take my hand good and firm, for I want to shake yours and wish you a merry Christmas."

John glanced backwards as he strode to his horse, expecting to see Abel waving. But, Abel was already asleep, his head firmly lodged between two sacks of hay.

"Extraordinary," muttered John.

On the 19th, with just six days to go before Christmas, John made it known that he was back at the farm after his travels. All the workers were summoned to a meeting. He had considered talking to Emmie separately, but decided it was far better for her relationship with the other workers to be treated equally.

They gathered in the dormitory, where Emmie stood alone in the doorway.

"Come on in," said Mark, beckoning her forward with his hand. "What's past 'tis gone."

"I'll stay here," she replied with unease, unsure if they could be trusted.

John arrived and immediately asked Emmie to sit with the rest, as he had no intention of raising his voice. She obliged meekly, sitting in the corner.

"First things first, I have added a few shillings to your pay to mark Christmas. You all have exactly the same as a bonus, no matter what you do on the farm." This was greeted with much pleasure. "Now, we come to more pressing issues. Oh, and while I remember, you might be interested to know this. The day before yesterday I spoke to Abel Tucker. He is well and sends his regards. He works in Glastonbury and is much settled."

"Only his regards?" cried Mark to Fanny as he nudged her in the back. "Why, that won't warm your bed much this Christmas."

"Be quiet!" commanded John, attentive to Fanny's feelings and alone in knowing how Abel truly felt. "I feel abhorrence for the general lack of grace sometimes shown for the feelings of others in this dormitory. My New Year resolution will be to root out any such bad blood. A happy work force is an efficient one."

"One bad apple spoils the rest. Is that what you say, Sir," said Mark once again, this time drawing Fanny's attention towards Emmie, "for I don't understand what 'abhorrence' means?"

"If that is intended to be another cynical remark against someone present, Master Gladtide, you may well be the first to feel the wrath of my resolution, which could come especially early for your benefit. Do I make myself plain?"

There was silence.

"I said, do I make myself clear?"

"Yes, Sir," came the reply.

"Good, then we move on." He looked at his notes, hastily penned on a scrap of paper. "Christmas money, done. Bad behaviour, done. Ah, now we come to Christmas itself. It is my intention to spend Christmas away."

Emmie lowered her stare to the floor.

"I have important matters to attend which are best served by my presence elsewhere. In so much as my decision will affect you, I have a new bailiff starting on the 21st. I have given him full authority. He will live in the little cottage over the road. You won't know him. His name is Cornelius Fairfax."

"Cornelius tooty-toot!" scoffed Mark without thinking, as was his usual manner to be quick to see the funny side of life." Then, realising his mistake, he turned desperately to John in apology.

John let it go, for he, too, found the name rather amusing.

"I had hoped to poach Samuel Nash from the big estate the other side of Muddleford, but he showed admirable loyalty to his present employer and I couldn't get him. Fortunately, my solicitor knew of a likely candidate from talking to a colleague practising at Brockhampton. Anyway, I have retained him, this Cornelius fellow. He is a gentleman farmer once of Chard. I am concerned that his general knowledge of farming is incomplete, but he is used to handling people despite his young age and will command respect amongst you. It is a short-term contract, until I find someone more suitable. Whatever he says is gospel. I will not question his decisions, including, Mr Gladtide, any matter of hiring and firing. Do I need to say more on the subject?"

They shook their heads.

"Finally, we come to Christmas day itself. With the stock to attend and other pressing work, the only person I can spare over the festival is Emmeline Sturry. The rest of you must plough on as usual, although I have ordered several geese and plum puddings for you all to enjoy as a reward, and hired a cook to prepare the feast. As I may not be using the house, Emmeline alone has the choice to stay or go to see relatives." He rose. "I think that's everything. Carry on."

"When do you intend to leave, if you do?" asked Emmie quietly.

He turned at her voice. "I will speak to you later. It wasn't my intention to single you out, but private things between us need to be said."

"Really?"

For Emmie in her expectations, the day seemed to be one of never ending disappointment. She watched as John came and went around the farm, never hurried and never indicating why he wanted private words. It was an unbearable period, with her entire future seemingly balanced on a knife edge.

As the sun gradually set on the day and she began her round of grate cleaning and fire lighting, John finally called her into the kitchen. He had two cups of tea waiting, steaming in the chill air.

"I have lit the fire in the drawing room, Sir. Would you like to sit there for warmth?"

He declined, indicating that he had, indeed, put a match to the stove only seconds before and was waiting to see the first signs of life. She sat by him, cupping the brew and shivering.

"I expect you've been wondering what it is I have to say?"

"I haven't given it a second's thought, Sir," she replied, hoping her demeanour would not betray her true feelings.

"That's good," he replied. "The thing is, Emmie, I find myself in a confounded mess. If my mother was still alive, I would ask her advice. As it is, I have been travelling around Wessex to meet up with old friends and seek their guidance, amongst other business. It is a matter of some considerable unease to me."

"Does it concern marriage, Sir?"

"How the devil would you know that?"

"A guess," she replied shyly.

"It was talk of Christabel that set my mind racing. It made me think of all that I have missed in my life as a bachelor. I quite like solitude, or at least solitude and I have become enforced bed-fellows. Yet, many things have happened recently to make me reconsider my position."

"Yes, Sir?"

"For goodness sake, Emmie, why do you flit so easily between 'Sir' and my real name? It makes me talk to you differently, depending on the hat you place on my head at any particular moment. My name is John. I have told you to call me John time and time again. There is more to us than employer and employee."

"Is there . . . John?" she asked excitedly.

"Well, of course there is. We both know what passes between us, don't we?"

"I was hoping so."

"There. I was right. Anyhow, the facts of the matter are these."

Over the next fifteen minutes, John recounted all that had taken place in secret at the home of the Grant family. He told her of Elizabeth's recollections of that February night and of Unity Isobel's birth. Throughout, Emmie's heart jumped from hurt to panic, crisis to catastrophe. By the time the soliloquy ended, her spirit was utterly crushed.

"And so, I have to decide whether to take Elizabeth's word for it or . . . Actually, I'm not sure there is an 'or'. Isn't the welfare of the baby enough to make me do the right thing by her, whether blood related or not? You know what people are like and how they judge a fatherless infant by the sins of the parents."

With her dreams shattered, her forbearance stretched to breaking point, she bowed her head and asked if she could leave.

"What is it, Emmie? Don't be so distressed by *my* problems. At least they're not yours." He offered his handkerchief to wipe her eyes. She pressed it to her nose, tears running unabated.

"What is it? Please tell me. Do you think of Christabel, perhaps?"

She raised her stare, flushed with grief. "No, Sir, I think only of myself."

"None of this affects you. Your job is safe."

"You mock me, taunt me."

"I do?" he replied in astonishment.

"You don't know, do you? You have no idea," she said hastily, her words muffled by the handkerchief. "We share so much and have endured so much together. I am not at all surprised when the name Christabel is mentioned so regularly in your conversations. I understand all that she meant to you, for I feel a different kind of loss that is, nonetheless, almost as deep. But, John, can't you see, I could love you equally to her."

He was visibly shocked, paralysed, by the entreaty. She continued.

"Did it not occur to you that our mutual suffering provides a bond between us? Are we not suited by our common agony?"

John hardly knew how to reply. "Surely, you're not serious?" he blurted, his thoughts hazed in disbelief.

"Any man other than John Madden would know without requiring confirmation from a destroyed woman. You may be gentle and kind, but you have a blind spot where women are concerned."

"My God, Elizabeth said as much the night of the party. Is it true? Am I hurtful to all women?"

"You unknowingly deceive them by the care and attention you unselfishly give," she added, sniffing hard to end her tears. She wiped her nose on her sleeve and gave the handkerchief back. "If only I was born better, you would look more kindly on me."

That was too much. "Emmie, Emmie, Emmie, you are entirely mistaken. You know full well I have never been swayed by the graceful curve of high-fashioned hips, the perfect speaking voice of the idle wealthy, or the elegance of gracious living. I look deeper at womanhood, to what lies beneath. If the world was split between the 'have and have nots' and then again between the 'respectable and the shallow', such divisions would not be similarly composed. I, of all people, can vow to live to this philosophy by example."

"Then, why can't you see me as a wife?" she said dotingly.

"Because I do not love you, Emmie, and that is the butt of it. It is a matter of principle to marry only someone I actually love."

"She being Elizabeth Grant?"

He hesitated. "You have beaten my argument, but with her there are higher matters for concern."

"I could give you a child? I have good hips."

"No, Emmie, don't degrade yourself this way."

"Have you even kissed her?" she pleaded.

"Knowingly, you mean? In truth, only as a friend. Unknowingly, well . . . Who can tell anymore!"

"And have you ever kissed me, fully on the lips?"

"No, of course I haven't. Not even as a friend."

"Then why reject the bottle before tasting the wine." She gently closed her eyes and inclined her mouth towards his.

It was true that he was tempted by her willingness, if only because she offered him something that was, otherwise, quite beyond his immediate taking. It was seduction without consequence. With absence of mind he sat fast, watching as her face closed to his. His spine tingled in anticipation. As their lips met and her hand touched the back of his neck, he could taste the sweet essence of honey, alluring and soft.

"No!" he cried, pulling away. "This is entirely wrong. What am I thinking of? I won't take advantage when I know there's no future in it. I think better of you than that."

She shook her head with disappointment.

"I know what that look means, Emmie, and the answer remains *no*."

"But I ask nothing from you beyond a proper kiss between unattached persons. I am not offended one jot by your hesitation. It's rather sweet, in fact. But you miss the point. You're not taking advantage of me, John. I am offering myself to you. Where's the harm in that?"

"Please don't do this. I am baited beyond anything you can imagine, but it can't be allowed for both our sakes. It is one complication too many."

She shrank into the chair, rocking. He stood, kissed her gently on the top of her head and left the room. The fire in the stove suddenly flared into life, mocking her bitterness.

The next day was enacted in a strained atmosphere that was neither derision nor disgrace, but one which flouted the very notion of friendship, despairing of charm and devoid of anything beyond civility. In this strangeness, Emmie received an unexpected letter, hand delivered to the house. John thought it was probably from her parents and, believing it might cheer her, ordered Mark to find her quickly and hand it over.

Emmie was found in the scullery, where Mark read the lines aloud to the best of his ability. She was truly puzzled by the contents and, after some thought, scribbled a few words of her own on the back of the same piece of paper, asking if he would be kind enough to hand-deliver it back to the sender, due to its urgency. His natural reluctance to walk the few miles for someone he did not altogether like was quickly understood by Emmie, who reminded him of his involvement in her terrifying ordeal with the barrel and how the master had asked her to spill the names of the ring-leaders. The note was duly redelivered, as requested.

That afternoon, John saw Emmie sitting alone on a wall outside the kitchen. His first reaction was to give her a wide berth, not wishing to disturb her thoughts, but, noticing that she was merely kicking her legs against a bucket, he approached. She looked up without expression.

"Did you get it?"

"If you mean the letter, Sir, I did."

"Oh, we're back to 'Sir', are we? No matter, if that's how you want it. Anyway, was it good news?" he asked in carefree fashion.

"Depends on your point of view, I suppose," she replied in prickly tone.

He understood her implied indifference and chose to ignore it. "Oh, well, carry on."

Emmie watched until he disappeared into the house, angry at how little she meant to him. He had not even cared enough to pursue the enquiry, confirming that she was, undoubtedly, nothing more than a domestic in his eyes.

With that thought firmly fixed, she looked for Mark, offering him a kiss if he delivered another letter. He was unimpressed and said so, although he professed to 'warming' to her a little for not having squealed to the master. He begged her not to tell Fanny of this change of mood. Emmie agreed to keep it their secret.

"I have a wicked suggestion, Mark Gladtide."

"You do, Emmeline Sturry?"

"I do that. Only, you've got to understand exactly what I am offering without me saying the exact words."

"How's that?"

"Oh, shut up!" She pulled him close by the scruff of the neck and planted a long, moist and passionate kiss. It was clear to both that this represented merely a down payment if he did her further bidding as a private postman.

"By heaven, Emmie, you certainly know how to kiss. Where did you learn to do it like that?"

She grinned seductively. "I'm not without experience. If you liked it, just think what awaits your late return to the farm. Perhaps, I might even think of something more if it's a cold walk."

"Alright, Emmie, but don't mistake me for your lap-dog. Walking to Matchcomb twice in a day is payback enough for any part in your troubles. After that, we're quits. Do you promise that will be the end of it?"

She made that promise. That night Mark was late to bed.

For John and Emmie, the following morning looked set to be a repeat of the previous. He had left his bed late and was surprised to find no hot water to be had. On further inspection, he discovered the breakfast table had not been laid either. He called for Emmie. An empty silence greeted the rally. He looked in the drawing room and outside in the courtyard, but she was nowhere to be found. Cursing his stupidity, he leapt up the stairs three at a time and, after knocking, entered her room. The bed was made and the room was tidy, and in the corner sat Emmie, a packed bag resting by her feet. She was wearing her best straw hat.

"I don't need to ask what's happening, do I, Emmie?" he said, the corners of his lips sunk but his voice maintaining some semblance of calm.

She was beyond answering, but instead placed a note into his hand. As he unfolded the paper, she pushed past and ran along the landing. He watched her leave without knowing what to do. He could hear her bag bumping on the treads and risers as she descended the stairs.

"This is not as it should end, Emmie," he mouthed, not wanting to be heard.

Dropping the letter, he ran to a front window and watched as she walked away from the farm, leaving the white gates open. She stopped unexpectedly, turned, and looked up towards the window where he hid behind the netting. Although he could not be seen, she just knew he was there. She gave a little wave of farewell. A low wind suddenly blew, causing leaves to swirl around her.

As the wind rushed away through the leafless trees, she fancied she could make out a voice repeating words in ghostly tone, a voice she had heard before while tending the graves of the Mere family at Shalhurn.

"*God bless thee for going, this day and for always*," it repeated until it faded into the distance, the leaves settling once more on the path.

Despite misgivings, Emmie knew she had made the right decision. It had to be faced. John was Christabel's and nobody else's. Thus accepted, a spring came into her step as she considered Elizabeth's likely similar fate, which she would anticipate with glee. It cheered her immeasurably. She burst into a run, happy to start a new chapter in her life, while knowing she and John had unfinished business.

CHAPTER 16

The gentleman farmer

*E*mmie's scribbled note to John, although poorly written and generously sprinkled with spelling errors, spilled over with emotion. Nothing was left to be imagined. After reading it, John's arm fell to his side in despair. He felt tremendous guilt towards her, mixed with anger that she could so readily deride Unity as an '*elegitamat basturd*' with no real Pa. Whatever she felt, it was an irresistible fact that somewhere in the world was Unity's true father and, in all likelihood, that person filled his trousers at Nether Bow. The note did not specify her destination, but he assumed it was to be Stirminster Oak, where her parents lived.

As John threw the note into the bin, little did he know how quickly Emmie had got over such vile sentiments, disparagingly written during the night in the darkest moments of indignation. Indeed, she was already planning her future with the most unexpected of patrons.

Deeply hurt by Emmie's departure, but still with a farm to run, John idled away the rest of the day while waiting impatiently for Cornelius Fairfax to arrive. Although no definite time had been agreed, common sense dictated that it should be in daylight. In the event, his knock came a full hour after the sun had set, making any immediate explanations of farm practices pointless. Instead, a simple introduction to the cottage and dormitory had to suffice for the day. Nevertheless, John welcomed him with due affability and helped in the unloading of his belongings from the gig.

"Who should I ask to tend my horse?" enquired Cornelius, as the last two boxes were dumped on the cottage floor.

"Nobody," was John's forthright reply, mopping his brow. "This is a working farm, not an estate park for the pleasure of its owners. Everyone here has a role, and I keep nobody spare to run around after the whims of the employees themselves, of which you are but the newest."

"Wait up, I thought I was contracted as bailiff. Doesn't that give me certain advantages?"

"It most certainly does. You may sit at the head of the table when eating with the others. I can't think of anything else, off hand."

Cornelius looked at him with earnest surprise.

"I see you are perplexed, Mr Fairfax. Please don't be. I have a simple set of values. My philosophy is that a good bailiff achieves discipline by example. There can be no room for indulgent makeweights, whether in thought or deed. Nobody can be independent from the needs of the farm."

"I am in charge, aren't I?"

"Of course you are, and the workers will follow your every instruction to the letter or face the consequences, but only in so far as farm work is concerned. Beyond that, you are your own man and must tend to your own personal needs."

"I see. I just thought, well, being a gentleman farmer yourself, you would understand the need for a certain pecking order."

"Afraid not. I'm a liberal employer."

"Naturally, I am a Tory."

"And so you are, my good Mr Fairfax, and so you are. I never doubted it for a moment. You will find an empty stable behind the church. The gig may be wheeled into the back barn. More importantly for your own welfare, you will find the larder in the cottage well stocked for tonight with a steak pie, cheese, bread and much else besides. You will want for nothing. Now, if we are finished, I will bid you a very good evening."

"Before you go, Mr Madden, what time shall I start in the morning? I need to know what is expected of me, as I have travelled far today and would prefer not to rise before I am needed."

"What time is usual for you?"

"Early. I am an early riser. It's good to see daybreak. My bed is invariably empty by nine o'clock."

"Here daybreak comes before the first postman, Mr Fairfax, Summer or Winter. We observe no differences in the seasons, being somewhat short-staffed. What can't be done outside, in the dark, can wait while inside fixes and mends are undertaken. I would expect the bailiff to be the first up, to set an example to the rest of the workers, who would dearly love to stay in their bunks until at least half an hour past six o'clock. Still, I take your point and suggest that tomorrow you take advantage of a late rising. Let's say seven o'clock for you, shall we, although by then you will have missed first breakfast. From then on, you should be up fifteen minutes before six o'clock. And, while we are talking of meals, you should know that everyone in the dormitory takes a turn to prepare them, whether billeted in the women's room or the men's. The open space between is common to both. Our last bailiff lived in the dormitory with the others, but I can make no exception to this cooking custom just because I rent you a separate cottage. Can you cook for many mouths, Mr Fairfax?"

"I don't know. I've never tried."

"Then, good luck to you. Oh, and a word to the wise, as one bachelor to another. The secret of good cooking lies in getting the stove nice and hot. Allow yourself an extra twenty minutes or so to light the fire in the range on the days you cook and to collect fresh eggs by the basketful. The range can be slow to draw and may need relighting more than once, especially this time of year when the kindling is inclined to be damp. You'll soon get the hang of our ways. And, if I'm not around to guide you through our routines, ask Mark Gladtide. But watch out for his practical jokes, especially now that it's near Christmas. He usually sends newcomers to the village for a tin of elbow grease and a china hammer. Now, I leave the good running of our little ship in your hands. Steer it well." John smiled inwardly as he walked away, stopping after a few paces to see Cornelius standing with his hand on his head, bewildered at having to tend his own horse and still rise at seven. "Oh, and one more thing while I think of it, just to satisfy my curiosity. I hope you don't mind me asking, but what did you farm in Chard? You never did say in your correspondence."

"Mostly flying machines."

"Goodness! Is there a growing market? Do they fly off the shelves?"

"I'm sorry? I don't understand. I said flying machines, as in winged wooden models that fly."

"Do they make good eating?" he added sardonically. "Only, I thought the purpose of a farm was to produce food of one type or another. For my part, and talking of winged things, I'm partial to the odd duck or pheasant if I can bag one. They fly!" He could see Cornelius was totally befuddled. "Don't concern yourself, dear boy. It's just my humour. I've already been told you mess about inventing things with twisted rubber. What about food, though? Did you grow anything on the farm to be sold and eaten?"

"Not really. A bit of soft fruit, I suppose."

"Soft fruit?"

"Grown in a walled garden."

"It's hardly proper farming, is it? Anything else? A few cereal crops, perhaps?"

"No."

"Dairy cows or beef cattle?"

"No."

"Fattening pigs or sheep?"

"No."

"Goats, hens, geese?"

"No."

"Carrots, cabbages, turnips?"

"No."

"Potatoes?"

"Nothing like that."

"Not even a few bees about the place to make honey?"

"Not even those."

"Just wooden flying machines."

"And a bit of fruit."

"Oh, yes, mustn't forget the fruit. You were hardly dedicated to farming, were you Cornelius Fairfax!"

"No, Mr Madden, I leave that to the likes of you. We can't all farm in the same way. Farming is all about diversity. Oh, I forgot, I also had a couple of ducks waddling about the place for their eggs. But, I restricted the number to two. They are so messy with their, you know, rear stuff!"

"Forgive my curiosity, but how did you manage to live?"

"Others better off than myself helped out. I hardly have a penny to my name, if truth be told, and conserve every farthing as if it is my last. Prudence is my watchword. You will never find me spending a half-penny on a job that otherwise I could do myself."

"Ah, generous parents, you mean!" observed John in a less than generous tone.

"Actually, yes. That is their function, after all, to maintain their offspring."

"You have made quite an admission, Cornelius. I think this job may do you a great deal more good than anything you will bring to the farm. At the very least, it will certainly conserve your father's bank balance."

John walked away, laughing and mumbling to himself. "Flying machines be damned. Crackpot! Still, I only need you for a very short time, which is just as well, I think." Before entering his house, he made a quick detour. Minutes later, he was home.

Having stabled his horse, Cornelius sought Mark Gladtide. He was found sitting by the range in the dormitory, enjoying the warmth it provided and smoking a long pipe, a jar of cider at his feet. The others had already retired to their beds.

Cornelius introduced himself, accepting a pull at the jar. "Mr Madden, what's he like? Does he always act strangely?"

"Best master I've ever 'ad," replied Mark from the comfort of a battered rocking chair that used to belong to Abel.

"I see. And just how many farmers have you worked for?"

"Only him."

"Oh! No matter. By the way, Mark, how are you with horses? Only, I have a grey and it could do with rubbing down and feeding. I could find a sixpence for your efforts!"

"The master says I am to tell you that I'm rubbish at it!"

"What? When did he tell you that?"

"Just a moment ago. You must've passed him on the way 'ere. You asked me what he is like. Well I tell you now. He's nobody's fool."

With no further point in delaying the inevitable, Cornelius walked peevishly to the stable. Mark put a hand into the well-worn pocket of his trousers, feeling for the shilling John had just given him.

CHAPTER 17

Patrons

Six days had passed since the Christmas party and the Grants were becoming increasingly concerned by John's unexpected absence. Jeremiah had wagered five pounds with Daniel on John making a return call the day after the gathering or the next at the latest, when he would openly declare honest devotion to Elizabeth and Unity. Then, after being asked for his daughter's hand in marriage, he would wholeheartedly agree to the proposal following due theatrical reflection. Indeed, he had instructed Elizabeth to keep herself dressed for such company on each of the intervening days, so sure had he been that events would follow his orchestrated path. Unfortunately, the deficiency of the main player had ruined the plan and Daniel had collected his winnings with uncharacteristic reluctance.

"Family, we must face the fact that John has abandoned us," said Jeremiah, carving the ham for luncheon. Each plate was given two slices, which Collins carried to those seated around the table. He stood in despair before carving his own meat, digging the knife point into the sallow flesh of the joint as a gesture of despondency. "We must forsake our happy expectations and now put into action an alternative strategy to see us through this difficult turn of events."

"Do you know what he's talking about, Mother?" asked Elizabeth with concern.

"Your father has not confided in me," she replied, turning to her husband in the hope of an explanation.

"Joyously, I can reveal that such a remedy may already be at hand," he continued. "As I see it, we have only two possible courses of action open to us to keep our good name from inevitable gossip among those who would delight in our distress."

"Father, how could you think it!" exclaimed Elizabeth perversely, throwing her napkin to the floor, sure that she was about to be sent away again.

Harriet understood the gesture and gave Jeremiah a look of daggers.

"Will you women control your tempers until I have finished! Only then, if you still feel so disposed, may you give me the customary tongue-lashing that a husband and father receives for trying to undo the errors of his grown family for the benefit of all." His stare, which had moved from one face to another during the telling, now fell uncompromisingly on his daughter. "And no, Elizabeth, neither plan involves me sending you away, if that's what you presume, at least, not in disgrace. Nothing is amiss. No, I have formulated entirely better ideas. One, which I hold in reserve, is to send you abroad on a tour of Europe. By the time you return, the Summer will be upon us and we can concoct some cock-and-bull story of you having married in France, but that your new husband died of some fever or other. I favour food poisoning from eating those detestable snails. It is acceptably believable. Anyhow, the manner of his death is unimportant. You may decide yourself upon the method of his sudden and sad demise. Choose whatever gives you the greatest pleasure, but also the most visible grief."

"I have never heard such rubbish," returned Daniel with derision. "I might be dim-witted, but even I know Elizabeth couldn't marry and have a child in six months. Nobody would be fooled by it and we would be the target of every contemptuous remark throughout Wessex for trying to carry out such a deception."

Jeremiah's nostrils flared. Harriet knew the signs and jumped to rescue the situation.

"It is the instinct of every parent to look after their own, Daniel. Your father is merely trying his utmost in a most difficult circumstance."

"Thank you, dear," returned Jeremiah, plainly endeavouring to hold his temper. "As for you, sonny boy, let me remind you of the seriousness of the issue, which must be decided according to the possibilities, and these are few." He sat, taking deep breaths.

"Are you well, husband?"

"I will be, when I recover my composure."

"See what you've done, Daniel? You must take more care of your father's condition."

"What condition?" he asked with tolerable warmth.

"Disappointment!"

"It is no use complaining about wading barefoot through a stream while bareheaded in the rain," remarked Collins from the side.

"Be quiet," scolded Harriet.

"No, listen to Collins," cut in Jeremiah, who turned to face her. "Is that meant to mean anything?" he asked, sure that it must.

"Pardon my interruption, Sir, Madam, but I only meant that if you have to tread a rocky path, there's no point in worrying about the nettles in the way."

"I'm sorry, Collins, but I still don't understand what you're getting at."

"If you have anything constructive to say, Collins, for goodness sake say it plainly."

"My pardon again, Madam. I am thinking that if an arm has to be cut off, there's no point to trimming the fingernails first."

Harriet looked to Daniel for explanation, Daniel to Elizabeth and Elizabeth to Jeremiah. All showed confusion except Jeremiah, who alone nodded gratefully.

"Capital. I knew you would come up trumps," clapped Jeremiah. "As Collins so clearly puts it, we mustn't get ahead of ourselves. Of course my plan would appear to have shortcomings at first glance, that is until it is remembered that Elizabeth has already been away from the district for many months without anyone knowing her circumstances, other than those gathered here. So, and I quote Collins now, we mustn't allow the detail of the plan to scuttle the plan itself. Am I not right, Collins?"

"You are, Sir."

"And John," added Harriet. "He knows."

"As does Nurse Trimby" said Elizabeth.

"Alright, there are flaws. We cannot account for the nurse, but I'm sure John isn't likely to contradict us in anything we say, knowing how he would be implicated in an ungentlemanly act. So, I repeat, to all intents and purposes we are alone in the knowledge. That gives us a great advantage, not least in fabricating timing. Who outside our circle would actually know when Elizabeth left for the continent? As far as the world in general is concerned, she might already have been there for months. Under such a ruse, a moiety of honesty could serve to disguise the other half of fable, so liberally entwined as to make the unabridged story believable. However, whilst I see this plan working, it has one distinct disadvantage. It does not solve the actual problem facing us, that Elizabeth needs a husband willing to accept Unity."

"And your second idea, Father," asked Elizabeth with renewed interest, believing the first was possible.

"I fear you would all shout me down in unison if I told you without first explaining a few wider issues. So, with a promise from you all not to interrupt, I will begin."

Everyone nodded.

"What about Collins, here? She has overheard everything."

"No, Madam, I pay no attention at all," was her polite, but ridiculous, reply.

"Thank you, Collins," said Jeremiah, "but you are as much

involved as anyone in our little deceptions. Even you cannot be expected not to know the things you already do know, or, indeed, dismiss your own contributions." He turned to his family. "So, it is my intention to allow Collins to share in everything and play her part. She knows the penalty for betrayal, don't you Collins?"

The servant stepped forward, said that she did, and stepped back to the wall.

"Right, well, this is my preferred plan, which I have given considerable thought to. It occurs to me that if John *has* decided not to marry Elizabeth, and all indications point to this, then the most likely other candidate for his affections is that little dairymaid, Emmeline something-or-other we met the other night. Do you agree?"

They agreed it was possible.

"Excellent, we are united so far. It seems strange to me that anyone in his position would look at her twice, but, then, he previously liked that other dairymaid and so anything is possible."

"Christabel," interrupted Daniel.

"Yes, that's the filly. So, we have to face the fact that John is partial to third class goods. I may be wrong, but I have a hunch he only brought Emmeline here to show her off, as a way of breaking the ice with us, his closest friends."

"You could be right, Jeremiah. Well, what an imposition!"

"Quite. Anyway, under the circumstances, the worse thing we could do would be to leave Emmeline in his close company. It just beggars trouble. So, yesterday I wrote to Emmeline, asking if she would like to join us here."

"You did what?" exclaimed Harriet incredulously.

"Oh, Father! That's too much," cried Elizabeth.

"Good for you, Pa," smiled Daniel, happy at the prospect.

"And you can keep your hands off her," scolded his father. No ifs, buts or maybes. Now, if I may resume centre stage? Where was I?

"Telling my brother to keep his depraved hands off her."

"Oh, yes, I was dealing with Emmeline. I can see you all think

I'm quite mad, but there's a point to my reasoning. Firstly, such a plan removes temptation from John's immediate company."

"If it isn't already too late," barged Daniel.

"Yes, boy, that is something we must all pray about. But, more importantly, from our own home we can use Emmeline as bait to attract John into visiting us. The rest will be up to Elizabeth. Yes, I know the plan involves elements of our last unsuccessful effort, the party I mean, but it really is quite different. Anyway, daughter, John has harvested you once and now you must ensure he is attracted again. Do you all see the merit of my plan?"

"A little," replied Harriet. "Is there more to it?"

"There is."

"Then, tell me this. Is it your intention to reform Emmeline, to raise her into society? Because, if it is, we might fall into the trap of making her even more acceptable to John."

"Actually, Mother, I'm beginning to understand Father's reasoning," exclaimed Elizabeth with elation. "Father believes that by making the plain-minded thing think she is worthy of being above her station, even intelligent, it will be the quickest route to exposing her shortcomings. Conversely, while she is left to be a dairymaid and acts like a dairymaid, and John likes dairymaids, she exposes nothing, except maybe her bloomers, which must be avoided at all costs! You know country girls are fairly free with their favours."

"Just so, Elizabeth. Well done for reading my thoughts." He turned to his wife. "I learned the very same truth long ago, my dear, but we had better not pursue the matter. However, in this case, little Emmeline is not invited for general advancement. But, nor must she be treated as a servant or John will take pity on the creature. I see her only as a companion to Elizabeth, initially at home and later while despatched with Elizabeth to foreign parts. In so doing, John is bound to pursue them, and what better way of getting him into Elizabeth's company while exposing Emmeline as a charlatan."

"Foreign?" enquired Harriet, worried at the prospect of losing her daughter again. "Why does every plan have to include sending our daughter away?"

"Bath, actually."

"What?" scalded Elizabeth with disappointment, "you mean *our* Bath, on the River Avon? Not some beautiful, sunny, foreign part? The place you always say you so despise? Am I to be sent there? Whatever for?"

"To wine, dine, be seen by the right people from north Somersetshire who we do not already know as acquaintances, take tea at the right places, and dance in that elegant city of strangers. By and by, though, you must waterproof yourself from the place with appropriate clothing."

"Without Emmeline, such an invitation would be a dream. With her, it's more likely to become a clumsy nightmare."

"But it will expose her for what she is," he returned. "However, there is more to tell, if you will allow me. To my letter, she replied in singular fashion that she would not come. At least, I think that's what she wrote. The letter was a forest of misspelling."

"Well then, that's an end to it," punctuated Harriet.

"Not so, as it happens. You see, not six hours later a second letter followed upon the first. She is to come after all."

"When?" asked Harriet in shock.

"Anytime now," was his happy reply.

"Good gracious!" uttered Elizabeth. "I am not at all convinced haste is well considered. We should've slept on the scheme to properly discover its pitfalls. As it is, it could cause tears before bedtime."

"Only for you," cried Daniel excitedly, "if John still prefers Emmie when he finds you two together. That's if he takes the hook at all."

"Then, my misfortune will be shared by you," she exclaimed. "I saw what you did under the table."

"What did the scallywag do?" yelled Jeremiah.

"By heavens, Sister, we must ensure you win his hand at all

costs," he returned. "Just as Father said, John must be the king at harvesting women and you must be his plucked queen. Long live the Harvest King!"

"Put your glass down, Daniel, and stop acting stupidly. Answer my earlier question!" demanded Jeremiah.

"Leave it, husband. Remember your irregular heart."

"Women!" he exclaimed, slicing his luncheon.

With the meal finished and cigars smoked, Jeremiah retired to his study. Collins entered carrying a tray of coffee and two sweet biscuits.

"Do you think they took to the idea, Collins?" he asked, using silver-plated tongs to drop a small sugar lump into the cup.

"Like a duck to water, Sir."

"It was frightfully clever of you to come up with such a plan, Collins, and cleverer still to suggest it to me in huggermugger. If I had said the plan was all your idea, why, I doubt we would have got past the starting gate. Now, it seems we have a proposition that is up and running."

"Yes, Sir, it is one of my better schemes."

"What would I do without you, Collins?"

"As to that, Sir, I am confident in the thought that you could manage perfectly well by your own ingenuity."

"You underestimate yourself, Collins, and your worth to me. When confronted around the dinner table by the faces of women, all with their own opinions on the way I should run my business, why, without your sound advice ringing in my ears I fancy I would be as ignored as a sneeze in a hurricane."

"With respect, Sir, I am inclined to believe Master Daniel is a male."

"He's the biggest old woman of the lot! No, you are invaluable to me, as always, and that's an end to the argument. But, our little tête-à-têtes must continue to be kept firmly behind closed doors."

"As you say, Sir. Is there anything else?"

"Only the usual when we are alone."

"Advice, Sir?" she smiled.

"Damn your impudence and come here."

She placed the tray on a table and walked to his side. "Is this what you want . . . again?" She tugged at her hem and lifted her dress enough to kneel comfortably at his feet. Prising his knees apart and raising a trouser leg, she removed his shoe and began to massage his foot.

"Flaming gout. Ah, that's wonderful, Collins. As I said, what would I do without you?"

"Get the doctor, Sir?"

"That quack? Why, he's as rough as coal. Anyway, I swear he's the one who, years ago, talked me into taking a season in Bath, to sample the water as a cure for my indigestion, which plagued me like the devil at the time. Bath, he said, do you the world of good. Ha! Didn't tell me the place was damp, fit only for fishermen and mermaids. And the water, if you can call it that, tasted like a glass of boiler-stoker's sweat! Exchanged me belly cramps for this damned gout, I shouldn't wonder. Paid the quack a guinea for the advice, too. All the good that came from the expense was to send the devil a few feet south. No, does me no good to take his treatment or look at his ugly face while he pummels my foot like so much dough. You are much more to my liking."

"As you please, Sir," she responded, following his eyes and hitching the bodice of her dress to cover the gaping cleavage. She rearranged his trouser leg, retied the shoe and stood. "Have you considered what is likely to happen when Emmeline Sturry actually arrives, Sir? It could be any time now."

"Have *you* given it any thought?"

"I have wrestled with the problem, Sir. This is how I see it developing. . ."

For some minutes she explained her thoughts, during which Jeremiah nodded constantly in agreement. Her counsel appeared wise. At least, it avoided the need to think for himself. This is not to suggest Jeremiah was foolish. Far from it. It was just that he could not cope with enigmatic situations. His normal world was in monotone, free from plotting and scheming, and one that valued the guidance and concord of a servant with whom he had shared many difficult problems. The very absurdity of this relationship guaranteed its continuance.

"Therefore," she added as a codicil, "I think you were clever to suggest everyone should treat Emmeline as a guest of sorts. I believe she will best expose her shortcomings in public if she is encouraged to adopt a position somewhere between an uninvited guest and a lady's companion. Did you give her any indication as to her forthcoming position?"

"No. I wrote no more than you suggested. I merely said how much we had enjoyed her company and would be pleased to take her into our household. That left the door fully open."

"A well constructed reply, Sir, if I may say so."

"But, Collins, I see one enormous drawback to the scheme. Once here, she will know Elizabeth's secret. Doesn't that add to our problems? Another voice to silence? Surely we can't be expected to keep it from her?"

"No, Sir, and nor should we try. As I see it, if we are right about certain feelings between Emmeline and Mr Madden, then the lady is likely to try to use Miss Elizabeth's difficulties against her. As Mr Madden already knows about Miss Unity, it's my view he will jump to your daughter's rescue, and much will change in his feelings accordingly. It is human nature to protect the downtrodden. In essence, you are cleverly transposing the onus of victim from Emmeline to Miss Elizabeth."

"I've just had another terrible thought. What if John has already told Emmeline about the baby? Won't that disarm us?"

"Not if Emmeline still rails against Miss Elizabeth or Miss Unity. As I judge it, Mr Madden would find it impossible to stand aside and quietly listen to harmful scorn."

"Doesn't that assume he cares? Aren't we scuppered if it backfires?"

"With respect, Sir, I don't think so. Because, if the plan doesn't work, it is my belief that your singular kindness to Emmeline is bound to endear you in her thoughts, providing the means for you to manipulate her loyalties. It could even have the added bonus of making Emmeline despise Mr Madden for his part in Miss Elizabeth's ordeal and the consequent difficulties heaped upon your shoulders as head of the family. No, I think it's a win-only situation. But only time will tell, and we may have to cut our cloth according to unfolding eventualities."

"A situation of mixed metaphors."

She grinned. "I am reminded, Sir, of something my uncle used to say to my mother. I can see him now, sitting by the fire, smoking a clay pipe and telling her how she should refrain from inviting any guest to the table who hasn't been involved in some scandal or other. Only a scandalous guest makes interesting conversation and suffers no inhibition in probing for indiscretions in others, he would argue."

"A risky formula for a pleasant evening."

"I think he spoke from experience. He told me at a very young age how, in the sacred game of marriage, women hold all the aces but deliberately never play them to win."

"I'm confused!"

"You see, it works just as he said, even between master and servant. At your pleasure, Sir, I come up with suggestions and you use them as your own."

"Ah, I see! Manipulation? Is that how you see relationships, Collins?"

"Of course. Is there anything more likely to achieve advancement in life?"

"I must say, Collins, you do seem to come up with comments far above those expected of a servant from humble background. Is your background humble, Collins, or have you hidden depths?"

"It was my grandfather who lost our family's position amongst better folk, Sir. We didn't always live in a hamlet among men wearing battered top hats and women in rags who talk free and common after gin has massaged their larynx. Two generations ago we were merchants with two shops, one in Sherborne and another in Dorchester. Staymakers of repute were we. Only, as quickly as my grandmother could make the garments, my grandfather would gamble the profits away, resulting in ruin. Married three times and widower twice, although after drinking he would say that my grandmother displeased him so much that he was married twice and widowed thrice."

"Enough depression. Let me know when Emmeline arrives," ordered Jeremiah.

Collins took the tray.

"Oh, and while I think on it, show Emmeline to the smallest guest room on the second floor. She must feel welcomed as a companion to Elizabeth, but there is no need for her to be too closely billeted."

"As you say, Sir," replied Collins abstractedly, bearing a smug look.

Two hours later, in the diminishing daylight of this December afternoon, Emmeline joined the household. She had walked between the villages, finding the journey easy, even with a bag, and now stood anxiously at the front door. Dwarfed by the portico, she tugged at the bell-pull, wondering why she had come at all. It had not been her only option, but, then, she was no stranger to difficult situations.

To her relief, anxiety seemed misplaced once she had been ushered inside, where her hat, coat and bag were taken by Collins and Harriet led her into the drawing room, where a pot of full-bodied tea and a plate of rich cake soon arrived.

"Won't you sit next to me," suggested Harriet in a pleasant tone, patting the cushion with the flat of her palm.

But Emmie was captivated, staring through the mullion windows at the garden beyond.

"What do you look at, child?"

"I fancied I saw Miss Elizabeth talking to John Madden across a holly bush. But I must've been mistaken. I left him in Nether Bow without any explanation of where I was headed."

"I assume you walked here."

"I did, Ma'am."

"Then, there is your answer. He could've ridden here at any time between. He isn't a stranger to us, you know. He comes and goes as he pleases, according to his particular wish at the time to visit Daniel or Elizabeth. I doubt he would bother to come all this way because of you."

"I suppose. I was fanciful anyway. It was Master Daniel wearing a similar jacket."

"Do you always call Mr Madden by his Christian name?"

"He encourages it, Ma'am."

"Are you comfortable with that familiarity?"

"We have known each other a very long time, only in the past weeks as employer and employee. Before that we met through a mutual friend."

"If I may enquire further, how did you view your recent situation?"

"My situation, Ma'am?"

"Your relationship, if you prefer."

"Why, as I said, employer and employee. There is nothing more between us."

Harriet's heart leapt. "Is that completely honest?"

"Yes, Ma'am, it is."

"You see, child, John is inclined to be a bit familiar, as he has demonstrated. It's very much in his nature, but you must not misunderstand the meaning. Better if you resist it."

"Except, we kissed a couple of days ago."

She jumped. "Kissed?"

"We did. Not in a passionate way, you understand. It was . . . more of an experiment."

"What a peculiar thing to say. Tell me more."

"There's nothing much to add. We kissed once, he pulled away and we parted. That's the story completed."

"Nothing else, before or after?"

"He's too much of a gentleman, Ma'am. We remain just good

friends." She paused for reflection. "No, I am wrong. We are not even friends now, I think."

"Really? Your doing or his?"

"Equal, I suppose," she said, more coldly than before.

"Then, my dear, have your tea while it is good and hot. And help yourself to cake. I do hope you will delight in our park land and come to think of Nether Bow as nothing more than a place worthy of leaving. Meanwhile, we shall ignore all men and be the best of friends. I warm to you with every passing moment."

"Thank you, Ma'am," was her innocent reply.

"Afterwards, I shall ask Collins to show you to your room. It is our earnest wish for you to keep Elizabeth company, which means a jolly spending spree for you both. Tomorrow, you and my daughter shall take a trip into Sherborne, where you can buy some new clothes for many exciting outings to come. Scriven's has new Christmas stock fresh from London. That will do Elizabeth very nicely. She can then accompany you to Swain's dressmakers, where they sell plainer clothes of reasonable fashion. At least, anything bought there will fit you. I will organise an allowance from my husband. He is sure to agree with me that Elizabeth cannot be seen in your company while you dress as a country girl. Are you very grateful, Emmeline?"

"I am, Ma'am, very. I should like it a great deal. I have been expecting a new dress from my parents, but I don't think it will come."

"While you're there, you may ask Annie Swain if she has any off-cuts. It's all very well thinking of ourselves, but we have the poor to consider at this time of year. Can you sew?"

"A bit."

"Excellent. You can occupy the dark Winter evenings making clothes for the poor. However, be forewarned, we have a matter of the gravest importance to discuss regarding Elizabeth. But, that can be for another day."

CHAPTER 18

Decisions

The good cheer normally expected of Christmas Eve and Christmas Day was nowhere to be found within the Grant and Madden households, although the workers at Wheat Sheaf Farm had merriment in abundance. Their revelry merely added to John's feeling of isolation. The Grants, whose main fortune was based on numerous enterprises in far off places, were spared the galling excitement of labourers. Their surrounding land being mainly laid out as a park meant that, for those working within its boundaries, a certain degree of dignity was expected while feasting in the servants' hall.

With no further contact from John, it appeared to the Grants that using Emmie as bait to attract him into their lavish net had been nothing short of another gross misjudgement. It was the second failed attempt to reel him in and probably their last. Clearly, despite their best efforts, John went about his business indifferent to their concerns and aloof to any relationships past. It, thus, became a bleak time of little joy, the short days and long nights after the 26th of December and the end of the main festivities proving fertile for thought, misunderstanding and reproach.

Only Emmie appeared free of such melancholy, unaware of the

greater game being played out around her. She had made good use of any vacant sprigs of mistletoe whenever Daniel appeared, and in her giggling company he too avoided a measure of the general air of depression that seemed to accompany his sister and parents in whatever they did. Collins spent longer in Jeremiah's company, whose gout throbbed harder than ever, and Elizabeth stayed much in her room, keeping Unity away from Emmie. This often left Harriet sitting alone in the drawing room among the paper decorations and festive baubles that gave no seasonal cheer. Even the Christmas geese, now finished as pie, had been consumed in near silence, beyond the odd compliment that they had been fine, plump birds, the best anyone could remember.

With inevitability, and a vacant chair at the table, came the time to share with Emmie the dreadful truth regarding Unity's parentage. Yet, even this did not go as expected. Emmie's carefree attitude at hearing what should have been devastating news greatly perplexed them, but they quietly put it down to a general lack of moral standards among the poor. The more obvious reasons for indifference – that she might have heard the gossip or heard Unity cry, or John had taken her into his confidence and put before her all that he had found so hard to accept for himself – merely passed them by as unlikely.

Notwithstanding such misgivings, Emmie was genuinely content, settled to the idea that she would probably never be the subject of John's admiration and, thereby, cared little if Unity was his or not. Indeed, it went beyond this. The possible distress he might feel due to uncertainty over Unity gave her a tinge of revengeful pleasure. For, it is a profound truth that the more help a good man offers to others for no benefit to himself, the quicker they are to turn on him in return if he is unable to fulfil their every subsequent wish. Conversely, it is equally recognised that people who care only for themselves never run the risk of being asked to help others in the first place, thereby never having to refuse anything. It was this baleful circumstance that now befell John, the man who had been Emmie's greatest benefactor during periods of her deepest distress.

Whatever misgivings and misdeeds engrossed the minds of the Grant family, the strange truth was that John had not deliberately shunned them at all, but was fully and unexpectedly occupied with more immediate problems of his own. For, whilst he had engaged the services of Cornelius Fairfax to take over the duties previously encumbered upon Abel Tucker, the appointment had not given him the expected freedom of movement needed to determine his own future.

Instead, in the loneliness of an empty and cheerless house, John had become increasingly aware of new problems surrounding his business, with jobs not fulfilled efficiently as they had been previously. The workforce, normally independent of his direct supervision, had become unmotivated and ragged.

This weighed heavily on his mind, compounding all other personal problems. It was as if a chill now enveloped every room of his once happy home. Emmie leaving Wheat Sheaf Farm under a cloud for a destination unknown, but presumed to be Stirminster Oak, and his own doubts regarding a future with Elizabeth, were matters of serious concern but still secondary to the running of the farm, his very livelihood. Thus, with one dilemma added to another, it merely retarded into near lethargy any decisions involving romance.

Unnoticed by everybody, but almost from the outset of his employment, Cornelius had forsaken many of his more arduous farm duties for time spent in the barn workshop, a place where farm equipment was usually repaired and new hand-tools made, but no longer so usefully occupied. Long into the evenings he had been heard sawing wood and beating metal by the dim light of oil lanterns strategically placed around a large area of the workshop, giving the impression of devotion to the farm and its needs. But, nothing could have been further from the truth, and if this needed confirmation, it came when John received by second post an invoice from an engineering company in Yeovil for two clockwork motors and a quantity of gummed lightweight fabric already delivered from stock, plus a separate invoice for a small steam engine with a lightweight boiler and a condenser awaiting full payment before assembly and delivery. Such equipment of little sturdiness, being of no practical use about the farm, had to be for another purpose, the discovery of which had a profound effect on John's ability to leave the farm.

John stood squarely in the doorway of the barn, silhouetted against the twilight. The other workers had already retreated to the dormitory, leaving Cornelius as a Machiavellian figure to work on into the evening.

"I've been caught out good and proper," was Cornelius's furtive response to stern enquiries as to what he was doing and at John's great expense. "I hold up my hands to everything. I can explain if given the chance."

"You'd better, because this bill is for ninety-seven pounds."

"As much as that?"

"It is. It seems engineering a condenser to your own design is twenty pounds by itself, Mr Fairfax. Take note of the words 'your own design', because it has nothing whatsoever to do with me. And perhaps you can tell me what I wanted with forty square yards of gummed fabric?"

"Ah, the fabric. That is a lot, isn't it?"

"No, Cornelius, one square yard is a lot when it is not required for use on the farm. Forty is a gross fraud upon my purse. I suppose the clockwork motors were for cuckoo clocks to ward off the rooks?"

Cornelius threw his tools onto the bench and walked gingerly to John, stepping over fragile structures lying hidden on the soil floor. His features glowed unrepentantly.

"If you had discovered me a day or two ago I would've been in deep trouble, without any visible means of explanation. But, you see, I have made such progress in a short space of time that our names are assured to be emblazoned in history books."

"You've lost me already."

"Mr Madden, Sir, tell me what is meant by a misanthrope?"

"A person who dislikes society, I believe."

"Then I use the wrong word. What about sceptic?"

"What I am at this moment, Mr Fairfax."

"Please, Sir, bear with me a little longer. It is all very exciting, so much so that I find myself tongue-tied. A sceptic is someone who questions accepted opinions. Do you agree?"

"Make it short, Mr Fairfax. I find myself becoming seriously irritated by your manner."

Cornelius became nervous for the first time, having believed his work would, without needing the verification of others, be universally recognised as genius.

"Of course. Well, it has always been my belief, and that of others of greater intellect than me, that it is possible to build a man-carrying machine that flies without the need for gas, as used at present by airships and balloons with all the associated dangers."

"No gas?"

"None. Not a drop of the stuff."

"I assume from the direction we are headed, we are about to plunge into your theories for a machine of a new and untested type, and all at my personal expense?"

"We are, we are!" replied Cornelius, renewed with enthusiasm. "Great joy is upon us, for it is no longer theory alone. It is an unwise man who reflects on the cost without understanding the worth. With respect, it isn't a matter of what this or that costs in monetary value, but what can be achieved by their clever conjoining. Here, laid out across the floor, you see nothing but a very large tarpaulin. I now remove it with care. Your help in this would be appreciated."

John took a corner, lifting it gently from the structure it obscured.

"Now, I expect you see only curved wood, partially covered by gummed fabric costing so much a yard. I, on the other hand, see the future and I offer you a part in it."

"A share in a bonfire? Because that's all it is, so much wasted material."

"No, Sir, trust me, on this occasion you are wrong. The craft I have nearly completed *will* fly."

John gave the object a measure of closer inspection. "How, in heaven's name?"

"How, what?"

"How the devil will this thing fly?"

"That I can answer. Over more than a year now, in one place or another, I have conducted a series of what I call aero-forceful experiments, aimed at replicating the flight of birds, which, incidentally, are creatures not filled with gas, except for farting that is." He bowed his head in sudden thought. "Actually, I wonder if birds do fart. Expelling gas rapidly from the rear could be a form of motive power." He shook his head as new thoughts appeared. "No matter, no matter. Forget I said that."

"Easily done, Cornelius. Now, get on with it, please."

"Forget also the fact that birds beat their wings. As far as I can discern, and this may be new thinking among my peers, they do so merely to gain speed and, therefore, height. You see, it's the air flowing at speed over or under a wing from its forward motion that generates an invisible lifting force, of that I am certain, although I confess I don't understand how or why. It might have something to do with the way feathers are formed, but I think that's unlikely."

"If God gave feathers to birds, and no other creatures have them, then that's proof enough for me, Cornelius."

"But it's unscientific."

"Not everything in our world can be proven by science. It's called faith in nature. Use your eyes and see creation, man. You can't fly, but birds do. That's me totally convinced at a stroke. "

"Bats!"

"Pardon?"

"Bats fly, but they don't have feathers. But, what bats and birds have in common is curvature of their wings from front to rear. It goes mostly unnoticed, but I think it's vital. So, if a man-made machine with fixed but curved wings is forced forward through the air at a sufficiently high velocity, then, in my estimation, it's bound to fly."

"Using an 'invisible' lifting force?"

"Yes."

"Invisible?"

"Quite."

"If it's invisible, how do you know it exists?"

"Hydrogen is invisible, but, being lighter than the surrounding air, it enables airships to fly. I merely use similar reasoning."

"If you are even remotely correct, how come I see birds of prey hovering at a constant height above the ground without flapping or moving forward at all, while they hunt for food?"

"I didn't say I understand everything. But, in answer to your comment, I suggest that birds can only hover at a constant height if the wind is blowing particularly hard head-first to create that force without forward motion."

"Could a man-made machine hover in very high wind?"

"I doubt it, because it would weigh far too much in comparison. There are limitations to this replication of nature. But, I could be proved wrong in the future. Who knows? No, as I see it, balloons and airships are likely to remain the only made-made objects capable of hovering. But, then, they will never be capable of making long-distance journeys in planned directions and at acceptable speed. The opposite of this will be true for heavy flying machines using engines, and the discovery of how to achieve it will make someone very rich."

"All fine and dandy, but still you don't say how a heavy machine could gather sufficient forward speed to attract this invisible lifting force."

"By using an engine to turn a multi-blade screw. The screw, or propeller as aeronauts now call them, will drag the machine forward at ever increasing speed until it flies. Such a device replaces flapping wings. It all makes entire sense.

"You have proof? Show me how a turning screw could make a heavy object move forwards at great speed."

"I can't, at least, not yet. But I have achieved limited success with one of my previous small models."

"Weighing?"

"A few ounces."

"Good grief. It's no proof at all."

"But the theory is sound, I assure you. I've read a great deal, including the way Brunel used a multi-blade screw to drive his revolutionary *Great Britain* steamship through the water."

"That was decades ago."

"Of course, but it was so revolutionary in concept that screws became generally used in steamship construction thereafter. Since then, the design of screws has vastly improved. I merely intend to adapt the idea in a lighter, wooden form."

"*Great Britain's* screw drove it through water, Mr Fairfax, water. Not the air! I have never read anywhere that the ship had even the slightest tendency to fly."

"Of course not. You make mockery of me. It had no wings for a start. And, as for its size and weight . . . well! Apart from that, it was made of iron. No flying machine can never be constructed of metal. That material is just too heavy. Wood will be the stuff of flying machines, or bamboo because the hollow stems are incredibly light, flexible, yet strong. But, returning to forward motion, screws turning through water or revolving through the air do have one similarity, the creation of forward motion. You must see that? It's a scientific fact."

"Even if you're right, this thing at my feet has no screw that I can see, or any means for turning one."

"That's correct. What you see here is an unpowered craft, intended only for experiments into defining wing shape. Interestingly, a curved wing flies better than a straight wing, but too much curve destroys the lift. It's a question of getting the shape just right. I recently met a man in France who can adjust the shape of his machine's wings using an ingenious mechanical crank. Such cleverness is beyond my understanding at present. So, I have tried out different wing shapes using small models, some powered by twisted rubber and some by clockwork motors, but always driven forward by a fast-turning screw. I think I now know the shape to use, resulting in what you see before you. My craft might look large, but my calculations show it is only big enough to carry a light man in descending flight. It is my first full-size craft of any type."

"Is that why you've missed meals, to keep your weight down?"

"I've been too busy, too excited, to eat. My appetite has flown away."

"Lucky something has!"

"You will see."

"Let's hope so. Anyway, what possible use to man or beast is a machine that can only descend?"

"As I said, it's a first step, a stepping stone. If it's successful and doesn't plummet to the ground after launch, I will build a slightly larger version fitted with the small steam engine and a screw."

"Why don't you fit an engine to this thing and save the expense of building two, that is, if I don't cancel delivery of the engine to limit the extent of your debts?"

"It's a question of power-to-weight ratio. The heavier the machine, the more power it needs to sustain it in the air and the larger the wings have to be. Everything on a flying machine has to be weighed, lightened and accounted for. Light weight is crucial to flight. I am gaining experience with every day that passes."

"The clockwork models, did they fly well?"

"Afraid not, but at least they didn't fall out of the air like bricks. Both achieved a steep but steady glide before they destroyed themselves on impact with the ground."

"I just knew you would say that."

"Yes, but I'm convinced I know why I didn't have better results. As I said, I'm gaining necessary experience. You see, the same old problem applied. A clockwork motor is just too heavy for the energy it produces. It's like using the mechanism from a grandfather clock to power a sparrow."

"Experience, my dear Fairfax, is another word for errors. It is one thing for you to fund your own mistakes, but it is quite another to reach into my pocket."

"Oh!"

"Remind me who funded you before, when you didn't grow carrots in Chard?"

"My father. But, I cannot ask for his help any longer or, indeed, experiment anywhere where I am known. I have my reasons. I need to be in hiding."

"More debt collectors?"

He considered the truth, but trembled at the possible consequences. "Yes, something of the sort."

"This steam engine on order, it will do the job expected of it?"

"No, not really. Steam is a lame duck for the same reasons as clockwork. But, I have no alternative. So, by careful design to minimise weight, it might just bridge the gap between a glider and a future petroleum-powered machine. It will not enable me to achieve level flight, of that I'm sure, but it might help reduce the rate of descent. It's merely another step to eventual success."

John picked around the craft, pulling and poking at the various strut, wires, fabric and brackets.

"It certainly looks a fine piece of workmanship. Shame your skills aren't directed towards maintaining the farm machinery. Alright, Cornelius, I have made my decision. If you want to kill yourself, that is entirely your business. As for me, I will forgive you the deception and the raids on my purse on two conditions. The first is that I take the cost of the wood and fabric from your wages. The second is that I cancel the engine until such time as I see this thing fly without one. It may cost me a penalty to cancel, but I'm willing to risk that. After, well, we will see. Are you agreeable?"

"Agreed." They shook hands.

"Oh, one more thing," added John in serious tone. "You must

work on that flying contraption in your own time, not mine. Understand? I want the farm running like . . . clockwork."

"I do, and thank you. You won't regret it, I assure you."

"I think I will, when I have to scrape you off the road and explain to your parents that the mess I return in a wheelbarrow is none other than their beloved son. By the way, how will you test it?"

"I've already thought of that. There's a good place to the north of the county, near Marlborough, called Silbury Hill."

"I know it. It's in a group of about thirty barrows known as Snail Down, said to be the burial place of warriors killed in battle and that of a king. There used to be an iron-age hill fort around there somewhere."

"That is not strictly right, with the greatest respect. Silbury Hill is as old as Stonehenge. It is believed to have been a shrine of sorts, man-made in three stages from layers of gravel, turf and chalk, but only that."

"What of King Zel?"

"That old myth. Ancient stories tell of Zel being buried in the hill, alongside a solid gold image of himself on a horse. But, the hill predates any human knowledge of metals of any kind, so that's a pile of nonsense. Others have said Silbury was the work of the Devil, who was carrying the hill from Bristol to London when it became too heavy and was abandoned there. Such a place invites fantasies, giving the hill significance beyond it's actual worth as a monument to human endeavour thousands of years before the birth of Christ. Still, no matter, it's a perfect place for going to the devil!"

"The Devil again. He played quite a part in the ancient monuments around these parts."

"Your meaning?"

"Stonehenge. Wasn't it the Devil who supposedly flew the stones from Ireland to this part of Wessex, having stolen them from an old Irishwoman? He then built Stonehenge to Merlin's design."

"Merlin? You mean, King Arthur's mythical wizard?"

"Wizard, warlock, sorcerer, said to be buried inside a hollow hill. The man who helped Arthur slay giants and become a fairyland being, according to legend."

"Fairyland?" turned Cornelius breathlessly.

"Yes, that's the tale, and all the bunkum that goes with it. Although, how Arthur could ever have become a fairy, even in the minds of ancient writers, heaven only knows."

"Perhaps he was born a fairy, but lived as a mortal?"

"Yes, and I was born a pumpkin and lived as a carrot! Anyway, as a man of science, Cornelius, what's your interest in myth?"

"Cadbury was Arthur's fort!"

"I know."

"Blimey!"

"It could be true," added John, breaking Cornelius's trance.

"What could be?"

"Zel."

"Zel? I thought we were talking about Merlin and Arthur."

"My mind's moved on. What about King Zel? Buried in the hill or not?"

"Oh, not, I'm afraid," responded Cornelius. "That we do know for sure.

"How?"

"Easy. In 1776 the Duke of Northumberland funded an experimental dig. A vertical hole was dug into the hill from the top, which is flat, but nothing of consequence was ever discovered. Later this century, a Dean named Merewether dug a horizontal shaft into the hill at base level. Again, the survey found nothing. No, it has to be faced, Silbury is nothing more than a huge pile of dirt, built for reasons unknown, but probably ceremonial."

"It's a lofty place, right enough, but an awful long way away. Can't you find somewhere nearer?"

"The effort involved in getting there will prove worthwhile, I feel sure. It's a high mound in the middle of open fields. That's important, as I can launch off the top in any direction, depending on the wind. Anywhere else and I would have to wait for the wind to blow in a particular direction and also I would have to face the possibility of being blown back against a hillside or cliff face. No, it's ideal, as if built for the purpose. I'll have the machine hauled to the top when it's finished, where I'll jump off when the wind blows hard in my face."

"Rather you than me."

"So would I, Sir, so would I."

CHAPTER 19

Across the divide

$\mathcal{E}$ very hamlet and village in Wessex had its own unique character, more often influenced by its inhabitants and their eccentricities than by any number of geographical features. Yet, the opposite was true of the towns. Sherborne, with its abbey, magnificent castle and grand estates, had flourished because of its strategic staging position for coaches travelling between London and Plymouth and, to a lesser extent, between Bristol and Weymouth, while the market town of Glastonbury had expanded beyond all previous recognition due to its location on the Exeter to London route. Commerce in Glastonbury had been further boosted by the construction of a canal, which reached a coastal port, but eventually this succumbed to the railways, which throttled the trade of the slower and less adaptable barges. Good transportation links had been the very key to the growth of local enterprise and the new prosperity of Glastonbury, with goods as diverse as bricks and gloves boosting the traditional farming economy.

These towns were places of grandeur and elegance, fine shops and gas lighting. In marked contrast, many of the hamlets and villages seemed locked into the past and would have been entirely recognisable to the long dead of merry England. So, a divide had grown between the towns and their surrounding villages, the eminent in their bow-fronted or sash-windowed houses and the agricultural poor living under failing thatch. To travel between town and hamlet was to step across time itself, punctuated by the grand houses of land owners who lorded over both and alluded to neither, and who made traditional country pursuits the grandest of all modern occupations.

Five days after the New Year began, chance news of Emmie's whereabouts became the hottest gossip at Wheat Sheaf Farm. Fanny had unexpectedly met her in Cerne Abbas, when, with barely the time to take in the circumstances of Emmie's indulgent appearance, she had been overwhelmed by her free flowing tongue.

The workforce being inconsiderable, it was not long before word of the meeting came to John's attention. He greeted the news with great excitement, having been concerned for Emmie's safety ever since a large parcel had arrived for her as a late Christmas present from her parents. This had alerted him to the worrying prospect that she had not reached Stirminster Oak safely.

"I hear you have spoken to Emmeline Sturry, Fanny. May I ask where?"

"In Cerne, Sir. I saw her riding in a horse-drawn carriage of all things, dressed like a proper lady."

"Good heavens. Did you have a chance speak to her? Is she well?"

"Oh, yes, Sir. She be very well. She spotted me from the window and immediately ordered the carriage to stop. It took me a few seconds to catch up and by the time I got there the coachman had already opened the door and lowered the step."

"What does it mean, Fanny? Did Emmeline say how she came to be in a carriage?"

"I couldn't stop her talking, Sir. She was bitterly anxious to rub me nose in the dirt of her success. She wasted no time in reminding me of how I lived in a hamlet and she resided among sumptuous wealth, two sides of the Cerne divide, as she put it. I said none of it be hers to keep, but such observations made no difference to her attitude. Strange as it seems, the manner of her tone and the cut of her clothes somehow forced me to speak up to her as if she be truly my superior. Imagine that. The more I think on it, the crosser I feel."

"Yes, Fanny, but *what are* her circumstances? What do you mean by, not being hers to keep?"

"Your friend, Daniel Grant, Sir. She be living with him."

"Really? Are you sure?" he asked in disbelief, followed by a shivering sigh of the type experienced only when hearing damaging news for the first time.

"Quite certain, Sir. It seems the Grants took her in to be a companion to Miss Elizabeth. She has her own room inside the house and everything."

"My word!"

"Me feelings exactly, Sir."

"Did she mention a certain Unity?"

"No, Sir, nobody of that name. She said she and Miss Grant be soon travelling to Bristol and Bath, as family expectations have altered."

"Meaning?"

"I don't know."

"Was I mentioned at all?"

"Yes, Sir, but I can't remember how. 'Twas only in passing."

"Think, girl. It's important."

"No, it's no use, the reason has fled me brain. Be there anything else I can help you with?"

"No, Fanny, you've done well. Run along." John suddenly reached out to stop her. "Oh, Fanny, before you go, how would you feel if I offered you the job of housekeeper in Emmeline's place? I can't stand my own cooking a moment longer. I need a hot pie, not constant cheese and cold meats."

"I would decline, Sir."

"Decline? Goodness, I wasn't expecting that. Of course, it is your choice not to take it, but may I ask why?"

"You sent Abel away. I don't think I would want to eat meals opposite you as if nothing had happened to spoil my prospects, if you don't object to me speaking so freely."

"No, Fanny, that's fine. I just thought. . . Oh, well."

She looked at his dejected expression. "If I change me mind, Sir, may I come back and say so?"

He smiled pleasantly. "Of course you can, most acceptably." She turned to leave. "Fanny," he called, "I am most dreadfully sorry!"

Without gesture to acknowledge or refuse his apology, she ran back to the dormitory, where she recounted the conversation to her friends. John heard the laughter and felt particularly alone, almost damaged by their companionship.

It was then, as he walked back to the house, a strange emotion came over him. He felt the need to reaffirm his own important friendships before it was too late, most particularly with Elizabeth and Daniel. Yet, worryingly, he also felt an alarming longing to 'chew the fat' with Emmie, about nothing in particular, but merely to hear her voice in idle and silly chit-chat. Maybe the imminent departure of the ladies to the north of Somersetshire, with or without Unity, had focused his mind towards rebuilding a social life.

On the 7th of January, in the emptiness of another year without Christabel and a day that was itself benign, John decided to visit the grave of his late mother. It was a place he disliked intensely, for it held none of the warmth he had always felt for her. The headstone was grey and cold, with creeping algae, and the January chill seeped into the very soles of his boots as he stood on the frosted grass. Yet, even with these discomforts, a subtle diffusing atmosphere was ever present, as if he could see beneath the soil at a happy and smiling face that held nothing but love for him. He glanced at the next grave along, noticing its headstone, which was unkempt, its letters peeling. Leaning across to clear the overgrowth, he revealed the full inscription:

BE FAITHFUL NOW FOR DEATH DEVOURS ALL
BEAUTIFUL THINGS

John remembered reading the inscription the day the headstone had been laid on its side against a mound of soil, next to the newly dug hole awaiting its eternal occupant. The inscription had inspired him to look for Christabel, a search which began with a letter to Mr and Mrs Sturry and ended in his cradling Christabel as life ebbed from her young and wounded body. The memory brought tears to his eyes. Here and at Shalhurn were the two greatest loves of his life, now both taken away. Only once had he visited Christabel's grave, an experience so emotionally damaging that he swore he would never return. He hated the fact that she had been buried outside the church's consecrated ground. Besides, he needed no marked grave to remember her. She was engraved permanently in his heart.

Gathering together bits of weed he had pulled from the grave, and after brushing the stonework, John prepared to leave. He was filled with an uncontrollable desire to have his old life back, when he was happy to be idle and insincere, and when Wheat Sheaf Farm resounded to familiar voices. But, as with all impossible wishes, the realisation of its hopelessness quickly gave way to more practical thoughts, uppermost of which was that nothing would improve without effort. He was a different man, living at a different time, and no amount of desperation to grasp the happiness he once felt could actually bring any of it back. Yet, in little Unity Isobel, Elizabeth had reintroduced his mother's name to a living person. That was it, he realised. She held his future happiness and fulfilment.

"Thank you, Mother," he uttered as he ran his fingers over the letters forming her name. "You have guided me once more. God bless you. Oh!" he added as an afterthought, "you have a beautiful granddaughter, at least I think you have. You would be so proud to see her."

John hurried home as a man on a mission, wasting no time in writing a letter to Abel Tucker, enclosing a five pound note and asking if he would reconsider the offer to return to the farm for considerably higher wages. The money attached was, indeed, unbelievably generous. As an excuse, John wrote how Cornelius Fairfax had been found to be a very poor bailiff indeed and the farm was in urgent need of proper supervision or it ran the risk of bankruptcy. The truth was somewhat less dramatic, but needs must, he thought. Understanding his own heartbreak for Christabel, John was also unwilling to inflict similar pain on Fanny. He would pay the price for her happiness too, whatever it cost. The letter was addressed *care of Mr Ellis, owner of the lime works, Canal Wharf, Glastonbury*.

John's letter duly arrived in Glastonbury by first post on the 9th, handed to Abel from a large soft bag strung across the postman's shoulder. The task completed, the postman rode off on his tricycle.

It was well received. It seemed his former master always wanted to give him money, not an unpleasant experience for any young man, but a strange one, nonetheless, for somebody born among the mud lanes of Parviton, where saving a few pence from meagre wages had never been an option. Indeed, so little spare money circulated within the village, it had become a place of medieval bartering, where the very notion of 'putting by' was unknown unless the item in question was one to be salted or pickled.

Parviton folk were raised under the umbrella of the Church to know the evil of strong drink, the resulting violence and poverty it heralded being seen as an almost inevitable consequence. Yet, somehow, the gross inadequacies of their lives detached them from moralising platitudes, making ale and gin an established part of their diets from a young age and as necessary to the adults to see them through the next harsh day as air itself. The men folk were, in particular, renowned as hard workers and heavy drinkers, content to view charitable parish relief as a fully established arrangement against starvation in old age, when no money could be earned.

Abel read on, noticing how Fanny was mentioned several times for missing him greatly, although John had been careful not to emphasis any deeper feelings. He also made much of the fact that Emmeline no longer worked at the farm, cautiously omitting the circumstances of her departure, so giving the impression that somehow justice had been served.

Fair though the written words were, Abel could hardly read Emmie's name without thinking harshly for her indifference to his downfall, disdain having turned during the intervening period into anger. The final lines of the letter were more general and included the polite phrase: *You are a much missed man, both worker and colleague, and missed also as a good friend by all in the dormitory*. John ended by wishing him Godspeed in whatever decision he made, adding that if he did not want to use any of the five pounds for the return fare, he was at liberty to keep it anyway as a gesture of the greatest goodwill between former master and employee, nay, between friends.

Having despatched the letter to Abel, John felt free to focus his thoughts towards the Grant family and their guest. This was a more complicated matter, requiring much greater consideration. Yet, knowing the ladies were to leave the area, a measure of haste appeared to be the wisest option.

As luck would have it, several days earlier Emmie had eagerly told the Grants of her encounter with Fanny, her enthusiasm showing no social constraint. She had emphasised with zeal the belittling attitude she had adopted in conversation, somehow believing that it would rub-off on the entire Madden farm, its owner and labourers alike. To this ploy, she had expected to win the tacit approval of the Grant family. Yet, to her gestures of self-satisfaction, the Grants had displayed a singular degree of contempt at this misuse of their property and their kindness towards her, so much so that Jeremiah instructed Daniel to ride to Nether Bow in the coming days to make amends for any misunderstanding and appeal to John's forbearing nature. The conversation that followed had taken a predictable course:

"That makes me look a fool," proclaimed Emmie, unable to understand why they thought she had a duty to be magnanimous. "The one thing John Madden should have done by now is visit Elizabeth and Unity. But he hasn't. Surely you want revenge?"

"Dear Father, please don't encourage Daniel to go," pleaded Elizabeth unexpectedly, ignoring Emmie's outburst, but agreeing in part with her reasoning.

"I'll hear no such nonsense, Lizzy. I desire you merely to await the outcome of our new proposition and put on a vexed look should John call as a result of your brother's success. Believe me when I say, we only have your best interests at heart, and Unity's, of course."

"I understand that, Father, but if John has not come of his own free will after such a long time, then what could be achieved by embarrassing us further over such an insignificant incident."

"Embarrass?" he replied sternly.

"Of course! We cannot force John into responsibility, and nor would I want his affection if it was not offered freely, without coercion. There would be no future in it for either of us. I couldn't live under such a cloud, knowing how his affections were entirely false. How could I endure such a thing? No, under such terms, I would refuse to accept his hand, even if he proposed."

"Who, in God's name, said anything about proposals of marriage? I am merely attempting to keep friendship alive after the damage done by our so-called house guest. That is my primary aim."

"In that case, is it worth the trouble? He has let us down, yet you offer apologies. I see no sense in it."

"You question my wisdom, Elizabeth, and would deny me my will in the matter? Understand this. At the present time we are only asking for John's forgiveness for Emmeline's rude behaviour towards one of his employees. If more comes from the contact, all well and good."

"Lizzy has a point," added Daniel in all seriousness, ready to crush Emmie with comments that took no account of her presence among them. "We must listen to her. We can't be certain John won't view any approach as a lame attempt to reunite him with Elizabeth. After all, what in reality is Emmie to any of us? He is bound to see evil intent in it."

"Have you finished?" rebuked Jeremiah.

"Not quite. We don't want to add fuel to past mistakes."

"What mistakes, Daniel?"

"Oh, Father, where do I start? We were all wrong to assume John could possibly want someone else here in preference to Elizabeth. Yet we let this belief influence our actions. Trust me, I know John and I'm certain he would've found some excuse or other to see either lady if he truly wanted to. No bait at all was dangled by your earlier plan and we haven't had the courage to recognise it until now. Perhaps, it's time to face the facts and let sleeping dogs lie. We have lost!"

"What are you all talking about?" enquired Emmie.

"I smell a rat," suggested Harriet. "Are you sure you aren't saying that just to keep the bait at the end of your own rod?"

"Who's rod? What bait?" asked Emmie in bewilderment.

"Shut up!" shouted all three in unison.

Emmie stomped from the room, leaving the others to formulate a compromise in a less-charged atmosphere. It was agreed. Daniel would pay his respects to John at Wheat Sheaf Farm on the 13th of January, which gave several days' grace in case, in the meantime, matters developed of their own accord. Then, if nothing intervened, he would make his apologies on behalf of the whole family, with no particular reference to any individual, and explore the circumstances for John's absence through light and general conversation. Any covert probing would be subtly wrapped in fellowship. Until then, life with Emmie should continue as before.

"You had better go to Emmeline, Elizabeth, and comfort her," said Jeremiah in a kind voice. "I think we have been unnecessarily cruel. But, whilst I desire to see her consoled, the fact of the matter is that we no longer have any use for her here and I, for one, wish her rid."

"Amen to that," expressed Harriet.

"I agree," added Elizabeth, rising from her seat.

"I could go to her?" suggested Daniel, looking between their faces for approval."

"Certainly not," replied Harriet. "This is far better left to your sister. I refuse to foster any vested interest." She turned to Elizabeth. "It would be wisest to get it over with as soon and as gently as possible. Spare her feelings, but be firm in your message."

"Which is?" she asked intelligently.

"That she should seek alternative arrangements, as circumstances have altered. Tell her, the trip to Bath is cancelled."

"That will not do at all," she responded. "It offers no rational excuse. Heaven alone knows how she would react to such news. I need to say more to stop her erupting, something less brutally final. After all is said and done, she knows nothing of our original scheme and nothing to cause us to change our minds over her need to be my companion."

"I so love a good argument," remarked Daniel with roguish expression, putting a hand into his pocket and pulling out a gold sovereign, "it's so improving. Here, give her this and send her packing." He flicked the coin to Elizabeth, who let it fall on the floor, where it rolled under a chair." Daniel scrambled on his hands and knees to recover it.

"Oh, cheer up, ladies," said Jeremiah, watching the seat of Daniel's trousers wriggle from side to side as his hand searched blindly between the wooden legs, "at least Daniel is now showing us his best side."

"Then," added Harriet, once the giggling died, "you, Lizzy, should give Emmeline your sincere thanks for her companionship over the Christmas and New Year period, adding that you now realise how emotionally damaging it would be to leave the area without Unity. Affix how the weather has turned too bitter to take the infant away from her home comforts. Tell her the family is to rally around and that we can best get through the coming weeks and months if left alone. Say her close friendship has been most amiable, but it has to come to an end. That should do very well."

"I've never heard such tripe," declared Daniel in unusually strong tone, having found and pocketed the coin. "She knows a great deal about us and particularly of Elizabeth's circumstances, most of which we certainly don't want publicised. Believe me, if this is handled badly, she will tell everyone she meets and add how she was unfairly dismissed for discovering our skeleton in the cupboard. Goodness, she has already demonstrated a capacity for vengeance. No, we need to sweeten the pill, making her beholden to us in some way. Only then will we be safe."

"He's right," exclaimed Elizabeth, sitting back. "It's a tricky one."

"Instead, listen to this suggestion," asserted Daniel. "I will pay her extra attention, to make her feel I care. In fact, you all could play a role. Then, when this is achieved, I will wish her every happiness in the future and suggest I help her find a new position elsewhere so, occasionally, we can meet as equals away from your prying eyes. She should find that alluring."

"A very dangerous game!"

"If it's played badly, yes, Father, but I have control over it. I can further suggest that schemes are afoot to change her role within the household from companion to one of servitude, as the trip to Bath has been postponed. I could then imply how she is likely to become unhappy here if she stays."

"She must not return to Wheat Sheaf Farm. That would be a disaster."

"Then, we must use a certain degree of cunning. I could find out who needs a servant and suggest she goes there by direct route, with our highest recommendation."

"Tell Collins I want to see her in my study," commanded Jeremiah, gesturing towards Daniel. "I need my foot eased."

Collins duly arrived in the small but elegant room of books, finding Jeremiah standing by the window.

"Put that stuff away," he ordered, walking easily to the desk. "It's your brain I need, not your healing hands. I have a thought."

"I am relieved to hear it, Sir," she replied suspiciously.

"No, more a concern actually."

"Oh, I am sorry to hear that, Sir!"

Over the next few minutes Jeremiah explained all the proposals, ending by asking for her opinion.

"And this was Master Daniel's idea?"

"Yes."

"Don't you smell a rat?"

"A rat?" he replied, looking around the floor.

"A metaphorical rodent. Master Daniel's suggestion may be considered to be biased towards his inclinations."

"My thoughts exactly. He has a soft spot for her."

"You must ask yourself 'why?'."

"I think that's entirely obvious, even to you. He's a randy young man and she's an available wench of dubious past."

"Precisely, Sir. The skill will be to turn that to our advantage."

"How?"

"By treating him as a man of experience in affairs of the heart."

"But, he isn't. He's far too young for that."

"A grave error, if I may say so. Age has no bearing on how often a man loses his heart, it merely places hurdles in the way of expressing it to affect the desired result."

"Meaning, Collins?"

"Meaning, Sir, Master Daniel would undoubtedly run a mile if he thought any dalliance with a dairymaid would commit him to a life with her."

"There are dairymaids and dairymaids. That Christabel woman was a cut above, by all accounts."

"But Emmeline isn't. She has little common sense and even less physically to offer him except for certain, shall I say, fundamental experiences which, if I am not mistaken, he would treat as merely a step up the long ladder of life. He will become bored by her shallow mind once he has taken from her the little he actually wants."

"Her very ample bosoms?"

"Yes, among other anatomical parts."

"That's awful!"

"It's nature."

"Are you telling me he *wants* to be seduced?

Collins said nothing.

"You are, aren't you? Are the young really that debased nowadays, what with Elizabeth and everything besides?"

"I am, Sir, but it's far from new. In fact, compared to our grandfathers' time, the young nowadays are moral saints. Like it or not, certain facts have to be faced. One is, if the woman in question is willing, there is little to stop Master Daniel from gaining the desired experience if he sets his cap on it. However, the very offering of it might frighten him away. That is equally likely in my opinion."

"Guaranteed?"

"No, Sir, gambled. But, Sir, if I may speak my mind, Master Daniel is all hot air and fancy pants, beneath which he is commendably good, much like you."

"You have no idea what I am like, Collins. You are not privileged to my mind."

"I think I am, Sir. You like me massaging your foot in a way that ought to be done only by the mistress, a mistress, or a qualified doctor. And, if I am not mistaken, the pleasure is more than relief from common pain."

"Collins, what are you suggesting?"

"You also get a certain pleasure from my frank speaking. But, then, you know I do it out of fondness, not duty."

"The point being?"

"The point is, you know exactly when to ask me to stop, preventing any impropriety. So will Master Daniel."

He considered the advice. "You must allow me to know how I feel about your hands on my leg, but I take the general point about Daniel."

"Shall I raise your trousers, Sir?" she said slyly, a twinkle in her eye.

"Yes, Collins, I think you might."

CHAPTER 20

The Levels

The early morning mist on this 10th day of January had lifted, leaving in its wake an atmosphere of warmth that was almost Spring like. After the bitter weeks of November and December, when thick clothes and roaring fires had not managed to take away the chill, it had came as a surprising, almost astounding respite to the rawness of Winter, an oasis of pleasure that lifted spirits. It was almost leonine in its furtive unobtrusiveness, unexpected and graceful in its coming and, yet, all powerful in its impact.

Daniel had chosen this very day to invite Emmie to join him on a business trip to Tant Suthern, a village generally thought to be as near to idyllic as anywhere in the West Country. It was intended to be the overture to his plan to move matters along.

At the centre of the village was a large area of green, fully common land, understood to be manorial waste. Paths cut hither and thither through the grass like a spider's web, connecting cottages, shops and other buildings standing at its edges.

Owned by nobody, the grassland had been used freely and happily for grazing small numbers of animals and other traditional country purposes for centuries, without difficulty or interruption to everyday village life. Then, the 1857 Inclosure

Act had been passed in Parliament, which had made certain activities a criminal offence, followed by the 1876 Commons Act which had further tightened the noose under the guise that nothing should be done on common land that could be deemed a 'public nuisance'.

These sanguine Acts, intended only as blunt instruments to maintain the character of villages with greens and stop common land from becoming little more than fenced-in farmland, had unintentionally heralded an unexpected consequence, particularly to this village. The Acts had provided the means by which certain land-owners and self-interested busybodies had been able to disrupt the lives of innocent villagers who had traditionally used the wasteland to help eke a living, while also unreasonably legitimising the prohibition of virtually any other use of the common area found to be irksome to the elderly agitators. Their greatest tool was the vagueness of the term 'public nuisance', which could be manipulated to fit virtually any activity they wanted to stop. Those without land or public influence merely complied with the will of the powerful, while those with power showed only contempt for the legal provisions of the Acts if they disrupted their own personal enjoyment.

Thus, the very threat of criminal prosecution had been enough to turn the meek into diffident onlookers within their own village, transforming the grassland into a virtual park for the socialites, who allowed their own mounted horses to graze the lush grass after fox hunting and turned a blind eye when their own heavily-laden farm wagons recklessly passed over the grass and churned deep grooves into the soil. Such abuses were openly committed, so sure were these privileged few of their invulnerability within village hierarchy. It would take a brave and steadfast man of considerable means to challenge such abuses and crush the worst excesses of the busybodies, probably an incomer to the county with little regard for anyone who did not truly merit respect by their actions: A DFL no doubt – a Down From London-er. Unfortunately, at this time no such man had yet appeared in the village. So, the double standards prevailed in an unhappy but silent truce, which left the village tense and the majority of villagers poorer.

Dominating the best view over the green from its elevated position was an imposing new village school, built of heavy stone in 1880 on the former site of a dainty row of thatched cottages. The school's impressively tall mullion windows and pointed gables, each topped with the carved figure of a saint, announced its Christian link to the neighbouring 14th century church and the adjacent village hall.

"I won't be a moment, Emmie," said Daniel as he climbed from the rented gig. "I have a parcel for the school." He grabbed a box, struggling to carry its weight.

"What on earth is in it? Bricks?"

"Books, very heavy books," he replied, using his knee as a prop while fumbling to find a balanced grip.

The books took only a few minutes to deliver, by which time dozens of little girls wearing shawls over white pinafores and boys in grey snaked out from separate arched doors and into the playground, where hopping, skipping and rolling of hoops began in at atmosphere of released laughter.

"There," said Daniel as he returned. "That didn't take long."

"It's an odd place to give books. Why here of all places, miles and miles from home?"

"It was John Madden of all people who encouraged my family to do it in the first place, as an act of charity. We started giving a year or so back. It seems John knows a young man who used to live in Westkings, but is married now and has moved away with his new wife of considerable fortune. Damn lucky fellow! Anyway, the young man in question and John used to be enemies, but have since made up due to a shared loss, both being older and wiser. They also now live in the same area of Wessex, making contact inevitable. Now, apparently this fellow is related in some way to an ex-teacher who used to give books to a school in

Westkings and, well, you know what it's like. Feeling obliged by the new friendship, John also offered to donate books as a gesture of charity to the poor. Then, when John dined with us and told us about his philanthropy, well, you can guess the rest. A glass of wine or two during a pleasant evening and, before we knew what we had signed up to, we had volunteered to do the same, and so it goes on. Regrets are bad form if the offer is withdrawn by the first light of dawn."

"But still you don't say why here, in this village, and not Sherborne or Cerne?"

"Oh, that's also down to Father. He knows the chap who donated the land for the new school. So here we are, and jolly inconvenient it is, too."

"I knew that man, the one you said John met unexpectedly. His name is Edmond Elvington. I'm right, aren't I?"

"What a coincidence," he replied through a yawn of noticeable size, having risen from his bed particularly early.

Emmie let the subject drop. With a flick of the reins, the gig moved off and was guided to a back street.

"Before we go home, I thought I would show you this." He jumped down, helping Emmie from the opposite side. "Quite a view, isn't it?"

Emmie stopped at a five-bar gate attached to a pretty farm cottage, stepping onto the bottom rung to look over the many acres constituting this part of The Levels. It was a low area of agricultural land, criss-crossed with ditches in an attempt to keep it drained, yet which flooded into jewelled lakes whenever continuous rain overwhelmed the meagre defences. For those who worked The Levels for a living, a constant battle ensued with nature, completely expected and yet still provoking, as ordinary and regular as the rain itself. It was not so much *if* The Levels would flood in Winter, but by how much.

The day being exceptional, it seemed everybody felt the invigoration of a snatched moment of warmth, those better off and with time on their hands grasping the unexpected opportunity to walk or ride the muddy lanes, their faces absorbing soft rays of sunshine, their fashionable shoes unsuited to the conditions. But, nowhere on the hundreds of acres of grassland that spread before them was a single four-legged animal to be seen beyond a black and white dog running happily around its rustic master, who alone trod the pastures.

The Levels here were not entirely flat, nor generally raised to any extent, but a mid-way between the two, with slightly rolling fields sliced through by straight outcrops of trees at near, middle and far distances, erratically placed but overlapping in perspective at various points to give the deception of merger into a single entity. The individual branches of the first line of trees were easily discernable, but those of the next line formed a sepia mass, while the farthest were little more than shadowy hazes ahead of a hilly backdrop. Here, at the extreme distance, The Levels ended and low clouds became gently illuminated into an orange-red.

To Emmie's left was the only nearby rise of a substantial nature, too small to be called a hill and, yet, too steep to climb without the expenditure of considerable effort. A single skeletal tree stood defiantly at its crest. Farm tracks wound their way around the base and into the next field, ending in puddles beneath another gate.

Only a fortnight before, heavy rain had caused considerable flooding, turning the land into a shimmering lake of grey-blue. Waterfowl of many types had flocked to the scene, some birds perching on grassy tufts that stood as little isolated islands. But, now that most of the water had receded, the birds had gone too, leaving behind saturated grass that was less green than elsewhere. In all, it was a picture of tranquillity, where nature gave gentle reminders that man only rented occupation of the land, but never fully controlled it.

"'Tis a lovely spot you have brought me to, Daniel. Look, the whole place sleeps, ready to wake bright and fresh in Spring. You can just feel the shallow breathing of the soil in hibernation."

He stared at the pastures, damp and green. "I've never thought of it that way. I just like the place."

"Do try."

"Alright, alright, for your sake, Emmie. But you must realise, a man is made differently from a woman and sees things his own way."

She looked at him thoughtfully, observing how he tried to understand nature the way she did, but was failing in the effort.

"Give yourself time, Daniel. Try to breath with the land. It will come to you with patience."

"I should like to, but I fear it looks too much like ordinary grass to me," he persisted, standing in despair. "How did you learn such things?"

"I once worked in a factory in Dorchester. It was the worse time of my life, forced on me by poverty brought about by relying on a corrupt man. Such experiences of hurly-burly cities, where there are vast numbers of people who don't care if you live or die, but would trample over your body if it quickened their journey, and where every brick is owned by someone or other, have a tendency to affect the way a village girl sees the open countryside. Can't you feel it? It's a place of free spirits and free food if you know where to look."

"I've always thought of Dorchester as being rather fine."

"That depends on the circumstances of the visit, I expect. If I went there with money in my purse, wining and dining at the best hotels and shopping in its elegant streets, and with no greater worry than what time I should leave, why, I would be bound to love the place too. But, if fate casts your body asunder to live in a rat-squalid room, fearful of any knock at the door in case it brings the next demand for rent, and with nothing in your pocket but the space where a few pennies had once been, it takes on a different character entirely."

"Have you lived like that, Emmie?" asked Daniel, genuine pity in his voice. "Only, if you have, I didn't know."

"Why should you? It isn't something I like to remember, let

alone talk about." She looked to the horizon, gaining strength from views familiar to much of Wessex. "Look, Daniel, there's a balloon in the sky."

"I see it," he yelled in excitement, pointing to the far distance. "I wonder what it must be like to be up there, to be as free as a bird."

"I wouldn't want to find out," she returned, watching as the round, dark object slowly moved where the wind demanded. "How does it stay up?"

"Hydrogen gas or hot air from a burner. No, I can see the envelope is perfectly spherical, so it must be gas."

"Where does it come from?"

"I'm not entirely sure. I think it has something to do with sulphuric acid and its chemical reaction with iron. I could be wrong. All I know is, hydrogen is highly explosive if it catches a spark."

"So, those poor people are flying under a bomb?"

"Yes, you might say so."

"Shall we watch a little longer, in case something happens to it?"

"Emmie," he reprimanded, "the countryside is not a place for tragedies, so a young lady once told me. That is kept for the cities!"

"It can be," she concluded, lowering herself from the gate, "but of a different kind."

He helped her into the gig.

"Will you allow me to buy you a late lunch at the inn on the green?"

"That would be nice."

They stopped outside in full view of the owner, who ordered a lad to lead the horse to the rear. Before entering, they took time to admire the view across the green.

"Have you eaten here before, Daniel?"

"I have, but irregularly. In truth, I am virtually a stranger."

"With other women, I shouldn't wonder, under an assumed

name." Her playful remark earned no response. "Now, it's my turn to join you. My parents in Stirminster Oak would be amazed at my elevated position."

Together, they entered the establishment, where a good table was provided under a window.

"Regarding what you said outside," faltered Daniel, as he edged Emmie's chair towards the table, "it seems my sister has decided not to travel to Bath, after all. It would be unfair to Unity. In consequence, it has come to my notice that my parents may be looking for changes."

"Oh, yes," was her innocent reply, enjoying the smell of freshly cooked food coming from the kitchen.

"The oldies are of the fickle variety and I fear they intend to change your role amongst us to one of a more domestic nature. I'm sure you would hate it."

"A servant, you mean?"

"Yes. Isn't that dreadful?"

"I suppose I always thought it would happen eventually, when the fairy tale ended. I knew I would wake up from the dream and be back in the cowshed. It's just come a bit sooner than I imagined. Oh well. It's alright, Daniel, I don't really care. Work is work and we can still see each other, if that's what you're worrying about."

"Of course," he stammered at the unexpected emotionless nature of her reply. As she became preoccupied by the soup heading their way, he pulled his thoughts together. "Only, I thought you might prefer to look for different employment, as a means of maintaining your present standards, now you've tasted the better side of things."

"No, I'm happy in whatever your parents decide for me," she said glibly, as if rehearsed. "I have no particular expectations."

"Oh!"

"Daniel, please, it really is alright. I was made for the bucket and cow, or, if your parents prefer, the bucket and mop."

"Oh . . . right . . . well . . . good," he muttered into the soup, which he consumed in thoughtful silence. The main course arrived as a platter of roast pork.

"My problem is," he eventually continued, "my parents would take a dim view of me if I spent any meaningful time in the company of a servant. You can see their point, can't you?"

"Like your father does, you mean?"

"What?"

She grinned knowingly, while spreading apple liberally over the meat as if a sweet gravy. "I doubt your father would treat me in the same manner he treats Collins, for various reasons," was her wickedly intentioned riposte.

"Meaning?"

"Oh, nothing," she teased.

"No, you meant something by that. I want to know. What has Collins to do with any of this?"

"Oh Daniel," she continued through a sigh of scepticism. "Have you really no idea what Collins does for your father?"

"I don't know what you mean."

"Then, I'm not the person to tell you. Ask him yourself, man to man."

With incredulity, he dismissed her words as rambling and turned his attentions to more pressing matters. "Anyway, I just thought you would be happier to find another job where, occasionally, we could meet as equals."

"Equals?" she gulped. "Hardly. It could never be, unless you have a marriage licence in your pocket." Her ready laugh faltered at the severe look appearing on his face, which showed no sign of conviviality, but was racked with seriousness. She stopped chewing. "No! That can't be it? Are you asking me..?"

"No!" he shouted, inviting the sudden attention of other diners. He nodded to each apologetically before leaning towards Emmie. "No, that's not what I meant at all and you must make no mistake on that part. Of course," he added as an afterthought, once he noticed several diners still attentive to their conversation, "I am sensible of the honour your acceptance of a proposal would do me, if made, but that is not what I meant. No, not at all."

"The man's a complete bounder," remarked an elderly gentleman who had strained to hear the conclusion to Daniel's conversation, but now turned away.

"What did he say to the maid? I couldn't hear," enquired his portly wife.

"He won't marry her."

"Is she in trouble?"

"Must be. She's clearly not of his class."

The wife turned to Daniel and frowned. "Do the decent thing, young man. Your conduct is contemptible."

Daniel, who remained poker-faced throughout the short scolding, smiled slightly, acute embarrassment paralysing his tongue.

"If I see you here again," she continued, "I hope it will be with a wedding ring on the lady's finger. Think on and do the right thing by her and the child, you wicked man."

Daniel withered, pale and broken, staring wide-eyed at Emmie.

"Upon my word, Daniel, you've turned the colour of cauliflower."

"Did you hear that woman," he asked Emmie nervously. "Our private conversation is being overheard and my intentions misinterpreted. She thinks you're having a baby."

"That's what comes of eavesdropping."

"Do I need to say more to clarify matters of marriage, Emmie?"

"I don't think so," she returned mischievously through curling lips. "Yet I think you propose too hastily."

"What!" he exclaimed, almost leaping from his seat.

"You can ask much of me and I would consider a reply, but we are too much strangers at present for any proper long-term commitment."

Relieved, he sat back, his pulse dropping. The circle of misunderstanding had been broken.

"Now that's settled," he said, "can we get on with our meal and forget the whole sorry business?"

"However," she crowed, "I've been engaged to be married twice, both times before my twentieth birthday, no less, and found the experiences pleasant ones until circumstances brought the engagements to a halt before the nuptials."

Daniel was shocked, but wanted to engage in conversation, any conversation, which estranged the earlier misunderstanding of marriage. Talking about Emmie's earlier life offered such an opportunity, or so he thought. Yet, without realising, he was being manoeuvred by Emmie's worldly ways into a new trap.

"Did you love both men?" he asked innocently, foolishly.

"Yes, and bedded them too," she added with bravado.

Daniel buckled. "What a thing to admit to anyone," he whispered in rebuke. "You make yourself appear so cheap."

"You asked."

"I didn't want to know that," he replied.

"Ask the next question."

"What question?"

She closed the gap between them. "If I would have bedded you if circumstances had been similar."

"The thought never crossed my mind."

"Anyway, answering the unasked question, I only bed men I love."

"And you don't love me," he said with relief.

"I could, for the twenty minutes required."

"Let's get on with the business in hand," he blustered anxiously, taking up his knife and fork.

"Alright, alright. If it tickles your fancy, I suppose I can oblige. After all, you have bought me dinner. But, you must respect me afterwards. Come on. You carry my favour for such a brief moment, there's no time to waste." She rose.

"No, Emmie," he pleaded, staying firmly fixed to his chair. "I meant the business of eating our meal."

"I realised that, Daniel, you goose," she said puckishly, sitting again. "I was teasing you. Anyway, twenty minutes is nothing but a warm-up period."

There was a long, stunned pause. He turned away, swallowing hard. Emmie's stare remained focused. She was enjoying his discomfort.

"As to marriage, Daniel," she added, "I will give you hope by adding this."

Daniel spun back, fearing what would come next from her runaway tongue.

"A woman might reject such an offer, not once but twice or even thrice, without expecting her suitor to give up heart. A refusal to marry can, sometimes, be seen as good manners. Now I am elevated in position, albeit temporarily, I can risk turning each card as it is played, fearless of losing the game."

"My goodness," he cried once more, no longer worried if he made an exhibition of himself. "Aren't you listening to anything I say? For heaven sake, woman, you've got it all wrong. You misquote my words and turn my intentions upside down."

"What did she say?" enquired the portly wife.

"She's already been engaged twice, to other men."

"Strumpet! He should save himself for someone more worthy."

"Shall I tell him, dear?"

"What did you say?" she asked, cupping her ear.

"Shall I tell him what you think?"

"Ignore them, Ernest, the pork's arriving."

Emmie smiled generously, noticing how the steaming food gained their full attention. She had lost her audience. She placed a reassuring hand on Daniel's. "Calm yourself, I was just playing with you. We may have our fun in whatever way pleases you, but I've set my cap elsewhere."

"You have? Oh, good. Where, for goodness sake?"

"That's for me to know. Of course, I don't expect anything to come of it, but you are too much of a boy to interest me beyond a bit of inconsequential flirting."

"I don't know about that!" he bluffed, throwing his napkin on the table in red-blooded fashion. "I see I'll have to think of a way to prove I'm not!"

"I thought you would never ask."

Before Daniel had time to realise the imprudence of his words, she beckoned the landlord.

"A room if you please, for one night only to begin with."

"Oh, Lord," murmured Daniel nervously.

CHAPTER 21

Explanations

*I*t was done. It had taken Emmie less than three weeks to manoeuvre Daniel into spending his first night away in the company of an unattached woman, and she intended to see it through.

As the evening drew in and fires were stoked, lamps lit and curtains pulled, the inn took on a romantic atmosphere, delicious, alluring. A piano played softly, its ivory notes adding an eloquence that drifted imperceptibly through the rooms, sweetened by the gentle bouquet of claret and Madeira.

Emmie excused herself from the table, making her way up to the room where she removed the fichu that covered her shoulders and had been tied at the front in a loose knot, exposing the low, rounded cut of her dress. Minutes later she returned, bending over the table to reveal the fullness of her breasts as she plucked a tiny morsel of food from Daniel's mouth with the corner of a napkin. Daniel looked askance, his eyes straining to see if anybody else noticed what she was doing. His embarrassment at her forward ways and obvious gestures was acute.

In her enthusiasm for the evening, and enjoying the attention she brought, Emmie at one point deliberately pushed a fork onto the floor by the feet of a young man who now sat at the next table.

She bent down slowly, provocatively, to pick it up, knowing he would act first. Their heads bumped hard, his eyes diverting to her breasts before amorous smiles were exchanged. The man looked up at Daniel, who wore a cold expression that displayed both foolishness and mistrust. Realising her mistake, Emmie sat back up in silence, nursing her head and leaving the man to place the fork onto the table without receiving gratitude.

The hour of 7 o'clock struck on a morning that was as slow as the deepest dawn. At the inn on the green, few visitors had risen from their warm beds, leaving the staff to occupy the communal areas. Emmie, having lived a life of early starts, was up and awaiting Daniel, who, on this occasion, had leapt from his bed and hurriedly readied himself to avoid further censure from the other guests.

The two breakfasted together before returning home in frosty silence. They were estranged in all ways except for their physical closeness on the seat of the gig. Emmie felt anger, misused at his hands, for Daniel had dipped a toe into her world, delving into the ethereal wiles of womanhood, and had been drowned by the experience. What passed as flirtation and romance to the girl had been repellent to the frightened boy.

Emmie jumped off the gig even before the horse had pulled to a halt outside the Grant family house, bursting through the front door and running towards her room. Harriet watched as Emmie pounded the stairs. She rushed to meet her son.

"What's amiss? Where have you been? We've been out of our minds with worry."

"Not that worried," remarked Jeremiah, casually joining them at walking pace. He winked towards Collins, who stopped herself from laughing by staring hard at the floor.

"I can explain," said Daniel, his earnest expression passing between them. "I think I've achieved your bidding."

"Bidding?" shouted Emmie, without regard for any

embarrassment she might cause herself or others, having crept back onto the landing to hear what passed between the Grants gathered below.

Her distant voice seemed to came from nowhere. They looked up at their tormentor. She had her audience.

"Have you been using me, and Daniel in particular?" she asked forcefully. "Am I of so little value to any of you, so low in your estimation, that you think I have no feelings?"

"Go back to your room, Emmeline," demanded Harriet, her face showing all the signs of controlled irritation. "This is a private conversation, in which you have no right of participation."

Emmie leaned further over the banister rail in defiance. "Which involves me!" she screamed. "Tell them, Daniel. Tell them what we did last night, before you so cruelly scolded me for leading you on! Tell them what sort of boy you are. A viper in the nest."

Daniel winced, the words astonishing him by their bluntness. She was beyond control, with no restraints of class.

"Daniel?" pleaded Harriet.

"Well, go on," taunted Emmie from high above. "If you don't, I will."

"Daniel?" commanded Harriet once more in dreadful tone, leaving no room for manoeuvre.

Daniel gawped at Emmie. "We did absolutely nothing to be ashamed of," he said, daring to look her in the face. "Nothing whatsoever!"

"What?" exclaimed Emmie in a hysterical outcry. "Tell them how you made sure we were cut off from here by talking the whole afternoon through, leading me to believe I could trust in your protection. Tell them how you wanted to take my hand while we sat in close company at the inn on the green. Tell them how you talked of marriage, spoken loudly so others who dined in close proximity could hear."

"Daniel?" bellowed Harriet once more, astonished by the suggestion.

"What complete rubbish. Don't believe her, Mother. Marry her? I think not!"

"You must not believe him," Emmie shouted recklessly. "I tell the truth. Tell them, Daniel, what happened as the evening drew in. Tell them how I lay still against you, your arm around me, never moving and always expecting your kiss to touch my lips. Then how I slipped down to sit on the floor at your feet, by the open fire, where your arm reached over my shoulder and I took your hand. Tell them how, later, my soul trembled with the atmosphere in the bed-chamber, which carried the air of passion."

"Stop that," beseeched Daniel, turning scarlet-faced. "Sit kissing, and you slipping to my feet in a public place? The very suggestion is remarkable. Honestly, Mother, Father, we did nothing. It is possible to stay away without evil inclinations, you know. This is pure fantasy."

"Ha, ha!" expounded Emmie once again, making a mockery of his softer eloquence. "The errant boy re-emerges from the skin of a man."

"Shut up, Emmie!" he exploded. "Father, Mother, I will tell you exactly what happened in a full and honest account, which must be believed. I am your son; she is, well, we all know what she is. Indeed, I know more than most. Don't listen to anything she has to say until I have finished, and even then you must take my word over hers."

"That's it, cosy up together. Very well, listen to his lies. Truth be told, I can't wait to hear them myself."

"I haven't been allowed to say anything, yet," he raged in return. "Why can't you be quiet for a moment?"

"Because I know what's going on inside your little head."

Harriet showed ambivalence, but gestured for Emmie to be quiet with a wave of her hand. She turned to her husband.

"I just knew something like this would happen if we left Daniel to his own devices. No good has come from it."

"That's so unfair," Daniel replied in injured voice.

"Go on then, Daniel, I'm listening. Just ignore her if she interrupts. Convince me of the merits of your stay away."

"Well, it was like this," he began. "After delivering the books and taking a brief walk, we ate a meal, and what remained of the afternoon we idled away in conversation of absolutely no particular importance. I hadn't reckoned on the dark settling in so early, because the day had been bright and Spring like. Yet, almost without warning, the warmth and sunshine turned chilly and dim, making the long journey home a dull prospect. So, we stayed at the inn on the green and enjoyed supper before retiring."

"I told you," shouted Emmie, now paying them little attention while she untied her shoes.

"She's trying to mislead you with innuendo," rebuffed Daniel. "I know I messed about with her over Christmas, but now she's taking revenge by making mischief."

"Revenge for what?" asked Harriet.

"Answer that," bellowed Emmie.

"I told her she was no longer invited to stay here as a guest."

Harriet gazed up to the landing. "Is this true?"

"What?" replied Emmie nonchalantly, now dangling her shoes over the edge in licentious manner.

"Is it true he told you of your changed circumstances among us?"

"He mentioned it in passing, after I told him I couldn't possibly accept a proposal of marriage so unexpectedly delivered."

"There we are," said Jeremiah. "Daniel's telling the truth."

"Hold on," cried Emmie in ear-splitting pitch. "Which part do you believe and which do you choose to ignore as never said? Didn't you hear me? I said he proposed marriage."

"And we choose to call you a liar," returned Harriet. "It is an obvious falsehood, intended to gain sympathy."

"Anyway," replied Emmie, horrified her ace had been trumped, "I told him I didn't care one way or the other whether I was regarded as a guest or a servant. So, what are the odds?"

"You don't care if you return to servitude?" yelled Harriet. "You would have us believe that?"

"Believe whatever you like. Tread me underfoot. You intend to, anyway."

Harriet was overcome with disappointment, for the truth in Emmie's words rang clear from the tone of their delivery.

"I'm unsure what to think. Who is spinning me a yarn? Is it you, Daniel?"

"Ripe, that's what this is, ripe. I do your bidding and what do I get in return? Not a vote of thanks, but an inquisition." His own words seemed to astonish him, as if his brain acted independently, over which he exercised no control. Yet, the eloquence was praiseworthy.

"Very well," said Harriet, "I've heard enough for the time being. At least you are home safely and most probably unscathed. We can reconvene later, when I've had time to think what to do with you both." She turned to go, leaving the truth as the only casualty.

Watching her turn, Emmie flared into indefensible madness, releasing her shoes to fall over the rail. They dropped like stones and crashed onto the tiled floor below. Harriet froze, her arms folded defensively above her head.

"Ask him!" Emmie yelled, her face contorted with fury. "Ask your precious Daniel to explain the sleeping arrangements."

"Be still, Emmie," screamed Daniel. "What makes you think anyone wants to listen to any more of your crazy talk. You've done your best to make me look foolish and failed miserably. Now you give my sainted mother heart failure. This must end at once." He began to walk away, but Jeremiah grabbed his arm.

Emmie saw the intervention as licence to continue. "I don't care what any of you think of me, but you should know what sort of son you have."

The promise held in the revelation was scarcely likely to be courteous to anyone. Daniel stopped struggling.

"Ah, so at last I regain your attention," added Emmie. "Ask the landlord of the inn. That's what I say. Ask him if there was only one room unoccupied, which Daniel paid for. There. It's in the open. And, by the way, you may all now close your mouths."

Harriet shook loose from the revelation, endeavouring to appear unemotional. But, insomuch as she strived to remain dignified, she was not altogether succeeding, her strength and solemnity slowly ebbing away.

"I held no fear to hear that," she said in straightforward reply. "You are desperate, Emmeline, racked with delusion and headstrong. They are not qualities I admire. God may strike you dead in the midst of your outrageous histrionics."

"If He doesn't launch a thunderbolt at your son first, or do all men stick together?" She stopped, horrified at her own words, said in anger. "I'm sorry. I didn't mean that. But, I am sure the Good Lord would know who deserves His wrath."

"And so do we, Emmeline. Make no mistake on that score and pray for forgiveness."

It was a war of words Emmie was losing on every front. She was again thrown by her lack of success in raising the stakes, when the weapons she held at the outset seemed overwhelming against any defence Daniel could muster. Surrender to the closed ranks of the Grants now appeared inevitable, the terms for a truce becoming uppermost in her thoughts. And, in this way, she calmed, weakened by failure. She stood erect and humbled, wanting to offer no further ill-will if reconciliation was still possible.

"You need have no fear of me, any of you, if you treat me properly and not like the house cat to be kicked. I don't care what work I do. Don't you see, I have nowhere else to go."

"You should've thought of that before making such a mommet of yourself. It is too late to adopt a contrite tone now, my girl, or think we should care. The harm is done and cannot be undone. You have been listened to, judged and found wanton." Harriet allowed herself a moment of triumph at the witticism.

"I'll pack my belongings," Emmie muttered, turning towards the door, but stopped to peer down to her accusers once more. "I suppose this is only what Daniel said would happen. I never stood a chance."

"It is the way of close families, Emmeline. You must learn to know your position and be happy with it."

"I am."

"Then, all is settled. You can return to your old world and leave us to ours."

"For shame; for shame! You all disgust me," she said sullenly. "But, I warn you, as God is my witness. If any of you do me harm in the eyes of others from this day forward, you have no idea what horrors might slip from my lips."

"Damn you, Emmeline."

"I think I am already damned. But thank you for the sentiment."

"Is she trying to blackmail us?" bellowed Jeremiah, reddening about the cheeks as he looked to his wife for reassurance.

Harriet had no answer, but thought it wisest to find out.

"Where will you go, ungrateful girl? The further the better, I am thinking."

"You would like that. Silence me by distance. Buttered, trussed and basted like a turkey. Well, at least that's something outside your control. I'm free to do and go wherever I please. On the other hand, it's you lot who are rooted to family skeletons, which are popping out from their hiding places. I pity you, but mostly I feel sorry for Unity for being part of such a family of schemers."

"I repeat, girl, where will you go?"

"Back to John Madden's, if he will have me. It's not far enough away, but at least he'll recognise the truth. He will know a stitch-up when he hears it."

"Does she mean what I think, Jeremiah?"

"How do I know? Everything's been such confusion since Elizabeth returned."

"No, Jeremiah, tell her she cannot go back to John!" cried Harriet, her brow furrowed.

"Alas, my dear, we have no means of stopping her."

Harriet looked up. "You intend to spread rumours?"

"I intend to live my life without concern for the Grants. If I say anything to John about my time here, it will be entirely truthful. If that hurts you, so be it."

The slam of her bedroom door echoed throughout the house. Unity began to cry.

"Do something to stop that howling," bawled Jeremiah in despair. "That's all we need, for the dairymaid to go to Wheat Sheaf and put paid to John wanting anything to do with Elizabeth or any of us by association. We'll be back to square one."

"Excuse me, Sir," interrupted Collins in respectful voice. "May I suggest that *I* speak with Miss Emmeline? She might view me as impartial. I might be able to influence her in some way."

"I suppose you could try. You can't do worse than we have," reflected Harriet, speaking for her husband and now more than a little frightened.

"I thought I might break the ice by taking her a nice pot of tea to start with. After that, I think she will confide in me as a friend of her own class."

"Apply grease, Collins," added Jeremiah blandly.

"Your leg, Sir, is it playing you up again?"

"No, Collins, not that type of grease, although I do feel my gout coming back. Maybe later. No, I meant take this message to the wilful wretch. If she goes straight back to her parents for three months, not a day less, mind, she can keep all the new clothes and I will give her full wages for that period. I think she may bite the hook."

"So, she remains bait after all," remarked Daniel, hoping his responsibility for events unfolding would be overlooked.

"No, boy, she's no longer the bait. By your actions you've made her the hunter and us the hunted."

"Hunt, hunted, what are you two talking about?"

"Madam," said Jeremiah abruptly, "allow me the luxury and presence of mind to have some independent opinion."

"It's alright, Mother, we have it under control."

Harriet left the hallway, too distressed to listen to any more argument. Jeremiah placed his arm around Daniel and together they walked into the study.

"Do you want to tell me what actually happened?" appealed Jeremiah in relaxed tone, as he sat at his desk.

"Nothing, I assure you."

"Come, come, there's more than a hint of truth in what she said. Look, son, I don't blame you if anything took place of a remarkable nature. Male to male, I would have found resistance difficult in early manhood. The single consolation of ageing is a reduction in inclination towards women. That, and having a wife of a certain disposition." He laughed. "Anyway, rights and wrongs aside, it would be best to be frank in our discussion, in case anything develops from it in the future that I need to take control over. Damage limitation, you might say. We should be prepared for all eventualities, if we are to learn from Elizabeth's circumstances."

"Develops?"

"Around October time!"

"Sorry?"

Jeremiah coughed knowingly.

"Oh, you mean. . . Good gracious, no. There's absolutely no worry on that score. I never went near her, whatever she intimates. If she's pregnant it won't be mine, and I'll tell you why. When the innkeeper said he had only one room unoccupied, I magnanimously offered it to Emmeline. She stayed there, alone. I lodged at the headmaster's house over the road. He didn't mind putting me up once I explained everything."

"So, what was all that nonsense Emmeline was preaching?"

"Just that, so much nonsense. To be blunt with you, Father, she scares me to death. She knows too much and is too worldly for an unmarried woman of her age."

"I think you've learned a valuable lesson, Daniel, and you're a better boy for it."

"Man, Father. A better *man*, trust me."

* * *

An hour later Emmie emerged from her room, well dressed and carrying two unmatched bags. She wiped her nose on her sleeve. Nobody greeted her as she walked down the two flights of stairs and into the hallway.

Outside in the courtyard, Collins waited patiently. She held a small purse of coins, a full three months' wages as promised. She had not been allowed into Emmie's room and had relayed the terms offered through the closed door, leaving the tea abandoned on the rug outside. On the other side, Emmie had listened dolefully.

Seeing Emmie close up, Collins was horrified.

"When did that happen?" she asked, looking at Emmie's bruised forehead developing into a shade of blue.

"Early this morning. It was Daniel's parting gift. My way of remembering Tant Suthern."

"Daniel? Surely not?"

"No, of course not. I lied. In fact, stupidly, I hit myself."

"How?"

"Oh, Collins! Of course he hit me."

"Why?"

"I think he blames me for our little excursion. We quarrelled and he lashed out." She squeezed a tear, which she dabbed melodramatically.

"What in heaven's name caused such a reaction? Usually, the only wicked thing about him is his humour."

"Oh, I suffered some of that, too. He was a different person this morning from last night. I think it came as a shock to jump the nest."

"That's no excuse. Will you tell the police?"

"And get him arrested for assault? No, I don't think so."

"It's your right. Nobody should get away with that unpunished."

"Even when it's deserved?"

"That's a different matter. Are you telling me you deserved to be hit?"

"No, of course not. Only, I took something from him that he prized."

"What, may I ask?"

"His dignity. Maybe also his youth."

"Did you..?"

"I don't think you should ask," said Emmie, handing her bags to the groom. "Anyway, there's a deal more to it than that. At this moment, I'm more afraid of my defender than my assailant."

"I don't understand. Who's who?"

"My defender? John Madden, naturally."

"Was he there, last night I mean?"

"No, Collins. Daniel was my assailant, but John Madden has always been my defender. I'm afraid of what he will do to Daniel when he finds out."

"But he won't, surely. You're going straight to your parents. That's the agreement."

"Of course," was her simple reply, feeling the weight of coins. She mounted the gig.

"If it helps," Collins added, "you should know that I've never known Daniel to be violent or, for that matter, to stay away without telling his parents first. I think he may have fretted the consequences."

"He's always acted badly around me. It's what he does," said Emmie while arranging her dress to fall neatly over the seat.

"Only in his own pond, where the edges offer safety. It's quite another matter for him to swim in uncharted waters. Poor Daniel, I suppose he has a deficient character."

"And his looks are not altogether handsome."

"Yes. For a young man, he is incomplete. Poor thing."

"Poor Daniel, be blowed! Anyhow, he's likely to walk with a limp from now on, at least for a while."

The groom took up the reins. Seconds later Emmie had gone.

"You'll soon get over her," remarked Jeremiah, finding Daniel looking through a window as the gig disappeared into the distance. "There are plenty of finer fish than her in the sea. The world is your oyster."

"Do me one favour, Father," responded Daniel with kindness. "Now that she's left, can we please stop talking about hooks, bait and fishy things. Oh, and by the way, can I borrow Collins? I have an acute pain!"

Knowing the Grants would be unable to admit to the bribe, Emmie cunningly decided to take the money and still return to Nether Bow, where she would ask for her old job. But Jeremiah had anticipated this possibility and had given strict instructions to the groom to release his charge only after the first day's stopover at Axminster, although better still if not before Stirminster Oak itself. Even the offer of a florin failed to change the groom's mind, but Emmie had to part with the coin anyway to stop him from telling Jeremiah of the attempted diversion. Thus, as the gig wound its way between distant villages, only she knew how close she had come to rejoining John's employment. She felt no shame for her attempted deceit, or the other involving Daniel's reputation.

CHAPTER 22

Somerset Apple Play

*E*mmie's unexpected return to Stirminster Oak sent her parents into a spin of elation. They had endured a period of deep gloom since the New Year. Her return to the fold was the fillip they needed to believe that life was still worth living.

The journey to this village, set on the southern edge of Dartmoor, midway between Plymouth and the Forest of Bligh, had been exceedingly long and physically demanding, requiring three stops once Nether Bow had been circumnavigated. Yet, the depth of the greeting made all the effort worthwhile.

The Sturry's home was a small mid-terrace in a block of four, somewhat better kept than those adjoining each side. It maintained the same stern and uncompromising appearance as when, in what seemed like a lifetime ago, Christabel had walked there alone to alert the Sturrys of Emmie's elopement with Lieutenant Longborne Charles, a journey of great personal sacrifice. The current circumstances were in some ways much happier, in others darker.

"Did you like the Christmas dress? Although, looking at you now, it must seem a pretty poor effort," said her mother, bursting to appear cheerful.

"I haven't had it yet, but that's another story for another time. Tell me, are you alright?" asked Emmie, her mother's strange disposition all too apparent. "Something is wrong, I can tell it. And you seem to have lost weight. In fact, you both have."

The question barely touched Rachel's consciousness, so resolute was she to make the most of the reunion. But, her attempts to smile failed to mask much inner anguish pinching her features.

"I wish I had known you were coming, I could've baked a cake, the kind I know you most love. And look at the place. Not tidy at all. What must you think of me? You look well, dear. What happened to your eye? Oh, goodness, I'm so pleased to have you home."

"Please, Rachel," said Joseph softly, placing his hand sensitively on her shoulder and squeezing gently. "Give the girl a moment to catch her breath." He removed a Bible from the mantel before taking a seat by his wife's side. "You must forgive your mother. She is overwrought for quite another reason."

Rachel's jaw dropped, her eyes turning from clear to sallow.

"First things first," Joseph continued. "We must thank God for the safe return of our daughter and remember other things important to us." He opened the Bible at the bookmark, but flicked over a few pages until he found a familiar text. "I am reminded of Isaiah 49:15. *Can a woman forget her sucking child, that she should not have compassion on the son of her womb? Yea, they may forget, yet will I not forget thee.*"

"Father," said Emmie, "what's going on?"

"Shush for a moment, child, while I read 52:7. *How beautiful upon the mountains are the feet of him that bringeth good tidings, that publisheth peace; that bringeth good tidings of good, that publisheth salvation; that saith unto Zion, Thy God reigneth.*" He closed the Bible. "Amen."

"Amen," repeated Rachel.

"Mother?"

Despite extraordinary effort, Rachel's spirit evaporated as the texts were read, as she was again reminded of the sadness that made joy inappropriate. She sat deeply into her chair. Joseph, too, struggled to remain strong.

"It's your brother, Robert," said Rachel after a reflective pause. "We received terrible news on New Year's Eve. Your brother, our wonderful son, has died from the bite of a poisonous spider."

"No! What are you saying, Mother? He can't be gone from us."

"Alas, it is true. With gladness we had received a long letter from him only in September, full of good news and much happiness. Robert said he prospered in Australia and was about to expand the flock of sheep. With sadness, a second letter followed, written by his business partner, Monroe. So, my dear, sometime between the two letters your brother became ill and passed over to the mercy of God. He suffered and we knew nothing about it!"

"Come, come, my love. Dry your eyes and tell Emmeline the rest. He is at peace now and the poison hurts him no longer."

She nodded in resignation. "There is no consolation to be had in the words of the second letter, although well meaning and intended to be of comfort to us. Monroe spoke well of Robert as a good friend and took much trouble to express his own feelings of tremendous loss."

"We were much moved and gratified to read it," added Joseph.

"After considerable sentiment was expressed in the lines, he concluded by saying that Robert's share in the business would be sold and the money raised would be forwarded to us. Any bits and bobs he thinks are personal and we should have will be sent on board a wind-jammer that regularly makes the crossing between Australia and England. He says we should look out for an old iron-built ocean liner now used as a sailing ship, but still holds proud at anchor." She dropped the letter. "So what? What good are these things? What is money to us without gladness?"

"Gracious, Mother! No wonder you were struggling to be

jolly. I hardly know what to say." Her voice dropped to a whisper. "'Tis strange to imagine all that happening on the other side of the world while we were going about our mundane lives in ignorance. He should never have gone. Poor Robert and poor you, my darling parents." She wiped her nose on the sleeve of her dress.

"Family needs to stay together," cried Rachel. "Are you staying, at least for a while this time?"

Emmie flung her arms around both their necks. "I am, Mother, I am."

Rachel sobbed without shame, possibly of sadness, equally possibly of relief. "Please say *it is*, Emmie, never *'tis*," she blubbed, trying to smile just a little through the tears as she pulled free. "You really should improve your speech."

"I rarely say *'tis*. It only comes out naturally when I'm upset and forget myself."

"Robert is with his Maker," said Joseph, placing the Bible into its accustomed position. With his back turned, he wiped his moist cheeks.

"It is done," cried Rachel, "and I must see that some good comes from it. When one door shuts, another opens. Isn't that what we've always thought, Joseph?"

He said it was.

"We must all hold steady in our work and our beliefs, although there's no denying it will be hard. We must remember the good times. But, how dark our lives will be now a light has gone out." She placed a reassuring hand on Emmie's with all the love a mother holds for a naughty child. "Please, dear, use my handkerchief. You are ruining your fine sleeve."

"'Tis. . . *It's* already damp, but yes, I will use it. Why wasn't I told earlier?"

"We were about to, but you must forgive us for having to come to terms with our own grief first. A letter would have been sent to Wheat Sheaf Farm in a day or two. But, by God's grace, you have returned to us before we had to put our sadness onto paper."

"Are you really staying for a while?" asked her father.

"There is nowhere I would rather be."

"Be praised," exclaimed Joseph, hugging his daughter again with uncharacteristic tenderness. "But life goes on, and what better tribute to your brother than to continue our charity work in his honoured name, as a family reunited. Tomorrow, you can begin helping me feed the miners scratching a living in the bowels of the earth. That will be our testament to his life!"

With the removal of Emmie from complicated family issues, resolved by their separation measured in miles, and still with no contact from John Madden, Harriet and Jeremiah Grant decided the time was right for Daniel to fulfil the original plan to visit his friend on the 13th of the month. The ladies of the house remained particularly anxious to know what position, if any, Unity Isobel held in John's life.

Yet, to the resurrection of the plan, previously agreed and held in abeyance, Daniel suddenly, unexpectedly, declined to co-operate. He was now less sure of the plan's merit and said so in forthright manner. His experiences with Emmie had shocked him into taking a new view on life, and relationships in particular. He realised how easy it was for those not privy to the most intimate facts to misunderstand a disputed situation. His parents had found it difficult to believe his account of the night at Tant Suthern and, therefore, perhaps he and his parents similarly misunderstood John and Elizabeth's true relationship. And so, against all expectations, Daniel resolved to finish with imbecility for good. He now wanted nothing better than a settled and ordered lifestyle, free of controversy and free from imprudent opinions.

In essence, a metamorphosis to his character had taken place. He had been aroused by Emmie and was now inflamed to fully experience a woman, but not in a wild manner. The route to this fulfilment was clear. He would make himself attractive to a future wife in the normal way of things, a woman of good family who would, and could, be presented well in company, without any of the worry that accompanied a dilettante in society.

"I don't understand your change of heart, Daniel. You and John have shared a friendship that has been steady for years. How could you want to see it end?"

Daniel deliberated. "I don't necessarily want it to end, Father. I just want it to be based on an equal footing, as men, and not as man and boy. I am no longer the joker in the pack. If he continues to want my company, it will be for my companionship and not my idiot ways."

"I'm sure John never viewed you as a fool."

"I know he did, because I played up to that image, believing it made me popular. As I see it, we had a considerable opposition of character which sparked our friendship, matched by our difference in ages. Since his mother died he has been steady, reliable and open, with no duplicity that stains his character. I, on the other hand, could not have been of greater divergence, and this is what gave our friendship its momentum. Can't you see, I want to change too, and in so doing I have to accept that we may no longer have a bond?"

"What of your sister's predicament? Is she to be a casualty of your whim?" begged Harriet.

"That depends on my role. I'll not play games, nor make unfounded or unverifiable accusations against John."

"Shame on you, Daniel," said Elizabeth. "You do this purely out of spite. You'll never convince me of any change in your make-up, at least not after one day. Anyway, you have always appeared to be fully satisfied with yourself. Why change a habit of a lifetime?"

"And your friendship with John? Where's that disappeared to so rapidly? No, we must all face facts. For far too long we've looked upon John as someone whose opinion we depend on, whose friendship we place in the highest esteem. Yet, when Isobel Madden was alive, John was entirely feckless. I remember all too well you, Mother, and you, Father, saying John was a waster who should be kept at arm's length from Elizabeth. Not that you managed. Elizabeth herself saw to that. Yet, he changed overnight into your perfect man, and that is the course I now set for myself. I'm done with the boy and rejoice in the man! I want to be more like John."

Harriet, Elizabeth and Jeremiah gazed in amazement at his eloquence.

"Don't look at me like that," he continued. "I rather fear I may never match my own expectations. John has a disposition that is generally liked, a pleasing manner that is at times reticent and meticulous, at others clever, outgoing and euphoric. He has the rare skill of being popular, partly because he never judges people on a whim. Maybe, with changes to my character, I may be the opposite and give offence wherever I go. But it will be the genuine me. It's a risk I'm willing to take in my transition to manhood."

"Gracious," gasped Jeremiah, taking a cigar from a wooden box, "is this Daniel or an apparition in our midst?"

"It's a selfish boy who's thinking only of himself," barked Elizabeth. "He's too frightened to confront John, that's all."

"I forgive that outburst," replied Daniel calmly.

"Father, please, make him go. How else are we to know what goes on in John's head?"

"Will you go, if I ask you to reconsider in all sincerity?"

"Is it an order, Father?"

"No, just a request between men."

"Then, as it is between *men*, I will. But, don't raise your hopes as to the outcome. I will not cajole him."

The 13th day of January saw Winter return in its full fury. As Daniel rode through the tempest and struggled to open the gates leading to Wheat Sheaf Farm, he could see his friend once more battling with the hurdles, which he had re-erected and were again in trouble. The wind streamed through John's hair, his coat billowing.

Daniel tied his horse to a gatepost and fought against the gusts to reach the work in progress. John looked up as a pair of spare hands grabbed the hurdle with determination.

"Daniel! What a turn up! Thank goodness you're here. Glad to see you, my friend."

Together, they managed to lift the hurdles free of the stakes and stack them on the ground, using strong rope to bind them together.

"The damn things never did any good. They were a bad idea from the outset. Thanks for your help. Coming in? I have a pot of mulled wine inside with your name on it."

"Sounds good to me," replied Daniel.

Inside the kitchen, John and Daniel removed their coats and shook hands. The glasses, filled with the cinnamon-scented brew, were quickly emptied, leaving a warm and pleasant sensation.

"It's been a while, John. How are you keeping?"

"Pretty well in myself, I suppose, but the farm's been going to rack and ruin since Abel Tucker left. I have Emmeline Sturry to thank for that. I hear tell Elizabeth and Emmie intend to travel as a party. I can hardly believe it. How on earth did that unlikely couple come about? Have they left yet?"

"One thing at a time, John. Travelling was the original intention, but many things have since moved on. Emmeline is no longer with us and Elizabeth is preoccupied looking after Unity Isobel."

Nothing had prepared John for hearing the child's name so blatantly mentioned. He felt the awkwardness that accompanied his inactivity towards her.

"You say Emmie has left?"

"I did. She didn't fit in and has gone."

"Where? I suppose some disgrace was involved?"

"I'm not at liberty to reveal the reasons. Enough to say, she was not cruelly treated."

"Was she able to walk to wherever?"

"We provided not only a gig, but a rather handsome purse. She will be happier elsewhere, among her own."

"More wine?" asked John with relief.

"Not just yet." There was a moment's hesitation. "What's going on, John, if I may presume to ask?"

"Is that why you're here, to check up on me?"

"Not entirely, but I suppose there's no point in denying it has some bearing. Everyone is worried by your absence."

John opened the small trap door to the stove and dropped an extra log into the furnace. Heat and sparks burst into his face. He closed it quickly with arm outstretched, cheeks burning hot. A damp cloth cooled his skin.

"That was a close call."

"Your answer?"

"I know I've been negligent in the matter of Unity," he said as he sat, having tossed the cloth into a bowl. "There's no denying it. But that shouldn't be taken to mean I don't care."

"How could it be taken any other way? A written line to Lizzy would have sufficed."

"Yes, of course you are quite right. I've been selfishly remiss for far too long, putting my own problems first."

"It's so unlike you to be cruel."

"Is that how I'm seen?"

"I would dearly like to say otherwise, but I cannot. Everyone is greatly disturbed at your abandonment."

"But, I haven't given my response."

"That's the problem. You've left everything hanging and everyone in a state of suspended anguish. Just say *no*, if your answer is *no*, and our lives can move on. But, my friend, speak you must."

"You assume my reply will be negative?"

"I think we all believe it will be."

"I seem to have ill-used everyone close to me. What can I say?"

"Just a simple *yes* or *no* to Lizzy will do. Are you really in such torment? Can't you decide and put an end to the affair one way or the other?"

"You have me all wrong, Daniel. Knowing Elizabeth's problems would be unaffected by a few days' delay, I suppose I thought I could prioritise and place the running of the farm at the top of my to-do list. The place is in serious disarray. This Cornelius Fairfax fellow I hired is a dead loss. Still, I should've recognised the distress my decision to prioritise would cause Elizabeth. Believe me, she is a cherished friend. Anything that hurts her also hurts me."

"And Unity?"

John became introspective. "As to the baby, I can honestly say I've spent many hours in joyless monotony contemplating her future. It's been a hard taskmaster, with uncertainties crushing my will to see anything plainly and with confidence." He turned to Daniel, who hung on every syllable. "What man could find such a situation easily resolvable?"

"I understand."

"Do you, Daniel? Do you really?"

"Of course. I've tried to put myself in your shoes and they don't fit. If it was me, I too would resist deciding until every aspect of doubt had been met. Yet, knowing the number and complexity of uncertainties remaining, I think I would have to be deceitful to myself to ever believe all the answers were in any way obtainable. A rational mind would conclude they are not. No, I have to say I'm glad it is your problem and not mine. Nevertheless, just as the moon follows the sun, so you'll have to find an outcome which you can live with sooner or later. It can't be avoided forever."

"I know. I even sought solace from my mother's grave, and thought I had the answer. But the cold walk back renewed my doubts. Can I ask something of you, so damning in its inference that it will test our friendship?"

"You had better, if it means that much."

John played with his empty glass, rubbing the stem between his fingers. "I have to ask, Daniel..," he said with stiffness.

"If, in my opinion, Unity Isobel is really yours?"

"Yes, am I that transparent?"

"It's the nub of the problem."

"I'm so sorry if the question seems dreadful. It besmirches your sister's good name, but I have to know."

"I would be foolish if I was offended by it, John. It's a perfectly correct question under the circumstances and one I would ask in your place. My answer is that Lizzy is as trembling as a bled calf, waiting upon your decision."

"Maybe, but is Unity mine?"

"I could say 'yes' and be insincere. In truth, how can I know any more than you? Normally, it would be the man and woman involved who would know what went on. All I can do is venture an opinion based on my sister's disposition."

"You surprise me with your wisdom, Daniel, but it doesn't help. Apparently I was there on the day Unity was conceived, and yet I have no recollection. It seems extraordinary, unbelievable. Where does that leave me?"

"Up the creek," was Daniel's honest answer. "Look, surely you must remember something about the day? Anything, however trivial, might trigger your memory into greater recollections."

"I can, but nothing after a certain time. The rest is a total blank. I don't suppose you could tell me if Elizabeth has courted other men? I haven't seen her for months, and little before that. It would help me make sense of it all."

"Could or would?"

"Would."

"Will you believe my answer?"

"What choice do I have? Anyway, I can always tell when you exaggerate. No, Daniel, I must have absolute honesty."

"Very well. I asked Lizzy the same question and she replied that she had met many men in social company, but none to be alone with. I believe her. Certainly, no man has ever called at the house in a way that would lead me to believe there was anything more than friendship involved, and I've never been aware of any letters delivered of a passionate nature. Lizzy is the kind to let it slip at breakfast if any had."

"Yes, I believe she is. Then it's probably true what she says?"

"Only you can judge. I'm biased on the point, although my deepest feeling is that she has acted properly."

"Is she always so sensible in her dealings, Daniel? Only, when I saw her bedroom at Christmas, it was ... How can I put it without causing more offence?"

"Childlike?

"Indeed."

"Don't concern yourself over that one jot. Lizzy would be the first to have it redecorated if she was allowed. But, Father won't have it."

"Can I ask why?"

"It was given that frightful wallpaper by my grandfather, soon after officers began returning from the Napoleonic wars. You see, many soldiers were hideously tormented by their experiences and could no longer sleep in the normal way of things, in regular rooms. The idea of giving a bedchamber the look of a campaign tent came from France, and one or two were kept in this manner for visiting military. Such was the calming affect on the uniformed gentlemen, the decorations have remained there ever since, just in case the Frenchies don't know when they're beaten."

"So, nothing to do with Elizabeth herself?"

"Not a thing."

"Thank you for being so honest, Daniel. It has helped a lot."

"Do I have your permission to repeat the things we have spoken about? The family will ask."

"I think not," he replied unexpectedly. "I need more time to consider everything. I don't want to give false hope. A day or two will suffice. But, you can carry a message to Elizabeth from me. Please ask if she would do me the great honour of accompanying me to a Wassailing. I will collect her soon after dark on the 17th. Tell me, how will I know if she refuses?"

"Oh, she won't. Believe me, she won't."

* * *

The very next day John received an unexpected letter. It was signed 'Your dearest friend, Elizabeth'. He took a deep breath before embracing the lines so beautifully written.

My dear John

I am writing to thank you for the invitation to the Wassailing. I am extremely happy to accept and wait in patient anticipation of the evening.

Daniel has told me only scant details of your frank conversation and the ugliness of the situation in which you find yourself. I understand well the dilemma. For, had it not been the case that I was actually present at Unity's birth, I too would have found the story incredible. I say no more on the matter, as it is not my intention to influence your final decision.

For the sake of a happy reunion, I wish to make it clear that I see our outing as one between old friends and not necessarily as a sign of accord over Unity's parentage. If there was a way to confirm such blood relationships, through magic or science, I would not hesitate to seek that authentication, knowing it to be true. But, there is not, and it is of little value to you that nature alone goes some way in addressing such doubts by giving a child much of the father's appearance. I am of the recent opinion that life is not so much the quantity of happiness discovered, but the quantity of pathos endured. A centre path is probably the most enviable route between birth and death.

I really cannot brave much more uncertainty. Come to me if you will as a friend, and that alone, or yield to your instincts over Unity. Whichever feeling you most trust, it will be your one and only opportunity to affect my life and Unity's. There shall be no second chance. I could not be happy, ay, content, to live a lie, knowing that acceptance of Unity as your own would, inevitably, lead to our marriage. I

would rather be your friend than your wife under such
circumstances. My broken heart awaits your decision.
  Your dearest friend.
  Elizabeth

P.S. My parents are now supportive of Unity, so nothing
further threatens us. Keep that as good cheer, knowing that
your decision, whatever it is, cannot harm us.

As luck would have it, the early evening of the 17th remained
clear and, as yet, dry, although bitingly cold. Elizabeth sat away
from the window, fully dressed and readied an hour early,
listening for any sound approaching along the drive. It was a time
of fretfulness, for she was far from convinced he would turn up at
all. Yet, as the clock chimed each passing quarter-hour and her
expectations fell to their lowest ebb, so at 7pm the crunch of
carriage wheels suddenly became audible. Unable to exercise
restraint, she was standing at the door when he arrived, a large
cape with fur trim covering her from head to foot.

"By George," said John on seeing her resplendent in green
velvet, "you look an absolute picture."

"Daniel thinks I look like Father Christmas."

"What does he know? Come, we have a fun evening ahead."

The carriage moved off on its short journey to a local
commercial apple orchard, well known in those parts for its
Orchard's Path. No mention was made of Unity, Christmas or
earlier events, allowing the conversation to remain light and
constructive upon their renewed friendship. Presently, the
carriage pulled off the road and between tall pillars, where
upwards of one hundred people gathered around lanterns
suspended on spikes driven into the hard ground.

"It's like fairyland," said Elizabeth. "It's so beautiful."

"Have you never been Wassailing?"

"Never. What happens?"

"I'll not spoil it by telling you. You'll find out soon enough."

To the sound of a band striking up, the revellers formed an orderly line and followed the music as the players walked the Orchard's Path, which took a circulatory course through and around the open fields of apple trees, like lifeblood circulating around a body. At the largest and most productive tree the revellers halted, forming a circle around its leafless branches.

"The Apple Tree Man," whispered John, "guardian of the orchard."

"Now what?"

"Just watch and learn!"

Again the band struck up, the music pervading the still night air as a spellbinding life-force of pagan ritual. Several men walked forward, each emptying a pitcher of cider over the roots.

"That encourages a good crop of cider apples," said John. "Next, you will see soaked toast and cake spiked onto the branches to attract robins."

"Why?" she enquired, memorized by the scene.

"They are the guardian spirits of the trees. Look, other boys are pulling down the lowest branches, to dip them into pails of cider."

Earthenware cups were now passed around those gathered, filled to the brim with cider. Elizabeth lifted the cup to her lips.

"No! It's not for drinking. When everyone has a cup, we all toss the cider into the branches."

The ceremony followed John's description. Elizabeth complained at the waste until the cups were refilled as the next step in the solemnities.

"Can we drink it this time, John?"

"Only in small sips as the Wassailing song is sung, to toast the trees."

A chorus of voices gave the evening a rousing harmony. As the singing ended, shotguns were fired into the highest branches and cow horns blown in a cacophony of sound. Other onlookers beat trays and pans.

"They are driving away any evil spirits and re-awakening the trees for the new season."

Finally, the procession headed back to the starting point, where a further brew awaited, a blend of warm ale, sugar and spices, mixed with eggs. Cream floated on the top, hiding roasted apples that had been finely chopped and stirred in.

"This is absolutely lovely," said Elizabeth, as she downed her cupful. "Aren't you drinking yours, because, if you're not, I'll have it?"

John passed his cup.

"Are you sure you don't want it?"

"I'm stopping at one cup of cider. One of us has to remain upright. If not, heaven knows what might happen later!"

The inference to the General Gordon celebrations passed Elizabeth by.

"Do we go home now?" she asked in bacchanal manner, tipping her cup upside down to show that it was completely empty. "Only, I'm really enjoying myself."

"There's the Apple Play to come. Several of my farm-hands are taking part. We should watch it."

"Oh, yes."

"It has been written by a fellow from Montacute, a certain Master Tupton, one of those arty sorts you get in the theatre. Look, here they come now, each to play the part of an apple."

From the direction of a small stone building several men and women appeared, dressed in brightly coloured costumes festooned with ribbons. They headed for a makeshift stage, illuminated by more lanterns and two flaming braziers. Loud clapping greeted their arrival. A middle-aged man in rags, wearing a battered hat, took centre. The crowd roared their approval as he struck up in good voice.

> *We are just actors bold*
> *Never been on stage before*
> *And we will do our best*

> *And the best can do no more*
> *We are just actors bold*
> *Some are young and others old*
> *Our story we'll unfold*
> *Our sad story must be told*

"If you lot can remember the words," shouted a small boy from the audience, pushing to the front. "You were rubbish last year."

A swift clip around the ear from his mother stopped him in his tracks.

"Take no notice of my Harold, Master Tupton," she beseeched, pulling him back. "He's only having a bit of harmless fun at your expense."

"Look, Elizabeth, here comes Fanny," remarked John, offering a slight wave of encouragement.

Fanny crept forward in nervous panic.

> *My name is Merry Greenfield*
> *And if you'll care to stay*
> *Upon this very green we'll*
> *Show our humble play*
> *Walk in . . . er, er!!!*

"*Old Pearmain*," prompted Tupton from the side.
"Oh, yes, I forgot."

> *Walk in Old Pearmain*
> *Your stirring lines to pray*

"*To say*, Fanny. The line is *to say*."

"She ain't much good, is she Ma?" Another clip followed upon the first.

"Look, Elizabeth, it's Mark Gladtide's turn, acting the part of Pearmain."

In comes I, Old Pearmain
The oldest in the land
I have been an apple here
Nigh since ploughing first began
Throughout old Somerset I roamed
And in Montacute I'd sit
I used to know old Gordon Geard
When he was just a pip
I was here when the crusaders
Left to fight their holy wars
But now another dark invader
Threatens with afflictions sore

"Oh, here we go again," joked Harold to another small boy as Fanny reappeared. "It's the f-f-f-orgetful lady with a stut-t-t-er!"

Fanny took a deep breath, searching for her lines.

Afflictions sore yet more you'll hear
Of battles soon we'll tell
But first a Midlander in will steer
Whose name you'll know full well
Walk in bold, bold, er...!

"She don't know his name, full well or other-wise! Look, Ma, she's dumbstruck."

"*Worcester*, Fanny. It's Worcester next," shouted Tupton in frustration.

"Oh, yes, sorry Master Tupton. *Walk in bold Worcester. Speak clearly as a bell.*"

In comes I, bold Worcester
Of noble stock and English bred
My flesh is clad in rosy red
Countless generations on me fed

But though my taste is crisp and pure
For many now I've lost allure

Worcester bowed, not once but twice and then again for good measure, only leaving centre stage when forcefully removed. Fanny stepped forward.

"Come on, Fanny. Give it your best."

"Shush, Elizabeth. You'll put her off."

Alas, alas! There's more to hear
For Pippin too is drawing near
Walk I, proud Pippin, play thy part
Show one and all, er . . . er. . .

"*Thy noble art.* For goodness sake, Fanny, *Thy Noble art.*"

"I be trying, Master Tupton, honest I be. 'Tis only first night nerves that tie me tongue. I know all the words at home, but here in front of all these people they just flit away. I'll do better next performance."

"In a year's time, Fanny. We only do it once every twelve months. You make the same promise every January."

The crowd roared at the entertainment. Fanny run off, crying.

"Now what do we do?" quizzed Tupton, his play in jeopardy.

"We can leave her out, Master Tupton," suggested another player in appeasement.

"No narrator? I suppose we could. Carry on everyone. It's going pretty well so far. Keep it up."

"Did you hear that, Ma?" said the boy. "That man says it's going well. I'd love to see a disaster. Ouch! I didn't mean any harm, Ma. I'm quite enjoying it really."

In comes I, proud Worcester
Of noble. . .

"Get off, Charlie," shouted Tupton. "You've done your bit already."

"So I have, Master Tupton, but I enjoyed myself so much I thought I'd give it another go."

"Nobody gets a second bite of the apple. Get off and make room for Pippin!"

The youngest of the actors pushed past, taking a Shakespearian pose and waiting for complete silence before beginning.

> *In comes I, proud Pippin*
> *I am known the country round*
> *For classic taste I am renowned*
> *In royal fruit bowls I've been found!*
> *But though I'm noblest apple of them all*

"You stand up now and act a fool," cried Harold to riotous laughter before dashing for cover, his friend close behind.

Pippin, too, ran off, throwing her hat to the ground, followed by her sister who was to play Bramley.

"This is becoming a tragedy!" bellowed Tupton, watching Pippin and Bramley disappear in the direction of Fanny. "I'll have to be Bramley as well, I suppose." He grabbed Pippin's hat and exchanged it for his own, sure that it would be adequate disguise.

> *In comes I, brave Bramley*
> *The pride of England's past*
> *'Twas I of all this valiant cast*
> *Had a future sure to last*

An ear-splitting crack overhead heralded a sudden and unexpected downpour, bringing the play to an abrupt end. Edward Tupton stood his ground, watching the audience and most of the players run for cover. Only Mark stayed behind, his sodden hat flopping about his ears, drips falling from his nose.

"Well, that went pretty well, Master Tupton."

"Yes, I think it did. Alright for next year?"

"Most certainly. The show must go on! Next year it is. Come on, Master Tupton, let's have a go at the finale despite the rain. One, two. . ."

We're one two three jolly folk all in one mind
We've come to act for you and we hope you'll prove kind
Pray give your attention and hark to our play
For we'll come no more nigh you for a year and a day.

"No such luck," shouted Harold from the cover of a wall.

John looked skyward from the shelter of a stone archway.

"We'll give it a minute or two more and then make a dash for the carriage. It'll be pretty muddy underfoot, but better that than freeze to death here."

He brought Elizabeth close, to protect her from the cold. Elizabeth was captivated by his strong arms, her bibulous smile proclaiming her readiness to do his every bidding.

At the first sign of a let-up, John took Elizabeth in a firm hold and dashed for the carriage, where the coachman sat patiently in his oilskins, rain dripping from every part of his body.

"Oh, John," said Elizabeth, as he arranged her dress and cloak to fall neatly about her, "I am exceedingly sorry."

"What for?" he asked with genuine curiosity.

"I fear I am an excessively selfish creature."

"Why?" he replied.

"Because I have drunk too much and will be of no ass . . . ass . . . for the return journey."

"Ass?" he asked.

"Ass-ociation," she replied through a slur.

He was quietly pleased when she fell asleep, resting her head on his shoulder. The return would be unexpectedly carefree, he thought.

* * *

John felt uncommonly awkward as he helped Elizabeth from the carriage and into the house, where she fell into Jeremiah's arms.

"What must you think of me?" he said as Harriet approached to see what was going on. "It took no more than three small cups of cider to bring her to this state."

"She hadn't eaten anything all day," said Harriet with concern. "She was so excited. Ale on an empty stomach has that effect on any young woman. You should know that, as a worldly man."

"He probably did," was Jeremiah's ill-conceived response, intended to have a humorous slant.

"No, really, I had no idea she had missed meals."

"An impressionable young woman in love, John, has many ways of expressing her feelings. Not eating is just one."

The word 'love' was not lost on him.

"Now see what you've done," rebuked Jeremiah. "You've embarrassed John unnecessarily."

"Not so," he replied, having fully released Elizabeth into their keeping. "I believe I have been a narrow-minded, self-centred and ungenerous man towards your daughter. I shall return in a day or two, perhaps three, but no more than that, to speak to her on matters of utmost importance."

Jeremiah looked joyfully towards his wife. "And for my part, John, I apologise for our unkindness in thought towards you. In protecting our daughter, we have besmirched your character among ourselves. Now, I realise, we were unfair to do so. Speaking also for my wife, we are most anxious you do not leave here without first knowing this. Any approach to me regarding my daughter will be greeted with the utmost approval. Do I make myself understood?"

"You do, Sir."

"And, please be assured of our unerring affection for bringing Elizabeth back safely, without any degree of advantage taken due to her disposition."

"Thank you for that, too. It means a lot. But, much as I respect your sentiment, I was thinking only of Elizabeth, who was in my care, and not of your approval, which is secondary."

"I stand chastened," declared Jeremiah.

"Was that necessary, John? My husband only wished to express gratitude."

"I know and I thank you both. But, I believe you consider Elizabeth to be too much a frail girl, when you have the proof that she is a grown woman. It would be well not to smother her with inducements to meet your standards, when she needs to decide her own path to happiness. That might, or might not, include me in the long run. That is for the pair of us to discuss at the appropriate time. I say this as a friend and not to be rude in any way."

"Then, no offence intended or taken. Oh, and don't forget, John," added Harriet as he turned to leave, "you did say a day or two."

"Or three," he added.

"Oh, yes, or three." She felt the noose slipping from the commitment. "By the way, how is the shooting on your farm?"

"We do very little, as it happens, if you mean game birds. Our usual targets are vermin and poachers."

"Well, we have excellent shooting here. Feel free to come to the district whenever you please and shoot all you like – rabbits, hares and birds. We even get the occasional stag roaming the fields."

After John had gone, and with Elizabeth passed to Collins to prepare for bed, Jeremiah and Harriet sat in the drawing room where a full fire raged, the crackling logs drowning any sound of outside rain. Jeremiah poured two glasses of Madeira, passing one to his wife.

"Do you think we overdid the gushing affection towards John? We don't want to frighten him off."

"I don't think we could, husband. I am now inclined to believe it has only been embarrassment that has kept him away. As a family we owe him nothing, but I'm sure he feels he owes the Grants much."

"All of us?"

"Why ever not? He has defiled our daughter, which affects us all and has caused us a deal of misery."

"Are you exempting Elizabeth from guilt?"

"Most certainly. She is a woman, and women are to be cherished."

"Yes, that is the usual way of thinking. But, why is it so? In our case, doesn't Elizabeth bear a large degree of guilt for her actions which led to the birth of Unity?"

"Is it a hog's fault when it is caught by the horseman and speared?"

"I beg your pardon! Are you suggesting my Elizabeth is like a pig, caught by John and brought down by a long stick? For, if so, it is a most unfortunate turn of phrase which should not be repeated in company."

"Cleverly, you twist and turn my meaning, Jeremiah. I only meant a woman is easily aroused to have passions that are beyond her simple control, because such feelings are new to her, overwhelming and entirely untested. It is for the gentleman to know when to show prudence."

"Balderdash! It is an historical fact that men are made to be the hunters and, therefore, chastity can only be guaranteed by the strong character of the woman and her refusal to go further than correct society allows. Why, if a woman permits her hand to be held too quickly or her lips to be kissed, surely it can only be taken by the man as a sign of willingness. And so it progresses."

"And what of fidelity? Is that in a woman's hands too?"

"That is entirely different. Faithfulness is the right and left hand gloves of marriage, both being required to make a pair. However, I was reading in the newspaper that one in every five men is thought to keep the company of other women. Of course, I don't believe it. Not one jot. Society would break under such immorality."

"I think our conversation wanders, Jeremiah. Shall we for our beds?"

"Our separate rooms again tonight?"

"What else?"

"You see. You exercise control over the bedchamber. I make my point!"

CHAPTER 23

A halfpenny a pasty

A few days after Emmie had settled in with her parents at Stirminster Oak and begun helping in their charity work, she came across five wretched children playing on a stone bridge spanning a fast-flowing stream that burbled its way over rocks at one end of the village. They dropped twigs into the cascading water, rushing to the opposite side to see whose stick emerged first. As she passed carrying a basket of pasties for the miners, she noticed the hunger on their dirty faces.

Emmie stopped to look at them playing. All were dressed in rags, the girls kept warm only by the meek provision of frayed shawls pulled tightly over their heads and across their thin bodies. The pasties, being freshly baked, gave off a smell that wafted delightfully through the air.

One girl, being the oldest and tallest, and well-favoured for her age, stopped playing and glared in Emmie's direction. She said nothing, but her eyes flicked between Emmie and the basket of food. Emmie removed the cloth covering the pasties and picked out the largest, holding it at arm's length. The girl stood her ground, shaking her head. Emmie offered the same pasty to the others, but they too followed their sister's example, although the pain of refusal showed on their lustreless faces.

"Why won't you take it?" said Emmie at last, adopting her softest tone.

"We haven't a halfpenny between us," was the reply.

"I'm not asking for money. Just have it. I have lots of others for the miners."

"We don't beg, lady. Ma says it's wrong."

"It's a gift, not alms."

Hearing this, the oldest girl walked slowly towards Emmie, her countenance still sullen. She stood a pace away with her hand outstretched, unwilling to take what was not hers. With tender touch, Emmie placed the pasty into her upturned palm. The girl's mouth curled almost inconceivably at its edges.

Now, the other four children ran to her, hands begging for crumbs like so many chicks feeding in a nest. The delicate precision with which the pasty was broken into five broke Emmie's heart. The smaller children were each given the parts containing meat and potatoes, the oldest girl keeping only the thick pastry edge for herself. Emmie was transfixed, watching as the little mouths licked their hands to mop up any lingering grease and any remaining taste of the food now consumed. With the feast devoured, the oldest girl returned to Emmie. She curtsied.

"Thank you, lady."

Emmie felt humbled by her piety. Like these little wretches, she too had known hunger in her wanderlust days and times of extreme poverty, but even in the worse moments of her plight she had always known in the back of her mind that she had parents to call upon who could and would provide for her in abundance. It was clear from the merest glance these children had no comfortable retreat, but a home where poverty was a shared experience between the whole family.

"What were you doing?" asked Emmie.

"Playing sticks."

"I haven't seen you here before."

"No, lady, we usually work at the quay, breaking stone into

powder. We all do it. The little ones use lighter hammers. Only, our Pa is now on strike, which puts us all out of work."

"Strike?"

"Yes, lady. The owners want to cut men's pay by a shilling a week and by a penny a day for the women and children. They say the mine is running out. Pa says we can hardly manage on what we all earn now, since the last cut, and wants pay left alone. He says it's the last straw and we must all fight for our rights or starve. We can't even go to school anymore, as it has to be paid for and mother says every penny we have has to go on important things."

"But you look as though you're half-starving now."

Quietly, the child turned and picked up a new twig to throw into the stream.

Emmie continued towards the mine, still wanting to deliver the remaining pasties to any miners staying underground during the night, whether strike-breaking or in protest. The reason did not matter.

She passed the chandlers, where normally the bustle of business began. But, today, the shop was empty. Both quays were also deserted, the two moored ships devoid of their cargo of arsenic powder, their crews of three resting below deck in tiny cabins at the bow and stern of the hulls. The captains, paid by productivity but now idling the time away in slim wooden beds, worried for their income; the two deck-hands of each boat swung in rope hammocks, smoking and playing cards.

The mine was approached along a path that gently snaked through an area of thick forestation, gradually rising until the newest working entrance was reached, dug into the hillside. A steam engine used for pumping water stood idle. Alongside the path ran the twin tracks of a narrow-gauge railway, to take the plunder away.

Emmie hesitated as she stood at the entrance, staring at the absolute blackness beyond. With the men on strike, there was no money to be wasted on illuminations. She called out, her voice echoing along the winding passage and into the depth of the hill. Only the sound of dripping water returned.

"There's nobody down there," came a voice from behind, startling her rigid. "Haven't 'ee heard there's a strike on?"

She turned. "All the miners?" she replied.

"Come, see for 'eeself," he said, putting a match to a lantern and holding it high until the glow brightened.

"I don't know. It's awfully dark."

"Hardly any darker now than when the miners are working. They mine by candlelight. Coming, or not?"

"Not, I think," she replied politely, looking again into the uninviting hole. "It's less intimidating to go down when lots of people are about."

"I'll go without 'ee, then, if that's 'ee decision. 'Tis me job to inspect the shaft for flooding, as the steam pump is not fired up. If I see anyone down there, I'll tell 'em they've missed out on a hot treat."

"No, don't do that," she called, as he stepped ahead. "I've been entrusted by my parents to help them."

He turned. "So, you're a Sturry?"

"Yes. How did you know?"

"Not by magic," he grinned from a little way inside the mine, the lantern casting an unnaturally long shadow on the wall and ceiling. "The Sturrys are well known and much despised by the mine owners for their interference. Filling the miners' bellies with free food stops 'em buying at the company shop."

"I'm sorry to hear that said of my parents, who act out of kindness."

"Little Emmeline, aren't 'ee?"

"Yes."

"Well, I'll be jiggered. I know 'ee."

"How?"

"You don't remember me, do 'ee?"

"No."

"Miss Simmons' class? I sat in front of 'ee at school. Once 'ee drew a chalk donkey on me back and I got the stick for it."

"That was you? Good gracious, you're Alfred Lewis."

"The very same. I can still feel the cane across me arse. Twelve lashes and me being only eight, the sadistic sod."

"My goodness, I would never have recognised you. You're all big and. . ."

"Haggard?"

"Well, I suppose you are, just a bit."

"Comes with the work. Anyway, I'm going to where the sun never shines, or I'll lose me job. There's little enough to justify me pay right now and the owners are looking to make more cuts." He continued into the tunnel.

"Hang on, Alf, I'm coming with you." She ran forward and put her arm through his.

"No funny stuff," he said with a smirk. "I'm a married man with six kids."

"Really?"

"Don't talk daft. I be the same age as 'ee."

"Married with no kids?"

"Not even that. Who would give me a second look?"

Together, they probed the hillside, the occasional vertical ventilation shaft providing the only contact with the outside world.

"Looks dry enough," he concluded, having penetrated as far as the rectangular holes cut into the wall where miners sometimes slept on straw to save having to walk home between shifts.

"What's that?" screamed Emmie, dropping the basket and dancing on the spot.

"'Tis only a little rat, nitwit. Must expect a few dozen down here."

"Come on, Alf, let's go back."

"Do 'e have to, straight away, I mean?"

"There's nothing keeping us here and I loathe rats."

"Perhaps there isn't, perhaps there is. We're all alone, with nobody to check up to see if I be working or having an idle nap. And, 'ee has a basket of food by the smell of it, with nobody to give it to. I'm hungry. We can sit in a hole and 'ave a jolly old time without anyone knowing. It's a right tidy place for a picnic and a chat about things."

"I'm not sure. I'd rather get back, if I'm honest."

"No, Emmie," he said, dropping to his knees to look inside the basket, 'ee must do as I say, as before."

"No," she answered in surprise. "It was your brother, Tom, who was so horrible to everyone. You were always nice."

"'Ee would say that, after good and reliable old Alf took the caning for the donkey to stop you getting a ruler across the hand. Anyway, little Emmeline, 'ee has it all wrong. I'm not Alfred, I'm Tom."

"Tom?" she gasped, her senses tingling. "You can't be. Tom's long dead and buried."

"So everybody thinks."

"What?"

"Alfred was always everyone's favourite. I can hear 'em even now whispering: *'Shame Tom can't be a bit more like his twin. Why can't 'e learn his times tables like Alfred? Why, Alfred's such a nice boy – pity about Tom. They might be identical, but Alfred's the little gentleman and Tom the roughshod'.* I was only a tiny, lost boy and it really hurt me to hear it. Well, Alfred died and I became 'im to the real world."

"That's impossible."

"Oh, but it is. See, I was sick and tired of Alfred and his goody-goody ways. So, one day, when 'e offered to chop fire wood at home, I said I would help. I got 'im to hold the logs while I swung the axe. I deliberately missed and sliced off two fingertips. It was only meant to be spiteful, but it worked better than that. The axe was old and 'e died horribly of bad blood soon after."

"I don't believe any of it. You're playing a joke on me, aren't you Alfred?"

"How can 'ee be so sure?"

"Because, the police would've got you."

"But they never did. That's the clever bit. I told Ma, Alfred had chopped his own fingers by mistake. Of course, she didn't believe me. Why should she? I was the one with blood splattered all over me clothes, as I pushed him over and threw the axe next to 'im. Curled in agony, 'e was. I felt like laughing as 'e cried his little heart out."

"You sadistic horror."

"I be called a lot worse than that. Anyway, the good news was that Alfred never did let on, more fool him. I told him what would happen if he did. The sop died with the truth stuck to 'is lips. When Constable Harris arrived to take statements, we knew 'e would never suspect Alfred of doing bad to his own brother. So, Pa told him I was Alfred and Harris believed every last word. After that, I became Alfred and Tom was dead."

"Why would your parents lie about such a sinful act?"

"Simple. They couldn't afford to lose both sons, as bad as I might be. 'Ee must see the cunning in it. A mystery play couldn't be better written. I had done the perfect crime, and me no bigger than a chaffinch."

"You murdered him!"

"I suppose I did, well, sort of. I cut the surplus population by one and rid me-self of a brother who kept me down, killing me with his superiority as surely as I killed him with the axe. The hardest bit in the swap was to be good, like Alfred. Fortunately, me parents realised how hard it would be to pretend, day in and day out. So they took me out of school and put me to labour, where I would be among rough folk twice me age. I took me anger out on the rock face, the pounds of stone turning into a hundredweight as the pile grew about me ragged shoes, me little hands becoming raw and blistered until even the blisters were calloused. As I took on the years, I learned the need to be submissive, more like me brother whose air I so happily breathed. But, as nobody could possibly know how Alfred would turn out, the pretence became easier and I could slacken off a bit."

"Why are you telling me this?"

"I want 'ee to know the pointlessness of resisting me. If I say we stay down here, that's what we do! I am, at this moment, like a cat with a rat in a pipe. Do I play with 'ee *or* eat 'ee, or play with 'ee *and* eat 'ee? I know I'll have 'ee, if I want."

"Have what?"

He slapped her violently, unexpectedly, across the face.

"You stupid, stupid trollop, mocking me as if I'm muck on the sole of 'ee shoe," he scolded scurrilously. "See how 'ee changed the moment 'ee knew it's Tom standing here, not Alfred. See what 'ee did? Made me hurt 'ee, when I really didn't want to."

"So, why do it? It's not normal behaviour." she replied, holding a hand against her stinging cheek.

"There 'ee go once more, telling me I'm unnatural and a queer thing meant only for the gutter, inviting me to lose me temper again, when all along I only want to be friendly. Scum, that's what 'ee has always thought of me."

"Not so! I can promise, girl or woman, I've never given you a second thought of any kind since you left school so unexpectedly. In fact, I don't even like you enough to want to be near you now. Please, show me the way out at once."

"You don't like my world down 'ere, do 'ee, where the devil takes his filthy pleasure? But, this be my world, where grime is as natural as skin itself."

"Then, I want to leave your world for mine."

"Too grand for it?" he barked vengefully.

"I've told you already, I don't want your company."

"Don't anger me again, Emmeline Sturry, I warn 'ee."

"And I warn you of the consequences if you don't show me the way out immediately."

"Oh dear, I've gone all a-trembling! See, me hand shakes with fear." He raised himself to full height, towering above her small figure and touching the rock ceiling. "Go on, then. Hit me if 'ee likes, if 'ee can reach me, 'ee being a short-arse."

"Why should I?"

"Because, if 'ee don't, I'll know 'ee to be weak, frightened to death of me."

Hesitantly, she raised her hand. But, before it reached any height, he grabbed her wrist with fearsome speed.

"So, 'ee really would strike me after all. The mouse has a temper!"

"It's only what you did to me. Oh, yes, I see it now. You're Tom alright, the horrible school bully."

Such an unwise reply was bound to invite a cruel response, yet the viciousness returned was beyond all measure. He wanted, no, more than that, he needed to strike out violently, for his nature dictated nothing less. His jaw twisted in rage as he looked her up and down, hardly able to hold himself in check. Her dress being the most visible evidence of her better life, he seized the moment and tore at the bodice, the aggression bursting the seams.

She staggered in disbelief. With one arm held outstretched in defence and the other holding her dress together, she stepped back submissively, choked for words. But, the Rubicon had been crossed. He had broken cover in the madness of the moment and there was no going back. The only way of guaranteeing his continuing freedom from this point forward would be to kill her or frighten her into silence, forcing a solemn promise from her trembling lips. Either strategy was to his liking, as it involved terror.

Lunging forward, he grabbed her wrist uncompromisingly and twisted hard, forcing her arm to straighten and turning her palm unnaturally upwards. The pain was intense, bones strained to breaking point. Doubled-over, she circled under the pressure until a heavy push from the sole of his boot sent her crashing to the floor. She fell hard, her knees and palms skating across the damp, rough surface. He watched as she turned yieldingly, her bodice left to hang loose.

"Give up?"

"Of course I do. Please, I beg you, don't hurt me again."

"'Ee yield to any demand?"

Her head dropped. "Not any," she stammered nervously.

For several moments he stood rigidly in front of her, his stare malevolent. He had already decided her fate and merely wished to prolong the agony. Then, licentiously, he stepped forward, releasing the buckle to his thick trouser-belt with all the confidence of a conqueror among the spoils of the vanquished. The gesture needed no explanation. She writhed in fear.

"Don't you dare touch me!" she screamed, crawling backwards. "I won't tell anyone what's happened, honest I won't. I'll keep quiet about everything. I'll tell everyone you're Alf. Yes, you are Alf, aren't you? I'll say I tore my dress down here. Nobody will think anymore about it. I'll say I fell over in the dark. You can trust me." She glanced in the direction of escape, but only pitch blackness filled the void between floor and ceiling. It was hopeless. She turned back, hoping for any sign of reason. There was none. "Why do you like inflicting hurt on those who are too weak to fight back?"

"Because I can," was his murderous reply. "It's the one thing I've ever been really good at. Made me friends at school."

"Only out of fear. Nobody wanted to get on your bad side."

"Maybe, but I wasn't lonely then."

"Friendship through pain? Hardly something to be proud of. Your parents must be so pleased they got you off."

"They knew what they'd get if they dobbed me in!"

"You would hurt your own flesh and blood?"

"I did before to my brother. They're no different. I look after number one. Anyway, pain and me are old friends, Emmeline Sturry. Here, share my friendship."

His boot struck her ribs, a blow which lifted her physically off the ground. She fell back, curled, fearful and trapped. The agony was intense. She glanced up at her tormentor, shocked to see no remorse. His face held only gratification.

"Save me someone," she screamed, cradling her ribs. "Help, anyone, I'm down here."

"Shout all 'ee like," he returned, savagely dragging her back to her feet by the hair. "Nobody can hear 'ee. The strike, remember?"

A rat appeared out of the darkness, attracted by the food. He watched as it came close, pushing a finger hard against Emmie's lips. The rat stopped at the basket, climbing onto its back legs and sniffing around the rim. Raising a leg, he crushed the animal in a single barbarous strike, grinding his boot hard into the rat's body until its bones cracked and blood seeped from its gaping mouth. Then, once all life had gone, he kicked it away, where it bounced limply off a wall.

"See," he said through a merciless grin, "down here I have sway over life and death. Scream 'ee lungs out. See if I care. Nobody for miles around, except for the rats in my trap. The question now is, do 'ee want to do it standing up or on 'ee back? Either will do me just fine. See, I can be the gentleman!"

"Don't, I beg you," she pleaded, her hands now pressed hard against her head to relieve his pressure. "I'll agree to anything."

"Too late for that, Emmeline Sturry. I can feel me blood pumping hard and there's no going back. I fancy seeing what 'ee got to show a boyfriend! I want it my way, rough and ugly."

"Get off me, I said!"

"Don't speak to me like dirt!" he bawled, his eyes held inches from her face. "'Ee knows I get very angry."

Without warning, he tossed her back to the ground. Her involuntary cry echoed through the chamber, ushering such a blow to the crown of her head that she dropped in a stupefying daze. Even he was stunned by her comatose state. Nudging her with the toe of his boot, he tumbled her over, watching for signs of life.

She remained completely still. He leaned down and pulled the two halves of her bodice apart. Almost immediately he could see her breasts heaving. Satisfied, he stood astride with fevered desire, fumbling for the hem of her dress and lifting it to above waist height. Then, grabbing at his trousers, the leather belt was ripped free and buttons were pulled open with a trembling hand.

Throughout, Emmie remained barely conscious, her unfocussed eyes swimming in the semi-darkness. He slapped her face, not once but twice, wanting her to participate willingly, or unwillingly but consciously, in all that was about to follow. Her awareness was part of the ritual, part of the punishment.

She whimpered to the second slap, her eyelids flickering. That was sufficient for his morbid needs. He knelt over her and leaned forward, taking his full weight on one outstretched arm. Emmie stirred a little to the nauseous smell of stale body sweat, close and repugnant, but remained insensible to the befalling crime.

He closed towards her lips, then, raising his head and crying out, his body slumped heavily across her slight frame in an unwitting collapse. Air squeezed from her lungs as she took the full force of the unexpected crush, her mouth gasping for shallow breaths.

Starved of air, Emmie writhed briefly before sinking back, her head dropping to one side, her mind spinning and light. For seconds everything went silent, moments held long in the strange atmosphere of the damp mine. A warm trickle ran slowly over her face, finding a downward passage around her ear to the rock below. Although enfeebled, she slowly diverted her eyes to a small glistening pool reflecting red in the dim light of the lantern. It had to be blood.

Weakening by the second, her panting breaths shallow, confusion set in. In this exhaustion, her thoughts travelled back to a time when she and Edmond Elvington had walked through woods to a disused windmill, flashes of happier days offering comfort as she slipped into unconsciousness.

It was then, at that snatched moment of calm, his weight miraculously, incredibly, fell to one side, releasing her chest to heave in the first of several tender breaths. She convulsed as air rushed into her lungs, as cold as the surroundings. Her eyelids parted, the fog of insensibility gradually lifting as she focussed on the body by her side and then, to her horror, on another figure which stepped out of the gloom, a silhouette as menacing in the confusion of the moment as the attacker himself.

There, above her, stood a small figure, pulling at her attacker's arm.

"It's alright, lady, it's me and me little brothers and sisters. We didn't know what to do, so I crept up behind and sloshed him with a shovel."

Emmie, confused and fragile, her face seen as ghostly white, burst into uncontrollable weeping.

"Please, little ones," she cried through her tears, "get him away."

With the smallest children pushing and the largest pulling, they managed to roll his limp body over. The girl returned and dropped onto her knees, offering Emmie the meagre warmth of her shawl.

"That bad man won't bother you none more. But we'd better get out of here before he wakes up."

"How. . . How did you know I. . .?"

"You were here, lady? We liked your pasty so much we followed you in, hoping we might have another to take home for Pa and Ma. We wouldn't eat it ourselves, honest. After all, you did say they were for the miners, and Pa is a miner, so no harm would be done asking. Lucky we did."

"God bless you," said Emmie faintly. "Can you help me stand?"

"Of course we can, lady. Come on kids, all grab hold."

Once Emmie was on her feet, the little children picked up any spilled pasties and placed them into the basket, discarding only those with blood on the pastry. One was thoroughly crushed and the smallest child asked if she might be allowed to divide it among them.

"Stop it, Dotty," rebuked the oldest, shamefaced. "We've had our share already."

"Have them all, my darlings," said Emmie with gushing gratitude. "There's enough to go round your whole family. Please, take them all."

"I think there's one each," gasped the smallest in delight, her nose close to the basket. "A whole one each and still three left for Ma and Pa! It's like Christmas all over again!"

"With some over," replied Emmie. "And there'll be more to come until the strike is settled, I promise you. I shall help you, as you have saved me. Now, can one of you run ahead and tell your Pa to contact the police? This dreadful man can't be left to bleed to death, even if he deserves to."

Constable Harris, being older but no wiser, cycled furiously to the Sturry's house that evening to take a statement in his capacity as part-time police constable to the district. It was his first major crime for years and the anticipation excited him.

He entered the Sturry's home as puffed as a peacock in his blue uniform, which he wore with pride. Removing his helmet, he chose to stand erect by the fire where he felt he dominated the proceedings. He took a notebook and pencil from his pocket to record the spoken facts. With the pencil point licked, he was ready to start.

The story that unfolded was beyond fiction in a place where the harsh reality of life was usually the only crime committed.

"We found the spade with blood on it," said Harris, writing his own words in the notebook. "The evidence was quite plain to see."

"I doubt he was in any condition to move it himself," remarked Emmie in a co-operative, but sarcastic, voice.

"Make no mistake, Miss Emmeline. There has been a serious crime committed."

"Against our daughter," said Joseph, wanting to establish the ground rules.

"That, we are yet to establish. Alfred Lewis could be the victim for all I know. His head wound indicates that he probably was."

"What!" exclaimed Emmie.

"Calm yourself, Miss Emmeline. I accuse nobody. It's the job of the police to get at the truth, to establish the right side of events. And, on that score, I must say here and now that I'm worried. Your description seems to be almost word perfect to the statement I already have from elsewhere. In fact, so word perfect, I want to know if you have colluded to conceal darker deeds still to be uncovered?"

"There is only one right side to events, Harris," barked Joseph. "It's called the truth, which stares you in the face."

"With respect, Joseph Sturry," "it's my job to tell everyone what the truth is."

"Pardon?" gasped Emmie. "That can't be right. Your job is to verify what I say. You are not here to judge me or twist the facts."

"But, what are the facts? So far, I've only heard what you want me to know. I have to decide whether it fits the evidence that stains the mine floor, and write my report accordingly. The truth, in my experience, is like a tricky little animal. Ferret-like, I always think. It pops its head out of holes and has a sniff around in the open, only to retreat back into the dark when it wants to be hidden away."

"What are you rambling about, Harris? Get to the point, man," censured Joseph.

"Ferrets."

"Ferrets, be damned. What are they to do with the price of bread?"

"Now *you* are confusing the issue, Joseph Sturry. Come, come, let's stop this time wasting on groceries and hear anything else Miss Emmeline has to say."

"Sense, at last," scolded Joseph.

"As for me," exclaimed Rachel, "I'm as bemused by Harris' attitude as a badger balancing on a bald man's back." She turned to her husband. "The man's a complete imbecile."

"Now, now, Mrs Sturry, enough of that. Being rude about my bald head is hardly likely to help your daughter's case. And, I remind you, in this uniform I am Police Constable Harris."

"I couldn't care less about you being bald. It's what goes on beneath that bothers me."

Joseph glanced a desperate look towards his wife as a warning. "Pardon her theatricals, Harris, but you *are* making rather a meal of a perfectly simple situation. I suggest we all keep calm and listen again to Emmeline, making no further judgements until she finishes."

General agreement followed the proposal. And so, Constable Harris listened to Emmie's final appeals, writing notes in a slow hand and asking for several passages to be repeated. Finally, he looked up.

"I don't like it! I've already spoken to the Cotwell children and they give the same version of events. It's all very suspicious."

Rachel stood, offering support to her daughter by placing a hand on her shoulder. "Surely, Harris, it's your job to find discrepancies? If there are none, then the opinion must be formed that you have heard the authentic story."

"Don't you worry on that score, Rachel Sturry. I'm trained to sniff out lies. Little gets past me. Why, only yesterday some twisted old relic tried to tell me he couldn't have stolen apples at his age. How old are you, I asked? 'Old', he replied, 'but not as old as my great-grandfather had been, who had lived in three centuries!' Of course, I laughed in his face. Impossible, said I. He was red with guilt, so I arrested him for scrumping."

"Perfectly possible, Harris."

"What is, Joseph Sturry?"

"To live in three centuries."

"Don't you take the fun out of me while I wear the Queen's uniform. I can count as well as any man. Nobody lives to be three hundred."

"Who is this man?"

"Percy Pullbright, out in King's Ashon."

"Oh, yes! The one whose great-grandfather was famously born in 1699 and died in 1801, aged 102."

"Be that as it may," Harris replied defensively, "but that doesn't explain the blush on Percy Pullbright's face? Guilt, if ever I've seen it."

"He lived the life of a ruddleman, Harris, supplying red ochre to mark the farmers' sheep before tupping. Years of work tinted his skin the dreadful colour of the dye."

The difficulty I have," continued Harris with embarrassment, ignoring Percy's miscarriage of justice, "is that, to believe Miss Emmeline's claim, I must first accept that all those years ago I was foolish enough to be hoodwinked into believing Tom Lewis was actually Alfred Lewis?"

"I have no problem with that," berated Joseph.

"Or Alfred was Tom Lewis, whichever way around you want to look at it," remarked Emmie unwisely.

"Well, young miss, which are you now claiming?" he asked with incredulity.

"Either is correct," she replied.

"Oh dear!" exclaimed Joseph in irritated tone, seeing the puzzled look on Harris's face. "Look, to clear up any misunderstanding, Harris, the surviving child was Tom, called Alfred by his parents for the convenience of the dreadful situation he had caused. The dead brother from the original axe incident was Alfred, called Tom as a cover up."

"Were you present at the event, Joseph Sturry?"

"No, Harris, you know I wasn't."

"Then, kindly keep your opinions to yourself."

"Father said it right, though," added Emmie in a matter of fact tone, taking her father's hand. "He told me so out of his own mouth before he attacked me."

"Your father attacked you?"

"No! Tom did. My father wasn't there."

"Exactly what I've just established. Now we're getting somewhere."

"Let me repeat myself," added Emmie. "Tom said he was only pretending to be Alfred."

"Well, he won't be speaking much now," said Harris.

"I suppose not."

"So, if I understand you correctly, Miss," rubbing the pencil tip against the wet of his tongue, "it was Tom who had his fingers severed as a child?"

"Tom, yes, if you are referring to the person buried as such with that name engraved on his tombstone."

"Like it or not, Harris, that's the fact of the case."

"But I don't like, not one little bit. Because, Miss Emmeline now claims dead Tom attacked her."

"Damn it, Harris," interrupted Joseph again, "that isn't what she claims at all. Emmeline says it was Alfred who lost his fingers but was buried as Tom, and Tom attacked her, having called himself Alfred for years and years."

"Alfred lost his fingers, not Tom?"

"Correct," replied Emmie.

"And he died?"

"At last you understand!"

"Alfred died?"

"Yes!"

"Then how come, Miss Emmeline, you said you met up with Alfred and went into the mine with him, where he later tried to interfere with you? How could he, with no fingers?"

"Oh, for pity sake, man, get it right," shouted Joseph in frustration.

"Now stop that at once, Joseph Sturry. In this uniform I am the law which must be obeyed. I warn you, do not look at me with respect and see only Harris the plasterer."

"Oh, I think I can manage that!" returned Joseph.

"God help us," whispered Rachel to Emmie.

"I warn you once and for all to respect the uniform and the dreadful power that comes with it. Now, let me tell you this, the person critical in hospital has all his fingers intact. What do you say to that?"

"He would have," replied Emmie.

"Because he is Alfred?" uttered Harris.

"No, because he is bloody Tom."

"Tom?" said Harris in puzzlement.

"Yes, Tom," shouted Emmie. "He has only been pretending to be Alfred, after he attacked Alfred with an axe. But, actually, Alfred died."

"Alfred died? When I came here he was still alive in hospital."

"Tom!"

"You said Alfred died."

"He did, years ago, under the name of Tom."

"Then who, in heaven's name, attacked your daughter today?"

"Good gracious, Harris. Tom did!"

"Dead Tom?"

"No, alive Tom."

"Alive Tom? So, who is dead?"

"Alfred!" they all shouted.

"But Alfred is in hospital, although he might be dead by now, as this is taking so long. The blow to his head by the attacker was of a very severe nature."

"Attacker?" exclaimed Joseph. "Tom's the attacker."

Harris sucked his pencil again in consideration. "So, you are now claiming that the man lying in hospital attacked himself. Alfred."

"Tom! Tom is alive, Alfred is dead!"

"Alright, there's no need to shout! Even if I believed you, he could hardly attack himself."

"You complete dunderhead, Harris!"

"Stop that! There's no need to take that tone. I'm not an idiot, you know. Now, where are we?"

"Right up the creek," shouted Joseph.

Harris wrote it down. "With or without a paddle, Sir."

"Suffering Jehovah!"

"Who's this Jehovah? Is he a witness?"

"Shall I make some tea?" begged Rachel through a pained expression, attempting to bring a measure of calm to the proceedings.

"Right, we are gradually getting near the truth. Tell me, Miss Emmeline, and think carefully before answering, was it Tom or Alfred who was attacked by you today?"

"No!" said Emmie. "Neither."

"Neither? Now I know you lie. We have the wounded body of a man."

"No! You misunderstand everything. *I* was attacked."

"You continue to claim that? Yet, you appear to be remarkably well, except for a bruised eye and wrist, and the lump on your head, oh, and bruised ribs which I have not seen. Compared to the man in hospital who had a shovel struck across his skull, who I shall call Tom Lewis for the sake of argument even though the tag on his toe says Alfred Lewis, you seem to have escaped the fracas lightly."

"Oh, my forehead was hurt before today."

"Oh, no!" exclaimed Joseph, turning to his daughter. "Why did you have to say that?"

"You want her to cover up the truth, do you, Joseph Sturry?"

"Of course not. Emmeline is only trying to help you understand."

"Ah, but I do, Sir, I do. As I said, for argument sake I shall call the patient Tom."

"Thank goodness," gasped Joseph.

"Thank goodness?" wrote Harris in his notebook. "You think it is good that a young man lies critically injured?"

"Given the circumstances, yes I do."

"You want him dead?"

"Tom or Alfred?" demanded Emmie, "because you have absolutely no idea what you are doing, have you Mr Harris the plasterer?"

"We are lost!" bawled Joseph, sitting deeply into his chair. "How long can we go on like this, Harris?"

"However long it takes for me to understand everything."

"Do we prepare you a bed or call for your superior?"

"Stop that, Rachel Sturry. I take a dim view of you all trying to make a monkey out of me. I can manage perfectly well by myself." He stopped, recalling his own words. "No matter, I think we had better start again, Miss Emmeline. Now, let's have the truth this time."

"Hang about, Harris," jumped Joseph with understandable impatience. "Are her wounds a figment of her imagination?"

"No, of course not. They are clearly visible, but are somewhat slight in nature. Look, I have to get my report written, and I can't start by saying your daughter was attacked by someone who has been dead these past dozen years and had no fingers anyway."

"Lord, help us!"

And so it went on. Late afternoon, Harris finally left. The bicycle ride home gave him time to think. He pedalled hard. It could be his first serious arrest.

By the time he pulled the cycle clips from his legs, he was sure he knew the culprit. He would recommend to his superiors that Emmeline Sturry should be arrested without delay for grievous bodily harm to person or persons unknown, 'persons' including her possible complicity in the earlier death of Alfred or Tom, whichever was buried. As the only person who seemed to know what had befallen both brothers, her complicity in their mutual downfall was obvious.

Before nightfall, a police wagon pulled by two dray horses arrived at the Sturrys' home. A policeman jumped down, joined by a second who had travelled in the cubicle cell. To much protesting, Emmie was bundled into the cell, the door locked and guarded from the inside.

"Don't fret too much, Miss Sturry. If you're innocent, we'll soon have you free," remarked her captor, as he lit a pipe for the journey.

"I'm the victim. Why is this happening to me?"

The guard could see Emmie was shaking.

"It's only the slow grind of law and order. Calm yourself,

Miss, please. Going back to the station for questioning doesn't mean a thing in itself. There's no presumption of guilt at this stage, other than in the arresting officer's mind. Taking you into custody is merely procedure in such serious cases. If PC Harris hadn't said you were likely to bolt, we might have waited until morning."

"What if they don't believe me? Harris couldn't be persuaded! I could be hanged for doing absolutely nothing."

"Alfred Lewis isn't going to die, according to the doctors. You see? Nothing to be fearful about, after all. The worse you could face is a long spell in prison."

"Is that supposed to cheer me?"

"Doesn't it? I would be extraordinarily happy to be told that I wasn't to have my neck stretched."

"If found guilty! I would have to be found guilty first, and I'm not. I tell you, I gain little confidence from the fact that you still believe Alfred Lewis is in hospital."

"PC Harris says he is, and so do his parents."

"Heavens above!"

"If you're innocent, as you claim, it will soon become clear through investigation and you will walk away free as a bird."

"How soon?"

"How long is a piece of string?"

"Oh dear!"

He took a long pull on his pipe, releasing the sweet scent of tobacco into the confined space.

"This wagon is called a *Black Maria*," he said between puffs, to ease the tension.

"What?"

"A *Black Maria*. This wagon. I heard say police wagons got the nickname from a lodging-house keeper in Massachusetts, America, who used to help the police arrest drunks. She was a great big black lady called Maria Lee, hence *Black Maria*. The name stuck when the London police started using similar vehicles." He paused, watching her peer longingly through the open bars in the door. "Didn't you listen to any of that, miss? Believe me, talking helps pass the time."

She turned, frowning. "Do you honestly think I care how this mobile jail got its name?"

"I was only trying to be friendly, to lift your spirits."

"Maybe, good Sir," she replied in muffled tone, "but I no longer trust the police or the British legal system."

"You mustn't say that!"

"I just have. If you want to help me, keep your thoughts to yourself. I need to think."

Back at home, all was pandemonium.

"What should we do, Joseph? We must do something at once to end this injustice. Our little girl is in such trouble."

"Again. You should've added 'again'. Good grief, she jumps from the frying pan into the fire, always needing others to pull her out before she gets burned."

"Stop it! This isn't her fault. She was only doing our bidding."

"This time, maybe. But, the result is the same for those who continually protect her against herself."

"You sent her to the mine, Joseph. If you hadn't, this would never have happened."

"She was taking pasties, for goodness sake, not robbing the chandlers! What harm could be expected to come from that?"

"We need a solicitor."

"Do you know of one, 'cause I don't?"

"No. We could approach John Madden for help. He's always ridden to her rescue in the past. He's bound to know a solicitor."

"I expect he does. But, this time we have to think hard before involving him. You know what Emmeline said took place between them."

"Yes, but I bet that's more to do with our wayward daughter than any change in his good character. I think we could chance it, for her sake."

"We could try the Elvingtons instead, her old employers," he interrupted, ignoring the earlier suggestion. "They are bound to know someone suitable."

It was agreed that they would ask the Elvingtons.

The next day Joseph rode long and hard in the direction of Westkings, staying away overnight and arriving the following morning. He was taken aback at seeing James Elvington, fresh from straightening a ploughshare and appearing little better dressed than a field hand.

"I see you stare at my stump," remarked James, wiping his face on a cloth. "It's alright, I'm used to the attention it brings. It's the result of a burn that happened many years ago."

"Oh, no," replied Joseph, still finding his eyes drawn to James' general appearance. "Sorry if I gave that impression."

James pulled a shirt sleeve over the mutilated flesh and grabbed his jacket, tucking the empty sleeve into a pocket.

"There, I'm presentable again. Now, what can I do for you?"

Joseph explained his connection to Emmeline and of her arrest.

"I see. That is serious, even by her standards. Come along and join me indoors for a drink? We can talk more comfortably there."

"It's very urgent."

"Then, there is no time to waste."

He led the way into the drawing room, where he rang for a maid.

"I'm not a big drinker, especially in the morning," said Joseph, perched on the edge of a chair.

The maid entered.

"Tea, please, Chambers. And perhaps some buttered bread with jam." She left. "You see, neither am I any longer, not since the accident. Now, Mr Sturry, you were saying?"

"Please, I would be obliged if you would call me Joseph Sturry or plain Joseph if you think it appropriate."

"My pleasure, Joseph. Funny to think on it, but your runaway daughter came uncomfortably close to being part of my family once upon a time. Did you know?"

"Something about it came to my ears."

"It wasn't to be and that, I have to say with due deference, was to everyone's good. I hope I do not speak out of turn. By the way, please call me James in return."

"Knowing my daughter, James, I take no offence by your expression of relief."

"So, tell me every detail. Hold nothing back. What's she done this time?"

Joseph was crushed by James' expectation of the worst and took several moments to recover. "She's been taken into custody in Exeter of all places. Why such a long way away, I have no idea."

"My goodness, that's a first. But, what for? You still don't say."

Joseph looked up from the floor, shame written across his face. "Grievous harm or even murder if the worst happens."

"By George!"

"It's a huge mix-up, of course, caused by the blithering idiot we have as a part-time police constable."

"You know I'm the magistrate? I shouldn't be listening to any of this."

"I didn't know."

"Come, come. Isn't that why you came to me, to help in some way?"

"Help, yes, but only as her former employer. If I had known you were a magistrate, I would've thought twice." He rose to leave.

"Please sit, Mr Sturry. . . Joseph. We haven't had our tea. Let's start afresh, and to the world we will call this meeting nothing more than a social visit. How does that suit you?"

"Very well," was his desperate reply.

And so, with full explanations, the seconds quickly passed into minutes, the minutes into an hour.

"I know John Madden," exclaimed James. "A fine fellow who once pursued one of our dairymaids. That, incidentally, got my son out of another certain depth of hot water, so to speak, until we realised who the girl actually was. Still, that's another story. As to the matter in hand, yes, I agree with you. Perhaps, on this occasion, John should be side-lined." He rose and went to the bureau, where he lifted the roll-top to extract a pen, ink and paper. "Look here, I'll write down the name of my solicitor. He's an excellent fellow who has never let me down." James almost sniggered as he wrote the words of explanation. "Don't look so panicked, Joseph," he added, blowing the drying agent off the page. "Mix-ups on a monumental scale occur sometimes, as my solicitor will bear witness and I have personally experienced in court, on the right side of the dock, you understand. Yes, indeed. As I said, he is an excellent fellow, but even he was once implicated in a plot that nearly drowned someone very close to me. Still, I can hardly blame him for that. No, that was more my wife's fault, as it happens."

Joseph looked aghast.

"Don't look so worried. It was more a case of misunderstanding than misdeed. In reality, our Sir Schofield wouldn't hurt a fly. I'm merely playing with words. Well, even that isn't strictly true," he muttered to himself, remembering how Schofield had sacked Augustus Fly, an event that ultimately led to Fly's horrible fate at the bottom of a collapsing wood pile. "You know, Joseph, my many moments of private contemplation since then have made me realise how easy it would be for a totally innocent person to be convicted of wrong doing. Therefore, I am resolved to intervene now in any way I can within the confines of my office. We must do all things possible to save your daughter. In fact, now I think on it, we will go to Schofield's office together, this very moment or even sooner, and no arguing."

"I wasn't going to."

"How unlike your daughter you are."

Three days later, with Schofield's professional intervention and new testimonies hastily gathered from everyone present in the mine when the attack took place, Emmie was back in the bosom of her family.

Joseph shook Sir Schofield's hand vigorously after he had personally accompanied Emmie back to Stirminster Oak, to ensure that everything was done according to the letter of the law and without complication from Harris or anyone else.

"It was God's will that you were seen to be innocent so quickly," said Joseph, as he hugged Emmie with all the passion of a relieved father.

"And Sir Schofield's timely intervention," added Rachel.

"That goes without saying. My wife and I are deeply indebted to you."

"It was my pleasure, Mr Sturry. And, so that you have no sleepless nights, I should tell you that my fee will be settled by James Elvington. I have been so instructed. I am extraordinarily expensive, so it is a gesture of unique generosity. You should make your gratitude well known to him. Now, however, with my charge safely delivered to the keeping of her family, I must take my leave. Keep up the good work."

"Good work?" enquired Joseph, as Schofield walked away.

"The pasties, man. Don't let this untidy episode stop your charity."

"No, Sir, I won't, although I doubt my daughter will want to help again."

"Her loss," he shouted back from the inside of his carriage. "Goodbye and the very best of luck to one and all. You have my card should anything go amiss."

Following an extended period in hospital, Tom Lewis was taken into custody. On the first day of his trial, he was dragged out of a *Black Maria* and mobbed by the crowd, only to be rescued by Police Constable Harris who had been shamed out of his former beat. Lewis was eventually found guilty on two separate charges, with no recommendation for leniency in the harshness of imprisonment to be endured.

Within days of his incarceration, the stone marking his brother's grave was removed and replaced with another bearing the inscription:

ALFRED LEWIS
AT LAST RESTING IN PEACE AND JUSTICE

CHAPTER 24

When all has flown

While the drama at Stirminster Oak took its course, many miles away at Wheat Sheaf Farm, John Madden had been fully occupied keeping Cornelius's flying ambitions under control. He had begun the task of separating Cornelius's duties from those of Abel Tucker, who had thankfully walked away from Canal Wharf and used some of the five pounds to purchase new clothes that were free of lime dust before returning to his former job, and all this sooner than expected. But, there was a consequence. The additional administration had kept John away from Elizabeth Grant far longer than the two to three days promised. Yet, at least, the farm would recover some sense of order.

Fanny, as might be expected, had been quick to embrace Abel on his return, only to discover that he intended to bring someone else to the farm, a rather beautiful glove-maker named Delysia. They had met in Glastonbury only days before and had immediately, irresistibly, fallen deeply in love. They expected to marry at the earliest convenience. Fanny had skulked away, broken hearted.

"We welcome you into our little band of workers," said John cheerily on the morning of Delysia's arrival, checking first that Fanny was out of earshot. "But, we have a bit of a problem.

Cornelius occupies the only cottage suited to two. I shall have to move him out. In the meantime, I could arrange. . ."

"That won't be necessary, Sir," interrupted Abel, with the touch of his forelock. "Delysia is content to live separately in the dormitory until we are wed. In fact, we would prefer it."

Delysia nodded in agreement.

"Excellent! Well, with that settled, all I need to do is to think how we might put a glove-maker to work. Such an occupation might be needed in Glastonbury or Yeovil, but at present I cannot think how we can use your unique skills in these parts."

"That's alright, Sir," said Delysia, "I don't mind any honest work."

"You've found a good woman, Abel," he acknowledged, "a good woman, indeed."

"I know it."

"And I a good man," she replied, squeezing Abel's hand.

"I can wholeheartedly confirm that without reservation," chirped John. "Only, Abel, please go easy with Fanny. I don't want to see her gone. Perhaps a few kind words?"

"Of course, Sir."

"Right away, I think."

"Oh, yes, if 'ee think haste be necessary."

"I do. After which, I want to have words with you and Cornelius, together."

That evening, John summoned both Cornelius and Abel into his home, where glasses of Madeira stood ready poured.

"Lovely," said Cornelius as he took the fortified wine. Abel grimaced after the first sip.

"Not to your liking, Abel?"

"Not really, Sir. Such refined taste in a little glass isn't to me palette. Would I be forward in asking for ale instead?"

John left the room, returning with a tankard. He smiled.

"I see, Abel, you've finished the Madeira anyway. It wasn't that bad, after all?"

"That was me," said Cornelius, pointing to the empty glass and with another measure in his hand. "Waste not, want not."

"Anyway, now to business. We must sort out sensible working arrangements. We can't carry on expecting you both to do the same job in name, but with Abel alone doing most of the work."

"I protest," returned Cornelius.

"Noted," replied John casually, not to be diverted. "I have been giving this some considerable thought and have come up with a solution."

"I was here first," said Cornelius sheepishly. "I have a contract."

"And so you do, one that you have been content to ignore up to now." He watched for a reaction on Cornelius's face. The truth was acknowledged with a slight nod of resignation. John continued. "No, we must agree on change, not look for rivalries. As I see it, the way forward is simple. I have given you, Cornelius, a great deal of latitude to complete your aero-forceful flying machine, or whatever you call it."

"Be that the contraption in the workshop?" asked Abel with more contempt than enquiry. "Where do 'ee harness the horse?"

"It is, and it doesn't use a horse, as I think you know full well," Cornelius replied condescendingly. "I would be obliged if you will continue to keep well clear. It is extremely fragile."

Abel turned to John for guidance. "Then, how do I mend the coulters and other farm tools when they break?"

"That sort of common sense issue is the very reason I wanted you both here tonight. Look, as I see it, the flying machine is nearly completed. Isn't that so, Cornelius?"

"Correct, except that it isn't a machine, as such. It has no mechanical moving parts. It's built to glide."

Abel looked askance. "What possible. . ."

"No, Abel, don't ask," cut in John, to avoid ridicule from a practical man. "I struck an agreement with Cornelius a week or two ago to let him complete the *thing* and then end his contract here. So, if we all rub along together for a little longer, helping each other the best we can and being patient when it comes to the inconvenience of having the workshop crowded, then we will all prosper in our respective occupations. Is that agreed?"

"If that suits 'ee, Sir," acknowledged Abel. "'Ee pays the wages."

"It does, in the short term at least. And then, after Cornelius breaks his silly neck jumping from Silbury Hill, you can move into his cottage."

"Thanks for the thought," retorted Cornelius, unhappy at the prospect of losing the best-equipped workshop he had ever had.

And so the farm and its band of workers settled into purposeful routine, tending the animals, making dairy products, clearing ditches, mending boundaries, turning the soil, gathering fallen branches from leafless trees, and such else besides. In this consummate landscape the maids and men, dressed against the cold, laboured contentedly, almost blithely. Abel was of particular cheer, pleased to be back among friends in an occupation he enjoyed, although Fanny's stares as their paths crossed dug into this happiness.

Just one week later Cornelius made the announcement John longed to hear. The glider was ready for testing. He had tried to delay the bulletin, believing the warmer weather of Spring might be more conducive to making the glider stay airborne. Unfortunately, however, it had been generally noticed how little noise now came from the workshop and how early Cornelius retired to his cottage of an evening, making the declaration inevitable. His stomach churned with the mixed emotions of excitement and apprehension, in equal measure.

Two days later, preparations began to transport the glider to Silbury Hill. John asked Cornelius if he had invited his parents to the launch. His reply was to the negative.

"I don't understand you at all," said John, as the glider was carefully moved from its resting place and onto a large flat-bed wagon with the help of a specialist remover who came with the hired vehicle. "Don't you want them to see what you've been up to, your moment of triumph?"

"I don't want them to see me injured," was his curt reply.

John stopped in his tracks. "Surely you don't really think that's going to happen?"

Cornelius could hardly say the words. "It's possible. I can't rule it out. I wouldn't be the first."

"No?"

"No. Think of Icarus escaping from the Labyrinth in Crete."

"Oh, but that's mythology."

"Of course it is, but history abounds with foolhardy attempts to fly, not just in legend but actual documented events. One of the best remembered was made by a Benedictine monk named Oliver, who leapt from Malmsbury Abbey and broke his legs."

"When?"

"1020AD."

"Good grief, Cornelius, that hardly counts. Britain is in an industrial age, full of scientific wonder. You shouldn't concern yourself with medieval history."

"Are you becoming convinced by my experiments?"

"I suppose I must sound like it, but let me assure you that I'm not. No, you are every bit as foolhardy as the monk. Believe me, if God had intended man to fly, he would've provided. . ."

"Wheels!"

"Wheels?"

"Yes, bicycle wheels. God didn't give man wheels, but we cycle. The same will be true of wings."

"You should leave flying to the angels, Cornelius."

"Man will fly one day, believe me, but whether it will be now, heaven only knows. I think I will fly, of course, but I have some remaining doubts."

"Then, why try at all? Go home and take this silly thing with you. At least that way you will give yourself time to reconsider."

"A tempting offer, but I remain resolved. It has to be now.

Anyway, I need a bit of wind, as long as it isn't too strong. Come, let's send the flying machine on its way."

With Silbury Hill being a good three or even four day's slow journey north, the wagon was sent ahead. John and Cornelius rode out the following afternoon, intending to stop for the first night in Castle Cary.

By the time they breakfasted in Marlborough, their second overnight stay, only the last few miles of the journey to Silbury Hill remained, allowing a leisurely pace to be adopted past little thatched cottages and unusual thatched walls. John had been sorry to leave Marlborough so quickly, being a place he much admired for its wide high street, elegant shops and monumental architecture, but rarely visited. Yet, despite any lack of urgency on their part, by the time the hill came into view the wagon and its freight were already parked up, the horse loose-reigned and nibbling at long grass growing where a dried stream had once wound an irregular path. The driver lay against the slope on top of a tarpaulin, which he had used as an overnight shelter when draped over the cart, and now smoked a pipe while admiring the fields of pale cream soil and stone. The remains of a bread and ale meal lay beside him.

"Heaven forbid," exclaimed John, the hill growing ever higher as they approached. "It's massive."

"I reckon about one-hundred feet at its peak," replied Cornelius in admiration.

"You're going to jump off the top of that?"

"Of course."

"I've never heard anything so daft. You risk your neck, you foolish boy."

"It's a *calculated* risk. Look, the top is absolutely flat, making preparations easy once I'm up there. And the sides form gentle slopes. If I have an accident, it won't be like falling off a cliff edge. That's why I chose the place. Plus, the wind gusting up the slopes should help the glider stay airborne. It's perfect."

"Perfect lunacy!"

"We will see," returned Cornelius with a twinkle in his eye.

John cursed the slope as being anything but gentle to climb as the three men manhandled the fragile glider to the top, the leather soles of his riding boots constantly slipping on the dewy grass. The driver had already staked a rope from top to bottom, and grabbing this one-handed had, alone, prevented John from sliding back down on several occasions. All collapsed on the grassy plateau.

"Good heavens, Cornelius," panted John as he doubled over, hands on knees, "you've certainly made a bloody nuisance of yourself since you arrived in my employ. I could be home enjoying myself, not up here freezing cold and thoroughly exhausted."

"I'm with you, Sir," offered the cart driver, who suffered the most, being somewhat older and overweight.

"Be quiet," snapped Cornelius. "You're being paid. *We* do it for science, not for profit."

John looked critically at Cornelius, but said nothing. The look was sufficient to prompt an apology.

"Right, let's get on," said Cornelius brightly, jumping up with all the vigour of youth. He plucked a handful of grass and threw it skyward to determine the wind, which would dictate the direction of launch. "You can go down once I'm ready to fly."

Cornelius stepped to the glider, taking a central open position within the area of the wings. With John and the driver supporting the wingtips, the craft was raised to a midway point between his waist and shoulders and the leather harness fastened to his body.

"Are you sure you want to go through with it? We'll think no less of you if you decide to abandon the flight."

"No, Mr Madden, I must go now or be frightened forever."

"Then, good luck and God speed."

Even before John and the driver reached the bottom of the hill, Cornelius had jumped, moving his legs pendulum-fashion from side to side, struggling to maintain control. From the look on Cornelius's face, the rate of descent was unexpectedly rapid until a gust suddenly caused the wings to rise up alarmingly, stalling the craft and sending it nose-diving into the side of the slope.

John scrambled up the hill to where the glider had landed with a chilling snap.

"I'm alright," said Cornelius, extracting himself from the wreck. "The willow hoop at the front did its job in absorbing the impact. It worked exactly as I had hoped."

"Shame the glider as a whole didn't," replied John, his look of panic subsiding.

Cornelius ignored the comment. "I think I know what went wrong. I've made the wings too large, too stable to be controlled. Whichever way I shifted my weight, it made not a jot of difference. I need to cut the wings back a little. When we get back home, if I work all night, we could be back here within the week to try again. Does that suit you?"

"Do I have a choice?"

Cornelius could find no answer.

"Alright, it's your neck, old man."

And so, mid-way through the following week, the modified glider was once again to be found at the top of Silbury Hill. By now, word had got around of the peculiar experiments and a small number of local villagers gathered to see what would happen next.

They were to be disappointed. The glider, after a running launch, was gusted to an immediate stop. Again it stalled, this time slipping sideways through the air before crashing into the hillside.

"He'll be dead," said one villager to another. "No doubt about it. Shall we go now and feed the chickens? By the way, how's Charlie's leg since he. . ."

John rushed to where Cornelius lay winded.

"I'm alright," he panted, wanting a few moments to recover before having the harness unbuckled. "I know what caused it."

"You said that last time," barked John, believing it had all got somewhat out of hand and was no longer sensible.

"No, this time I really do. Alright, help me out, if you would." The driver lifted a wing while John cupped his arms around Cornelius's back, ready to lift. "Damn, I've twisted my foot really badly."

"That's an end to it, then," scolded John once more, leaving no room for manoeuvre. "It's bloody madness."

"Not so," reposted Cornelius. "I'm so close to success. It would be foolish to stop!"

"'Twas an awful long way to come for such a short flight," added the cart driver sardonically. "Still, 'tis your own money."

"Then, please remember it," riposted Cornelius, conveniently forgetting the leading role John had played in funding the expedition.

Limping to the wagon, Cornelius sat on the flatbed alongside his damaged glider as the procession began the long trek back to Nether Bow, his rider-less horse tied to the rear. With all three men now needing to travel in close company, the tarpaulin remained folded throughout the return journey, the cart driver enjoying luxuries in Marlborough and Castle Cary that were new experiences to a poor man.

The very moment the cart stopped in the grounds of Wheat Sheaf Farm, and with no dignified pause to thank the driver for his efforts and see him properly rewarded, Cornelius hopped to the barn to ruminate over his designs and calculations. Perplexed, the driver pulled the wagon around, leaving John to seek Abel's company, four guineas lighter. As anticipated, everything had run smoothly in his absence, with no problems to report beyond the anger of a local trader who demanded immediate payment of an overdue account for several lengths of belt leather and a number of strong buckles.

"I took the opportunity to pay him out of what remained from the five pounds you gave me, Sir, as he was so agitated. Did I do right? I suppose it was for that confounded flying machine."

"You did well, Abel. Come to me later and I'll settle the debt. I hope you'll also join me then in a glass of Madeira. I've had quite enough of Cornelius's company for the time being. You will come, won't you?" He noticed Abel's grimace. "Alright, you can have ale."

Recounting Cornelius's accident gave John a strong sense of mortality, so much so that he now viewed as urgent the need to get his own affairs in order. He might not take the sort of risks Cornelius chanced, but he knew fate had a horrible habit of throwing up the unexpected when least prepared. He shuddered at the memory of seeing James Elvington's withered arm when he had visited Christabel at Westkings years before, a vivid example of this depressing thought. He was unsure of the circumstances of that particular accident, but convinced of the likelihood that James's life had been one of quite ordinary experiences, visited by sudden disaster.

Top of this new *to do* list was a visit to the Grants, where he would discuss the possibility of marriage to Elizabeth, followed by the preparation of a legal will and testament to include provision for both Elizabeth and Unity, as principal beneficiaries. In many ways the latter was the more difficult, as he did not believe in unbridled wealth. He was not a socialist by any means or one of the new communists who wanted to ban the very act of inheritance, but, nevertheless, he recognised real danger in unearned riches. His own mother had disappointed him upon her death by staggering his inheritance. Yet, in retrospect, how wise she had been. Having become independent of parents, he had attracted new friends willing to spend his fortune, but who had disappeared equally quickly when it began to run thin. The wake-up call had worked, and the subsequent staged income began to turn the waster into a man of position and accomplished dignity, capable of running the farm within a budget.

The problem in the preparation of his own will was one of proportion, he thought, as it was reasonable to believe Unity might also inherit from her mother's family. As he saw it, it would not do to spoil the child by giving her further riches which, when stacked together, came to such magnitude that it guaranteed Unity would never need to be industrious in any way. Yet, who else would he leave the farm to if not his future wife and child? And, there was a further complication. What if the opposite was true and Jeremiah and Harriet Grant intended to bequeath all their wealth exclusively to their oldest son, Daniel? This would leave Elizabeth in desperate need of an independent income and provide no future inheritance for Unity beyond anything he bequeathed? No, there was only one answer to the enigma. He would have to speak to Jeremiah first regarding his intentions towards Elizabeth, and only then ask for her hand in marriage. This way he could apportion the estate appropriately.

All her life, Elizabeth had been an amiable but dilatory young woman, relying for her gracious position on the enterprise and accomplishment of her parents and forefathers, who had between them accumulated significant, though not limitless, wealth. With their business portfolio spread widely, generation after generation of Grants had ridden out the vagaries of the markets, unaffected when grain prices fell or money markets panicked during times of war and peace, instead steering a straight course which accrued prosperity like so many precious shells garnered upon the shores of a beach by the constant flow of the sea.

What was interesting, even astounding, therefore, was quite how well Elizabeth had managed to shake off the conventional constraints of her upbringing and rise to the challenge of single motherhood. Little or no practical help had been offered by her parents since she had come home with Unity, and yet she had met the challenge with a fervour her parents described quietly between themselves as *something quite marvellous*. Indeed, on one occasion Elizabeth had heard them saying this as she descended the stairs to join them for lunch, deciding instead to return to her room with the word *marvellous* ringing in her head. It was a new experience to be praised for something worthwhile, rather than being flattered for merely appearing in a new dress somebody else had created and in which she was nothing more than a fashionably attractive clothes-hanger. On this occasion, she had lifted Unity from the cot to consider the object of the compliment, realising that motherhood was not something she had worked at to conquer. Strangely, it had come quite naturally, as instinctive as a bird returning to her chicks. It was, indeed, a *quite marvellous* achievement.

In the early morning of the next day, John arrived unexpectedly at the home of the Grant family, hardly allowing time for the breakfast table to be cleared. He was resolved to get the matter settled and not suffer the agony of indecision. And, although he set about the business in the time honoured manner, with adherence to custom expected of a gentleman, he was shocked to find Jeremiah well rehearsed in his reply and ready to give his approval without any examination of income or prospects. Anyway, such questions as routinely asked on these occasions hardly applied to a suitor who was so well known to the family. Whilst glad the embarrassing interview was kept short, it gave John no time to enquire as to Jeremiah's will.

Meantime, the moment John's voice had been heard in the hallway, Harriet had raced up the stairs to prepare Elizabeth for an important caller. She was found feeding Unity and would not be hurried by her mother's impatience.

With time to kill, John waited patiently in the garden while Elizabeth readied herself. But, when she eventually appeared, she was still holding the baby in her arms, accompanied unexpectedly by her mother.

John bowed cordially to the pair, trying hard to conceal his feelings, which were divided in equal measure between distraction at the obvious bond of mother and baby and annoyance at Harriet's imprudent presence at such a moment. Little did he realise how hard Harriet had begged Elizabeth to let her take Unity before entering the garden.

"Now, Lizzy, give me Unity, so our dearest John might have your fullest attention," said Harriet, again trying to take control.

Elizabeth turned her back. "Dear Mamma, please don't go. Anything John has to say can be heard by you too." She looked down at Unity and then across to John as a gesture of prioritised loyalties.

"Don't be silly, Elizabeth, I'm not wanted. I cannot understand your reasoning to think that I would be anything but a gooseberry," said Harriet in a loud voice, hoping her facetiousness would avoid a scene. She closed discreetly towards her daughter's ear. "Have you gone completely insane?" she whispered.

Still Elizabeth would not part with the child.

Harriet glanced towards John and shrugged. "I am all a-fluster. What am I to do?"

"More to the point," returned John sharply, masking his embarrassment, "what am I to do? I can hardly express what I came to say within such a triangle." He turned to Elizabeth. "Am I to assume from this situation that I should go away?"

"You must do whatever you think is right," was her strange reply. "It's taken you long enough to come!"

"What are you doing, Lizzy?" begged Harriet in a soft but determined voice. "This is craziness of the worse kind. Is it a game you are playing at our expense, to jangle our nerves? Because, if it is, I can tell you that it's working. Days, weeks, what does it matter? He is here now and that's what counts."

"Perhaps Elizabeth realises why I've come, Harriet," spoke John distinctly, "and wishes to spare me the distress of rejection."

"No!" exclaimed Harriet, grabbing hold of John's arm to stop him leaving. "I am convinced that cannot be so."

"Then we must ask the same of Elizabeth," suggested John strongly.

Still Elizabeth ignored them both. She brought a smile to Unity's face by kissing her little cold nose.

"I'm all adrift to know what's going on. I shall get my husband at once."

Harriet stormed off, lifting the hem of her dress above the damp stones as she ran towards the house.

When Harriet had gone, John rounded on Elizabeth in bewilderment, wanting to say something profound but stumbling to find the right words. The entire mission had not gone as planned and he felt deep shock. She, in return, merely shrugged her shoulders at his silence and began humming a tune while rocking Unity in her arms. It was John who eventually broke the deadlock.

"What do you want me to say, Elizabeth? This is not at all as I expected. You know full well why I came. I thought it would be an agreeable prospect to you. I can only surmise one of two reasons for your disservice. Either you wish me gone without declaring my intention, or you court the idea that a smidgen of disinclination adds to the exquisiteness of womanhood. Which is it?"

"I have no idea what you are talking about," she replied, without raising her head. "Say it more plainly or not at all!"

John could hardly believe what was happening. His patience snapped, turning in a thrice from shaky composure to one of measured irritation.

"By God, Elizabeth, I fail to fathom you. Maybe it is well that I uncover this side to your character, before discovering it too late to pull myself free."

Hearing this censure was bait enough. She glared at John incredulously. "Almost from the day we met, John, I picked you out from my other acquaintances as the man I would most like to have as a companion in life, to be the father of my children."

"Which I am."

"Which you are by default," she countered with more fact in her voice than criticism.

"Are you saying I'm not Unity's father?"

"Of course not. You are, and on that there is no room for compromise. But you are a reluctant father, not because you are a bad man but because you are uncertain in your own mind. The delay in coming here is proof enough. Oh, maybe now you have decided to accept it as an actuality, but I can see deep into your soul and I know there will always remain niggling doubts over whether you raise someone else's child. It is not a prospect I can live with. It would be far better for Unity and I to manage alone than live under a cloud." She kissed the baby's cheek. Unity gurgled with happiness.

"How can you presume to tell me what I think or what I want?"

She listened, digested, and having understood the gravity of his snap reply, she suddenly felt strangely distant from her body, as if floating in a dream, in a world where anything could be said without consequence. Yet, just as quickly, she came back to earth with a thud, realising just how inappropriately she had responded given the fact that everything she had ever wanted lay before her for the taking. She shivered, not from cold but awareness. Quickly, she fought for a kind response, but composing an apology led to a pause which he took as indifference.

"Look here, Elizabeth," he said eventually, before she was ready with her own words, "I am becoming somewhat rattled by this morning's experiences. I came here in good faith, and so far you have humiliated me in front of your mother and made me feel completely worthless to both you and Unity. I think I should leave before I make matters worse."

"No!" she exclaimed. "Give me just a few more minutes of your time. You will understand when I ask you this." She hesitated. "Tell me truthfully, what were the reasons you gave my father for wanting to marry me?"

"On that, well, truth be told, he hardly cared to listen to anything I had in mind to say. I was in and out like a fiddler's elbow, without so much as a by your leave."

"Then, tell me, as if I was him."

"What?"

"Why you want to marry me. You didn't want to before, when

I would've bitten off my own hand and fed it to the pigs to have you in my bed."

"A bad choice of phrase, Elizabeth."

"By my side, then, if you want to be delicate after the event."

He considered the difficulty of being absolutely honest and still gain her trust. "Firstly, I suppose, it would be ridiculous for me to hide the fact that Unity needs a father. But, then. . ."

"Stop, you say it with your first breath. The offer is to ease your conscience, not out of love for me."

"Wait and hear me out," he demanded. "Admittedly, I might not have been encouraged to seek marriage to you or anyone else for that matter at the present time if Unity hadn't arrived on the scene, but there are two ways of viewing even that prospect. The *glass half empty* attitude would be to see Unity merely as a reason why it is necessary to marry, whereas to see the *glass half full* is to realise that Unity merely focussed my mind towards the happy prospect of sharing a life with you and our daughter."

His eloquence moved her. "Our daughter? I think that's the first time you've said that."

"Are you sure? I've certainly felt it before, even if the words stayed prisoner behind my teeth."

"Any other reasons for asking me? You implied there were more."

"So there are, too numerous to express. Well, for a start, your parents want us to," he said ill-advisedly. "Your father said to me as he took me by the shoulder and offered me his pipe, 'John, my boy, to achieve a successful marriage as a farmer you need a woman who will cook and mend, a woman who will turn the butter, and a woman who warms your bed. The secret of happiness is to keep the first two women away from the third!', or words to that effect."

"John!" she shouted, outraged.

"I thought he made a lot of sense."

"Damn you, John!"

"Oh, come on, Elizabeth, a bit of fun does nobody any harm.

For God's sake, you knew full well I was joking. The very idea of your father expecting you to get down on your hands and knees to polish a step is laughable. Nor would I allow it."

"Sadly, I would do all those things if your feelings were sincere towards me. I would take the rough with the smooth."

"The good times with the bad? No, Elizabeth, don't let us kid ourselves. You were not born for drudgery, and nor would I expect it of you. Mops are for cleaning, flowers are for admiring. You are a flower to look beautiful and smell sweetly, an English rose by any measure."

Her smile, so radiant for a few seconds, suddenly dropped as a new thought came into her head. "Christabel would have done any of those things for you, asked or otherwise. You said so before."

John shuddered at her name, so inappropriately raised.

"Well?" she repeated, a reply required.

"So, that's behind this fiasco. She's long dead, for goodness sake."

"Your heart was buried with her, I think."

"My heart was broken, that I admit. But, I repeat, Christabel is dead these past years. Nobody could be jealous of the long dead."

"I could be jealous of not receiving the same depth of feeling you had for her. Dead she is, but not in your heart. Tell me I am wrong?"

Her argument was complete. "I find myself unable to comment, Elizabeth. Not because I refuse to be honest, but because I live each day suppressing my thoughts towards her. I don't wish to bring them to the fore."

"There, you say it!" she cried. "She lives on."

"But, only in my thoughts. Surely a man can love twice."

"I think you have loved only once, John, and I am not that person."

"You are mistaken," he said, touching Unity with the tip of his finger.

"Maybe I am. But *if* you have loved twice, maybe the other is

Unity and not me at all. Now I think on it, that makes entire sense. After all, why should you love me? Am I not the same silly person you have befriended all these years without the slightest sign of special regard? I even think your sainted mother preferred me over Christabel, but we could not break into the ivory tower you built around the dairymaid."

"She certainly preferred the idea of you being my wife over a cheese maker."

"A cheese maker? You've said that before. It proves her ways are set solid in your soul."

"Just a silly, throw-away comment she once made. I remember other remarks just as clearly, on many matters and about other people. Forget it, Lizzy."

"Maybe Isobel should have been more forceful in her attitudes. If only she had kept you on a tighter rein, closer to your own kind."

"My own kind? You mean my own social class, don't you?"

"Have I wounded your liberal mind?" She looked deeply into his face. "Yes, I think I really have. I know well your perspective on social divisions, John. You admit to different levels of income for different grades of work, yet you deny a class structure. But, one is the same as the other, under different names, because one creates the other. Society cannot function without employers and employees. It's a fact of economic life. That alone dictates class structure, by a different route. Your mother saw the need for observance of the natural order. Those who gamble with their money, she would say, either create wealth for themselves and employment for others or go bankrupt in the process and end up in the poor house. Those who don't gamble, but instead take what is offered, are assured of income but denied the prospect of wealth."

"She adored Christabel's labouring father, Jack Mere. Doesn't that prove something?"

"Of course she did, because he was a good person. But, Jack knew his place and their friendship remained just that, cordial but distant."

"Am I a bigot in your eyes, for I feel in my soul that I'm not?"

"I would not be so bold as to imply it in words."

"Just in vague references? I think we should stop this conversation. It is derisive, when empathy is needed. And I don't want you blaming my mother for what has come between us. There are boundaries beyond which even a parent cannot properly exercise control. Emotions are for the individual, not for a committee to decide."

"It remains a fact, John, that Christabel made my life intolerable and even now she has control over you from beyond the grave."

"Maybe she does. I can do nothing to stop how I feel, even if I wanted to break from the past."

"Even if you wanted to?"

"A poor choice of words, nothing more sinister."

"Ask yourself this, John. Would you permit me to forge a chasm between the present and your past memories?"

"To be entirely honest, I don't think I would. Memories are the stepping stones of life, the only solace to growing older."

"Then tell me, where does your continuing infatuation for Christabel leave us?"

"Up a gum tree, I shouldn't wonder."

"You had better go. There is no more between us."

Inside the house, Jeremiah paced the floor in lonely contemplation, anxious for news of the betrothal. He held a bottle of champagne by the neck, ready to burst it open the very moment the engaged couple joined him. The wait was gripping. It had been some little while since he had wished John 'every happiness' and surely, by now, the words of love must have been spoken.

He looked through the window, but could see nothing. He had called for his wife, but she was nowhere to be found. Anxiously, he replayed the morning's events in his mind. No, he thought, it was a waste of time. There was absolutely nothing that could go wrong. He just had to be patient and the day would be one of unbridled joy.

At last, Harriet came scurrying towards him, news hot on her lips. He perked up and rushed towards her, embracing her warmly and lifting her in a full circle of delight without giving her any chance to respond.

"It is done at last!" he shouted with joy. "What happiness for us all. Where is the happy couple? We must toast them."

"Not done, but undone," she howled, fighting to be released and explaining at length all she had witnessed.

Jeremiah was dumbstruck.

Elizabeth and John stood apart in the garden, neither quite knowing what to say or how to leave, when Jeremiah thundered from the house. Harriet followed behind, battling to keep pace against the inconvenience of the many inner skirts to her dress. Their faces were strained and tense.

"Alright, you pair, explain to me what's going on," demanded Jeremiah in high voice as he approached, forgetting he still grasped the champagne as testament to his expectations. "Upon my word, Sir, you shall swing if you dishonour my daughter a second time."

"Stop!" bawled Elizabeth, taking a step backwards to protect Unity from the full force of his advance.

"I told you, Jeremiah," cried Harriet, having caught up, "it isn't John's doing. It's Elizabeth who's being perverse."

"Well?" rounded Jeremiah, snatching Unity from Elizabeth's arms and placing the child into Harriet's keeping. "What do you have to say for yourself?"

"She doesn't have to say anything," offered John, placing himself between them. "It's all amiss. I have come on a fool's errand and made a chump of myself. Elizabeth has explained in simple and kindly terms how she expects someone truer than me as a husband, and I am in agreement that she is right to want it."

"Damned if she knows anything" shouted Jeremiah fiercely.

"Please go into my study, John. I will join you shortly. I will get to the bottom of this."

"No, Sir, with respect, I shall not," he replied firmly. "There is nothing to discover. The unpalatable fact of the matter is," he paused, "Elizabeth has realised before it is too late that she does not love me. She thought she did, but now it's come to a head she realises that she doesn't. It's a burden I, alone, will have to bear and an admission that does your daughter the greatest credit in view of the fact that Unity needs a father."

"Not as much as Elizabeth needs a husband! If not you, then where will a husband come from? Who will have her now?" He turned to Elizabeth, anguish showing in every feature of his face. "You are undone by your own hand. If you do not accept John's proposal, I see no future for you in society. We are, as a family, ruined."

"You won't turn her out of the house again, will you Jeremiah?" uttered Harriet, wretchedly. "Ask this of yourself. What should she have done, be governed by her head or her heart?"

"Whichever led her to John's door. But, no, wife, I will not turn her out. We have travelled that road over the past months and it was a false destination. Yet, I fear Elizabeth will be shunned by the good and laughed at by the bad. Only the hard-featured won't care. I cry inside only for what might have been, for I fear above all else that Elizabeth herself will come to regret what she is now doing."

Harriet approached Elizabeth, putting Unity back into her arms and cradling the pair in her shawl. "Now, more than ever, she will need all her family around her." She squeezed Elizabeth gently. "It is a brave decision. I won't pretend to understand, but we are a family united. We will survive the crisis."

With a shake of her head and a compassionate smile to John, she led Elizabeth and Unity back into the house, leaving the men to stand in their awkwardness.

"I should go?" said John.

"No. . . Yes. Gracious, I really don't know. Look, perhaps all is not lost, if you are willing to lose the battle to win the war. Now I think on it, it is not entirely unusual for a young woman to say *no* the first time of asking, when later the answer is *yes*. I am by no means disconsolate for future prospects. Promise me you will not give up, John?"

"She had a reason for refusal that was beyond argument or explanation. It would be wrong to make a further attempt, as the circumstances for her rejection are unalterable."

"What about Unity? Have you considered her?"

"Leave her welfare to me. I might be rejected as a husband, but my fatherhood is unquestionable. I will honour and love my child the best I can."

"You are a good and honest man, John. I would've been proud to have you in the family. Maybe. . ."

"I think the matter of marriage is closed. I will keep you informed as to my arrangements for Unity."

At Wheat Sheaf Farm, Cornelius Fairfax was sitting at the bench in the workshop when John returned. The large barn doors were closed and the inside was dim. He was reflecting on the night's work and preparing to attach a tail to the truss-work frame of the glider, which was still undergoing general repair.

"Don't you ever sleep," enquired John as he entered, judging from the burning lanterns how Cornelius must have worked through the night. He held the latest bill for the leather harnesses and buckles in his hand. "Do you know what time it is?"

Rubbing his eyes, Cornelius replied that he had no idea.

"Lunch time, you goose. Get yourself some food, and clean this place up."

"I will, gladly, if you can indulge me a moment longer. Actually, I have some really good news," he said in a happy, but sleepy, attitude.

"Excellent, I could do with some." John stuffed the bill into his pocket, the time not being right for confrontation.

"You'll be pleased to know," he said, building to a crescendo, "I'll soon be out of your hair. I have the answer to my failure to fly. It's so obvious now I think about it. Tell me, what does a bird have that my glider hasn't?"

"A beak."

"Anything else?"

"Legs, eyes, guts. Shall I go on?"

"A tail. It doesn't have a tail."

"Is it important?"

"I think it could be. In fact, I am sure of it, even without testing my theory on a scale model. See, I have designed a tail and gone straight into constructing a full-size version. What do you think?"

"I think it's the wrong way around."

"What?"

"Your sketch shows it attached vertically, like a tennis racquet balancing on its edge. I'm no ornithologist, but I've never seen a bird whose tail feathers don't lie flat."

"Yes, at first I pondered the same thought, but what practical use is a flat tail? Surely it's merely an extension of the wing area. No, what I need for stability, to prevent side-slipping, is a vertical tail."

"Your neck!"

"My reputation and our fortune if I'm right."

"So be it. When will you try it out?"

"In a few days, if I'm lucky. I'll snatch a few hours of sleep and then work through the night. That way, if we can hire the wagon again, and if the weather is suitable, I will soar with the buzzards within the week."

"Or drop like a gannet."

True to his word, the following day a bleary-eyed Cornelius staggered from the workshop, hobbling his way to the pump where he let the icy water run over his head. He stretched upwards and back, straightening his spine after many hunched hours attaching the tailfin to the glider and securing the cotton fabric covering. He wore a satisfied smile, certain his life's ambition was soon to be fulfilled.

"Want some breakfast?" shouted Abel, as he returned from the fields. "I be cooking."

Cornelius nodded with appreciation and made for the dormitory steps, where the warmth of the stove allowed his coat to be removed for the first time in hours. Abel threw a rag in his direction.

"Dry your hair, man, before 'ee catch 'ee death of cold."

"What's the weather to be for the rest of today and the next four, Abel?"

"Not too good, I be thinking. The sky's full of bad omens. I have no hope for t'morrow, either, or the one after that."

"Damn. I suppose you're usually right about such things?"

"I'm a countryman, born and bred. Take it from me, it will rain on and off for days."

And rain it did, from mid afternoon until late evening, dotting the open fields with shallow ponds as the natural drainage failed to cope with the downpour and the small sluice gates struggled against the fast-filling ditches. Much the same followed for two days thereafter.

But, just as Abel predicted, on the fourth day the rain stopped and was followed by a noticeably brighter spell. This was encouragement enough to begin preparations for Silbury Hill.

On the day the wagon reappeared in the yard, Cornelius engaged Abel's help to move the glider into the open, where it was manhandled onto the flatbed.

"Is this to be the big event?" asked John eagerly, willing to lend a helping hand.

"It is, Mr Madden, God willing."

"I think you may need His protection more than His help. Are you sure you really want to go ahead with another leap into the jaws of death? Can't you put some weight or other on the glider to simulate an aeronaut, in case it crashes again?"

"It isn't the way of things, I'm afraid. It has to be a person, because every change in the wind, every new gust and blow, has to be countered by a shift in my body mass."

"On your head, then."

"I hope not!"

The now familiar journey to Silbury Hill began in good spirits and, as the day warmed, expectations grew. Abel had joined the wagon driver, intending to take over the heavy lifting from Cornelius, whose foot remained fragile. He also drove, which seemed to hasten the journey. Two days later, and with the hill in view, John and Cornelius caught up with the wagon party after stopping over in Marlborough, travelling in Cornelius's gig. Enthusiasm reached fever pitch.

With a rope attached to his waist, Cornelius was assisted to the top, where he joined Abel in hauling the glider ever upwards. From below, John and the driver pushed the best they could against the slippery grass. Then, with the direction of the wind determined, Cornelius once more stepped into the gap in the glider's wing and the leather harnesses were fastened.

"This is it. Good luck, old thing. See you at the bottom," said John with little actual confidence.

"Don't look so alarmed, Mr Madden. I'll take good care of myself. But, just in case I don't, I've written a letter to my parents. It's on the mantel in the cottage, just behind the clock. Please see they get it, if. . ." He stopped short of completing the sentence. "Of course, I shall tear it up myself in a few days' time. But, just in case, you understand."

John nodded and began the descent. But, Cornelius was again impatient to begin and, before John had taken many downward steps, the glider made a heart-stopping drop from the peak. John looked up in panic as Cornelius's feet brushed past his head. He ducked, the shadow of the glider casting its progress on the grassy slope. Cornelius stared ahead in terror. Then, suddenly, miraculously, the glider picked up speed and was carried level on the wind, beginning an amazingly steady descent.

As the height increased between the slope and Cornelius's dangling feet, so it became obvious that man and machine would overshoot the foot of the hill by a considerable distance. John, Abel and the driver scrambled down the rest of the hill at speed, running to where they thought Cornelius would land.

Almost effortlessly, and quite by accident, the glider stalled just yards off the ground, allowing Cornelius to use his feet to stop, resting the glider gently onto its nose.

"My goodness, Cornelius, that was absolutely terrific."

"I knew it, Mr Madden. I knew it would work. This is history being made. Remember the date. We need a photograph next time."

"Next time? Are 'ee mad? Surely there won't be more flying?" said Abel, delighted at the spectacle but anxious not to push luck.

"There won't be today. Anyway, I don't have photographic equipment with me, which I must have as a record.

"I have a Camera Obscura on the wagon," interrupted the owner. "I carry it everywhere I go in a wooden box. I fancy meself as a bit of an artist, but I be hopeless getting sizes right from a distance. That's where the Obscura has use."

"I'm not familiar with the term," puzzled Cornelius. "What does it do?"

"Bless you, Sir," said the driver, "that's because of your tender age. Hardly anyone uses them anymore. If the lens be pointed in the direction of the scene to be copied, an image appears behind on the glass screen. If paper then be placed on top of the glass, a picture can be traced by hand. Mind you, the paper has to be dampened with light oil to make it transparent or nothing can be seen through it. Then, with the outline just right, the paper can be dried and painting by hand can begin. It makes me seem proper clever and no mistake. Still, Obscuras are mostly out of use nowadays."

"Thank you for the explanation," offered Cornelius kindly, "but I need a genuine photograph to be believable. A drawing would be no proof at all. Anyway, I have an even better idea. Now I know my glider works, and realising how my previous attempt attracted onlookers, I think I will wait a few weeks and see if I can sell tickets to the public at sixpence a go. I can advertise locally and place an advertisement in the paper. Only those who buy a ticket will be told of the day and time I will fly. It will be the beginning of our fortune from flying."

"And the beginning of reimbursing me," added John.

"Of course," agreed Cornelius painfully.

CHAPTER 25

The legacy

E mmie stood by a window, watching two tom-cats fighting over the remains of a squirrel. The head had been eaten. She pounded the frame, paralysing the larger cat and giving the smaller the opportunity to drag the body under a ledge that was too low for the other to reach. The larger cat, no longer distracted, slashed its paw into the void, hoping to hook its claws into the dead fur. The fury of movement, born of frustration, proved enough to frighten the smaller away. Yet, despite desperate effort, the squirrel could not be recovered and the larger cat slinked away, stopping to turn every few paces to ensure the smaller cat did not return to claim the prize.

The drama over, Emmie closed the window. She had recovered from her frightening experience at the hands of her attacker and the police, and considered it time to find a place back in the real world.

"What do you want to do with your life, Emmeline?" asked Joseph, bursting with excitement but showing none of it.

She shrugged her shoulders. "I suppose I could go cap-in-hand to John Madden's farm, if he will have me. Or back to Westkings and the Elvingtons. Either way, it will mean moving from here. Would you both mind if I do?"

Rachel lifted a bag off the floor and took out her knitting. She casually unravelled a length of wool and tucked a needle under her arm. "You said some of the labourers didn't like you. Can you face more trouble?"

Resignation writhed across Emmie's young features. "I'm tired of trying to be liked. Maybe I prefer the company of those who hate each other. People who hate are generally so much more interesting. Funny enough, Mother, I received a letter from Edmond Elvington only the other day. It came out of the blue. Father read it to me. Didn't he say anything to you?"

"I thought it was your private business," admitted Joseph, "and yours alone."

"Oh! Anyway, James had told Edmond what had happened to me and Edmond wanted to know if I was alright. It was so kind of him. Maybe, despite being married, he still fancies. . ."

"Don't even go there!" shrieked Joseph.

"No, you're probably right. After all said and done, Lily is almost as pretty as me!"

Joseph shook his head. "Just finish what you began to say to your mother."

"Oh yes, well, apparently Edmond met up with John Madden in Sherborne, who told him about Abel Tucker. Now, my point in telling you this is that Abel is the most placid man you could ever wish to meet, with a beautiful nature, yet even he has apparently created quite a ripple of trouble in the dormitory."

"How so?" enquired Rachel.

"By bringing his fiancée to the farm before properly jilting his old girlfriend. I know Fanny, the abandoned woman. She is the person I most despise. So, I can believe it when I'm told she has daggers out for Delysia, the fiancée."

"What a tangled web," remarked Rachel.

"Have you quite finished your story, Emmie?" asked Joseph.

"I think so. Why, Father?"

"Because it's not customary to hear you speak so well of a man, whose name you don't follow by saying that he fancies you. I begin to wonder if you really are fully recovered from your ordeal."

"Stop that! You know I am. You've no need to remind me of my past mistakes with Edmond, Longborne Charles, Daniel Grant and John Madden. I was particularly wrong to believe John ever wanted me at the farm for personal reasons. As to the others, well, they did fancy me."

"Quite a list."

"Quite a life, Mother."

"Well, Emmie," interrupted Joseph, "that's all about to change."

"How do you mean?"

He took an envelope from his pocket. "I have such very good news for you, born out of our sadness. You remember me saying some time back that your brother's partner wrote saying he would sell Robert's half of the sheep business and send the proceeds on? Well, it's arrived. It provides the opportunity for a brilliant future, and your mother and I have decided to hand the entire amount over to you. It's a very worthy two hundred pounds, plus a few pennies."

"Gracious me!" was all Emmie could say, as she dropped onto a chair in disbelief. "I'm almost rich."

"You have most certainly been given a fortunate leg-up, and it's all down to your brother's hard work in Australia. We said some good might come from it."

"Can we pray for him, Father? I need to thank him."

"I never thought I would hear the day when you would ask such a thing. Of course we will." He took the Bible from the shelf. "Before I select an appropriate text, I am reminded of something attributed to Samuel Johnson, a hundred years ago. He said *'no man but a blockhead ever wrote, except for money'*. I think he was foolish in this remark, as it implies that every effort has to be rewarded. It would be well not to take the same attitude, Emmie, as the charitable work we are renowned for doing has its own rewards. However, I hope you can make this inheritance work for you, to provide stability for the future when we are dead and in the ground. In the meantime, I select John 3:17. '*If a man says, I love God, and hateth his brother, he is a liar: for he that loveth not his brother whom he hath seen, how can he love God who he hath not seen*'." He snapped the book shut. "Amen."

"Amen," said Rachel.

"Amen," said Emmie. "Two hundred pounds!"

"Just so. I wonder where it will take you."

"To Wheat Sheaf Farm, if I'm not much mistaken."

"But I thought it would provide the means for a new and better life?" said Joseph with concern.

"It will. My reason for going is not the obvious one. I will ask for your guidance, Father, but I might have the very business in mind which would give me that security. You remember I mentioned Delysia, Abel's fiancée? Well, by all accounts she is a skilled glove maker recently from Glastonbury, at present doing farm labouring which she is totally unsuited to. This is according to Edmond's letter. Now, what if I offered to set up in business in Cerne or Sherborne, with Delysia making gloves and me selling them from a little shop? What do you think?"

"I think it sounds wonderful," was Joseph's reply.

"And you Mother? What do you think?"

"Wonderful," she repeated.

"Then I will see to the arrangements in a week or two, after I have given it a little more thought. It is such a lot of money."

"Is this Emmeline in our midst, Rachel, or has she done a Tom and Alfred on us?"

CHAPTER 26

The unexpected hero

"*H*ave you seen the newspaper, Charlotte?" bawled James Elvington some time later, rushing to meet his wife in the hallway and waving the broadsheet wildly above his head.

"What is it, James? Is it dreadful news?"

"Depends entirely upon your personal feelings, I suppose. No, I would say, quite the contrary. It's that bloody fool, Lieutenant Longborne Charles."

"What's the rogue done now?"

"You'll hardly believe it when I tell you. That scoundrel, thief, debaucher and generally bad lot has only made himself a national hero."

"How?" enquired Charlotte abruptly in disbelief, unable to comprehend any possible situation in which he could distinguish himself favourably.

"Let me read to you what it says. Under the heading *The Gallant Lieutenant*, the newspaper says:

January 29th, 1885. As Scotland Yard's Special Irish Branch and the Government attempt to untangle events and lapses in security which led to the Fenian attack on London on January 24th, as previously reported and which caused damage to

Westminster Palace, the Chamber of the House of Commons and the Tower of London, a particularly courageous act of unselfish heroism has been uncovered independently by this newspaper. This may be seen as the one glimmer of light in an otherwise infamous day for the Union, in which two policemen were hurt in the first explosion.

Unaware that nobody had been seriously injured in the second explosion, Lieutenant Longborne Charles, a British Army officer, reputedly rushed single-handedly into the fray to save his sister, who had entered the building moments before the catastrophic event. Without fear for himself, and presumably understanding the possibility of further explosions occurring, he is said to have carried Miss Catherine Charles out and into safety before re-entering the Commons to take charge of the evacuation. His role in the rescue and the confused events that followed are, as yet, officially unconfirmed, but reports from bystanders suggest that this is an accurate summary of what took place.

Lieutenant Charles has not courted publicity for his heroic act. Despite vigorous efforts on our part to interview the gallant gentleman, we have been unable to locate him. According to War Ministry communications, they too are unable to shed any light on the reluctant hero. His sister, Catherine Charles, however, who was rescued from the Commons screaming, has shown no such reluctance in co-operating with the Press. Unlike the gallant Lieutenant, she has been exceedingly ready to tell her story.

According to Miss Charles, Lieutenant Charles has recently returned from a tour of duty in the Sudan, where, as the entire nation knows, General Gordon has been besieged by the Mahdi army since last April. Given her recent experience, there is understandable confusion over this posting, however, as she also claims the Lieutenant had been despatched to Southern Africa. In a monstrous attack on the integrity and heroism of the Lieutenant, an anonymous source suggested that this shadowy figure never reached either battle ground, an accusation Miss Charles vigorously denies.

~

On other matters concerning our forces in the Sudan, unsubstantiated rumours are rife regarding the fate of General Charles Gordon, Chinese Gordon as he is known to the troops under his command, suggesting he has since been killed in Khartoum. This has not been officially confirmed or denied by the Ministry. We must trust in hope that the foreign report circulating the world by telegraph may yet prove to be unfounded. The entire British nation awaits news with bated breath, particularly as Sir Garnet Wolseley should by now have relieved the garrison at the head of the Anglo-Egyptian army. The nation is asked to offer prayer for the safe keeping of our Christian soldier, who leads his troops into battle carrying a cane and a Bible."

"What do you make of that, Char?"

"It's unbelievable."

"Yet it says he saved Catherine. You know, I was never fooled by her, yet I couldn't help liking her all the same. I'm glad she's safe. Do you remember the business with the magic lantern all that time ago, when she first came to stay? It still makes me laugh when I think of it. What did she say? Oh yes. She said how she was totally mystified by the workings, a science which was over her scatty female head."

"And Longborne replied that her head was like the horse she rode, exceeding small!"

They laughed heartedly.

"Let's hope for the best, as long as it doesn't encourage Catherine to come and visit us again, or try to force Longborne into our society. Hero or not, he remains a downright rogue in my eyes. I wonder if Longborne knows where Edmond is now living, or Emmeline for that matter. It's best if he stays well away."

"I won't tell him if you don't. He's caused all the damage I can face."

And, an unbelievable story it was. In reality, the 'gallant lieutenant' had never been part of any great British enterprise to the Sudan. Yet, even if he had, he would have been neither missed nor venerated for any military prowess displayed in the jaws of an enemy. For, he had always made himself undistinguishable, nay invisible, amongst the ranks of real officers who wanted more than a fancy uniform to wear. His philosophy for armed service had always been to avoid exertion and danger whenever possible, however slight or conspicuous, and this same ideology was applied with equal vigour to work in general. He wanted the uniform only for the esteemed position it held in good society, but with none of the consequent dangers such colours could attract. His fellow officers knew this only too well, commenting among themselves how the only time he was likely to be found at the forefront of his troops was when they were in full retreat, yet even this prospect presupposed that he would ever have reached the front line in the first place. Like so many officers of low rank, he was entirely unsuited to the task and 'magnanimously' stood aside to let others prove themselves in battle.

Overall, Longborne had spent his adult life living off the admiration which came from being a British officer and a gentleman, yet his conduct embellished neither occupation. He made a career of 'leeching', sucking from the generosity of friends and colleagues, without the slightest outward sign of compunction. After all was said and done, he brought amusement into their drab lives by his self-assured manner, and this alone made everybody cheerful to be counted amongst his innermost circle, or so he thought.

As for Catherine Charles, she was vexatious and affected, as counterfeit as her brother but with none of his craftiness. She merely wafted in and out of people's lives like a gentle breeze, with all the graciousness of high society and the impoverishment of unseated gentry, taking in her emanating flurry all that was freely given or won by her silly, yet, appealing ways.

What actually took place on the 24th was somewhat different from the newspaper reports, but was unlikely ever to come into public domain, leaving the Lieutenant with an estimable character as far as the papers were concerned.

The old year of 1884 had ended and the new year begun as so many years previously, with Longborne and Catherine Charles away from their duties and homing in on a new victim to snare as a reluctant benefactor. This time they were aiming high, leaving behind the country squires and knighted gentlefolk in an attempt to catch a greater prize. And now, at this enlightened time, there were few bigger prizes than the poet laureate, Alfred Tennyson.

It had been widely reported in the previous year how Tennyson had become a firm favourite of the Queen, sparking a tender friendship which led to the bestowal of a peerage on the elderly scholar. Tennyson was also known to be an extremely rich man from his writings, his most attractive quality as far as Longborne was concerned. The challenge presented to the pair was how to make his acquaintance and win his favour, and in this contrivance possibly also effect an introduction to the Queen herself. It all made perfect sense if planned with military precision.

> *"Her court was pure; her life serene;*
> *God gave her peace; her land reposed;*
> *A thousand claims to reverence closed*
> *In her as Mother, Wife, and Queen"*

Tennyson, To the Queen

For some weeks over the Winter of 1884 and the beginning of 1885, the brother and sister had billeted in London, courting Members of Parliament and scouring newspapers for any news on Tennyson's whereabouts, sure he would be summoned to the

Palace over Christmas or New Year. Moreover, he would not be difficult to spot, his favoured big cloak and wide sombrero-type hat hardly able to disguise his tall figure, ragged hair and beard, and prominent features.

More importantly to Longborne, Tennyson's temperament was well documented, leaving him in little doubt that he could use his considerable charms to win over the poet. It would be a case of opposites attract. Tennyson's inability to hide his genuine sincerity – laying himself naked through his belief in simple truths – would be easy prey to a cunning mind already well versed in false humility, flattery and a well-prepared order of conversation.

Yet, despite such preparations, nothing went as planned. And so, when their plan failed to materialise by the third week of January, Longborne came up with a new strategy of even greater daring. He would abandon Tennyson. Instead, he would somehow court the company of the Prime Minister, William Gladstone, who needed friends in the military since his popularity among the public had taken a severe knock due to the Government's delay in authorising a relief expedition to save General Gordon. The consequent logistical muddles with the troop-carrying steamboats had only added to this public contempt.

Therefore, it became Longborne's new plan to get a message to the ministers in London, advising how he could be of practical help in the restoration of their failing image. Of course, in the reality of politics, this proposition was neither realistic nor truthful in its achievability. Nor, for that matter, would the offer ever have been accepted if it had reached Gladstone's hands. Nevertheless, believing in his own invulnerability, the plan was set into motion on the 24th, with Catherine taking the said letter into the House of Commons, on Longborne's behalf.

The communication itself, dictated by Longborne and written in copperplate style by Catherine on regimental paper, suggested in no uncertain terms that his superior officers were fools, how General

Gordon had put himself into harm's way by taking up residence in the palace at Khartoum, and that without his assistance the Government could find itself facing terrible, and as yet unforeseen, consequences at the hands of the public and military alike.

Then, all hell broke loose. Following the chaos caused by the first bomb, the Chamber of the House of Commons emptied of Members just as Catherine entered the building. Unimaginably, a second explosion then followed upon the first, a highly destructive bomb planted on seats known as 'Under the Gallery'. Detonating with tremendous force, the Peer's Gallery was completely destroyed. The nearby Speaker's Chair also suffered considerable harm, as did the Government front benches where the great and the good had been debating only a short time before. Even the Member's Lobby and post office took damage, smoke and dust penetrating many corners of the ornate building.

Catherine stood paralysed in this pandemonium of shouting, rushing about and confusion when, out of the gloom, Longborne rushed into the fray, grabbing her purse and immediately turning for the door where he used the first bit of clear light to look inside for his letter. It was not there.

"Help me," Catherine screamed, still static with fear, her clothes covered in plaster.

Scowling at the misfortune of having to go back, he covered his mouth with a handkerchief and unceremoniously bundled her over his shoulder, throwing her to the ground after reaching the first available outside space.

"Let me have it," demanded Longborne.

"What?" Catherine responded through choking coughs.

"My bloody letter. They'll think I had something to do with this if they find it with my signature at the bottom."

"I don't have it."

"What!"

"I must have dropped it in the panic."

Longborne looked back towards the entrance in dismay.

"You stupid idiot."

Bounding back into the building and pushing past the human traffic anxiously going in the opposite direction, he searched the inside until he found the letter on the floor, well trodden but safe. He stuffed it into his tunic and headed back out, for the last few yards reluctantly assisting an elderly man with a top hat and cane, wing collar and long grey sideburns, who blocked his exit. Unknowingly, Longborne had come tantalisingly close to meeting his intended target.

* * *

Epilogue to Longborne and Catherine

That April, William Gladstone asked the House of Commons to allocate £11 million to purchase war matériel, as the Russians were expanding ever closer to British India, having seized Penjdeh in Afghanistan. This left only the mountain ranges as a division in the east between the two huge empires. Once again, a new battle front loomed ever more likely.

Despite strenuous efforts to relinquish his commission, Longborne's unmerited reputation as a hero made the Army reluctant to accept any such gesture at a sensitive time. But, while the Afghan front did not develop into immediate conflict, and British nervousness proved to be beyond reason, Longborne became involved in the separate annexation of the Kingdom of Upper Burma later that year, as part of a force of ten thousand troops under the command of General Prendergast. To Longborne's delight, the action cost few casualties and he was courted by the newspapers to give account of further heroics. With his reputation complete and his company sought, he remained in the East, leaving his sister to find her own place in the world.

Happily for Catherine, deliverance from obscurity came sooner than expected, when Charlotte Elvington made it known that her help would be appreciated in supporting Mrs

Josephine Butler in the final round of her fight with Gladstone's Government over repeal of the notorious Contagious Diseases Acts. By then, Catherine had woken to her brother's selfishness, confirmed by his abandonment. She also harboured resentment for his fame, achieved only with her collaboration.

Charlotte's unlikely choice of Catherine as a helper had been entirely at James' suggestion, however, believing Longborne's celebrity status could be brought into play by his sister in support of their pressure group. And so, with Catherine taking a small part in subsequent protests, eventually – by April of the following year, 1886 – the threat of prison for ordinary women wrongly suspected of prostitution had been lifted.

"You see, Catherine," said Charlotte on that glorious day of repeal, "Mrs Butler spoke truly when she said men made prostitutes the scapegoat of their brutishness . . . their animal passions unhallowed by affection. But, don't get me wrong, dear. Those of us of the National Association do not encourage prostitution, or condone a quarter of our armed forces contracting venereal disease, but we have fought gallantly for the right of accused women to refuse medical examination and not to be thrown into prison merely for the defence of their liberty and defiance of the law. I feel sure from now on women will no longer be punished for men's hypocrisy."

"Men will always have the upper hand," replied Catherine, having read in the newspaper the latest report of Longborne's part in King Thibaw's deportation from Burma for supporting French interests.

"Maybe, my dear," replied Charlotte through a grin, "but the fools hardly know when they are being manipulated by women. I wonder who really wears the trousers."

CHAPTER 27

A respectable woman

*I*t was the middle of March 1885 before Cornelius had sold sufficient tickets to make his aeronautical efforts profitable. Sales had been slow to start with, but had gathered pace with the publishing of the advertisement in a local paper. The final few days of sales became a torrent, creating much alarm at the prospect of having possibly sold so many tickets that all the landing space would be compromised by curious onlookers hungry to see the spectacle. Still, at sixpence a head, it was worth the risk of packing them tightly, even if he had to land on their heads.

John took a more considered approach, arranging for farmhands from an estate near to Silbury Hill to erect temporary hurdle barriers at the base of the hill. The final decision as to the exact location of the barriers would be left until the morning of the demonstration, when he would be able to calculate the direction and strength of the wind and, thereby, leave an appropriate area.

And so came the morning of the demonstration. Cornelius, John, Abel and the wagon driver were already on top of the hill at daybreak to check conditions, having erected a marquee in a nearby field the previous day to serve as a base camp and a hangar for the glider. The night had been cold, leaving everyone chilled and ready for a hot breakfast provided by Fanny and Delysia, who had arrived even earlier. Despite their combined role in the proceedings, the ladies disliked each other and avoided speaking. Such close company was more than Fanny could stand and, thus decided, she knew she would leave the area for good, setting off even before the breakfast plates had been washed. Anyway, with so much going on, nobody would notice her absence.

At eleven o'clock the first onlookers began arriving, when the glider was carried to the summit to avoid a crush. A light canvas sheet was carefully pulled over the frame, pinned at the corners to short posts. By twelve o'clock the place was teeming with life. The noise was tremendous and expectations high. Most had come to see an accident, many of the rest to see a folly, with only a few expecting a successful flight.

At twenty minutes past twelve, Cornelius stepped inside the wings and the glider was lifted to above waist height. Belts and buckles were fastened and Cornelius nodded to show that all was ready. John and the driver let go of the wingtips and stood well back, unable to risk descending and getting lost amongst the crowd.

With final words of farewell and hearty handshakes exchanged, Cornelius took a deep breath and ran forward. But the ground remained slippery and his metal-studded boots skated on the wet grass. Unbalanced, he tripped where a depression was forming in the chalk, caused by the first signs of collapse in the Duke of Northumberland's 1776 shaft. With Cornelius falling forward uncontrollably, the glider's tail shot skyward, a gust catching the fabric and blowing man and machine sideways. John leapt to pin the glider to the ground, while Abel extracted Cornelius's contorted body. The crowd roared with laughter.

"Is it damaged?" pleaded Cornelius.

"More to the point, are 'ee alright?" asked Abel.

"I'll live. How's the glider?" He took a few awkward steps, but fell to the ground. "No I'm not. I think I've broken my ankle."

"I knew something like this would happen," scorned John, aware of the laughter turning into jeering as the crowd became impatient to get its money's worth.

"I'll try again, if you two can hold the tips of the wings and run alongside to support the weight until I take off," suggested Cornelius through his pain.

"And land how?" retorted Abel.

"On my bottom if I have to."

"And steer how?" asked John.

"Oh dear, it's not going to happen, is it?" admitted Cornelius in frustration.

"Not today," accepted Abel sensibly.

Cornelius looked at the simmering crowd below. "They'll have my head for giving up. Do you think they'll disperse quietly if we offer them their money back?"

"I very much doubt it. Their blood be up," counselled Abel, fearing the worst. "I think we all be in considerable trouble."

"I could explain that it's entirely my fault," suggested Cornelius, far from convinced anyone would take notice.

"Offer theeself up as the sacrificial lamb? Not a great idea," replied Abel unenthusiastically. "Look, I've an idea. There doesn't appear to be much to this flying malarkey. It's more dangling than skill, as I see it. Why can't someone else take 'ee place?"

"Who would be foolish enough?" enquired John.

"You, Sir, I be thinking."

"Not bloody likely. I've seen too many of the consequences of playing God. My feet are staying firmly on terra firma."

"That's it then. We're in trouble," remarked Cornelius bleakly, noticing the more rowdy elements below already tearing at the barriers. "I think they intend to storm the hill."

"Come on, Abel," said John in more desperation than kindness, "you give it a go. I'll pay you twenty pounds if you try."

"Twenty pounds be a fortune, Sir, but my life be worth more than that."

"Twenty-five, then," he offered hurriedly, noticing the first onlookers climbing the slope. "You would have to work most of the year for that much."

"Alright, alright, but if I die, I'll ask 'ee for five pounds more."

"If you die, you can ask for whatever you like. That's a promise."

Cornelius and John manhandled the glider until it rested around Abel's body.

"Now pay attention, Abel," demanded Cornelius in a controlled tone, despite more people taking to the slope. "If you feel the glider tipping left, swing your legs right. If it tips right. . ."

"I'll swing left."

"That's it. It's only a matter of natural balance, like riding a bicycle."

"But I can't ride a bicycle."

"Well, come to think of it, it's nothing like a bicycle actually."

"What if it nose dives? Should I undo myself and try climbing on the tail?"

"No! Everything must be gentle. Little movements. If it dives, bring the nose up by shifting your weight to the rear. Otherwise, pray hard and hope the hoop at the front absorbs the impact."

"Thanks," he replied with sarcasm.

"Remember, height is your friend, so try to climb on the breeze."

"What are 'ee talking about? The ground be me friend, as long as we meet each other at a respectable speed."

John and Cornelius retreated, as Abel prepared to run forward.

"Twenty-five pounds, mind. Don't. . ."

Mid-sentence, the wind suddenly, unexpectedly howled into a gust, catching him off-guard. His knees buckled as he strained to hold the glider level. With enormous effort, he recovered an awkward pose, his hair streaming back. But, the wind remained strong and the nose fought to rise, lifting him clear off the ground before John could grab a wingtip. The spectacle caused those scrambling up the hill to turn in panic. Then, just as quickly, the strong wind stopped and the glider plunged back to earth, tipping onto its nose before turning upside down on the plateau. Before the others could reach him, Abel had pulled himself clear.

"Are you hurt?" asked John with genuine concern, looking him up and down.

"Please, Mr Madden, I wish to give me notice. I was hired to be a bailiff, not a pigeon."

"That's it," said Cornelius with resignation, exhausted from hopping against the wind on one good leg. "This time we have no choice but to appeal to the crowd's better nature. We had better announce our intention to refund all ticket money and hope it's enough to appease them.

"Is the glider damaged?" asked John forcefully.

"Does it matter?"

"I'll do it!"

"Do what?"

"Fly the bloody thing."

"You want to try?"

"Not particularly, but needs must. Just tell me the bloody thing is okay."

Cornelius gave it a quick check. "It looks alright at a glance, but it really needs much closer inspection to be certain nothing is fractured."

"Then I will fly," said John in defiant tone. "But, let's get on with it before I come to my senses."

"No! It can't be allowed," demanded Abel, wishing they all could be magically spirited back to the farm. "It not be safe."

"Is it, Cornelius?" enquired John with serious expression.

"Probably," was the reply, "but, there again, the whole business of flying isn't safe."

"You didn't say that when Abel tried, or yourself for that matter."

"That's different. Anyway, the glider has taken quite a battering since then."

"And you think we're any safer up here, do you, doing nothing to appease the crowd? This is what comes of greed, you know. If they weren't here, we could pack up and leave."

"I'm beginning to understand that for myself."

"Listen to me, Cornelius. If it's concern over my name being in the history books and not yours, then. . ."

"Of course not, I was thinking only of your welfare."

"Well then?"

"Go on, if you must."

"My mind is set. I will fly."

Purposefully, the glider was turned over and carried back to the mounting point, where mud and grass were scraped off the fabric.

"Do you understand what you must do?" entreated Cornelius. "Be as one with the glider and try to feel every slight movement, and let your body take the opposite action. The wind will do the rest. It should be quite natural. Mostly, don't let the nose rise up too much, or it will stall. Equally, don't let it drop too much, or all the lift will disappear."

"Not too much up, not too much down, and feel for every sideways movement. I think I have it. Come on, let's get this bloody nonsense over with and have a cup of tea."

As the glider was raised to waist height, the crowd became silent, the occasional *hush* reprimanding the slightest interruption to their concentration.

"Are you ready?"

"As I'll ever be."

"Then hold tight to the bar. Get ready to run forward on the count of three. One, two, three. . ."

John was airborne, rising higher than ever achieved by Cornelius and making controlled progress. The glider descended steadily, the wind now constant. John felt remarkably at ease, moving his legs from one side to the other to see how the glider responded. It followed his every command, gently banking to the left and then to the right. The crowd cheered with admiration as his shadow danced against the grassy slope, ever downwards. Then, when half the hill had been conquered, the stress-carrying wires suddenly, dreadfully, snapped in quick succession, immediately followed by an ear-splitting tear of wood and cloth that ripped through the silence. The glider collapsed in mid air, its wings folding inwards and upwards above John's head. He dropped to the ground with tremendous force, bouncing off the slope as he impacted. He came to rest in a crumpled heap among the shards of the glider at the base of the hill.

"That was worth coming to see, worth a sixpence," said one man to another as the crowd lunged forward for a better view. "I wonder if they'll do it again."

"There's a caller for you, Ma'am," said Collins to Harriet Grant, keeping the visitor waiting impatiently at the door. "It's somebody called Delysia Gray from John Madden's farm."

"Ask what she wants and then send her away with a flea in her ear."

Delysia heard. She barged her way into the house, urgency overcoming any fear of reproach. Looking around to see who was present, she singled out Elizabeth and took her hands in a firm grip, pulling her close to whisper solemnly.

"You must come at once. All is amiss in a most terrible way. It's John Madden, he's seriously hurt. The doctor doesn't think he'll last another day."

"Oh my God," screamed Elizabeth, running one way and then the other until Harriet caught her, holding her in kindly restraint.

"What is it, child?" asked Harriet, alarm churning her stomach.

"I cannot speak of it. "I cannot get breath," panted Elizabeth. "Ask the Gray creature."

"John Madden has fallen from a great height, Ma'am. He's busted up something rotten."

"Go with all haste, Elizabeth. Go now and take Unity with you." She turned to Delysia. "Where is he? Has a doctor been summoned?"

"He's at Wheat Sheaf, but the accident happened near Marlborough several days ago. He was taken to Lacock, a nearby village, but he insisted on being brought home, strapped to a board. He knows how bad his injuries are and wants to be among familiar things."

"Yes, yes, but have they called a doctor?"

"They've called the vicar to pray over him. It's very bad. John knows he hasn't long to live."

"Has a doctor been summoned, I asked? It's better to hold onto his life than pray over his spirit.

"Yes, Ma'am, he too."

Rushing out to the awaiting gig, Delysia, Elizabeth and Unity sped off in the direction of Nether Bow, Jeremiah and Harriet following in their own carriage. They arrived together and were ushered into John's bedchamber.

The scene greeting them was beyond all hope. John was conscious but paralysed from the neck down, his ghostly face reflecting the light of candles glowing on bedside tables. His arms were unnaturally hidden below the blankets, unfeeling of life and straight. The curtains were pulled. Cold enveloped the room, a Macintosh waterproof cloth spread over the bed laden with crushed ice around the shape of John's broken body. The general aura was one of calm, where all was peace and sadness.

"Can he hear us?" asked Elizabeth, as the doctor re-entered carrying a bowl and cloth.

"Of course I can hear," murmured John. "I'm not dead, yet."

"Is the ice absolutely necessary, doctor?" beseeched Elizabeth.

"Merely an idea of mine, to freeze his limbs. I couldn't think what else to do," came the reply.

"Will it help?"

"Probably not. It gives me time to think."

"Remove it at once, if you please," she demanded.

The ice and waterproof sheet were taken away, leaving Elizabeth free to sit lightly on the edge of the bed, as close to John as she could. He looked up, smiling, before turning his attention towards Unity, who was too well protected from the chill to be seen. Elizabeth gently unwrapped the covers and lowered Unity towards him, allowing her tiny cheeks to flop against his. He could feel her warmth against his skin, her baby smell filling his senses.

"She is mine, you know," he said, "now and for ever. I love her so much."

"She knows that, John, and I will ensure she remembers this moment."

"I have made provision for you both. I did it last week. You are all the family I have and I have provided well."

Elizabeth kissed him, her tears finally joining them completely. "I'm so sorry for what I did."

"No, Lizzy, it's for me to be sorry. I've cut my life short by my own recklessness, my only, singular reckless act in years. I didn't even get a cup of tea! Just goes to show how foolish it is to be too good." He managed what passed as a painful laugh. "I have one regret above all else, Lizzy, that we didn't marry. Forgive me my stupidity, my behaviour."

"Oh, John, that too is my deepest regret." She turned to all those gathered solemnly around the bed. "Could we have a few moments alone? I need a few minutes to say all the private things that need to be said between us."

Outside, Cornelius slumped with his head in his hands, hardly able to bear the terrible responsibility of his ambitions.

"Why should John suffer the fate of the talisman?" he repeated to himself in castigation. "It was never meant to be that way. Fate got the wrong victim. It should have been me at the foot of the grassy slope."

Nobody heard.

Harriet, in her agitated state, took the vicar to one side and spoke earnestly, shaking with fear at his possible reply. He shook his head to her enquiries. She took ten pounds from her purse and placed it into his hand, closing his reluctant fingers around the bundle. He shrugged, then nodded in agreement. Harriet gently knocked on the bedroom door and re-entered.

"What is it, Mother?"

"I have a little good news, if such is possible. I may be interfering, but I would like you to know it all the same."

"Come closer," whispered John.

"It's the vicar. He's agreed to perform a marriage ceremony here and now without waiting for all the usual pomp and paper, if you would like it. It isn't regular, you understand, but he's willing to bend the rules on this occasion. What do you think, my dears?"

John looked hard into Elizabeth's eyes. They shone with approval. "We would like that very much," he said, crying inside.

And so it was done. Two hours later John passed away, the Madden family alone in the room.

Elizabeth was helped from the chamber as John's eyes were closed for the last time and his head covered by a sheet.

"Is it over?" enquired Jeremiah, having sat on the landing, his emotions too strong to bear in company.

"Is it, Father. He is gone from us."

"I'm so sorry. So very sorry. God bless him, God bless you and God bless our wonderful Unity."

"Amen to that," said Harriet.

Elizabeth walked down the stairs and into the drawing room, where she sobbed uncontrollably. Harriet followed after a discreet pause. Her daughter's anguish cut her deeply. She sat by her side, caressing her head in her arms as she had when Elizabeth had been an innocent child.

"How can I live without him? He was my world."

"You will learn to, my dear. You will manage, for Unity's sake. You must be resolute for her. We will help."

"I have lived my life wanting him, girl and woman. Why did I foolishly reject him? What was I thinking? I should have grabbed the moment. It might have changed everything. All his movements would have been different and he would now be alive. How sad is that thought to live with?"

"It is God's grace that he is taken from you, Elizabeth. If he was chosen to be called, the whereabouts of his physical being would not have made any difference. Depend upon it and gain some comfort."

"I am without comfort, without love, without life."

"He loved you just as much as you loved him. That is certain."

"I think he did love me in the end, but he really, deeply, sincerely loved someone else."

"You know this?"

"Oh, Mother, the last name that came from his lips was not mine, but Christabel's, the dairymaid. Even as he died, he was thinking only of her."

"That is not to be taken seriously, Elizabeth. He was in a confused and weakened state of mind, but he married only you."

"He said, because of Unity I now knew my place in the world, whereas, like the wind, he was yet to discover his."

"Delirium, nothing more."

Elizabeth ignored the well intentioned words, as if unspoken. "Do you know what else he said? He said as he stared at the ceiling, *at last I see the Herons*."

"What did it mean?"

"There was worse. With his final breath he uttered, *I am ready to die. Come, as you promised. Find me, Christabel. We fly together*."

"Oh, my poor, dearest, darling girl. You must let him go. His happiness is in the path to heaven, yours in raising Unity Isobel as a symbol of the brief love you shared."

"I am a widow on the day of my wedding," cried Elizabeth, gripping Unity tightly to her breast.

"No, child, today John has made you a respectable woman."

CHAPTER 28

Reunited at Shalhurn

*I*t was late March and in the hamlet of Westkings the carpet of snow recently covering the rolling countryside had suddenly, miraculously, given way to the sweet beginning of Spring, pretty wild flowers bursting into early colour along the myriad of hedgerows that criss-crossed the fields. It was a place of romance, of visionary beauty to be seen by anyone with the heart to understand, to be written about in tearful novels.

To the south, in Nether Bow, Wheat Sheaf Farm was now run by Abel Tucker for the benefit of Elizabeth and Unity Madden, who intended to live with Jeremiah and Harriet for the foreseeable future. The farm held too many sad memories to be made into a comfortable home. Cornelius had left, having burned his glider and all it represented. He knew one day in the not too distant future people would fly, but he would not be counted among them. In a nearby shop in Cerne, Emmie opened her glove business, assured of success by the skill and enterprise of Delysia.

Far afield, Fanny had found herself in the tiny market town of Hawkwood on Lady Day, the 25th of March. Although a traditional time for hiring fairs and all the merrymaking associated with the occasion, she had been unable to secure a position for the coming year. The small bag at her feet had shown her to be a single woman with no furniture of her own, and it seemed the attending farmers were looking for families. Thus, twelve days later she joined the transient massing of Flitting Day, moving from their former places of work to the next hiring fair, two or even three generations of families struggling under the weight of tables and chairs, bedding, pots and kettles, and all else they possessed. Shepherds carried crooks to show their trade, thatchers twisted straw into their hats or buttonholes and wagoners used whip-cord as hatbands, while a solitary foot haggler looking for better employment carried a live hen in a basket, its legs tied together. As before, Fanny stood with other single women.

As the day progressed and money parted hands as simple contracts for the next twelve months, so the number of hopefuls huddled together gradually diminished. By mid-afternoon, Fanny had given up. And so had a man in his early thirties who stood close by, a kindly-faced gentleman with a small girl hanging from one arm and a baby in the other. Fanny smiled compassionately.

"Where's their mother?"

"Dead this last month. Died at child birth. I'm at my wits end, with no roof to offer my girls."

A farm agent approached and enquired of his occupation and the whereabouts of his wife, a ritual already repeated throughout the day. The man shook his head in resignation, but said nothing.

"Oh, my lad, I need you to have a wife. I have a dairy to attend and my butter won't make itself. It's women's work while the men folk tend the fields. I can't have my cottages not fully occupied, either. I'm a generous man, but I have my need for workers."

"I be his wife," shouted Fanny, grabbing her bag and stepping to his side.

"You, missy?"

"Yes, Sir. I was just over there looking at the merriment. I be back now."

"Well," smiled the farmer, taking a half-a-crown from his

waistcoat pocket, "you are both hired as from now, and most happy you all shall be."

In Shalhurn, where Jack Mere and Verity lay at rest in the churchyard under the watchful presence of a tower with one crooked and three straight pinnacles, and where Christabel Mere was buried close-by on the other side of the collapsing boundary wall, in an adjacent field of unconsecrated ground, Emmie fulfilled her final act of contrition to her friend. With Elizabeth's unselfish approval, Emmie had arranged for John to be buried in the thin strip of consecrated ground that separated Christabel's grave from that of her father. At last, Christabel and John were joined forever. The disturbed forget-me-nots that had blossomed between the older graves now began to re-seed themselves towards the newest among them, with tiny salver flowers of radiant blue. John was happy once more.

"*God bless thee this day and for always,*" came the ghostly voice of Joseph Stone, carried low in the wind and heard only by Charlotte Elvington as she finally returned the confiscated ring to her errant daughter's grave, planting it beneath the soil. The story was complete. . .